MARIA

A Novel

Kris Heywood

MARIA

This is a work of fiction. All the characters, names, incidents, organizations, and dialogue in this novel are either the products of the author's imagination or are used fictitiously. Any resemblance to actual persons, living or dead, events, or locales is entirely coincidental.

Published in the United States by Siskiyou Press.

Library of Congress Cataloging-in-Publication Data
Heywood, Kris
Maria/Kris Heywood
2011910546

ISBN-10: 0615502881 ISBN-13: 978-0615502885
Siskiyou Press
1. Coming-of-Age—Fiction. 2. 1960s Munich—Fiction. 3. Bi-racial—Fiction. 4. Multi-cultural—Fiction. 5. German after-war years—Fiction. 6. American occupation—Fiction.

Printed in the United States of America

First Edition

Cover art by Leanne Zinkand, Silverlining Designs

Für die michliebende Mutti

For my mother
who loves me

MÜNCHEN, 1959

CHAPTER 1

THE FIRST TIME I RAN AWAY FROM HOME I was fourteen. It was the week after our Mutti (Mom) married Onkel (Uncle) Franz.* Behind his back, Anna and I called him O.F.— but he was *not* our uncle.

When he and Mutti left the apartment together, both wore gold bands on the left hand. When they returned a few hours later they'd switched them onto the right. She looked tired and pale, he flushed and triumphant.

In all the years Mutti, Anna and I had lived in Munich together, our sparse flat had been a happy place, even on the days Mutti didn't have a Pfennig (penny) left to stretch and we went to bed hungry. After her ill-advised "I do" and a hapless stroke of her pen, it had become *his* place, and the indoor temperature sank to Prussian lows as his pre-wedding tolerance vanished, leaving no doubt in my mind that Anna and I were the barely tolerated parts of a package deal that netted him an attractive wife *and* her precious low-rent Marshall Plan lease.

A few days later, while he was away on one of his weekly sales routes, the doorbell shrilled right before supper. Seppi gave a sharp bark from his blanket.

*GLOSSARY AT END OF BOOK

"Quiet, Sepp," Mutti told him, untying her apron. Turning to me, she added, "Marianne, it's time to put your homework away and help Anna set the table."

Seppi got to his feet and watched Mutti walk to the hall. He wasn't much taller standing than he'd been lying down. Although his father had been a German shepherd, his mother was pure Dachshund. Seppi looked just like his father except that his back was too long, his legs extra short, and his ears flopped.

"He has a loyal heart," Mutti said when we adopted him. "That's what counts most."

Now he listened carefully to the murmurs coming from the front door, tilting his head from side to side and doing his best to raise his ears. Then the hall door opened and Mutti preceded a strange man to the table, which took up most of our small kitchen. The man was dressed in sinister black from the shiny tips of his shoes to his hat. Seppi sniffed suspiciously at one of his heels. Frowning, the man shook the foot at my dog and adjusted his horn-rimmed glasses.

"Sepp, hinlegen (lie down)," Mutti gently admonished, whereupon he clicked across the shiny linoleum back to his blanket, plopping down with a sigh.

"Frau (Mrs.) Edel—" the man began.

"It's Hohner now."

"Precisely," he said with a glacial smile. "That's why I'm here."

"Oh?"

"As I said at your front door, I've come from the diocese. We are informed that you have . . . remarried?"

Slowly, she crossed her arms. "I have."

Anna stood at the silverware drawer with her mouth agape, clutching three soup spoons. I bent over my math notebook, sucking on my pencil eraser and shielding the complex division I'd been working on as if he meant to find fault with the sums.

He made no move to take off his hat. Mutti didn't invite him to sit. After a short hesitation, he raised a black leather briefcase, asking, "Gestatten (may I)?" Putting it on the tabletop before Mutti had a chance to respond, he pulled out a folder, showed her the typed form inside it, and said, "You are an adulteress in the eyes of Our Lord. A mortal sin." He slid the form in her direction.

Instead of picking it up, she raised her chin and said, "Ja, und (So what)?"

He squared his shoulders. "Frau Edel, it is my duty to inform you that you are hereby excommunicated from the Church."

I took the eraser out of my mouth. It was coated with spit and bitten half through. I broke off the dangling bit before writing down the x-word. Then I said, "Pardon me, please. 'Excommunicated'—what does that mean?"

Both of them glared at me.

"Ausgestossen, (ejected)" he explained with grim satisfaction. "No longer wanted."

I didn't get it, though I could tell from the red blotches forming on Mutti's cheeks that she did, and that it mattered more than she cared to admit. "Does it mean she won't have to go to Sunday Mass anymore?"

"Cannot go," he corrected, gloating.

"She never liked it anyway," I said. "What about Anna and me? Can we stay home, too?"

He snatched the form off the table and thrust it into Mutti's hands. "*You* will reap your just rewards, may God forgive you, but surely your wantonness does not include the reckless endangering of your daughters' immortal souls?"

"Of course not!" she sputtered.

My guess was that he meant to imply we were less lucky than she. But before I could ask him to clarify, Mutti sent me to my room. There I thumbed through the E section in my dictionary while their conversation faded into the hall and then to the front door.

Half a minute later he got into the ancient black Opel parked at the curb below and puttered away, spewing black smoke. It hovered over the tarmac like an arrow pointing to Mutti's sin.

*

THE next day, during last period, my teacher looked from the paperwork spread on her desk straight into my eyes and said in front of the whole class, "I see your mother has married again. What is your new father's full name?"

Stunned, I could only stare. Frau Bischof asked the question twice more. Annoyed at my lack of response, she finally shouted, "Speak up!"

"He's not my father," I said. "I already have a father. I don't need a new one."

Her lips white with fury, she scribbled a few lines and blotted the paper. Then she tore it out of her pad, folded it, and stuffed it in a small envelope. "Give this to your mother," she commanded, "and do not presume to correct me again."

Astonished at the turn of events, I slid the letter into my pack. After class I walked the whole eight blocks to my bus stop before I dared to retrieve it. She'd addressed it to "Frau Hohner—PRIVATE." Even though I knew it contained something bad about me I never dreamed of opening it. But why deliver the means to my own destruction? One moment I was staring at the unjust letter in dismay, the next my hand—without any help from the rest of me whatsoever—crushed it and dropped it into the nearest waste bin.

*

THE DEED sat heavily on my shoulders all weekend. Sunday morning in Mass I felt doubly unwanted for the sin of my mother and for my own. I took to my bed the rest of that slow-moving day, uninterested in eating my share of the traditional fatty pork roast with Knödel (dumplings) and my wedge of cheesecake. Just as well—that way, I didn't have to sit at the table with the man who was not my uncle and never would be my father.

On Monday morning, while he slept in, Mutti bustled around the kitchen preparing a meager breakfast. Anna malingered in the bathroom, applying a new face in front of the mirror. I sat on my bed and swallowed the entire contents of my multi-vitamin bottle. Then I got up and spun in the narrow space between bed and wardrobe until I was too dizzy to stand. Collapsing onto my mattress, I moaned, "Mutti! I feel like throwing up!"

It was the absolute truth.

She rushed to my side, assisted me to the bathroom, held my head over the toilet while I retched, and wiped my face with a cold washcloth. Then she helped me back to my bed and put the cloth on my forehead. Ten minutes later she took it off, pronounced me cured, gave me an unripe banana, and demanded I get ready for school. So I did.

After taking the city bus into Munich I walked the whole eight blocks, my feet getting heavier with each step. Gray clouds hung oppressively low. Half-hidden behind a thick layer of fog the school was equally gray. And foreboding. Try as I might I could not make myself cross the street to the entrance. Even though I had always loved learning above everything else, I stayed rooted to the opposite sidewalk, quite unable to step off the curb.

Cold sweat drenched my undershirt and made the cashmere pullover I was wearing smell like a damp goat. The bell rang faintly somewhere within the thick school walls. For the first time ever I was going to be late. No, worse—I was going to be absent, for my feet, suddenly mobile again, insisted on taking me to the next corner and out of sight.

Wandering aimlessly through unfamiliar city streets I wondered at what I had done and what I might do next. Eventually I found myself back at the bus stop, took the next bus to the Harthof, and arrived there after O.F. had left on his weekly route. I threw together a picnic lunch, stuffed it into my beach bag along with a swim suit and towel, clamped the bag to a frayed blanket on my bike's luggage rack, and rode out to the Baggersee.

A few prospective bathers, still in their coats, huddled at the shore waiting for the sun to appear. They paid no attention to me as I spread my blanket on a patch of weeds, sat, and put my nose in a book until the clouds burned away.

That day brought the start of a heat wave that lasted for the rest of the week. Each day was sublime. I brought a new book every morning and finished it in time to beat Mutti home from the office. In between, I let the sun warm my frozen insides, wading into the lake periodically to cool off again. The water was a tranquil, transparent satin.

On Friday the hot spell ended with a tremendous lightning storm. Ignoring Mutti's most dire warnings I swam all alone in the lake while thunder raged overhead. Water and air seemed equally warm. The trees on the far shore bent double. Fire bolts arced in every direction. Then it poured so hard I could no longer tell where the lake stopped and I began.

For as long as the storm lasted I was entirely free.

Afterwards the air chilled rapidly. It rained all weekend and showed no sign of slowing on Monday, when I was ready to fill my class-seat again. Frau Bischof had a knack for making lessons interesting, especially geography. We were studying our way from the Sahara to Madagascar, whose capital had the magical-sounding name "Tananarive."

Although Mutti missed noticing my healthy tan it did not escape Frau Bischof's full attention when I told her I'd been sick for a week. Staring at my forearms, where blindingly white sleeves contrasted beautifully with nut-brown skin, she demanded a written excuse, signed by my mother. When I couldn't produce it she pointed to the door and snarled, "Get out of my class and don't ever bother trying to come back!" All the girls in our sex-segregated school room leaned forward to see what I would do next, giving a collective sigh when I picked up my pack and obeyed.

Since the first day I'd followed my friend Gabriel to the Freidorf village school—when he was seven and I three—I'd been passionate about schools. I would sit quietly under Gabriel's desk, learning to read by osmosis. This year I'd even learned to love Frau Bischof—when I wasn't terrified of her imperious temper. She knew everything and was glad to pass it on. Until the fateful Monday morning of my banishment.

*

AFTER she threw me out I went home to console myself with my '45 Ricky Nelson record, humming along with his slurred American phrases. Unfortunately Mutti appeared right after lunch, wearing one of her best secretary outfits. To my surprise she'd arranged to take the afternoon off for a dental appointment. She was as puzzled to see me as I was to see her.

Demanding to know why I was not in school, she chased me around the table until I told her I had been permanently dismissed.

"Ausgestossen," I said. "Just like you."

She did not get the connection. "Von wegen (that's what you think)!,"she said, thrusting her chin at me. "Put on your shoes. I want a word with your teacher."

As Mutti dragged me to the bus stop, I couldn't tell whom she was angrier with—Frau Bischof or me. She kept a vice grip on my arm the whole time we were riding into town even though she'd already wedged me into a window seat to make sure I couldn't escape. I was beginning to suspect she meant to cause an embarrassing scene in front of the entire student-body, including everyone on the boys' side. At last we stepped off the bus and started crossing the street. Then an oncoming car ran the red light and barreled toward us. Startled, Mutti let go of my arm.

I turned and ran, ducking down alleys, around corners, through strange courtyards. Chasing after me in her spikes, she lagged farther and farther behind. Soon her voice, calling my name, grew ever fainter. Then it was gone. I snaked under a bush and lay flat until I was sure she had given up the pursuit.

I didn't know why I'd bolted any more than I knew why I'd skipped a whole week of school. How could I expect her to understand something I couldn't explain to myself? Anna would never have done what I did. It wasn't in her nature. Why was it in mine?

There was no way to fix what I'd broken. Once I ran I had to keep on running. Guessing Mutti would go on without me to lock horns with Frau Bischof, I decided I had better retreat. I got to the bus stop for the Harthof just as the bus pulled in. The minute I arrived at home I filled a couple of suitcases with clothes appropriate for a Mediterranean climate, said a tearful goodbye to Seppi, and struck out for Italy.

I had just enough change to take the streetcar to the southernmost tip of Munich. The rest would be strictly a walking tour.

*

GRITTING my teeth, I managed to tramp a few kilometers before the suitcases grew unbearably heavy. By the time a respectable-looking businessman, driving a dark-blue Opel, stopped to offer a lift, daylight was fading and my defenses were low. Having missed both lunch and supper, I was no longer capable of thinking clearly.

Grateful for his kind offer, I slid onto the passenger seat, one suitcase at my feet, the other balanced on my knees. The man had bushy eyebrows and hair curling out of his nose and ears. Lost in his own thoughts, he had nothing to say until it got dark and we found ourselves in a black stretch of the forest. Then he came to a stop, turned off the lights and the motor, and shifted towards me.

"Look here, Mädchen, (girl)" he said. "I'm not stupid. You're a runaway and I'm going to drive you to the nearest police station—unless you're nice to me. Now."

I had groped for the door handle the instant he put on the brakes. Before he finished his speech I was already shoving my suitcases out the car door. Diving after them, I snatched them up and dashed to a clump of inky underbrush. It swallowed me so completely that the dim flashlight with which the businessman was tracking me proved useless to him. Stumbling and swearing, he gave up when it started to drizzle. Car doors slammed, the engine restarted, the headlights came on, and the motor faded around the next curve.

I might have made it to the bright Italian sunshine and spent the rest of my life on a white beach, picking oranges straight off the trees and acquiring an even better tan than the one that had irked Frau Bischof—if the chilly and wet German climate had not reclaimed me that long, miserable night. I'd been so fixed on blue southern skies that I hadn't thought to bring anything warm. My featherbed, too big to stuff into a suitcase, would have been utterly useless during the extended downpour I soon found myself in.

I went to sleep in a soft, mossy hollow in a stand of young firs and awoke lying in a cold puddle. A faraway church bell chimed the night hours away as I shivered toward hypothermia. When the hour-bell struck four times I followed its sound across drenched fields, not daring to walk on the road. Dawn found me in a small village, hunched over the grated vent of its bakery. I basked in the heat rising from the basement ovens and savored the delicious smell of fresh baked breads and Bretzen (pretzels). I couldn't have bought as much as a five-Pfennig roll even if the shop had been open for business.

I didn't have the money to call home from a phone booth or to board a streetcar. So I aimed my feet northward and walked all day, stubbornly dragging the wretched suitcases step after impossible step. I didn't arrive at our front door till our own church bell struck midnight. By then Mutti, who sometimes had a better grip on reality than I, was so worried that she forgave me all my trespasses the instant I dared the first hesitant knock.

She stuffed me with as many hot sausages and white bakery rolls as Seppi and I could comfortably hold and let me sleep in. But after I woke up the next morning she insisted on accompanying me to my school one more time.

Frau Bischof, who'd obviously rehearsed her part of the drama during my absence, demanded an immediate apology for all my recent offenses, including the backtalk and the lost note. The penance the women considered appropriate for me was two extra hours of homework each and every day until I could finish a punishment workbook on geography in my best penmanship, complete with original drawings. "It will occupy your spare time for the remainder of the school year," Frau Bischof said with grim satisfaction. "And keep you out of further trouble."

I chose Africa, which had a history so ancient it was obscured by the mists of a million years. And since I loved to draw those daily two hours were among the most enjoyable I ever spent. Because I loved the palette of African skin tones, ranging from the lightest tan to midnight blue, I included tribes from Asante to Zulu. On my pages, graceful pygmies and Bushmen mingled with astoundingly long-legged herdsmen like the Dinka, Watusi, and Masai, who could jump higher than they were tall. I drew shorn women whose faces were pleasingly round in every feature and adorned with an opulence of beads; boys whose heads were carefully molded into exaggerated ovals; men with teeth filed to sharp points, every inch of their bodies painted with ochre and chalk.

Then I added exotic wild animals; endlessly undulating dunes; the Savanna; the Sahel; dense snake-filled jungles. Of all the places in the world, Africa held the most magic for me.

My workbook grew thicker each day. I handed it to Frau Bischof in the first week of November. She was so overcome she could not speak. But when she forbade blue jeans in her class-room she chose to overlook the fact that I continued to wear mine. And during cooking class she made all the girls except me wear old-lady hairnets. When the bravest of my classmates complained Frau Bischof told her it would be a shame to cover my curls, which were too tight to fall in the food, anyway.

That was as good as it could get in her classroom.

I didn't run away again until the summer after I turned fifteen.

CHAPTER 2

FOR MY FIFTEENTH BIRTHDAY IN MAY the only thing I really wanted was a life that excluded O.F.

Mutti said it couldn't be done. So I gave myself a new name instead. It was *Maria*. Three vowels, two consonants: a song. But what good was a name if no one would use it? Two months later everyone was still calling me Marianne.

Mutti did grant my other birthday wish. It was a tiny white mouse I named Elvis. Buying him was a considerable sacrifice for her because O.F. disliked pets and often gave Seppi a calculating look when he thought no one was watching. They had a talk about little Elvis behind closed doors. It quickly deteriorated into a shouting match. Mutti emerged from it with her green eyes shooting sparks. O.F. locked the living room door behind her and stayed inside, chain-smoking and furiously pecking on the little black portable typewriter he'd confiscated from Mutti last year, on the same day he had installed a lock on his side of their wardrobe.

In June they mapped out my vacation, also behind closed doors. Mutti informed me I was to be sent to summer camp from the beginning of July through August. She was not interested in my opinion on the subject.

As we drifted toward July I wished the calendar would skip all the weekends, sparing me O.F.'s disapproving presence. Then came that one Saturday when my childhood blinders finally slipped.

It happened while I was sitting by myself in the living room, Seppi stretched at my feet. I was waiting for the TV to warm up. A warm breeze billowed the long gauze curtains at the open balcony door. On the narrow street below, in deepening late-afternoon shade, children were laughing and shouting as they played with Wolfi's new ball. It was made of see-through plastic and gave a musical "ping" each time it bounced.

I held Mutti's old purse-mirror close to my face, staring fixedly into the reflection of my eyes, trying hard not to blink. I'd read a story about that technique in one of Frau Keppler's books of weird tales. It claimed if you stared long enough some invisible beast would rise from within, stare back at you out of your own eyes, and drive you insane.

I wondered what it was like to be possessed by an alien. Sometimes, between involuntary blinks, I sensed a dark thing crouching just out of sight.

An instant later it happened: my pupils grew fixed and expanded, crowding my hazel irises into tight bands at the rims. Through the black holes in the centers something glittered and sucked, trying to steal my place in the world.

With a gasp I flung the mirror onto the rug where it collected the green overhead light and sent a flare into my right eye, triggering an odd, silvery buzz. I pressed a hand over the eye, pulled the doily from under the ashtray with the other, and tossed it onto the glaring rectangle, breaking the evil spell. Then I squeezed my lids shut and massaged my rapidly numbing right temple.

When I opened them again it was as if I were seeing the living room for the first time: the moss-green couch, the matching chair I was sprawling on, the coffee table, the two-sided mahogany wardrobe on the opposite wall, the convertible desk squeezed into one corner; the console crammed into the other.

It occurred to me that nothing in the room was as it seemed to be. The couch hid a bed, the desk a sewing machine, the console the TV, radio, and record player, and O.F.'s locked half of the wardrobe doubled as a safe. It's where he stashed all the stuff he didn't want anyone—not even Mutti—to see.

Then the TV emitted the same kind of silvery buzz I'd felt in my light-stabbed eye and slowly the screen turned dull shades of gray. I gathered the courage to scoop up both doily and mirror, shook the treacherous glass-rectangle into the wastebasket, and replaced the doily on the coffee table, appreciatively sliding my fingers over its smooth surface. It had come with us from the village along with every other piece of furniture in the apartment except for the console.

Mutti had paid for the furniture twice. The first time, at Vati's insistence, she'd bought the pieces *for* him as part of her dowry before they got married. The second time he made her buy them *from* him after the wrenching divorce.

O.F. purchased the console with the first paycheck Mutti turned over to him once they were legally wed. When he was in one of his huffs he liked to say that only he could decide who was allowed to touch it and when.

The grays on the screen began to sharpen with contrasts while I sifted through the sounds coming from the kitchen. From the other side of two closed doors I could hear Mutti chop and stir while *he* most likely was shaving at the sink next to the gas stove. I strained to catch the first shrill syllable, a rising pitch inevitably followed by the harsh scrape of a chair, lids banging—or worse, the living room door flung wide with O.F. in the frame, itching to magnify some miniscule fault of mine.

Just yesterday, an hour before he came home, our kitchen had rung with laughter. For a sliver of Emmenthaler little Elvis had stood on my shoulder on his pink hind feet, his fragile toes tickling my skin, dancing while his namesake sang "Jailhouse Rock" on the AFN station. As I waited for the TV picture to grow focused I reached into my bushy hair to make sure he was still in his hideaway nest.

A documentary was in progress. I couldn't understand the narrator, whose voice remained garbled even after I increased the volume. He was speaking a nasal American English too fast for my unpracticed ears to comprehend. The accompanying film zoomed along a dim corridor between wooden bunks. Feeble near-skeletons cowered on the rough beds, their heads no more than hollow-eyed, skin-covered skulls.

The narrator's twang was a far cry from the King's English I was learning in school. My greatest achievement, so far, had been the successful recitation of this odd little poem:

> Swan swims over the sea.
> Swim, swan, swim.
> Swan swam over the sea.
> Swam, swan, swam.

It was fun to say the lines at top-speed three times in a row, though not very useful.

Overwhelmed by the narrator's rapid-fire English I leaned toward the set, fishing for one simple word I could understand, such as "it" or "that", but the American phrases stuck together like beads on a long, crowded string. Then a translator's voice overrode the twang to explain:

This was the sight that greeted the liberating forces: men and women shorn, in rags, starved and near death, left behind by the same Nazi jailers who fled with the Jews still able to walk . . .

The camera panned to a hillock outside the barracks. At first I assumed I was looking at turnips. On closer inspection I noticed odd protrusions—a stick-thin arm poking out here, a bare foot jutting out there. Then it dawned on me that I was seeing a pile of naked dead people, grotesquely entwined. The camera focused on the shaved head of a girl around my age, her eyes fixed in terror, her arms nothing but bones covered by skin.

. . . The story is the same in Auschwitz, Buchenwald, Dachau. The Germans called it 'the final solution.' The rest of the world calls it the cold-blooded murder of six million men, women and children, most of them Jews. Many were dragged from their beds in the middle of the night while their German neighbors and friends turned away so they wouldn't see. Hitler issued the orders. The German people obeyed . . .

The roar of my blood drowned out the rest but one word continued to toll deep inside me: *Dachau*. As far as I knew it was a boring little town just outside of Munich. I wasn't even sure at which end, although now I was hoping it was nowhere near mine.

Seppi put his muzzle on my knees. I touched my forehead to his, glad for his warm, comforting breath. And then the door really did thud against the wall. O.F. paused dramatically in the frame, his cold eyes raking my body.

"Are you deaf?" he said. "How many times must I tell you to keep the volume low? And why are you wasting precious electricity on the overhead light when it isn't even dark yet?"

I stiffened my spine and Seppi froze, flattening himself across my feet. I froze, too, but on the inside, where it didn't show. O.F. scowled, waiting for me to apologize in my most submissive little-girl-voice. Try as I might I couldn't produce a single syllable. He was sure to hold it against me. On the TV, the translator was saying,

These were the camp showers, but they did not hold
water. Through them, gas was piped to where the Jews
stood with raised faces, expecting hot—

O.F. crossed the room and clicked off the set. The sound stopped at
once but the picture shrank to the size of a white little ball and hovered. He
glared at Seppi, who was beginning to quiver, and shifted his gaze to my
knees and up to my face. His eyes glinted briefly at Elvis who had chosen
that ill-advised moment to poke his sensitive pink nose out of my hair.
Then he went to turn off the light and closed the door much too softly
behind him. For once I was grateful for I felt as if I were made of dust and
would disintegrate at the slightest agitation.

A copy of the white dot, now no more than a pin-point on the screen,
jumped to O.F.'s side of the polished mahogany wardrobe where it
expanded until it covered the whole wardrobe door. On it, nightmarish
pictures unfolded. Feeble skeletons trembled on bunks. Ragged men were
buried alive in mass graves. Children and women collapsed under lethal
showers-heads. The haunting face of the girl with the bald head appeared
last, her dead eyes drilling holes through my heart. Seppi's solid weight on
my toes was the only thing keeping me anchored in a world that was
shifting and spinning like an out-of-control carousel.

CHAPTER 3

I N SOME DISTANT PLACE glass and porcelain clinked to the rhythm of O.F.'s quarrelsome tones and Mutti's soothing replies. It was a weekend refrain I usually tried to ignore until the beat changed for the worse. That evening, I listened to the endless loop until it faded along with the dusk and the evening breeze became a chilly night draft.

Then I heard Mutti's quick, determined step. The overhead fixture came on, tinting the room a sickly green and causing Elvis to scramble deeper into his hairy nest. Mutti kept her hand on the switch while she looked to where I sat on the floor, cradling and rocking as much of Seppi as I could fit onto my lap.

"Marianne!" she said. "Dogs belong on the floor and people belong in chairs. How many times do I have to remind you?"

"Maria," I corrected in a hoarse whisper.

She dismissed my new name with an impatient wave. "You'll be covered in fur. Your clothes . . ."

Seppi wagged his apology.

"But I'm wearing my blue jeans," I protested. "You called them the only fitting replacement for Lederhosen (leather-pants) when you bought them for me. Because fur won't stick. Remember?"

Sounding flustered, she said, "I wish you wouldn't wear them on weekends. Franz told me he found you sitting in here with your knees obscenely apart. He said pants on young girls are indecent."

I wanted to laugh but shivered instead. She was at my side in an instant, one practiced hand on my forehead, the other checking the whites of my eyes. "Are you sick?" she asked. "Do you have a fever?"

It would explain my odd symptoms. "I don't know," I said, "but the room's rolling around and around."

She stepped away. "If this is some last-ditch attempt to get out of summer camp it won't work. You're still taking the twelve o'clock train to the Harz tomorrow, even if I have to carry you to your seat myself. Come, I've made soup. It'll thaw out your bones. Why were you sitting in the dark? Honestly, *Mariandl*, sometimes I think that the stork brought you to the wrong house."

I had played with that thought, myself. It was appealing.

She pulled at my arm. Obediently, I rose to my full height, dwarfing her by two heads, a recent development I still found confusing. It was hard to look up to someone you could look down on. "Mutti, what do you know about Dachau?" I asked. Did I imagine a tightening around her bottle-green eyes?

"No more than you, I'm sure," she answered, her voice guarded. "Only that it's somewhere on the other side of the forest and by all accounts an unattractive place. I've never had any reason to go there, and neither, I trust, will you."

"What forest? Which side of München?"

"The wrong side," she said. "And don't change the subject. O.F. promised to let you take the first bath tomorrow morning. I bought a new bar of soap for the occasion. Still sealed in its wrapper. I've put it in your underwear drawer. Please use it. The nuns are even stricter about cleanliness than O.F. is."

There was no use pleading again, as I had done every day this past month. Why couldn't I stay home like Anna and play with Wolfi and the rest of our friends? Because O.F. wanted me gone, that's why. So far he'd only managed to pry me loose during summer vacations but I suspected he was working on a more elaborate scheme and anything I said, did, or omitted was ammunition in his escalating war against me.

I fell easily into his traps because he was a careful planner and I was too impulsive for my own good.

"Come!" She took my hand and led me to the door. "You too, Seppi—straight to your blanket like a good dog."

Contritely wiggling his rear end, he followed us through the tight little hallway. In the steamy kitchen, the fragrance of Mutti's liver dumpling soup, which I loved to smell but hated to eat, mingled unpleasantly with the rancid odor of O.F.'s latest miraculous scalp tonic. He was bending over the sink, his face close to the wall mirror, rubbing his nightly dose into his faded, thinning hair.

The table was set for four: fluted white soup plate on top of matching dinner plates, dessert plates and glass tumblers directly behind them. Every dish was gold-rimmed except for the crystal salad bowl at the center. It was filled with the inevitable dull mix of watery iceberg lettuce and grated carrots. Knives, forks and spoons were lined up as precisely as tin soldiers.

Anna had laid out each piece of silverware according to some unshakable standard Mutti had taught her. My voluptuous older sister was standing in front of the open refrigerator, her hair ratted and sprayed into a stiff blonde beehive, her face as appealing as pink lipstick, tan makeup, caked eye-shadow, and a thinly-drawn line drawn with her eye-brow pencil could make it. She was clutching a bottle of *Limunade* (lemon soda) against her well-filled blouse. The matching blue skirt hid her only problem area— a pouch of baby fat as yet unwilling to melt. Sensing trouble, she deliberately turned away from me to stare at the refrigerator shelves as if they held her salvation.

Mutti nodded at Seppi. With a sigh, he plopped down on his blanket. She pulled out my chair, tapping the backrest. I tried to sit. And then it started, as it always did when O.F. was at home and we happened to be in the same room.

He tore himself away from the mirror to say, "Just a minute, you! I didn't see you wash your hands. Let's have a look. Come here at once."

I stiffened my knees but stayed where I was until Mutti gave me a small shove in his direction. Close up, the reek of his new hair oil put a knot in my throat. Reluctantly, I held out my hands. He studied each finger and when he was done he said, "Now show me the other sides." For one second I wondered what would happen if I refused. It was one second too long. He seized my hands and flipped them over with his paper-dry, loose-skinned, freckle-backed fingers, which were damp with sticky tonic and dusted with minute specks of white dandruff.

I snatched my hands back but already some microscopic O.F. germs had managed to burrow under my skin. Gagging, I ran to the bathroom and stuck them under the faucet, frantically rubbing them in plain running water. I couldn't use the family soap lying on the sink because it was covered with more of his germs—as were faucet handle, towel, and toilet seat. Nothing was safe from his taint. And then an invisible sword stabbed my already tender right eye, striking sparks. I wiped my palms dry on the jeans, dug a knuckle into the offending temple, and went through the kitchen to the bedroom Anna and I shared, mumbling, "I have a headache."

"You're not excused," O.F. said, his voice like steel. "Your mother went through the trouble of cooking you a delicious meal and the least you can do is show her enough respect to sit down and eat it."

"You eat it. I don't feel like it," I muttered recklessly over my shoulder.

There was a small, lethal silence before he mimicked in an exaggerated little-girl-voice, "*You* eat it? *I* don't feel like it?"

"Everyone here knows I detest liver," I unwisely explained.

Instantly, his face darkened. "You *detest* liver?" he shouted as if he'd heard that fact for the first time. "Who do you think you are, a princess? And how dare you talk to me in that tone!" He turned redder with each word, and the more he flushed, the more Mutti paled, wringing her hands.

Then she cried in a tortured voice, "Franz, please don't!" As if that would help. As if it had ever helped. Why hadn't *she* thought to remind me to wash my hands? Why hadn't she warned me that we were going to have liver-dumpling soup? Why did she even cook it when she knew how much I loathed the taste?

"In what tone?" I asked, just for clarification.

Struck speechless, O.F. leaped at me, claws extended. Nimbly, I pivoted into the bedroom, slammed the door, and turned the key—all in one fluid motion. He threw himself against the wood with an inarticulate scream of rage and hammered it with his bony fists until the door trembled and strained in its frame. "Open up!" he screeched. "At once!"

Nothing on earth could compel me. Besides, I was already tearing at the window, leaning out to gauge the drainpipe and wondering if I could trust it to bear my full weight should the need arise.

In the kitchen, Mutti cried again, her voice shaking, "Franz, *please!*"

I wasn't sure what I hated most—his unfairness, her submissiveness, or the pitiful excuse of a life I was forced to endure.

And then the drama was over. Having discharged his excess poison he allowed Mutti to lead him to his chair.

With trembling fingers I pulled Elvis out of my hair and deposited him in his cage. Usually I slid it under my bed but that night I left it right next to my pillow. I kicked off my slippers and crept under my enormous featherbed fully clothed in case I was forced to attempt the drainpipe at some point during the long night. Muffled by a thick layer of goose down, I unclenched my teeth and let them chatter, moaning softly at the piercing pain in my head. Pressing a fist into the right eyeball brought some relief, but only for as long as I kept it there. Since the top end of my mattress was only half a meter away from the door I could hear every word that was spoken in the kitchen along with each clink of fork against plate and glass against tabletop.

"That impudent girl!" O.F. grumbled. It was his favorite way of referring to me. "She belongs in reform school and I'll make sure she gets there if it's the last thing I do."

Anna had managed to remain silent during the unfortunate episode. I imagined her sitting across from my empty chair, back erect, chin up, elbows in, taking meticulous bites, her eyes averted, hoping O.F. would continue to ignore her. When he was at home my sister asked no questions, offered no opinions, and stayed as meek as she was able. Leaving me to do all the dirty work true resistance required.

But was my occasional backtalk enough reason to put me behind bars? Or the fact that I hadn't had a proper wash since O.F. decided that he should be the one to have the first bath on Saturdays? Until last month it had always been me. Mutti said it was because I was the youngest and the one in most need. I tried to adjust to being second but could not make my naked body lie where his had just been.

Every Saturday since I simply sat on the tub rim during my turn, swishing a hand through the water to produce occasional splashing sounds. Once, I heard stealthy footsteps outside the bathroom door and the sound of his heavy breathing. That's when I started to hang a washcloth over the keyhole and dampened my towel, knowing he'd check to see if it had been used.

In one of the letters he was forever composing to the Youth Authority he claimed I came out of the bathroom with my neck as dirty as it was when I went in. Mutti found an aborted craft on the bottom of the wastebasket, along with discarded sheets of carbon paper impossible to decipher because he typed on them more than once. He sealed the clean copies and the typewriter in his part of the wardrobe. She searched for the spare key, couldn't find it anywhere in the house, and decided he must be hiding it somewhere in his locked car.

Fist in eye, I curled up under my featherbed and whispered my nightly prayer. It was, "Dear God, please send me someone to love!" But no matter how precisely I steepled my hands, finger to finger, no one had come to me yet. Except for last week.

Hopefully, that didn't count.

*

IT HAD been near suppertime. I was out front, leaning against the rough stucco and waiting for Mutti to call me upstairs when Heinz came around the corner to visit Wolfi who lived next door. Heinz stopped to say hello. I wished him a good evening. Then we both stared off into the distance, too shy to find anything else to say.

He lived three blocks away but lately he had started to come around to hang out with Wolfi. They were the only two boys in the neighborhood with hair as dark as my own. I thought it gave us a lot in common. All three of us tanned dark, too. Or perhaps they didn't bathe much, either. While Heinz and I waited for an interesting conversation to spring up between us someone opened our kitchen window directly above. I looked up, expecting to see Mutti. Unfortunately it was O.F. who leaned over the sill and started bellowing at us like a mortally wounded bull. Still yelling, he thundered down the stairs.

Heinz looked as stricken as I felt. We both leaped to the corner and sprinted for our lives, he in one direction and I in another. My heart hammered as I plunged into the thistle patch across the street where I struggled to still my panting, not daring to move a muscle until long after Mutti called me upstairs for supper.

It wasn't fair. Anna got to go everywhere with her Peter. O.F. never bellowed at her. How come I couldn't even stand next to a boy? In front of the house? In broad daylight?

On Monday I saw Heinz duck into the little bakery next to the bus stop. I went in to buy a pretzel and said a cheerful *Grias Di* (hello). He froze, ducked out again, and escaped toward his apartment. On Tuesday, Wednesday and Thursday I haunted the nearby sidewalks but he always managed to avoid me. Yesterday I finally realized the whole ugly truth: he was afraid to ever come near me again—and so was every other boy in the neighborhood.

O.F. had given me a bad reputation.

Heinz couldn't have been God's fickle answer to my whole year of asking, could he? Maybe I'd better give Him a stronger hint in case He hadn't had a chance to think it through for Himself. "Dear God," I amended my prayer, "please send me someone from a different place. Someone who doesn't know us."

*

EVEN though the featherbed covered my ears I could hear the chairs scraping away from the table. O.F. withdrew to smoke and smolder in front of the TV. Anna helped Mutti with the dishes, neither of them saying a word. Then my sister took Seppi downstairs and up again. At last she tapped on the door and whispered my name. I half suspected O.F. was putting her up to it and was hiding behind her, but I forced myself to unlock the door anyway. What else could I do? It was her bedroom, too.

She squeezed in, affording me a glimpse of the kitchen. It appeared to be empty except for Seppi, huddled all alone on his blanket, looking at me with sorrowful eyes. I slapped my thigh. He came running. I relocked the door as soon as the tip of his tail cleared the jamb.

In silence, Anna felt her way through the dark to her side of the room. Our beds were joined lengthwise, foot-ends touching. She stopped by her headboard next to the window, her shoulders slumping in the faint rectangle of light. When she started to unbutton her blouse I discreetly turned my face to the wall. I could hear her slide blouse and skirt onto a hanger, slip on the nightgown she kept neatly folded under her pillow, rustle her featherbed, and wiggle underneath.

I stared up at the dark ceiling until the TV went silent on the other side of the wall. The couch squeaked as someone unfolded the mattress. O.F grumbled. Mutti peeped a timid reply. Bedsprings started to creak.

Once all was quiet I listened to the church bell chime every fifteen minutes and struggled toward sleep. But there were monsters everywhere, even in my closet. When a coat hanger mysteriously rattled I dragged Seppi up from the floor and stuffed him under my covers. He lay on my cold feet. While I was waiting for them to get warm I put a finger through the bars of Elvis' cage and he kissed it good night. Then I drifted, at last feeling secure enough to let myself go.

CHAPTER 4

THE MORNING SUN MADE EVERYTHING NEW again. It tickled me awake and drew me along its beam to the window. I pushed open both panes and leaned out. The sky was a blue dome fringed with angel-hair clouds. Somber family groups emerged from every apartment building, faced east, and migrated toward church.

I flipped Anna's covers away from her face. "Get up! We're late!"

She was sleeping on her back with her mouth open, her long nightgown twisted around her knees. The beehive had come undone, half the pins strewn on the sheets. Yesterday's artfully penciled-on eyebrows were smudged on her pillow.

If only Peter could see her now.

"Shall I douse you with a glass of water?" I asked, trying to be helpful. "It'll save you the five minutes you usually spend on washing your face."

She squinted at me out of mascara-smeared eyes and yawned. "Douse your own face. It'll be an improvement." She sat up. "God, I'm hungry! After you set him off last night I completely lost my appetite. I only pretended to eat so he wouldn't pick on me next. Good thing Peter's mom always invites me for hot cocoa and pancakes after Mass." She got up to finger the blue sailor dress hanging on the side of her wardrobe. "Not that again! You'd think Mutti would notice I've outgrown it. This is the absolute last time I'm wearing the silly thing."

With a sinking feeling I noticed an identical dress hanging on my wardrobe. Mutti suffered from the compulsion to dress us as twins even though we were two years apart in age and looked nothing alike.

"It's too warm for a wool dress," I complained.

Anna was already pulling hers off the hanger. "Outdoors, maybe. In church it'll be as cold as the tomb."

I caught a glimpse of myself in the dresser mirror and couldn't resist angling the long side panels until I could see an infinity of Marias raying off in every direction.

"You've got a thing about staring at yourself in mirrors, I've noticed," Anna said, searching her closet floor for matching pumps.

"It's you who has a thing about looking in mirrors," I corrected. "I'm just interested in what's behind them."

She raised her pitiful brow-stubs at me. "There's nothing behind them. They're as flat as you are. Now scram."

She wanted me to withdraw to my side of the room so she could change. Glad to oblige, I took Elvis out of his cage, put him in my hair, and gyrated in front of my wardrobe. Studying my blurred reflection in the high-gloss varnish, I wondered if I looked more like a belly dancer or a Gypsy.

Anna hid behind her open closet door, pulled off her nightgown, and tossed it onto her bed. It collided with the headboard and slipped down to cover her pillow.

Putting Elvis on my shoulder, I laced my fingers together, straightened my arms, hung my head to give him access to the back of my neck, and let him run a few loops. "I know Mutti promised to feed him while I'm gone—but Anna, he needs to come out of his cage every day. Would you . . ."

I could practically hear her shudder. "I will not!" she said. "He's cute and all. But to tell you the truth, I can't stand his naked pink tail. Reminds me of an earthworm."

Elvis stopped to sit on his haunches on the back of my hand, staring reproachfully into my eyes. Until that moment I'd thought the eight weeks of camp were strictly my problem. Now I saw them from his perspective. Two months of solitary confinement in his little wire-trap, subtracted from a life span of no more than a couple of years, had to seem endless to him.

Dressed and shod, Anna carefully brushed the top layer of her beehive until it was smooth. It was a pity she didn't like mice—Elvis would have adored that permanently ratted bubble of hers.

Anna collected lost hair pins from the sheet and used them to fasten her bubble. It wound up slightly askew, a fact I decided to keep to myself because we were already tardy and Seppi was peering out from under my featherbed with his urgent I-have-to-go look.

"Could you take him downstairs to pee?" I asked as my sister fluffed her featherbed over her mattress, meticulously matching corners.

"In the morning it's your job," she said. "I only have to do it at night."

"Just this once?" I pleaded. "I don't want to risk bumping into *him*."

"Neither do I." She rummaged in her powder-blue makeup bag, adding her comb and toothbrush. "Why do you think I spend so much time at Peter's? You ought to be glad you're getting away for a couple of months."

"But O.F.'s only home on week-ends," I pointed out. "I'd still have five days out of every week to have fun. Besides, you know I always get homesick at camp. And I hate nuns."

"That makes two of us." She slung a clean hand towel over her shoulder and slapped her thigh at Seppi as she went past my bed. He jumped to the floor and followed her into the empty kitchen. "You better hurry," she whispered, closing the door. "You don't want to miss early Mass. Not today, anyway."

Returning Elvis to his cage, I stuffed in a couple of my worn socks and a stained handkerchief to comfort him with my scent during our long separation and then carefully secured the wire door. He stuck his quivering nose between two of the bars and I touched it with a fingertip. "Now you can hibernate in style while I'm gone. Don't forget me. I'll think of you every day."

I pushed the cage under my bed and considered the stiff navy-blue dress. Two hours with that on my skin would give me hives that were sure to last for the rest of the day. I'd always been sensitive to wool. Not only was Mutti ignoring that fact but she made me feel guilty about it, as if I were manifesting red welts in order to score a point.

I grimaced at the blue dress with distaste. Next thing I knew I had stuffed it into the wardrobe and brought out my favorite outfit—a flaring black cotton skirt painted with giant red poppies and the short-sleeved white peasant blouse I always wore with it. Both were well used, soft, and exquisitely comfortable.

I took off the damp, wrinkled clothes I had slept in and got dressed. Then I got busy working nighttime snags out of my long hair with a wire brush. Staring at myself in the mirror, I felt a moment of doubt. Red poppies, in church? Maybe if I sat in the last pew no one would notice. I raised my arms over my head and twirled, watching with satisfaction as the skirt flared in the glass. Gypsy, for sure.

As part of my morning ritual I climbed on my mattress, gazed deep into Ricky Nelson's colluding eyes, and planted a kiss on his pouty lips. It had taken me months to collect all of his life-sized body parts out of *Bravo* magazines. They printed the head last but it was well worth the wait. Mutti was amused by my singular devotion and contributed the '45. I listened to the record every chance I got but unfortunately I had yet to crack the twang-code.

As far as I could tell "Thurlnerbeanionels" played on one side and "Imatravlimain" played on the other.

When I saw Anna hurrying across the street toward Peter's I ventured into the kitchen where Seppi was busy with an unusual breakfast consisting of leftover potatoes mixed with green beans and a liberal scoop of liver dumpling soup. I, on the other hand, found only the usual thick slab of dark rye on my plate. The bread was smeared with a transparent film of margarine and topped by a shadow of jam. That of itself wouldn't have been so bad if it hadn't come with the one thing I disliked even more than liver—scalded milk left to cool, covered with thick slimy skin. Propped against my cup was a sheet of paper. I recognized Mutti's meticulous script. She wrote,

Liebes Mariandl!

Herr Adler needs me to help him prepare for his trip to New York. Onkel Franz has volunteered to drive you to the Hauptbahnhof (train station) *without me. I'll meet you at the train. Your bath will be ready right after church, so don't dawdle.*

Wash thoroughly. Franz will inspect. Your suitcase is in the car.

Deine Dichliebende Mutti (your loving mother)

P.S.: Drink your milk!

Franz will inspect? Your loving Mutti? Hardly! With an exasperated groan I sent the note sailing to the floor.

It wasn't fair. Anna got to stay home with her Peter all summer. She'd be free to bike to the lake every day, play volleyball on our street until dark, and go to the neighborhood cinema on Saturday afternoons while I was banished to the same awful place I'd suffered through the previous summer. A ride in O.F.'s VW, which reeked of raw gasoline, was only the first part of a long ordeal.

At camp I would be forced to: kneel in chapel before dawn; gag on lumpy breakfast gruel; partake in endless hikes after lunch every day; pick at dinner salads gritty with sand and an occasional insect; pretend I didn't care when the other girls laughed at my broad Bavarian dialect, and cry myself to sleep every night. Try as I might I couldn't find one good reason to let O.F. drive me to the train station today.

And then it happened again. My brain meant to do one thing but my body did something else. I picked up the cup *intending* to go to the silverware drawer and get out a fork so that I could fish the disgusting skin off the milk before it had a chance to break into gag-sized pieces. But instead I found myself at the sink, tilting the cup and pouring every drop down the drain. The next moment I was retrieving the note, turning it over, and writing on the back in large, daring block letters:

I AM NOT GOING AND NOBODY CAN MAKE ME! —MARIA

I tore the crust off my bread, broke it to pieces, dropped them through the top slots of Elvis's cage as a good-bye present, carefully locked the bedroom door, and gave Seppi half of what I had left. "Hang in there," I told him. "It'll be Monday soon. Meanwhile make yourself small and pretend you're asleep so that O.F. forgets you're here."

Too bad I couldn't take that advice for myself. Crossing the cramped postage-stamp hallway, just big enough to hold four doors, I saw that the one to the living room was ajar. I could smell the cloying fumes of O.F.'s hair tonic wafting out from inside, mixed with old cigarette smoke and a night's accumulation of stale breath. Fortunately for me the source of the unappetizing odors was no longer there. Neither was he in the bathroom, where flames were already crackling in the boiler's firebox. Tiny brown bugs were crawling all over the linoleum, looking for cover. They'd hitched rides inside the decayed pine cones O.F. was fond of collecting from the woods to fuel our baths. The box he used for the cones was gone, too—which meant he'd taken it down to the cellar for a refill. And—oh horror—his bath towel and wash mitten, draped over the tub rim, were unpleasantly damp. Not only had he already been sitting on his naked red haunches in the tub but he wanted to make sure that I knew it.

Cautiously I opened our front door, unhooked my red anorak from the coat tree, and tiptoed down the stairs, admiring the shine Mutti had coaxed onto each step. She and Frau Forster, Wolfi's mother, took weekly turns waxing them and the landing, each trying to outdo the other.

A hugely pregnant Frau Huber was emerging from the apartment directly below.

"Grüss Gott, (God's greeting)" I murmured, giving her a quick curtsy in passing.

She was not about to let me get away that easily. "Hello, cuckoo-bird," she said, her gaze lingering on my casual skirt. "Is that what good Catholic girls wear to church these days?" I could hear the faint sound of a shovel scraping across the cellar floor. She moved closer, whispering, "He was at it again last night, wasn't he?"

I nodded, too embarrassed to speak. Last year she had yanked one of my dark curls straight, saying sweetly how odd it was that I did not look the least bit like Anna or Mutti. With her next breath she'd claimed she knew for a fact that Gypsies often steal regular babies to substitute their own, suggesting *I* might be such a cuckoo child.

It had stung. Now I was actually hoping she was right. If she was I could not be held responsible for anything I saw on TV last night. But if not I, then who? When parents refused to shoulder their own guilt it passed to the children and the children's children. It said so right in the Bible.

Rail-thin Herr Huber followed his wife to the landing, buttoning his coat with a polite smile and accusing eyes. "He kept us all awake again, didn't he?" he said, as if I had the power to change O.F.'s behavior. "Last week I spoke to your Mutti about it and she promised it wouldn't happen anymore."

She couldn't change O.F., either. Surely that must be obvious to them by now.

Frau Huber pressed my arm. "Do you want to walk to church with us, cuckoo-bird?" she asked in her sugary, eager-for details voice.

"Come, Liebchen, (sweetie)" her husband said. "She couldn't match our turtle-pace if she tried. You *know* she's never happy unless she's running somewhere."

I wasn't sure that was a friendly remark. The Hubers had been among the biggest gossips against us when O.F. first moved into our apartment—before he and Mutti were properly divorced from their previous spouses.

There was another faint scrape from the cellar, followed by a bout of hacking smoker's cough, growing nearer.

"Wiederseh'n," I gulped, sprinting down the rest of the stairs and out to the stoop. I paused to take a refreshing breath of cool morning air. And then, instead of turning to the right and heading for the corner and church, I turned left and hurried along the full length of the building past the other four lobby doors.

Frau Keppler, who lived in the last ground floor apartment, was leaning out of her window. "Hello, Marianne," she said. "Where are you off to in such a hurry? Church is in the other direction."

I stopped politely because she and I had become good friends after O.F. first moved in. That was in the days when Frau Forster was busy turning all the Catholic tenants against us. Back then everyone except for Frau Keppler took pride in ignoring my shy greetings. She, as the sole Protestant in the building, knew very well what it was like to be shunned. One afternoon she'd invited me in for cookies, chamomile tea, and a look at her latest carton of used-book finds, letting me borrow an armful. The invitations became a weekly event.

"Guten Morgen (good morning), Frau Keppler," I said, smiling up at her.

She leaned out even farther. "I heard the fracas last night. How that man shouts! I have another box of books waiting for you. Why don't you stop by after church so we—'

A primitive howl traveled from our kitchen window along the full length of the building. O.F. had discovered my note. "*Tschüs*! (Bye!)" I gasped, lunging toward the corner without further ado. For once I was grateful I had such a long name. By the time he could channel his fury into articulating all four of its syllables I'd be well out of earshot and out of his range.

CHAPTER 5

THERE WAS NO WAY HE COULD CATCH ME. I was a faster runner. And if he intended to chase me in his car—well, it was locked in one of the garages, halfway to church. Nonetheless, I raced at top speed across front lawn and road, diving behind the next row of apartments and the next, zigging here and zagging there until a side-stitch pulled me to a stop.

Too late, I noticed that I was standing in Heinz's courtyard. And there he was, crouching over an upside-down bike, wrench in hand, spinning the rear wheel. As I struggled for breath he looked up and wordlessly fled into his lobby.

He needn't have bothered; I was already swerving toward the nearest side street. Then I saw a quick flash of white and heard an ominous putt-putt. Surely it couldn't be O.F. But who else drove an obscenely white VW with an air-cooled engine that unfortunately required no warm-up time?

For a few helpless seconds I wheeled in a circle, feeling the settlement crowd in on me from every direction. This hardscrabble part of Munich was congested with Marshall Plan housing crisscrossing over soil mostly too poor for farming. To me, the endless rows of apartments were unsightly brick cages. For the other tenants, they were the first real homes they'd had in years.

After the war East German refugees who were forced to leave their whole lives behind, along with local evacuees whose homes had been destroyed by bombs, were billeted into the spare farm chambers and attics of outlying villages. The farmers accepted these unwanted intrusions grudgingly. Families of four or more crowded into each room. Many of these newcomers refused to assimilate into village life. Like Mutti, they put their names on Munich's housing list for the displaced and were eventually awarded one of the Marshall Plan units.

I pressed a hand over my side ache, pivoted away from the street, and limped along Heinz's narrow walkway through a labyrinth of similar courtyards leading to the main road, which I was hoping to cross as soon as I was certain the white VW was not coming back.

Mutti despised the neighborhood as much as I did, but she appreciated the foothold it gave her. The family residence had collapsed in an air raid, forcing her, Vati and Anna to flee Munich. They wound up in the village of Freidorf, forty kilometers away, and lucked into a dank, spiderweb-shrouded attic. Vati soon converted it into a respectable home complete with kitchen sink and cold running water. The toilet was a plank with a round hole cut in its center, a bucket underneath.

I was born on the farm and thrived among cows and pigs and chickens. I roamed the wide fields all day and often made my way into the surrounding forest, picking berries and gathering mushrooms. But Mutti, born and raised in Munich, frequently complained about primitive village life. She said she had more sophisticated tastes than the farmers and applied for subsidized city housing long before the divorce talk between her and Vati grew serious.

We moved when I was nine—with O.F.'s less than free help and advice. When the moving truck was fully loaded and ready to go I hid in the darkest corner of the Hilde's stable. For once my best friend Gabriel betrayed my trust by leading Mutti straight to it and to me.

I had hated our part of town on first sight, and even though I had to admit that Munich was a beautiful city, it had too many walls, too many squares and angles, too many people, too much traffic, too many rules. In my heart the green village fields awash with wildflowers lived on. Brooks continued to babble. The sun-drenched farm garden kept producing its fresh cornucopia of produce. The dark woods never stopped waiting for me to refill my bucket with berries and mushrooms. Every spruce tree whispered my name.

I had had to leave everything I loved: childhood playmates, my black-and-white cat Putzi, the tepid swimming hole around which our friends often gathered on hot afternoons, the chilly Mangfall river nearby. In all the years of pleading I'd done since, not once did Mutti relent and allow me to return for a visit. Was she afraid I would refuse to return to the city? Could be she was right.

My hollow footsteps traced a narrow walkway between two apartment buildings, from which I could see the unkempt field across the side-street. Beyond it was the long, anonymous brick barrier of the Kaserne (army base) the Amis (Yanks) had appropriated after the war. The top of the barrier was covered with coils of barbed wire and—rumor had it—sprinkled with glass shards.

There was an unspoken neighborhood agreement to pretend the wall wasn't there and that the occupying Americans did not exist. Although I'd walked down this street every school day since I was nine I'd never set foot on the field. I had no idea what the Amis had named this Kaserne or what they were using it for. I was not encouraged to ask.

"The Amis are dangerous," Mutti had preached the few times the subject came up. She didn't say why.

I could see the bus stop on Schleissheimerstrasse from the end of the walkway, and the shuttered bakery shack standing nearby. It was casting a shadow over the unsightly hut hiding behind it. My gaze fastened to the bakery shutters, envisioning my three favorite pastries languishing behind the Sunday-barred window: *Nusshörnchen, Bienenstiche, Negerküsse*. Discovering I was still clutching the remnants of my slab of dark rye, I sat behind a sheltering bush, chewing and licking my sticky fingers.

A girl I knew stood leaning against a sapling on a nearby front lawn, defiantly sucking on an American cigarette. Some months ago Regina had run off with an Ami soldier, leaving nothing but ugly rumors behind. Last week she returned to her mother's cramped upstairs apartment ringless and single, her mouth and nails painted blood-red, wearing neon-bright orange socks and pink plastic barrettes in her newly frizzed hair.

"She looks a fright," Mutti reported when she came home from work that day. "I pity her poor mother."

Now Regina was looking in my direction. I half rose and got ready to wave. But then I heard a fast putt-putt, saw another white flash, and dropped down behind the bush. O.F.'s VW stopped at the curb. He rolled down his window to ask Regina a question. She gave a lazy reply. He drove away. Painstakingly pulling my ankle-slumped socks up to my knees, I waited for the sound of his motor to fade.

When I was sure it was entirely gone I got up and went to the sidewalk. Regina was expertly knocking ashes from the tip of her cigarette. "Hello," I said cautiously, remembering Mutti's warning to stay away from the tarnished girl when possible and give short, polite greetings when it was not.

"Ja, servus, (well, hi) Marianne!" she said, the vulnerable look in her kohl-rimmed eyes at odds with her smug grin. "Your father was just here looking for you."

"He's *not* my father!"

Pursing her painted lips, she took another drag and then blew out the smoke in a passable ring, though I'd seen Mutti do better. Damping the grin to a placating smile, Regina got ready for intimate girl-chat. "A fine morning for a stroll, isn't it?" she began. "Where are you going so early? Church is in the other direction."

"I'm looking for a friend," I said coolly, picking up speed.

"Well, so am I," she shouted after me.

I should have stopped at hello.

Didn't she know the neighborhood verdict? She'd made herself cheap for a piece of chewing gum, a Baby Ruth, a carton of cigarettes. "An Ami cast-off," Mutti had called her over parsleyed potatoes and quark. "Does she think she can just come back here as if nothing has happened?" Passing out canned pineapple rings for desert, she'd added, "Eine gemeine Schickse (a common slut)." Her final comment came as she topped the pineapple with whipped condensed milk. "That's what happens to girls who crave Butterfingers and Coca Cola!"

I knew there was an invisible line good German girls never crossed. Since Regina had crossed it obviously she was no longer good. But what was it, exactly, that made someone a Schickse? And was a Schickse the same as a Hure (whore)?

*

WHEN I was six Mutti had taken me shopping for school shoes in a nearby market town. Right in front of us a woman with flaming cheeks ran out of a house door and fled down the sidewalk, pursued by a man shouting, "Hure! Hure!"

I stopped to take in the scene but Mutti yanked me into the shoe store. "What is he saying?" I asked, straining to hear.

"Uhre, Uhre (clock)," she said, blushing. "He's asking her what time it is."

It didn't make any sense. But because my tender age and Catholic upbringing forbade additional questions I'd merely nodded, filing the incident away for future reference. At six, it had not occurred to me that my mother ever spoke anything but the whole truth, no matter how nonsensical her words sometimes seemed. At fifteen, I still did not know the difference between *Hure* and *Uhre* but lately I'd begun to notice that she was capable of bending the facts.

*

HURRYING away from Regina, I allowed the blurred hut behind the bakery to come into full focus for the very first time. Unpainted, warped, surrounded by broken bits of glass glittering in sunlight, it had a sign affixed to its bolted door, right under a naked red bulb. It said, "ALABAMA BAR."

I had a mental glimpse of vague shapes loitering at night and imagined shrill laughter and the beating of drums. Once Wolfi claimed the bar was a place where black Ami soldiers danced with white-powdered, obese specters not seen in the light of day. I thought he was making it up. Wasn't there something about knives and blood, too?

As far as I knew this stretch was harmless between daybreak and dusk. What happened here afterwards had nothing to do with me. My bedtime was eight on the dot and Anna's was eight-thirty. In Mutti's opinion the best place for growing girls, after the sun set, was in their own beds.

I'd asked Mutti about the hut on our first day of school in the city, when she'd shown Anna and me the best route to walk to the neighborhood grade school. "Promise me you'll ignore that shack," she said, blushing. "It has nothing to do with us. The Amis can be quite wicked."

Yet last night on TV they'd looked like liberators to me. How could they be both at the same time?

Now I went to sit at the bus stop, patting every one of my anorak pockets for change. I'd neglected to bring so much as a Pfennig. Without the means to pay bus fare to town my options were narrowing. If I stayed in our part of town O.F. would find me for sure. But where else could I go? I considered the maze of identical apartment buildings to my left. Then I scanned the sea of tiny look-alike houses across the street to my right. Their proud owners considered themselves a cut above Marshall Plan tenants. Each of the miniature gems was surrounded by a little fenced yard crowded with small flower and vegetable beds and dwarf fruit trees. To own one of these rectangular slivers of paradise was Mutti's most ardent desire.

She paid just forty D-Mark rent for our no-frills one-bedroom flat. It meant she'd had to tack her own linoleum over the subflooring after we moved in. The new bathroom had been empty except for a toilet and the small sink beside it. She had to buy a tub. The kitchen only held a bigger sink and a wall-mounted gas ring with two turners. During our first years in Munich there were times she had to choose between groceries, home improvements, and rent. The rent always came first.

O.F. started paying it once they married. In return she had to hand over her entire paycheck to him. He deposited her salary in their joint Bausparvertrag (savings account) at the bank and gave her a meager weekly household allowance out of his income. For fifteen years her checks would feed that savings account and then they'd cash out to buy their own tiny house. In the meanwhile we were almost totally dependent on O.F. Sometimes she had to remind Anna and me that each bite we ate came to us from the goodness of his heart, for we weren't his natural children and he owed us nothing at all.

We should have stayed in the comfortable attic on the farm, with no O.F. to be grateful to, a lush garden, the soft lines of meadows and forest around us, the horizon framed by the Alps. So what if Mutti had to drag the poop-bucket down three flights of stairs to the outhouse at least twice every day? On the farm, Mutti swore regularly that one day I'd see the village for the mud hole it was. Then I'd be glad she'd rescued me from it.

Yet even she appreciated the wheat field adjacent to our city apartment. It was the last field of its kind in this hardscrabble place. Already, the new Protestant church had taken a chunk of it and soon the rest would be plowed under, yielding to the Marshall Plan march.

I was looking down the length of Schleissheimerstrasse, half-waiting for a bus I couldn't afford to ride on, half-wondering what to do next, when I thought I heard loose engine valves clicking rapidly closer. I ran across the intersection and dove behind the next row of apartments, walking alongside the back walls so that I wouldn't be visible from the street. Moving from one building to another, and another still, I aimed straight for the invisible forbidden line where Germany ceased and America began. He'd never look for me there. Across that line was new country where Mutti's strict rules did not apply.

Finally I dared getting back to the sidewalk and soon came to the scraggly lot at the end of our neighborhood. On its far side was a plant nursery, hiding behind a mound of steaming compost. A stooped elderly man was pulling his handcart along the nursery path towards the street. The cart was loaded with red geraniums in clay pots.

He got to the sidewalk in time to block my passage, dropped the handle and wiped his forehead with a crumpled kerchief, carefully dabbing at the wart on the tip of his nose. It sprouted a single white hair.

I offered him a polite "Grüss Gott" and tried not to stare but the wart was hard to avoid.

He wagged his finger at me and said in a gloomy, end-of-world tone, "Not Grüss Gott. Behüt dich Gott (God protect you)!" Then he blew his nose and asked, getting louder, "What are you doing here, mein Kind (my child)? Your place is in church."

Well, so was his! But instead of pointing out the obvious I silently curtsied, skirted around him and his old cart, and walked on.

"Who is your mother?" he called after me, his voice still rising. "Does she know where you're going?"

When I didn't answer he screeched, "Don't go that way! It's no place for a good Catholic girl!"

I lengthened my stride, embarrassed for him and for me. It wasn't as if I intended to do something bad. This was only an innocent Sunday stroll, after all—even if I *was* running away from home. His protest did pique my curiosity, though. Eagerly leaning forward, I quickened my pace to find out what it was he didn't want me to see.

CHAPTER 6

L AST YEAR MY FRIEND WOLFI got a brand-new bicycle for his birthday. With its shimmering marine-blue paint and slim racing wheels it was the wonder of the neighborhood. A swarm of kids surrounded it to run their hands over the smooth metal and the elegant leather seat. My favorite parts were the chrome handlebars, so bright they reflected my face like a fun-house mirror.

With all my heart I wanted a bicycle just like his. I might have mentioned this fervent desire to Mutti once or twice, for when my own birthday came around she beckoned me downstairs with an avid smile and pointed to a beribboned old-lady bike leaning heavily against the house wall. Its original shade of utility-black had been inexpertly covered with gooey pastel-green paint. The rust on the handlebars had almost disappeared under a layer of gray primer. Both balloon tires were worn, the seat springs permanently exhausted from its long association with a more ample behind. Worst of all, another beribboned old-lady bike teetered nearby, this one painted powder-blue.

I sensed a hapless design.

"Happy birthday!" Mutti sang out, beaming proudly. "The green bike is for you. It's your favorite color." She rubbed a thumb over a thick drop of hardened enamel. "It goes so well with your dark hair and eyes."

I wanted to remind her that my favorite color was poppy-red. But then I recalled the green wool cap and shawl she'd given me for Christmas, and the matching sweater that had been Vati's contribution, and knew they'd made up their mind on the subject and were not interested in my own humble tastes.

Gazing admiringly at the powder-blue apparition, Mutti added, "I know Anna's birthday's not till fall but you don't mind if she gets her present a little early this year, do you? So you can ride around together?"

Three months early? On *my* special day?

"We *can't* ride together," I said flatly.

"Why ever not?"

"Because green and blue clash. At least that's what you've always told me. You wouldn't want us to clash, would you?"

"But—I was talking about *clothes*, Marianne," she said, flustered. "Green and blue clothes, on the same person. Not bikes."

Anna, lagging behind, finally arrived on the stoop, blinking at her good fortune. While she gushed her gratitude I tried to work up enough appreciation for my second-hand bicycle to put a rosy glow on Mutti's cheeks.

Eventually I got over my dashed hopes and realized the plodding green nag did everything a bike should do, including racing its unlucky twin down the street to sure victory. Wolfi, with uncharacteristic restraint, never challenged me to a match, and I was wise enough not to suggest one.

*

ON THE Sunday of my unexpected and startling rebellion I broke out of my childhood prison to enter a world in which cerulean skies and emerald fields met a distant forest, tinting the horizon a misty turquoise.

For a girl whose favorite color was supposed to be green I had come to the right place. It also appeared to be the favorite color of the United States Army in this new world I had haplessly stumbled across. There was an unkempt grassy field on the other side of the highway, stretching to a long chain link fence. The rows of barracks behind the fence were painted light-green. Between fence and barracks scurried small ant-like figures who were dressed in drab-olive. On the tarred access road to a barred gate green trucks and jeeps stopped in front of a sentry who saluted the drivers smartly before and after checking their papers. Above him, a sign read,

H E N R Y   K A S E R N E

Apparently the Amis were no better Catholics than me, for the highway was abuzz with un-Sunday-like traffic. I was the only pedestrian in sight. It explained why the huge American cars passing were tooting their horns. A girl out walking seemed to be a novelty here.

"Hey, baby!" a man's voice shouted from a roundish green hulk screeching to a halt beside me. The passenger window rolled down. A hand emerged, holding a green pack of chewing gum. "Gum?" the voice asked. Then the soldier it belonged to stuck his head out of the window, his hair clipped to stubble.

"No, thank you," I replied in flawless English.

He seemed to find my response encouraging, for he asked, "Care for a ride?" with a boyish, winsome grin.

What kind of fool did he take me for? "No speak English," I said in a guttural accent as he climbed out, the pack of gum flat on his palm as if he were trying to lure a dog into grabbing range. I bolted across the highway and onto the field, not slowing until I heard him slam his car door and rev up his motor. Tires spun. The car sped away. Only when it was completely out of sight did I dare return to the highway.

No more than half a minute later an immense red convertible, its cream-colored roof folded down, slowed to match my walking pace. The driver waved a green bottle of beer, patted the passenger seat, and yelled, "Hop in, sugar!"

But after my experience last year with the dark-blue Opel I had no desire to get into a strange car ever again. So I kept my focus on the turquoise horizon until he drove off in a huff.

And then a transport truck veered onto the shoulder, the rear full of *Ami* soldiers, all of them wearing mud-green uniforms with matching caps. The driver honked, grinning from ear to ear and running his gaze over my body. I kept walking and concentrated on keeping my footfalls steady. Until a piercing police whistle nailed my feet to the road. I expected a squad of blue-coated Polizei (police) to surround me, snap handcuffs onto my wrists, and haul me away. Maybe there was some kind of law against a girl walking alone on the side of this highway.

Then one of the soldiers on the truck bed winked at me, held up two fingers, stuck them in his mouth, and whistled again. When I flinched he yelled something that made the rest of them laugh and slap their knees. Frightened, I scurried back to the field and cringed at the hilarity my evasive maneuver was triggering behind me. If I ran all the way to the fence, would the ant-like figures behind it rush to the wire and stick candy-bars at me through the mesh?

It was at that point that I suddenly remembered what I'd heard about the forest at the horizon. Just last week the German police had discovered the bodies of three German girls buried under the trees, each in her own shallow grave mulched with a layer of old leaves. Did they invite their own deaths simply by walking along this very road? Did they accept the offered gum, the beer, a ride in the pretty convertible? If American soldiers considered girls like me prey I had better find a way to discourage their attentions at once.

After the truck drove on I returned to the shoulder, switching my leisurely pace to a brisk stride. I'd often seen Mutti rush to the bus stop with the same air of importance. Once I had jokingly called it her efficient-secretary-trot. Now I copied it as best I could without the aid of her perilous spiked heels.

My business-like pace seemed to work for a while. I was making good progress. My shadow kept getting shorter. I began to relax. From directly overhead the sun was caressing my shoulders. Was it lunch time already? On cue, my stomach rumbled. I wished I had thought to bring something to eat.

With any luck, if I kept putting one foot in front of the other, the highway would take me all the way to the forest. I pictured myself under a canopy of luminous green, picking blueberries, scooping clear water from a nearby stream, nesting in a mossy hollow bordering some cozy little clearing, and whiling away the afternoon. I'd listen to bird song and watch white clouds drift past the tree tops. In the bright light of high noon those three unlucky faceless girls faded from my mind and were gone.

At dusk, I would watch the clouds turn silver and sail across the moon. I would have to stay in the forest well into the night, for I realized I could not return home until Mutti's anger had been transformed into concern and worry. By then all these bothersome Amis would be fast asleep, leaving the roads empty so that I could glide through the night unscathed. It seemed a good plan.

I passed another military compound. The sign over its padlocked gate read,

WILLIAMS KASERNE

Behind a long and high chain link fence endless rows of jeeps, transport trucks and tanks sat in a vast parking lot, aligned in neat rows. The base abutted a group of small houses sitting behind privacy hedges. Each of the cottages peering warily over its own picket fence looked more like a fortress than a dream home. The houses gave way to a cluster of storage sheds. Most of the doors were locked but one was partially open, revealing the rear end of a black BMW motorcycle.

All at once, without warning, a horn blasted immediately behind me. I could actually feel the heat of a radiator at the small of my back. I refused to react and kept my pace smooth and even, reminding my fluttering heart that I had no intention of being anyone's quarry. The horn blasted again, this time for a good ten seconds. I ignored it. Then an oversized yellow shark-finned boat of a car pushed itself into my line of vision, herding me against the nearest shed wall.

I was not impressed. After all, it was broad daylight; bad things only happened at night. Without missing a beat, keeping my eyes averted, I squeezed around the front bumper and crossed the road to the opposite shoulder where I continued facing the oncoming traffic. The yellow car must have found my maneuver discouraging, for it made a U-turn and sped away to Henry Kaserne. I kept up my pace and soon encountered a whitewashed brick wall running parallel to the road. It was too high for me to see over. Then came a gate, invitingly open, a sentry at each end. The sign above them, as white as the wall, read,

W A R N E R   K A S E R N E

I was impressed with the solid look of the structures inside. They seemed more like fancy apartment complexes than the barracks I'd seen at Henry Kaserne. Narrow roads curved pleasantly between and around buildings, giving the compound the cozy feel of a village. Amis strolled across the cobblestone pavement, enjoying the mid-day heat.

An American woman, driving a beige, topless convertible through the entrance, turned down the first lane past a sign shaped like an arrow, which spelled out the word "Library." It was the English word for *Bibliothek*. The woman was wearing huge sunglasses and jumbo pink plastic curlers half-covered by a fluttering scarf. Two toddlers were bouncing on the back seat. I wondered what kind of books she would borrow and how big the library was and if I'd ever get a chance to see it for myself.

The whitewashed wall continued on the other side of the gate. A stone's throw away stood a covered bus stop. Inside, an old man wearing a Bavarian Trachtenjacke (traditional jacket) had fallen asleep while waiting for the next bus. On the other end of the bench sat a slim woman wearing a tailored suit, impatiently swinging a crossed leg. She was drawing on a cigarette while she studied me from head to toe, raising judgmental eyebrows, her free hand drumming on the suitcase at her feet. I wished her a good day but she made no reply.

Most of the American vehicles on the highway were turning off at Warner Kaserne. The road between me and the woods was virtually deserted. Wide-open fields sprawled uninterrupted to the horizon, except for a solitary Gasthaus (inn) standing a few hundred paces ahead. It had a splendid beer garden, still empty, where red-checkered tables waited under blossoming chestnut trees for an after-church crowd of hungry customers. I caught a whiff of the meaty aroma of today's special wafting from the restaurant kitchen. It blended nicely with an equally mouthwatering smell of roasting onions, making me doubly ravenous.

I searched through my anorak pockets again but they were as empty as they'd been last time I checked. Oh why did I rush from the apartment without thinking? I could have upended my locked savings-bank, worked Mutti's surgical tweezers through the grated slot on the bottom, and fished out a few of the fat one-Mark pieces that were inside. That's what she used to do in the pre-O.F. days whenever we ran out of food.

What if I arrived at the forest to discover that blueberries and hazelnuts were not yet in season? The only things remotely edible growing in the field beside me were *Sauerampfer,* their leaves as sour as the name implied. The tantalizing smell of the restaurant's meat-drippings conjured an image of a juicy slice of roast, a generous pool of sauce, and a creamy heap of mashed potatoes. If one of those aggressive Amis came to offer me a Baby Ruth now, would I have the moral strength to decline?

*

WHEN I was halfway to the woods I saw a bicycle coasting out of the tree line, heading in my direction. I watched it grow from a toy to an indigo ten-speed French racer. The rider, wearing a red polo shirt the exact shade of my anorak, was the first real live black man I'd ever seen up close. His skin was the color of bittersweet chocolate, his brows and cropped curls so black that they shone blue, his teeth Pepsodent-white. He smiled and before I had time to think I gave him an answering smile.

"Gruss Gott, Fraulein," he said in passing.

"Grüss Gott, Frä*u*lein," I corrected, turning to watch him ride toward Warner Kaserne. From behind he looked like a Masai warrior wearing Western attire, or maybe a Watusi prince. No Ami I'd ever seen rode around on a bike.

Overhead, a fluffy white cloud-ship sailed in front of the sun. The air grew noticeably cooler. I tore my gaze from his shapely royal back and continued my walk toward the woods. A few minutes later I heard the soft clatter of his bicycle chain as he came riding back in my direction. He smiled again as he slowly rolled past me. I admired the clean, regal arch of his blue-black brows and his well-sculpted cheekbones. Because I'd been drawing faces since I was old enough to hold a pencil, I knew good lines when I saw them. His were better than good. But his skin was not the color of dark chocolate after all. It had a more coppery hue, a warm brown lit from within as if it had soaked up all of this morning's sunshine.

"Guten Tag (good day)," he said pleasantly, coasting more slowly still. Above us, the clouds were moving away from the sun, drifting off with the breeze.

I responded with "Good Aaafternoon," in my best King's English. He pedaled on, giving me another chance to admire his athletic shape from behind—broad shoulders, muscular arms, a slim, tapering back, and endless legs. He was growing rapidly smaller. Then he was gone. The ribbon of highway stretching before me seemed empty without him. I felt bereft. The temperature was dropping; a bank of new clouds, ugly and gray, were casting a deep shadow across the land as they neared the sun. I turned up my collar, stuffed my hands into the anorak's pockets, and walked on.

Miraculously, he reappeared just a few minutes later—a small dot traveling purposefully in a straight line toward me, gaining in size.

According to everything Mutti had taught me it was high time for me to cross to the opposite side of the road, signaling disinterest. But how could I when he seemed so familiar already? Familiar *and* trustworthy, because he had not offered me a stick of gum, wasn't wearing a foreign uniform, was not whistling at me as if I were a stray dog.

Restored to his full size he was achingly beautiful. He braked the bike beside me, planted both feet firmly on the ground, and said, "Hot day. Care for a Coke?"

I could only understand the first sentence. The clouds had begun to move on, allowing warm sunshine to caress my shoulders. "Hot," I agreed, folding my collar down, taking my hands out of the pockets, unzipping the jacket.

His long, slender finger pointed to the Gasthaus I had so recently passed. He said slowly, "A cold soda," pantomiming the act of picking up a glass and drinking from it.

"No, thank you," I answered. "I have no money today." I shook out my pockets to prove it.

He shifted his weight and tried again, his words even slower than before, pointing first at himself and then at me, "I—buy—you—Coca Cola." He showed me a fistful of coins.

"No!" I protested. "I do not want Coca Cola!" Surely, this was my cue to move on. But I stayed.

He eased the change out of sight. "What. Drink. You. Like?" he asked. "I buy."

I tried to ponder the ethics of his offer but the vision of a tall, frosty glass interfered. Creamy. White. Wholesome. And best of all, cold milk had no skin.

"Milk?" I ventured. "Cold?"

He grinned, once more displaying his flawless teeth. "Okay! Cold milk for two!" He got off, crooked an elegant finger, and started to push the bike toward the inn.

I stood undecided, counting pros and cons. True, he *was* a stranger— but it wasn't as if I was really going anywhere with him. The inn was a public place, the tables under the flowering chestnut trees perfectly harmless and benign. Besides, hadn't Mutti, in her terse note, practically *ordered* me to drink milk? And since I'd already broken so many taboos today, adding one more to the list would make little difference.

He beckoned again. Taking one small step, and then another, I followed—without realizing that huge and lasting consequences begin just that way.

CHAPTER 7

W E WERE THE FIRST CUSTOMERS in the beer-garden that early afternocn, choosing a table under the most massive tree, admiring its huge Chestnut leaves and creamy blossoms as we sat. Then we started with basics.

He pointed at his chest. "Joe," he said, "as in GI."

Already I was lost.

"*Your* name?" he prompted.

I started out saying, "Is Mariann—," then quickly changed my answer to, "Is Maria." Loving the music the three vowels made, I repeated, "Yes. My name is Maria."

"You sure?" he asked, looking amused.

I was sure.

The approaching waitress was the motherly sort, comfortably padded, wearing a pretty blue dirndl with the traditional low neckline and ballooning white sleeves. She pulled two menus and an ordering pad from her black apron and held her pencil at the ready.

"You're too quick," Joe told her. "Give us a minute here."

She acquiesced with a friendly smile, busying herself with rearranging the chairs at the other tables while Joe scanned the menu, hunting for recognizable items. Glancing sideways at me, he said, carefully enunciating each word, "So, you're out for a walk. Where are you going?"

"To the forest."

"Why?"

"Because I run away. It is a good place to hide."

His nostrils flared as he digested the unexpected information. Then he asked, "How long are you planning to stay in the woods?"

"To dark. Very dark."

He rubbed his strong chin, which had a cleft in it, just like Kirk Douglas'. "I see," he went on. "What'll you do in the woods all afternoon, by yourself?"

I gave a careless shrug. "Walk. Sit. Sleep."

He started to grin, covered his mouth, waited until he had his face under control, and tapped on the beverage list. "This word here. Does it mean 'milk'?"

"*Milch*. Yes."

Delighted, he said, "Hey, I'm getting good at this. By the time I leave Deutschland, I'll be talking like a native—if you'll pardon the expression."

Before I could confess that I didn't have the slightest idea what I should pardon or why the waitress was back at his elbow.

"Bitteschön (if you please)," she said, putting a towel-covered breadbasket between us. "Jetzat! (Let's start)" She brandished the pencil again.

"Svai milks." He held up two fingers in case she didn't get the point. "Cold."

"*Ja, gut*," she murmured, writing on her pad. "And?"

I was already lifting the end of the towel to examine an assortment of warm Bretzen and rolls. Right on cue, my stomach gave a loud growl. "Excuse!" I said, embarrassed by the rude noise.

Joe considered me thoughtfully and then pointed to an entry on the menu. "This here. Says wieners and sauerkraut, right? Two plates, bitte."

"Jawohl, (sure)" she beamed, writing.

"Only one," I told him. "For you. Nothing for me. I cannot pay."

"Who asked you to?" He shut his menu, took charge of mine, held them both out to her and repeated, "Two plates."

"No," I said again. "I cannot pay!"

But he waved the waitress away. When she was gone, he leaned toward me, suddenly serious. "Listen. I'd do the same for anyone in your shoes. You know why?"

I shook my head.

"Because I've been there myself. Ran away from home when I was no older than you. If I hadn't my dad would have kicked me out anyway. See, I was adopted when I was a baby . . ."

"Ach! Good!" I cried. "I, also. Perhaps." Clearly, we had something in common. Neither of us had been a wanted child.

He looked startled. "It wasn't as much fun as you might think. My adoptive mom died when I was fifteen, and my dad, he married again, lickety-split—"

Another near match. "Genau (Exactly)!" I said, tearing a roll in two and stuffing half in my mouth, the other in my pocket.

"You crack me up." He chuckled, shaking his head, then he leaned back in his chair and watched me chew. "Seriously, Maria, if you don't mind returning to our original subject—you don't have any money. What are you planning to eat for supper tonight?"

"Berries. Nuts."

"And wild mushrooms?" He sounded doubtful.

"We have start talk from you now," I said. "You have not finished your story. You are born in what state?"

"Maryland." Right away he could tell it wasn't one I'd looked up on a map lately. "Down by Virginia," he explained. "South. The stepmother didn't want me around. She was always complaining about me. Making me look bad."

Another near hit. "Yes," I agreed, nodding vigorously.

Somewhat flustered, he stroked the straight bridge of his nose before going on. "Finally one day she put it to him—either I left or she would. I could see where it was heading. I guess my dad, he only put up with me all those years because my mom loved me and he loved her, if you know what I mean."

I nodded sagely, tore a second roll, and squirreled half of it away.

But he was looking inward now and barely noticed. "Soon as I turned sixteen I went north. I could tell nobody would miss me. Meant to cross the border into Canada—by then I was sick of the states, you see—but I got stuck in Vermont. You know Vermont?"

"We learn from Africa now. North America comes next year. I know not Vermont."

"You should," he said. "Reminds me of your country. Cold. Very cold. I hung on for a year, doing odd jobs and starving between. Wore me out. By the time I turned seventeen I was so desperate that I lied about my age and joined the Army. It was that or freeze into a skinny icicle, see? I was tall for my age and they needed recruits, so—here I am. Been a GI for two endless years. One more to go before I get to go home. To whatever."

The waitress brought our tray, lifted off two sturdy, oval plates heaped with steaming sauerkraut and plump, rosy sausages, and placed an ice-cold glass of milk next to each. No sooner had she bustled away than I dabbed a spoonful of mustard on the rim of my plate, cut a huge chunk off my first sausage, savored the bite, and gave a contented sigh. "Eat," I urged Joe. "*Guten Appetit* (good appetite)."

"Right. *Gesundheit* (to your health), and all that. Don't forget to chew."

"I don't." Discreetly, I licked greasy juice from my lips. "What will you do when you go to whatever?"

His face turned dreamy. "What I should have done in the first place—hitch to California. Mild climate. Lots of jobs. And if your luck doesn't hold and you go broke you can always sleep on the beach and pick oranges straight from the trees."

"Same in *Italien*. How do you say—Italy? Where fathers love children. Bambini. California fathers also love children?"

"I wouldn't know about that. I'm not a kid anymore. Nineteen is full-grown." He drew an "M" on the mist that had collected on the outside his glass and took a long drink. Then he swiped at his upper lip, missing the milk-mustache under his nose.

"Nineteen is old," I agreed, thinking of Anna who was rapidly sliding in that direction. My wieners had disappeared, leaving me with a daunting pile of hot pickled cabbage, not nearly as easy to swallow.

Joe watched my indifferent chewing for a few seconds before forking one of his sausages onto my plate. "Don't you like kraut? I thought all you guys did."

"Only im Notfall (in an emergency). When all else is gone." I ate his contribution before he could change his mind. But he was growing pensive again.

"In the Army, they feed you and give you a bunk, but there's too many rules. Stupid ones. And the pay's lousy. Nothing but pocket money. Heck, I earned more cutting lawns. Hey, look a-here!" He tensed. "We have an audience."

He was right—we were no longer alone. Half the tables were now occupied by locals wearing muted church-type clothing. Everyone was staring at us. Joe clutched at his napkin, then he took a calming breath and waved regally in every direction until they felt ashamed of their bad manners and looked elsewhere. The waitress fluttered from table to table, carrying trays of foaming mugs and plates of the special, which seemed to be sliced veal with mashed potatoes smothered in gravy. It would have made a wonderful second course.

I scooped up a forkful of sauerkraut. "You like my country?"

He shrugged. "It rains a lot and I don't have a car, so I don't get out much. But I sure would like to see a castle or two if I knew what streetcar to take. Maybe you could show me sometime."

I said nothing, unaware he'd asked me a question.

"It would be nice to get away from the barracks on the weekends," he elaborated. "I could get a day pass. Have to ask permission for everything. Like a child." He frowned at his remaining three sausages.

"Eat them," I urged. "You will like."

He cut off an end-piece with his fork and chewed with obvious enjoyment. "I like," he said. "Better than any hot dog I ever had." Deftly, he sliced one of the hard rolls, stuffed the rest of the sausage inside, and smeared on a blob of mustard. "Ketchup?" he asked, scanning the table. "Never mind. You guys call it 'tomato-puree' and mix it with water." I was amazed to discover that he could stretch his mouth wide enough to accommodate half of what he seemed to think was a cooked dog. With one gulp it was gone. A line of yellow joined the white under his nose. Mutti would have lost no time pointing out both lines to him. If she had dared, she would have wet her napkin with god-knows-what and wiped them off without asking—which was precisely why I decided not to give them the slightest attention.

"Look up there," he said, licking his lips. "The weather in your country changes faster than you can blink." The sky had become engulfed by an ocean of clouds. One particular black spot hovered just above the horizon. "It'll pour in ten, fifteen minutes," he predicted. "And you don't even have an umbrella. I'm afraid the woods are out unless you're looking for a case of pneumonia. I best be getting myself and the bike back to Henry before the storm hits. What will *you* do?"

What, indeed. "I will sit in the little bus-house by Warner Kaserne until the rain stops. *Then* I go to the wood."

He considered. "What if it doesn't stop raining till dark? You might get arrested. Don't you know about the curfew?"

"What is a curfew?"

"Underage girls are not allowed around here after eight. Heck, if the Polizei saw you now, sitting with me, they'd drag you off somewhere. This area isn't a good place for you to be, even on a sunny afternoon."

"Why not?"

"Too many wolves."

I was almost sure there were no wolves in the forest. Foxes and badgers maybe, but no wolves.

He slid his remaining sausages onto my plate. "Eat up before they get cold," he said. "If I can get ahold of the CO I'll ask for an evening pass. It's almost payday, though—which means I'm very close to dead broke, along with most everyone else in the company. But I'll scrounge some cash somewhere and meet you outside of Henry at, say, six o'clock. Eighteen-hundred hours, that is. I'll ask around to see where I can take you. To keep you safe from the Polizei, I mean. And me from the MPs."

I was grateful for his concern, so like that of a big brother watching out for his younger sister. The word "safe" was especially endearing to me. "MPs?"

"Military Police," he spelled out. "If they find us together we'll both be in trouble."

"But why? We do nothing wrong!"

With a dry laugh he said, "I bet they wouldn't see it that way. Here, might as well empty the basket." He pushed it at me. "Stuff every pocket. You never know where your next meal's coming from and when. And don't forget to finish your milk."

*

HE WAS right about the weather. By the time we'd walked halfway to Henry the entire sky was an ominous black. My summer clothes were starting to feel uncomfortably thin. The first drops fell just as we arrived at the base gate. "What'll you do until six?" he asked.

I looked in the direction of the highway, trying to think.

"Here, squeeze into the phone booth for a minute," he said. "I'll be right back."

As soon as I shut myself in a thick curtain of rain dropped between Joe and me. He disappeared behind it. Ground fog swirled to embrace the booth, which smelled vaguely of urine and vomit. Even though I could see nothing outside and no one was near, I felt guilty for taking up such a valuable bit of public space.

A lot of people couldn't afford home phones. Public phone booths were always in demand. It was not uncommon to see five or six disgruntled people stare angrily through the glass at the lucky person inside, who was most likely leaning against the folding door to keep it shut, pretending not to see their collective scowls. If he hoarded the receiver for more than five minutes they would advance as a unit, rapping on every panel. And if that did not bring immediate results they'd force open the door to yell insults.

Thus, I felt guilty for being inside the booth under false pretenses. Every now and then I could feel the sentry's eyes on me. Finally I unhooked the receiver, pressed it to my ear, and engaged in an animated pretend-conversation just in case he was thinking of coming over to evict me from my refuge. When the rap I feared finally came I almost dropped the receiver in fright. But it was only Joe, dripping wet, pushing a fuzzy winter coat and an umbrella against the outside of the glass.

"Don't ask me why I didn't use the umbrella on the way over," he chuckled, opening it for me when I stepped out. "Not in the habit, I guess. Here, put on this coat. Hey, I think I can swing it." He guided my arms into the sleeves, not bothering to first remove the anorak. "Not by six, though. It'll have to be closer to seven. But don't hang around here, and don't walk along the highway by yourself anymore either. Take this." He transferred a handful of change from his pocket to mine. "Maybe you can ride on the bus for a while. Keep out of trouble."

On my way to the nearest bus stop I played with the coins, feeling uneasy. The way I understood the good-girl rules, the only way I could begin to use any of this money was to vow to myself that I would pay back every Pfennig out of my savings, first chance I'd get. Inside Joe's silk-lined coat and underneath the unwieldy umbrella, I managed to stay reasonably warm and dry. I sat in the bus shelter until the next bus came to take me into the city. At the Kurfürstenplatz I transferred onto a streetcar contemplating the extraordinary circumstances of my chance encounter with Joe and mentally listing the many things we already had in common, starting with the extraordinary combination of our biblical names.

At the end of the line I bought the latest Bravo magazine from a kiosk, stretched my legs, and got back on the streetcar for the return trip across town. Because my life was getting more exciting than anything the teen magazine had to offer I kept it closed on my lap as the streetcar clanged from stop to stop. Eventually I got hungry enough eat my stash of rolls, furtively chewing each bite with a minimal movement of my jaws, well aware that eating on a streetcar was strictly verboten (forbidden). I transferred to another line at the Stachus and rocked comfortably from one section of town to another, alternately nibbling, reading, and going over each word of my conversation with Joe in the beer garden.

Promptly at seven, last crumb long gone, I returned to the yellow phone booth outside of Henry Kaserne, ready to relinquish what was left of the change and wondering what my protector had planned for the evening.

CHAPTER 8

JOE CAME THROUGH THE EVENING MIST wearing a tan trench coat and a glad smile. As soon as he squeezed in beside me under the black umbrella I passed the handle to him. Promptly, he raised it to accommodate his height. "You're right on time," he said approvingly, giving the handle a spin. "I bought this thing in a German shop. The sales clerk called it 'the family model.' If we walk real close the rain won't dribble down our necks." He patted his side. "Got enough cash for two dinners in a nice dry place. That is if you're still interested."

"I am," I replied, pouring the leftover coins into the pocket of his raincoat. He offered me his arm. I linked mine to it. We synchronized our steps, and just like that, we were a couple—as Mutti and Vati had been, back in the village of Freidorf.

*

ONCE Vati began his civil service career in Munich he rented a furnished room for himself within walking distance of his office, leaving us on the farm. The ancient local trains were not set up for daily commutes. At first he came home every weekend, bringing small toys for Anna and me. On Sundays, while the traditional pork roast browned in the oven, we went for the equally traditional family stroll.

Mutti and Vati linked arms and began walking in step—he in black suede knickers and a gray Trachtenjacke, she in a hand-sewn maroon silk dirndl that showed off her hourglass figure. Anna and I basked in their glow. The villagers we passed always stopped to offer a friendly hello. Frau Meier, who lived in the last house down the lane, would hobble out of her garden gate to present Vati with a flower for his lapel, telling him what a handsome group we made.

"The perfect young couple," she'd gush. "The perfect little family."

Borrowing her admiring eyes, I'd see my parents in a new way, noting how prettily Mutti's skirt flounced, how her eyes lit as she gazed up at Vati. For a man, he had beautiful hair, dark and wavy and so thick his barber had to thin it every two weeks just to keep it half-tame. Vati liked to go hatless—a breach of good manners the villagers chose to overlook, making allowances for his strange city ways.

When all was well Vati held Anna's hand and Mutti held mine. Sometimes she rested her palm lightly on my shoulder instead, making me quiver with happiness. Then Vati's visits began to grow irregular. He blamed his workload, telling Mutti he was too busy to make the time-consuming trip every weekend. For a while he came every other Saturday, but soon he pared the trips down to once a month.

Mutti saved her discontent for those rare occasions. At first they kept their verbal battles behind the locked bedroom door but soon they were yelling insults at each other in front of Anna and me. Out of habit our Sunday strolls continued for some time although Mutti's hand no longer rested lightly on my shoulder. When I clung to her fingers, they felt slack and unpleasantly cold. Her face still presented the villagers with a happy-wife-smile, but her eyes refused to participate in the deception.

On our last few strolls Vati made Anna and me walk a few steps behind so that he and Mutti could bicker uninterrupted in fierce, undecipherable whispers. I focused on their arms, which were still linked, if only for the sake of appearance. I tried to will their steps back into alignment, determined to forget the slammed doors, broken plates, and the occasional hurled box of stickpins. And then one day Frau Meier came out of her garden gate with a red carnation for Vati's lapel and casually mentioned that her son had seen him climb the Zugspitze with his pretty young sister the Sunday before.

"I didn't know you have a sister," I told him. In the uncomfortable silence that followed Frau Meier threaded the trembling flower through my baby-fine curls and limped away, dabbing her eyes.

The void my parents' separation left inside me lasted until the moment Joe and I hooked elbows and he matched my stride. Then the old cloak of contentment draped over me once more. I could have walked at his side forever, oblivious to the foul weather, listening to his tender voice sing, "Smoke gets in your eyes," and "There are 99 kinds of candy bars; heaven knows there must be a billion stars; there are 99 kinds of magazines, but there's only one of you . . ."

Inhaling the exotic scent of his spicy aftershave, I felt as if it was Christmas Eve and I had just unwrapped my best present. Together, we crossed darkening alleys, vacant lots, housing tracts, until I had no idea in which direction we were moving. With our own portable roof over our heads and no rules to obey, I let my feet take me where his led.

At last we came to a barrier wall, stumbled alongside it and veered onto a pitch-black uneven field. We scraped our ankles against clumps of thistles until we found and followed faint tire tracks. Ahead, a red glow tinged the thick haze like a miniature sunset.

Joe said, "O-ho! This must be it."

A muffled drum-beat drew us to the blurred outline of an unpainted shack, the weeds around it flattened to form a narrow parking strip framed by unkempt brush. A row of battered American cars were half-hidden by foliage. The muted drums continued to pound through the shack's shuttered windows.

Two shadowy figures huddled on the makeshift stoop under a naked red bulb. Their cigarette tips were crimson pinpoints of light. One was a mountainous woman, her face powdered a ghostly white. She was staring fixedly at the ground. Her companion, an elfin man as dark as the night, stared just as fixedly at the rust-tinged horizon.

"Evening," Joe said cheerfully as we stopped at their feet. The mismatched couple reluctantly moved them aside to let us squeeze up the stairs. She blinked at us with black-ringed, unfocused eyes. He saluted listlessly with an empty bottle.

Joe opened the shack's door. A wave of deafening sound rolled out and broke against us. My feet refused to step over the threshold until Joe gently guided me into a dream gone wrong. Everything inside the inky room throbbed. Small candles trembled uneasily from the tops of rickety card tables set against the far wall. The only other source of light was a narrow shaft of suspended grease droplets oozing through the gapped kitchen door until it was snuffed by dense tobacco smoke.

Joe steered me past a miniscule dance space on which shadows clutched, rubbed and shuffled, to the one table that was most removed from the action. I stood rigid while he unbuttoned my borrowed coat and helped me out of the sleeves. He draped it over the adjacent table, tossed his trench coat on top, and pulled out two chairs, pushing me onto mine before sitting on his. He stuffed his long legs under our table and shifted both chairs until we faced away from the crowd. "So," he said, beaming at me. "Here we are, all cozy and dry. Spider said you can get a real hamburger in this joint. Ever had one?"

"Hamburg?" I asked, latching on to the only word I could understand. "From the North Sea?"

"Hamburg*er*," he corrected. "That's a patty of hambur—ground beef, see, on a bun." He cupped his hands together and hinged them open. "Similar to your bread rolls but soft and fluffy. Like cotton." He picked up invisible bottles with his free hand and shook them over the imaginary hamburger. "Ketchup. Mustard. Pickles. Onions. A bit of lettuce and hopefully a fat slice of tomato. A meal on a bun. All American. Want to give it a try?"

"Okay."

While we waited for someone to take our order Joe's fingers tapped along with the music. "You dance?"

A picture of Anna and Mutti waltzing around our kitchen table came to mind. While I kept poring over my homework, Mutti would switch to an elegant tango and slide into a rollicking Charleston, Anna adroitly copying her every move. Once she'd been thoroughly coached my sister enrolled in a ballroom dance class and began to bring home trophies. This encouraged Mutti to try her luck with me but I refused her kind offer. The idea of eventually being clutched by a total stranger, skin to skin with blackheads, pimples and sweat, did not appeal.

That was why I could now tell Joe truthfully, "No. I cannot dance."

"It's easy," he said. "Listen—I think this is a fox-trot. That's a fast kind of shuffle. One, one-two. One, one-two . . . Watch their feet. Child's play."

But their feet were not all I saw. Small, skinny black men were grinding themselves against the stoic flesh of their partners, grabbing at private parts without so much as a slap in return. The dance space was hardly bigger than a checkerboard. The black and white pieces upon it, turning around and around, were making me nauseous.

Every few minutes some couple slipped out into the night, to be replaced by another returning, their clothes mussed, the woman's hair askew. There was something insect-like in this busy-ness—the throbbing music, the sluggish queen bees, the little men swarming around them like agitated drones.

"We don't have to dance with *them*," Joe said, shuffling his fingers over the tabletop along with the beat. "We can do it right here, between the two of us—"

"I *cannot* dance!" To submit myself to the same rhythm surging through these unsavory females would make my corruption as inevitable as catching a cold was in a room full of sneezers. The difference between *Uhre* and *Hure* became stunningly clear: these women were whores.

Joe rose, one knee awkwardly knocking against a table leg, sending the candle dish scuttling across the top. He exhaled, rubbing the knee. "I best see what's keeping the waitress. She must be around here somewhere. I believe I'll get me a Coke to go with the burger. You?"

I shuddered, shaking my head.

"Milk, then." He pushed the wildly sputtering candle in front of my face. "You look cold. Why don't you warm your hands on this till I get back?"

As soon as he left I drew into myself like a snail surrounded by slime. There was no safe place to look except at the candle centered in front of my nose. Doing its own private dance, the flame changed from yellow to orange to red and to yellow again, a bluish streak at the wick, the hues blending, stretching, steadying. A few pulse beats later the music faded along with the room, leaving only the flame.

In it, the forbidding face of our parish priest unfolded, staring out at me. His dark brows had always reminded me of a hog-bristle brush. More hair spilled from his nose and ears. His bloodless lips were pinched in a habitual frown. He came to my class three times a week to teach catechism. As soon as he walked in Frau Bischof would rise, incline her head stiffly without speaking, and vacate the room for an hour, slamming the door behind her.

And what an hour it was—every girl sitting stick-straight in her cramped seat, hands folded demurely on her desktop as he marched circles around us all, his sinister brows knitted, his withering voice tolling like a cathedral bell. "Class," he'd start, his piercing eyes demanding undivided attention. "Repeat after me. It is a mortal sin . . ."

". . . a mortal sin . . ."

"To touch your own body . . ."

". . . to touch my own body . . ."

"Punished by the eternal flames of hell." He seemed to swell with each word. "Remember," he'd boom, rocking on his heels and unclasping his hands from behind his back to conduct his captive orchestra. "You will not *think*. You will not *look*. You will not *touch*. Even washing yourself *down there* in the tub is a mortal sin. Now repeat after me . . ."

Lesson by relentless lesson, week after week, he made us repeat his truth until we accepted it for our own. "Girls," he'd say. "Do you know how it feels to accidentally burn the tip of your finger on a hot iron or on a pan straight out of the oven? Now imagine burning like that all over, every millimeter of you aflame, not for an instant, not for a minute, but through all eternity, forever and ever . . ."

We gave a communal shudder. Somebody moaned.

He said he was in charge of our souls. His task was to keep them pure white and pleasing to Our Father. His instructions seeped deep into our flesh, muscles and bones, petrifying, locking, choking off the natural life-force streaming toward us.

With a dry sob I blew out the flame and bowed my head in defeat.

"Maria," Joe's voice called soon afterward. "Hey, Maria!"

Glancing up, I saw his blurred form push through the greasy murk. For a moment I could not remember who he was, or where. In the absence of an overhead light his skin looked tar-black. His eyes seemed to gleam with some internal, ungodly fire. Desperately, I rubbed both hands over my face and blinked my protector back into focus.

CHAPTER 9

H E PEERED AT ME, HOLDING TWO GLASSES. "You fall asleep? In this noise?" He set them down, pushing the white one in front of me, next to the candle. "It went out," he said, picking it up in its dish. "I don't carry matches. Let me just trade it for that one over there—"

I shook my head. "I like the dark, Joe. No one to see us."

"Not 'Cho'," he said, sitting behind the amber glass. "Joe. A soft sound. Not like a locomotive."

"Joe," I repeated, unable to tell the difference between his pronunciation and mine.

"Almost." He smiled encouragingly. "Now pretend there's a 'd' in front of your 'ch'. And change the c to an s. That makes it into a 'J', see. Soft. The hamburgers are on the way. I watched the waitress slap them into the frying pan myself. Turns out she's also the cook and bottle-washer. Hungry?"

"Always hungry, Cho." Now I could hear myself saying it wrong.

"D-show," he instructed.

"Very good," I said, and he laughed.

A dainty little man wearing a bowler hat and sunglasses tapped toward us with the help of an elegant ebony cane. His teeth gleamed white, except for the right canine, which was made out of gold. "Joseph," he said, pulling up the nearest chair to sit down, carefully pulling his pants loose at the knees. "I see you made it. Have any trouble finding the place?"

Joe shook his head. "Your directions were clear enough. You were right, it does look like it fell off the edge of the world. Especially in this weather. A little hard on Maria, though."

His friend leaned forward. "You kidding, right?"

"Say what?"

"This Joseph and Maria bit. Some kind of joke, huh?"

"Knock it off, man," Joe said softly. "Names happen. Like yours." He turned to me. "Maria, meet Spec 4 Spider. Spider, Maria."

Spider grunted and said, "That's not my real name and you know it. Shit—what's in those glasses, anyway? Milk? Coke?" He raised his brows. "Where you think you are, in a school cafeteria? You need you some beer, man, or wine. Hell, I've got just the thing to fix you guys up. Whiskey. Here, let me add a shot—"

Joe cupped a hand over his glass. "This is strong enough for me, Spider, especially in the company I'm keeping tonight."

Spider slid his shades to the tip of his nose and flicked oddly naked eyes over me as fast as a lizard thrusts out its tongue. "Boy-oh-boy," he said, sadly shaking his head. "You a cradle-snatcher, pure and simple. MPs catch you, watch out, man. Statutory rape. The stockade. The end of a brilliant career. Demotion. Scandal. Hell—dishonorable discharge. Me, I best be getting back to my piece. You-all . . ." He nodded at our glasses and leered. ". . . Enjoy yourselves, hear?" Rising, he tapped his cane smartly on the floor and sauntered into the smoke. A few seconds later he was on the checkerboard, leaning heavily into the wobbly flesh of his obese partner.

I occupied myself with the milk, carefully dabbing my mouth with a napkin once I'd drained the last drop. Joe rubbed at his temples as if to erase some bothersome thoughts. I had a few of those myself—a whole chain of them, starting with the word *if.*

If I hadn't stopped to talk to Joe I might have made it all the way to the woods before it started to pour. The air would be fragrant with pine resin. I'd have sheltered on a hunter's lookout, the kind that were on stilts and had roofs. Or I could have wiggled under the lowest branches of some dense-leafed tree. Better yet, I might have crept into a dry cave just big enough for one. I'd be curled on a cushion of moss right now, falling asleep to a soothing nocturne of rain cascading on to the forest floor just outside the entrance. *If* I hadn't stopped for Joe.

I watched him tap absentmindedly on his forehead, keeping pace with the beat. He was as dark as the other men in this place, but there the comparison ended. He was too tall and regal to blend with this crowd. Nor was I anything like the women. Too thin, for one thing, and too young, and maybe even too smart.

I allowed myself the first full breath since crossing the threshold. "Cho is for Choseph. That is true?"

He smiled weakly. "Joseph Duncan, that's me."

"I do not like your first name. I cannot say it right—and it is silly."

"Joseph, silly? How come?"

"Maria and Choseph are from the Bible, yes? People will laugh, like Spider. I call you Duncan, vielleicht (perhaps)?"

"I hear enough of that in the barracks. Duncan do this and Duncan do that. It's not friendly. There's Maddis, though Joseph Maddis L. Duncan, to be exact."

"I call you Maddis?"

"Naw. That's my father's name. My mom only stuck it on hoping he'd like me better. Madd-is, she used to call him. Mad is Maddis, she'd say."

I shrugged. "Not Choseph. Not Duncan. Not Maddis. I call you 'soldier'?"

"No, wait." He gulped some of his soda. "There's one more. The L. It stands for 'Lucius'." He looked straight at me. "It was my mom's special name for me. Her first baby's name, who died. She called me that only in private. Nobody's used it since she passed. I give it to you. Maria and Lucius. Lucius and Maria. How's that sound?"

"You have many names."

"One for each season. You like it?"

"I like it. And I can say 'Lucius' okay."

I studied his thick curly lashes, the high cheekbones, his proud almond eyes. *Lucius*, the African king. Prince *Lucius*.

I said it out loud.

"Just between *us* now," he cautioned with a quick look at the dance floor. "A private name. For a Private First Class."

He grinned. I stared.

"A joke," he said. "In case you need something to laugh about. You don't laugh nearly enough. I noticed that about you."

I managed a lopsided smile as the waitress appeared with our tray. I'd wondered what kind of woman would choose to work in this hole. She was about Mutti's age and could easily have passed for a neighbor—most likely she was.

"Here you are, soldier." Her voice was warm, even motherly. She plopped the tray down, looking at me, and stepped away for the long view. "What have we here? My, oh my, soldier, this will never do. She's a schoolgirl, much too young to be in a bar. You get her out of here, understand? Take her straight home and don't bring her again. I don't believe in sin, soldier, but this girl, in here, is one for sure."

"As a matter of fact," Lucius said, "I was just wondering if you have a phone she can use. To call her mother. But I promised her a hamburger, seeing how she's never had one. We get to eat first, I hope."

"You better, after I slaved to get them just right. Take her to the kitchen after you're done. Don't let her go there alone, you hear? She can use the phone behind the counter." Briskly, she unloaded the tray, knocked it warningly against Lucius's wrist, and hurried away.

Home. White linen tablecloth. The high gloss of paste-waxed linoleum. Mutti's blonde oaken hutch with its built-in breadbox. She'd bought it when she was eighteen and it still looked brand-new. A buttered slab of rye and honey-sweetened peppermint tea. Or better yet, my favorite—a bowl of hot Griesnockerl (semolina dumpling) soup. A wave of yearning swept through me, so fierce I could not move.

Lucius took the top off his bun. "Aw," he said. "No mustard. No ketchup. No pickles. She even forgot the lettuce. Never mind. It would wilt in this joint anyway. Now watch." With a determined grin he picked up the imaginary bottles again, pretending to shake and pour. Then he slapped on the top of his bun and twisted it around a few times. Raising the creation to his mouth, he took a huge bite and chewed. And chewed. At last he reached for his Coke. "They'd never hire her stateside. How hungry are you, really?"

"Not very," I admitted, watching him rinse out his mouth.

"Even *canteen* food tastes better than this," he grumbled, pushing our plates aside. "Wish there was a dog around I could throw this junk to. Come to think of it, I wouldn't want to endanger his health. Ready for your call?"

I jumped up. He fished two ten-Pfennig pieces out of his pocket and escorted me to the small kitchen, which reeked of burnt grease. An ashtray stood on the work table right by the stove. It was heaped with half-smoked cigarettes, their filter tips smudged with lipstick. He waited in front of the counter while I stepped around it to the wall phone.

Never before had I been so glad to hear my mother's familiar voice. "Hello?" she whispered.

"Mutti?"

"Mariandl! Where are you?"

"—It's Maria," I corrected.

"Mariandl," she repeated as if I hadn't spoken, "listen, you don't have to go away this summer. You can stay home with Anna, just as you wanted. Where did you say you are?"

"In town."

"Please take the next bus home. I'll meet you by the bakery."

"No, don't," I said. "Not in this rain. I can borrow an umbrella. Besides, I don't know what time the bus will get to the Harthof. What about O.F.?"

"Asleep. He's calmed down some but you better lock yourself in your room until he leaves in the morning."

"I will," I promised, a knot constricting my throat. "I'll be home soon."

I hung up, barely believing my luck. How come it had been so easy? Turning, I saw Lucius lean against the wall, his eyes on my every move.

"Everything work out?" he asked lightly.

"My mother wants me to come home." I loved saying those words but was immediately grieved because Lucius could never say that particular sentence again. All at once I was in a hurry to leave so I could begin to forget this whole day. On rare occasions Mutti turned out to be right. Not that she'd hear it from me.

Back at the table Lucius picked up his coat, put it down, grabbed mine instead, opened it awkwardly, and held it out to me. I slipped my arms into the sleeves. He buttoned me up.

"I cannot wear it home," I said.

"No. It's a man's coat. With an American label. I'll walk you a ways, though. Make sure you're all right. You can keep the umbrella for a while. Maybe you'll want to return it to me next weekend?"

He waited for a reply but I was already striving for the exit. Outside, the red bulb still bled into the night. The cars, half submerged in drenched foliage, reminded me of shipwrecks. The nearest, large, pale-green and rounded, rocked ever so slightly on worn struts. Nearby, Spider's mountainous woman was leaning against the shack wall, cigarette in a limp-wristed hand, eyes fixed on where a star might have twinkled on a clear night. One side of her dress was hiked up; Spider's hand was busy underneath it.

I froze rock-solid. Lucius bumped me from behind, saw my face, and turned it away from the spectacle. "Open up that umbrella, girl," he said gruffly. "These coats won't keep us warm if they get soaked."

I fumbled with the latch and released it. The umbrella spread wide. Lucius, stepping close, wove my arm through his but it was not the same as before. Our steps no longer matched.

Retracing our route, we soon came to Schleissheimerstrasse, empty and black, the streetlights ringed with diffuse halos. Lucius wanted to escort me all the way home but I stopped one block short of the bakery and pulled my arm free. "My mother might be waiting at the bus stop," I explained. We were standing on the boundary to my world. He didn't belong in it.

He took the first step away from me. The blurred light from the nearest lamppost barely had the strength to illuminate the top of his head. I put the open umbrella down next to my feet, took off the coat, and gave it to him. In an instant, the cold seeped up the anorak's damp sleeves. I held out my hand. "Thank you for everything, Lucius. Good-bye."

He peered at the hand with a puzzled frown, as if he didn't quite know what it was for. Tilting his head toward me, he said, "Can I . . . kiss you?" To our mutual astonishment my hand flew out, smacking him hard on the cheek. It sounded just like a shot. "Hey!" he yelped, outraged. Fists balled, he lunged at me but stopped himself in midstride before I could begin to dodge. Then he grazed one of his fists against the offended cheek and examined the knuckles as if expecting to find them covered with blood. His eyes, huge, bottomless, grim, locked onto mine. "Nobody gets to hit me. Ever."

I pushed out my chin.

He sighed, breaking the spell. "That crummy place was the best I could do on short notice, Maria. I don't go to bars. Don't even like liquor. I should have known not to listen to Spider—his advice has gotten me into trouble before. I'm sorry. It won't happen again." I said nothing. He swallowed. "I've been alone too long. It hurts, you know?"

"Yes," I agreed.

"I'd like to. Invite you. To a good meal. In broad daylight. Next Saturday. Okay?" I allowed my shoulders to give a small twitch. "In a respectable German restaurant," he continued. "Blue skies all the way. Where can we meet?"

Not in my world. In his. "Outside your gate," I suggested. "Eleven o'clock." I regretted the words as soon as they left my mouth.

He unclenched his fist. "Let's shake on it."

"I must go now." I picked up the umbrella. "Good-bye."

"Not good-bye." He extended his hand. "Auf Wiederseh'n." With trepidation, I placed mine in his, knowing that a handshake was as good as a promise.

CHAPTER 10

I COULD HEAR THE MUFFLED BOOM of American music half a block from the bakery. Two voices were shouting from the direction of the spectral Alabama Bar, still hiding behind it. I could barely make out the shop's chunky silhouette, shrouded by fog, or the bus stop a stone's throw away from the shuttered display window. With all my heart I wished Mutti had come in spite of my protestations. For a few seconds I could actually see her compact figure under our old plaid umbrella floating out of the shadows toward me. Then I blinked and she was gone. I stayed on my side of the street hoping to remain invisible to anyone lurking around the infamous bar.

"Find your own hoe and don't be hit'n on mine," the more high-pitched of the two voices was yelling. "Fore I bust you upside the head with this bottle."

The other voice growled, "Damn shee-at!"

A profusion of glass shattered against some wall. An unseen woman began to laugh but stopped abruptly almost at once. The bar door must have briefly opened, for a cacophonous din waxed and waned.

I reached the intersection and crossed into my Marshall Plan world, thankful for the three long buildings beyond the narrow strip-lawn that bordered the sidewalk. Even though all the windows were dark, at least they were within shouting distance.

The field buffering my world from the American barrier-wall was an abyss. The aura surrounding the nearest lamp post was quickly snuffed by hovering fog, leaving me surrounded by impenetrable night.

My feet were ice-cold. The rest of me was too tired to shiver. I passed the sapling Regina had so bravely leaned against this golden morning and raised my eyes to where I guessed her window to be. She had grown up with a bird's eye view of the bar, seeing too much too soon. Lucky for me *my* apartment abutted the wheat field instead.

Then I heard the careless scrape of a heel some distance behind me. My neck pricked as I peered around the umbrella. The sidewalk was empty. Nonetheless I quickened my pace, striving to reach the last building in this row, where the road would make a sharp right. Cater-cornered from that spot stood two more buildings between me and the safety of home.

I'd never noticed how many ornamental bushes grew on these lawns, tall enough for some ambusher to hide behind. There it was again—a stealthy scuff, and when I turned, nothing. I clutched the umbrella tighter and lengthened my stride, trying to keep my heartbeat from skipping. Could someone be deliberately holding back, counting on the fog to obscure him, matching not only my walking speed but my erratic stops and starts? If everyone who lived in the apartments I was passing was asleep, what made me think someone would rescue me if I screamed?

At last I came to the curve. Without breaking my stride I closed the umbrella, hooked the handle over my arm, and bolted. The first building passed in a blur. I darted up the walkway between it and mine and sprinted along the front, past Frau Keppler's shuttered kitchen window, then four darkened glass lobby doors. I came to a stop at the fifth. And there, right above me, was the only rectangle of light in the neighborhood—our kitchen window, with Mutti waiting inside it.

I pushed the handle. The door wouldn't budge. I was locked out.

I saw the curtain flutter as a vague shape paced behind it. My finger was a centimeter from the panel of bell buttons when a muscular brown arm snaked from behind me. A broad, fleshy hand sealed my mouth. Another clamped onto my shoulder, pulling me away from the door. I twisted free and dove for the buttons again.

The hands reclaimed me, one tight on my face, the other around my neck, cutting off my air supply. Although I struggled every step of the way the phantom, smelling of whiskey and cigarette smoke, dragged me to the back of the garbage shed bordering the field. He tried to force me to the ground. I kicked out to the rear, hitting a knee. He gasped and loosened his hold.

Then I found the umbrella handle still attached to my arm. Unhooking it, I stabbed its sharp tip blindly over my shoulder. He exhaled, stumbling. I slipped out of his grasp, twisted around, and thrust my makeshift sword at his face. He shielded his eyes. I poked the sharp umbrella tip at his hands and cheeks, then whirled and ran back to the lobby door and the bell panel. My finger tapped the right button before he caught up.

We both froze as an upstairs doorbell shrilled. It was a beautiful sound. With an angry hiss he melted into the fog, his steps quickly receding around the house corner. Above me the curtain parted and Mutti squinted out into the night. I rang again. The window cautiously opened.

"Marianne—is it you?" she whispered.

"The door's locked!"

"Well, of course it is. I'll be right down."

In seconds the stairwell grew light. Then she appeared on the inside of the glass door. The lock clicked. I pushed my way in, slamming and bolting the door.

"What is it?" she whispered. "Are you all right?" For one pulse beat, it seemed almost possible to tell her about the attack. But she was already busy, studying my bedraggled appearance. "You're soaked," she said in an accusing, critical tone. "What good is an umbrella if you don't use it?"

"I was—cold. So I—ran."

She gave a disapproving shake of her head and preceded me upstairs. I followed her through the open apartment door and the stifling hall into the kitchen. She shut us in and said with a sigh, "Well, here we are," spreading her hands.

Yes, there we were, in her spotless domain, where everything was in its rightful place. The refrigerator purred soothingly. Seppi's tail thumped a greeting. It was exactly how I'd envisioned it in the bar, down to the pot of Griesnockerl soup simmering on the burner, the waiting slab of dark, buttered bread. Mutti ladled out my soup, set it carefully before me and lowered herself onto the next chair. I held my raw hands over the steam rising from the broth. She cupped them with hers and rubbed them vigorously.

"So red and cold. *Sauwetter* (lousy weather)!" she said, handing me a folded towel. "Here. Your hair's dripping."

I shook off a cascade of crystalline drops. Most of them landed on the tablecloth. She winced and I hurriedly wound the towel around my head.

Pushing a soup-spoon at me, she said, "Eat while it's still hot," watched me savor the broth, and said what I didn't have the courage to say. It was, "I should have listened to you." I was amazed. She explained, "O.F. called my office to read me your note, so I went to the Hauptbahnhof (train station) to tell the Sisters you weren't coming. They were displeased. Quite Prussian. I found myself wondering which one had wound a tuft of your hair around her finger last year, pulling it until your eyes teared—and which one forced you to swallow a second tablespoon of cod-liver oil as soon as you finished vomiting the first one into the toilet. I wouldn't have wanted to go with those nuns, either."

"Don't make me go again," I said. "I don't need a rest-cure. I just want things to be the way they were before . . ."

Her slanted eyes grew veiled. "We were starving before," she reminded me. "I couldn't find a well-paying job, or enough food to put on the table. O.F. saved us from poverty. We must always be grateful." Her wan smile gave way to resolve. "It'll never be as it was. Vati and I are married to other people now. I wish you'd just try to be nice to your Onkel Franz. He's my husband, *gell*? That makes him your father, don't you see?"

I jumped up, toppling my chair. "He'll never be my father! *I* won't abandon Vati the way *you* did!" I rushed to my room, slammed the door, and turned the key from the inside, already regretting the meal I had so rashly deserted.

She chose not to follow. I heard her add some water to the broth and lower it to the floor for Seppi. No doubt she'd torn the rye into bite-sized pieces for him, too. He slurped my supper with almost indecent haste, giving a moan of pleasure when he was done. My stomach contracted with envy.

She righted my chair, rinsed and washed the tongue-cleansed dishes, opened and shut the refrigerator a couple of times, and turned off the light. The instant I saw the gap under my door go dark, I said "Good night" just loud enough so she could hear it if she chose.

"Sleep well, mein Schatz (my treasure)," she replied, closing the hall door gently behind her.

*

I PULLED off the towel, shook out my hair, and thought about my mother's prominent cheekbones and Mongolian eyes. Somehow a few renegade genes from ancient times, when Asian hordes overran Europe, had asserted themselves in my Bavarian mother. There was a photo album she'd managed to save from her childhood. In it were three pictures I loved. She was eleven years old—wiry, flat-chested, her brows thick, dark, untamed. These days, she kept them meticulously shaved, penciling in artificial thin arches every morning. I liked her natural face better. The fascinating thing about two of the pictures was that they were taken in Yonkers, New York.

From the age of eleven to twelve Mutti lived with her parents in faraway America and ever since I was old enough to talk I'd pestered her to tell me the story of that year until I knew it by heart. Now, I easily ran the script through my mind as I put my cheek upon my pillow.

In 1927 her father sailed to New York, promising to send for his wife and daughter as soon as he could. He rented a sparse room and worked several jobs, living on crackers and canned food until he managed to save not only their fares but the large sum he had to deposit with the U.S. government before they would allow Grandmother into the country. While working as a nurse at the Russian front during the First World War she had contracted rheumatic fever, which damaged her heart and made her an undesirable immigrant.

The first photo was of Mutti with Grandmother on the ship *Hamburg*, posing with a group of other German wives eager to start brand-new lives. Grandfather spoke six languages fluently and helped organize the effort to make Esperanto the preferred international language. By the time Mutti and Grandmother arrived he had rented an apartment in Yonkers big enough to accommodate the solid German furniture that had traveled with them.

"I didn't speak a word of English," my mother said. "In school they put me in first grade and moved me up every few weeks until I was in the class to which I belonged. But then a terrible thing happened. Papa got sick, probably from all the stress he'd put on himself and from those long months of eating nothing but canned goods and crackers. Stomach cancer. He died a few weeks after the diagnosis. Mama followed him a month later. Her heart just stopped beating one day. By the time I turned twelve I was a double orphan."

A social worker drove her to the orphanage. The good German oak furniture was auctioned off along with the other household belongings. Distant relatives were located in Germany and Mutti was given the choice of growing up in the orphanage or going back where she came from. She chose the relatives.

When she got to their house she realized she was to be their unpaid helper. They worked her relentlessly; she left them as soon as she turned eighteen. A few months later she married Vati to make a home for herself. "From the frying pan straight into the fire," she'd say with a laugh. Her dowry consisted of the money from the auction and from what was left of her father's savings account, minus burial costs and her return fare. The remains of her parents stayed in Yonkers; she never had the comfort of visiting their graves.

"The oddest thing was," she said, "that when I returned to Germany, I was no longer fluent in German and had to work my way through the lower grades there too."

Gradually, over the years, she lost most of her English, but the bits and pieces she retained she pronounced like a native.

"Say the English word for *Küche*," I'd beg.

"Kitchen."

"And for *Kirche*."

"Church."

"Count to ten again, please!"

I loved the round nasal sounds she could make with her mouth. Back in Freidorf, my favorite form of entertainment had been listening to her sing the English version of the alphabet song.

If she had stayed at the orphanage I would have been born an American.

I was determined to learn English at the first opportunity. It came when I enrolled in a new program for gifted children, with its mandatory English lessons. To speed things along I paid three *Mark* for the addresses of three English-speaking pen pals.

The first was fourteen-year old Zaghul who lived in Cairo. He sent me samples of Arabic script, described his Holy Days, and told me he fervently hated the Israelis.

The second was Zhang Yonglin, a Chinese boy in Singapore. He showed me the beauty of Chinese characters. In response I sent him a passage in Old German script. He hated the Japanese, calling them the world's most barbarous people.

The third was Sam Brown of Pocatello, Idaho. He wrote to me about the Russet potatoes his state was famous for, and about the car he was going to get on his sixteenth birthday. He hated all "niggers." I couldn't find the word in my Langenscheidt (a language dictionary) and asked him for a definition. He elaborated on the theme in his second letter.

What *I* hated most in the world was stupidity, so I decided to drop Sam at once.

In school I was considered a whiz in English but a few hours with Lucius had shown me how little I really knew. Although I understood a fair amount I'd been painfully aware all evening of how badly I spoke it. That was about to change. Starting tomorrow I'd work on a new project— improving my English. I'd buy a British newspaper and translate it syllable by syllable. I'd sit and listen to my '45 Ricky Nelson record on '33 for as

long as it took me to transcribe every slurred phrase. I'd even keep our
radio tuner to the AFN station until I could recognize individual words.

Ablaze with good intentions, I stretched out full-length until the soles
of my feet touched the cool foot-board. Drifting, I recalled the second
snapshot in Mutti's old album. She was arching her spine into a flawless
bridge for the benefit of her father's camera, her straight brown hair
flowing toward the American soil that her hands could not hold on to.

My most treasured photo was the third—a family portrait. Mutti was
standing next to her father, half his height, the white bow in her hair almost
as big as her head. And he, tall and capable, resting one tender hand on her
shoulder, exuded kindness and a clear, unmistakable intelligence I
fervently hoped he'd passed on to me. Grandmother, seated and pale,
looked up at him with eyes so naked with love that I was stunned anew
each time I examined the picture. Together, the three of them were one
perfect family unit, more whole than mine ever was or could be.

Lying in my bed that night I let my mind linger on the eleven-year-
old's happy smile until a wave of envy washed through me. I'd seen the
same kind of envy on Lucius's face when he watched me call home.

On the verge of sleep I raised my head and listened for some sounds
that should have been there but weren't. Something was wrong but I was
too tired to figure out what it was. I'd had an arduous day.

CHAPTER 11

I T WASN'T UNTIL I AWOKE in the middle of the night, desperate
to go pee, that I realized what sounds were missing. They were
those Elvis invariably made every time I came home. Since he hated
being locked up as much as I did he would rattle his cage to remind me he
wanted out. I risked turning the light switch to check under the bed. The
cage door yawned open. I recalled the care I'd taken to make sure it was
properly latched when I shoved it under the bed. The bread I'd stuffed
through the bars this morning was untouched. Elvis was gone.

Anna tossed from side to side under her featherbed, blinked at the
light, and made muffled protesting noises. "Okay, okay," I whispered,
grabbing the flashlight off my wardrobe shelf before plunging the room
back into night. The beam was weak. I wiggled under the bed, shining the
light into corners. It would have been a relief to find a dust ball or two big
enough for a mouse to hide behind but the floor was scrubbed Mutti-clean.
Same thing under Anna's bed. I checked all the dresser drawers and both
wardrobes, finally training the beam at the gap under the door to see if it
was wide enough for a mouse to squeeze through. I hoped it was not. Then
the flashlight went dead.

I promised Mutti to stay put but my bladder was about to burst. Since
O.F. was asleep surely Mutti wouldn't hold a quiet scurry to the bathroom

against me. My pulse raced as I turned the key so slowly that the click of the lock was a mere sigh. Barefoot, I felt my way through the dark kitchen into the hall. I could hear O.F. snoring behind the closed living room door. It took me a minute to gather the courage to proceed to the toilet. When I was done I used the pail of water Mutti kept filled next to the commode for after-hour flushing. House regulations forbade tenants to use the tank after nine.

As I retraced my steps through the hall a floor board creaked ever so slightly. The snoring continued and so did I, feeling better the closer I got to my room. My hand was already on the door handle when the kitchen light came on. O.F. was standing by the switch, wearing his hairnet and gray-striped, wrinkled pajamas.

"What are you doing up at this hour?" he asked, squinting at me.

All at once the flannel nightgown I was wearing felt much too thin. I muttered that I had just used the bathroom, silently wishing I'd thought to put on my robe.

"Don't mumble at me," he said irritably, his voice growing louder. "It's disrespectful. You woke me up. I don't appreciate that."

I stared at my nervously wiggling toes, remembering that direct eye contact only made him worse.

"And have the decency to look at me when I speak!" he said, still escalating.

I nudged my door open and gave an elaborate yawn. Keeping my voice low and steady, I said, "I'm tired. Good night."

"You have not been dismissed," he countered. "I asked you a question. What are you doing out of bed?"

"Nothing now," I said.

"Nothing? What kind of answer is that? You're trying to mock me!" With no further warning, he hurled himself across the room. I pivoted into the bedroom and almost succeeded in closing the door behind me but he got to it before I could click it shut. Shoving it wide, he grabbed my sleeve and dragged me to the kitchen. I yanked free, escaping to the far side of the table.

"What a sorry creature you are," he spat. "Insults and lies. Unwashed. Dirty inside and out."

"I'm cleaner than you!" I shot back.

The outburst rendered him speechless. Then he came at me, fists flying. I kept the table between us. We did a few rounds. I pulled out each chair I was passing to slow him down and he shoved them back in one by one. Then the floor rumbled under my feet. It took me a second to understand it wasn't God signaling His displeasure at our ruckus but only

Herr Huber, rapping his ceiling with a push broom. Seppi, hiding in his corner, flattened himself as best he could.

Mutti stumbled in wearing nothing but a sheer flesh-colored nightgown. It clung most shockingly to her curves. How could she let him see her like that? For the first time I pictured them in bed together and couldn't decide if my imagination or their reality was the greater sin.

"Franz?" she said, still groggy. "Franz!"

But he was beyond reason, chasing me like a hound after prey. He did a quick U-turn in midstride and I immediately reversed directions. The floor shook again, less politely. Seppi yelped. Like me, he was apt to forget his best intentions.

"Franz!" Mutti repeated, her hands rising in supplication as she stepped between us, blocking my escape route. As I faltered, trying to get around her, O.F caught up and rained blows on my head and shoulders.

Following my first impulse I cowered, shielding my face. Following my second I said, "You have no right!" and raised a fist against him. Then everything I was and had ever been recoiled from that act of aggression, paralyzing my arm. He cowered by sheer reflex, regretted it immediately, and erupted, face boiling, neck veins distended. I squeezed past Mutti who was still praying for peace and had almost reached my sanctuary when he managed to clutch at my gown. A seam tore. Trying for a more solid grip he pressed his talons into my nipples.

"Get your hands off me!" I yelled, sobbing. "Get them off!"

Seppi, driven beyond endurance, stumbled between us and seized the cuff of O.F.'s pajama leg with his German-shepherd sized teeth. It ripped. Behind us Mutti gave a small moan and slid to the floor, exposing far more lying than she had standing on her feet. Seppi and O.F. let go at the same time. O.F. rushed to Mutti's aid. I grabbed my savior by his collar and pulled him into the bedroom with me, locking the door.

In the kitchen, O.F. cried, "Lottchen! Mein Gott (my god), Lottchen!" Soft slapping sounds were followed by a weak sigh. Seppi and I stood pressed together, both of us trembling. I still felt the imprint of O.F.'s odious fingers on my budding breasts and whimpered with fury and shame. Seppi just whimpered.

I hated it when O.F. called her "Lottchen" as if she were his little girl. It made me want to kick in the wardrobe door, crack the magical mirrors, and jump out the window, all at the same time. Grinding my teeth, I stuffed Seppi under my featherbed and then slammed myself onto the mattress.

Why hadn't Mutti taken my side? Instead she'd merely chosen to swoon. It was the coward's way out. She was as awful as he and I was sick of them both, *and* of angelic Anna pretending to sleep through the commotion so she wouldn't have to get involved.

The only one in this broken family I liked—besides the missing Elvis—was Seppi. He was also the only one who had defended me. It was a fact O.F. was sure to remember as soon as Mutti was fully recovered. Lucky for us he had a schedule to keep. In a few hours he'd have to start on his weekly sales route. I'd have five blessed days of freedom. Enough time to bike to the lake with Anna and Wolfi and to lose myself in a different book every day. Didn't Frau Keppler say she had box full of new finds?

And then what?

I wiggled to the foot of my bed, put my face against Seppi's, and ran my hand over his fur until we both stopped trembling and slept.

*

IT WAS still raining in the morning. I was tempted to stay in bed but unlike Anna I'd never been good at sleeping in. A few strands of blonde hair above her featherbed were the only proof she was still in our room. I knelt on the cold linoleum and pulled the empty cage out from under my bed. "Elvis," I whispered, "Come back!" The dried bread bits were still undisturbed. I went to the window to study the clouds. At least the little guy was indoors, no doubt snug in some mouse-sized roost. Once O.F. was gone I'd tempt him out with a cube of Emmenthaler, a cheese he could never resist.

Catching a glimpse of myself in the mirror I positioned the side leaves until I'd created an army of disheveled curly-haired girls. I brushed the ends of my hair under, then up into a flip, then over to one side, letting the locks flow over a shoulder. Stewardess. Glamorous uniform. Travel to foreign places. I fingered the torn sleeve of my nightgown and scowled at the door. I had to go to the bathroom again but this time I'd wait until my bladder burst.

There was a tentative knock followed by Mutti's whispered "Mariandl?"

I turned the key. She slipped in, already dressed for work, the extra makeup unable to hide the purple rings under her eyes. She carried two things—one was a tray with the inevitable breakfast of bread and boiled milk, and the other a chipped chamber pot from our village days. Embarrassed, I slid my gaze from it.

She pushed it under my bed. "I should have thought of it last night. Before . . ."

There was no way I'd use it, even if my life depended on it. I held up the cage. "Elvis is gone. The latch was undone when I came home. I can't find him anywhere."

She swallowed, her eyes growing distant. Then she said, her voice strained, "You may search the house for him as soon as O.F. is gone. Until then, keep Seppi quiet, will you? For his own good. Starting next Friday I'll lock the door from the outside and give Anna the spare key. I'm sorry but I can't trust your judgment anymore. I have to keep you and O.F. apart."

"It'll be like being in jail!"

"Only on weekends. I'll bring you breakfast, lunch and dinner. Magazines. And if you have any girlfriends you'd like to visit on Saturdays and Sundays you have my permission to spend the entire day at their houses. Just be sure to be home by eight. He'll be in front of the TV by then. I'll stay in the kitchen, tidying up, waiting to lock you in for the night. I'm warning you—don't rile him again. He must be plotting something. He's positively gloating. Oh Marianne, you should have gone to the Harz Mountains when you had the chance."

"Can't we just be normal?" I asked. "Like Wolfi's family? And Peter's?"

Impatiently, she shook her head. "You know better. God! Sometimes you make me so tired. Why can't you be more like your sister?"

I gave her a hard stare.

She looked away. "Ich bin mit den Nerven fertig (my nerves are shot)," she said, addressing the wall. "The bombs. Vati's nasty Friday-night fights. I just can't take conflict anymore. Losing my parents on the other side of the world, miscarrying my three precious boy-babies during the war before Anna was born . . . I hope you'll be better at choosing your life than I was at choosing mine. Better at choosing husbands, at least." She put a damp kiss on my forehead and I caught a nauseating whiff of the *4711* she was fond of splashing on her wrists and neck. "I've got to run or I'll miss my bus." She fingered the tear in my nightgown. "Remember, don't come out until you see him walking down the street with his briefcase."

Seppi stuck his head out of the covers, beaming at her. She stroked his muzzle. "You stay put too. Quiet as a mm . . .' She glanced at me, offered a feeble smile, and dashed out.

I turned the key and rubbed a fingertip over the damp spot on my forehead. It came away red. Spit *and* lipstick. "Yuck!" I grumbled, peering in the mirror and attacking the spot with a handkerchief. In the reflection I saw that Anna was awake, observing my every move.

"If you weren't so flat you could get a boyfriend, like me," she said. "Then you wouldn't have to be home so much."

"And where would I find one? He won't even let me talk to a boy, except for Wolfi, who's like a brother." Although we used to play bride and groom for weeks on end back when life was still fun.

"Use a dab of Nivea on that lipstick," Anna said. "Oh, Marianne, I wouldn't want to be in your shoes. Since you're too scrawny to appeal to boys, at least do what Mutti said. Visit your school mates on the weekends. Now let me sleep in."

I wasn't about to confess that I didn't have any girlfriends either. At least not the kind who would invite me over from morning till night. How could I bear to be locked up in this narrow room with a chamber pot?

I'd planned to do no more than return the umbrella to Lucius on Saturday but maybe I should take him up on his dinner invitation after all.

Anna settled back, shutting her eyes.

"Wait," I said. "Will you help me find Elvis? His cage door—"

"Open. I know. So was the room door when I came home to change out of my church dress." Her eyes gentled with pity. "I'm afraid O.F. must have found the spare key while we were gone. I doubt you'll ever see poor little Elvis again."

CHAPTER 12

I T WAS ALMOST NINE A.M. WHEN O.F. FINALLY shut the front door behind him. True to my promise I stayed in my bedroom and stood behind the curtains to watch him come around the building and head toward the garages, swinging his briefcase importantly with each footfall. He stopped after a few paces, pulled out a collapsible umbrella, and decisively snapped it open.

Dancing desperately to the toilet, I barely avoided wetting my pants before I could get them down. Five minutes later I dared to take Seppi outside. He, too, peed like a fountain. Back upstairs I put the safety chain on the inside of the front door, just in case. Anna was in the bathroom taking an eyebrow pencil out of her makeup bag at the sink.

"There's something about the way the front door clicks when he leaves that wakes me right up," she said, reconstructing a brow. "It's like a big weight lifting off me."

I put a trail of tiny Emmenthaler bits from the kitchen to Elvis's cage, hoping he would eat his way to it. No matter what Anna thought I couldn't believe O.F. had done anything worse than turn my mouse loose.

We opened all the inside doors and every window to get rid of all the fetid O.F. smells, then we made ourselves comfortable in the reclaimed living room, Anna on the couch with her sketch pad and charcoals and I curled in the green chair with a book.

The phone rang precisely at noon. I lunged for the receiver but Anna snatched it up first. Her victory was short-lived. It was Vati and contrary to our combined expectations it was me he wanted to speak to.

"I have a belated birthday present for you," he said, sounding even more formal than usual. "Come to my office tomorrow, for lunch. I'll give you this month's support money too."

"Will we eat out?" I blurted foolishly.

He cleared his throat, not bothering to reply. "And bring your report card—it's about time I had a good long look at it. Servus."

"Ja, tschüs," I said meekly. "Auf Wiederhören (till we talk again)."

I hung up and crowed, "Vati wants to see me tomorrow! For lunch!"

"Oh goodie," Anna said. "Stale cheese sandwiches and watered-down raspberry juice."

Vati was an even more dedicated saver than Mutti. He didn't believe in restaurant meals. At least not for Anna and me. On our trip to Lake Constance last year he'd brought a rucksack full of stale cheese on rye. He packed twice as many the summer we tented on Sylt. His uninspired concoctions even accompanied us on our yearly ski trips to the Alps. The worst of the lot—and his favorite—was a combination of tomato paste and plasticized cheese spread. Hopefully Mutti would take pity on me and provide enough cash on top of the bus fare so I could fill up on something more appetizing on the way to his office.

"He has a birthday gift for me," I couldn't help bragging.

Anna snorted; his birthday presents were rarely more exciting than his lunches. But since he'd been on vacation in Greece all of June this year's present might at least be exotic. As part of his salary package he received free rail passes he could not bear to forfeit.

Anna returned to her drawing. I tried to refocus on my book, stealing occasional glances at her as she sketched the French door's gauze curtains and the drapery that framed it. She didn't seem the least bit upset that she had not been invited—but then, even though Vati had never ceased to adore her, she'd chosen Mutti's side that awful Christmas Eve when he had arrived unannounced in the village right after Mutti started the divorce.

*

HE HAD come to plead with her to forgive him for something neither wanted to explain.

Hard-mouthed and slant-eyed, she'd asked him to leave so that the Christ Child could bring us our presents. We escorted him through the woods to the depot in waning daylight and stood on the platform beside him in tense silence. As the train approached through the trees his eyes filled with tears.

"Bitte (please)!" he said.

"Never again!" she replied.

That was when I put my hand in his and chose him. Because somebody had to. He could not bring himself to acknowledge my gesture of moral support. After he boarded the train and waved disconsolately across the slowly widening distance between us Mutti was forced to restrain me, for I was determined to run after him like a loyal dog who had inadvertently been left behind.

On the trail back through the forest without him a velvet night sky sparkled with countless stars. The moon illuminated the snow-covered ground and every tree we passed was an ideal Christmas tree covered in white glitter. That Christmas Eve tinged all subsequent ones with a sense of sadness and loss.

*

THE DAY after Vati's phone call I awoke to a chorus of birdsong so intricate that I lay entranced for long minutes, listening. A splendid day was about to unfold before me. Mutti had given me enough lunch money to buy a juicy Polish sausage or even a spicy shashlik. I knew a little place behind the Kurfürstenplatz that specialized in both. If I could get to the Stachus early I'd have enough spare time for a stroll through the Kaufhaus to dab on a drop of demonstration perfume and try a sample of lipstick in the hope of impressing Vati.

As part of the plan I decided to put on the birthday dress Mutti had bought me in May. When I had unwrapped it she said with an indulgent smile, "It's a bit loud, gell, but when I saw it in the shop window I knew it was just right for you." There hadn't been a grand enough occasion to wear it until this perfect July day.

The instant I slipped it over my head I was transformed. Suddenly all things were possible. This wondrous gown could turn even strangers into friends. It worked its magic almost at once.

No sooner had I arrived at the bus stop than the bus appeared before me, braking so precisely that the door wooshed open in front of my feet. Inside, my favorite window seat was empty. And when I got to my little snack shop in back of the Kurfürstenplatz the cook was just taking a sizzling batch of my favorites off the grill. I counted my coins twice, wishing I had enough to buy one of each. With a shrug he speared the plumpest sausage onto my plate, added a skewer of shashlik thickly coated with curry and paprika, and said,

"I made too many of these. Mahlzeit (good appetite)!"

I wolfed my meal with great appreciation, sopped up the spicy grease with a roll, and tactfully turned my back on the other customers before licking the plate and my fingers clean. Fully satisfied, I strolled across the square toward the streetcar stop, catching a glimpse of myself in the nearest shop window—the dress great splashes of scarlet, maroon and green, like a field of roses, its low-cut bodice revealing an elegant neck and good shoulders. Another glance showed me a narrow waist, a flare of skirt, and freshly washed hair, rinsed with wine vinegar so that it shone red under a benevolent sun. It took all the willpower I had not to stop and stare at my own reflection. And then I noticed, in the glass, a man standing behind me, watching me admire myself. Before I had a chance to grow embarrassed at being caught out he moved closer.

"Excuse, please," he said. "Not be scared. I cannot help to see—your dress, your hair—reminds me of Hungarian Gypsy princess."

"Oh?" Nothing he might have said could have pleased me more.

"I tell myself she must be model and no other. I am photographer. I take pictures of you, enter in show. Win first prize."

"Ah!" I said, pleasantly tongue-tied.

He gestured at a green door. "Studio is upstairs. See sign in window? You can spare half hour, perhaps? To get started. For next sitting I talk to your mother. She say yes?"

"Of course!" How could she not? She'd be delighted for me. And proud. Anna on the other hand might be a bit miffed once I got famous; it had always been understood that she was to be the prettier sister.

Streetcar and Vati forgotten I followed the stranger across the square and up a dark stairwell to a room crowded with camera equipment, the walls covered with black-and-white samples of previous work. For half an hour I turned my head this way and that, tilted my chin up and down, and looked over my shoulder as he kept up a steady flow of words.

"I name Kadar Sandor. From small town near Budapest. Fled here when Soviets come. 1956. Deutschland (Germany) has cold heart. Cold eyes everywhere. Not like yours. Such honesty is what this place needs. We show them your soul, yes? I see your dress light up the square. The hair! The face! Is miracle. Germans too pale, you see? Not love color. Not love anything. Not know how to live. Is pity. See line on wall? Look there, no matter what. I come closer."

The camera moved in, its staring eye a meter away, then less. Forget stewardess. I was born to be a model.

"Half hour is gone," he soon sighed. "Like blink of eye. You have phone? Put number on this paper, please. Your name. Mother's name. So. Has been great pleasure." He shook my hand at the door. "When you come again? Tomorrow? One week? I talk with mother, we see. Will develop negatives in meantime. One thing you promise, no?"

"What?"

"Hair is like poem. Like song. No cut, no change. Okay?"

"Okay!"

*

I COULD still feel my cheeks glow when the streetcar pulled into the Stachus. It was too late to browse for lipstick and perfume but according to Herr Kadar I was dazzling enough without them. I ran to transfer onto the next clanging tram, this one headed toward the Hauptbahnhof. The busy train station was a good place to buy foreign newspapers. I chose the Daily Mirror, from London. Clamping it under one arm, I prepared to brave the detestable continuous-motion lift in Vati's office building. The last time I came with Anna there was a great uproar, screams and running. The lift had made an emergency stop between floors.

"What happened?" I'd asked Vati nervously.

He gave a disinterested shrug. "Someone got hurt. Happens at least once every day."

"How come?"

"These lifts are quite safe as long as you pay close attention. If you don't . . ." He'd shrugged again.

It was his unfinished sentence that started my phobia. How *could* a person step onto something that never stopped moving without getting stuck, hung, or squashed? How could one get off without falling? Paralyzed with what-ifs, I propelled myself onto the lift by sheer determination that day, knowing Vati would show his displeasure if I admitted my fear.

Now I confronted the same lift, sweating as I watched men in well-cut suits step matter-of-factly in and out of the contraption. I took a stabilizing breath and counted to three. Then I had a major revelation—the thing was alive and had already chosen me as its next victim. Stumbling backwards to the stairs, I climbed two flights, then took a short break so that I would not arrive in Vati's office all sweaty.

Last summer he visited me at the camp, claiming he'd had to travel nearby on business. Sister Geraldine came to fetch me to the guest-parlor, her cheeks even rosier than usual. He sat on the best chair, a cone-shaped bag filled with huge green grapes on his lap, surrounded by an array of twittering nuns who giggled like schoolgirls. Even haughty Sister Francesca thawed several degrees in his presence. And he, deep in conversation with Sister Abisinnia—who was my favorite, too—noticed me just long enough to pass me the bag before refocusing his full attention on the young nun.

Later when she walked me back to the hall she said, "You have a very handsome father."

I was surprised I hadn't noticed and she had.

For a couple of hours that day the Sisters were at their most congenial while trying to pump me for tidbits about my parents. But by suppertime everything was back to normal. Sister Abisinnia, who had taken charge of the grapes, insisted on giving one to each child present in the large dining hall. She had to remind me twice that God expects us to share with those who are less fortunate.

My grape was sun-ripened and unexpectedly sweet. Perhaps the whole bunch would have been overwhelming after two weeks of bland camp fare.

Dragging myself to the third floor of Vati's office building by the smooth wooden banister, I realized that he had an exaggerated effect on most women he met. He didn't have to say or do anything except be there to cause astonishing symptoms in otherwise level-headed females. Traveling with him was always less than satisfactory as his attention invariably wandered from his own daughters to somebody else's.

But today would surely be different. I'd open the office door in my enchanting dress and his eyes would be riveted on me. At last I'd bask in the glory of his undivided, admiring attention.

His eyes were indeed riveted when I made my grand entrance. But I should have realized that with Vati nothing ever worked out the way I imagined. He looked from my face to the wall clock, his expression souring. "You are three minutes late!"

I should have used the lift.

He waved away my stuttered apology and stared at my dress. "What ghastly colors. Now I'm glad we're not eating in public. I'd be ashamed to walk into a restaurant with someone so gaudy."

Hovering in the doorway, I stammered, "But—but it's my birthday dress. It makes me look beautiful."

"It makes you look cheap. Especially with your hair all bushy and wild. Now that you are fifteen, isn't it about time you learned to put it up decently to keep it out of your face? Why are you still standing at the door? Be so kind as to come into the room and be seated."

As soon as I moved the dress began to fade—and so did I. Like Cinderella's charmed gown, mine turned into ash-gray rags, leaving me unadorned.

"Did your mother buy this preposterous carnival costume for you?"

"Yes."

"An unfortunate lapse of taste. Nonetheless, I hope you had a good birthday. *My* present is bit more substantial than Mutti's, I must say."

Subdued, I took his gift-wrapped offering and sat in the visitor's chair. "May I open it?"

"That would be nice!"

The instant I tore off the white tissue paper I knew I'd made another mistake.

"If you had been more careful we could have reused it," he chided.

Flustered, I couldn't decide if I should throw the shreds away or hand them to him for repairs. I dropped them behind my chair, hoping he wouldn't notice.

"What do you think waste baskets are for?"

Blushing, I looked around the room but could not find one.

He nodded at the black camera perched on my lap. "Well?"

"For me?" I hedged, trying to work up some honest enthusiasm.

"I must be going blind. There's someone else in this room? I had to buy a new Leica for my trip to Greece so I'm passing the old one on to you. It still takes nice pictures."

I studied the black object with dismay. Did I ever give him the slightest hint that I might be interested in taking pictures? For the next few minutes he attempted to show me how the camera worked. Words like shutter, speed, feet and inches bounced off my ears as I struggled in vain to understand. Most likely he would consider me impertinent if I dared to ask how I was supposed to pay for film and developing.

Photography was *his* passion. He had a bookcase full of albums and boxes of loose photos stuffed in the side board, documenting our lives. The occasional guests, stumbling into his house for Sunday Kaffee und Kuchen (coffee and cake), were obliged to pay for them by leafing through those tomes and making uplifting comments about each picture they viewed.

"Ja, vielen Dank (thanks)," I said, carefully polite. "Anna will be delighted when I show it to her." She'd say that true to form he had given me another cast-off to save himself the trouble of throwing it away and that hopefully he would have run out of discards by the time her birthday rolled around, forcing him to buy her something new.

"Of course she will," he said, momentarily cheered at the mention of her name. Then he opened a drawer, lifted out a plate piled with belegte Brote (open-faced sandwiches), placed them precisely between us, and wiped his hands on a handkerchief. "Now that we got your present out of the way it's time for our lunch. I made these last night so they might be a bit on the dry side but I'm sure you realize day-old bread is far healthier than fresh baked."

I had a feeling that refusing his offerings was not an option, so I studied the array while he brought out a long-familiar aluminum flask and poured reconstituted, watery raspberry juice into our tumblers. I began to nibble on a square of black pumpernickel smeared thinly with Camembert, leaving the pink plasticized cheese spread to him.

"Well," he said when he'd finished swallowing his last bite. "We'd better take a look at your report card."

I pulled the envelope containing it out of my bag and yielded it to him with mixed emotions, suspecting he'd not be impressed by the fact that I received the best grades in my class. He slipped out the document, unfolded it, and studied it attentively for some time while a vertical frown line deepened between his brows. Until that moment I'd actually believed my five Einser (A) were something to be proud of. On a scale of one to six it could hardly get better. But he skimmed over all five of them to focus on the two Zweier (B).

"Two Zweier!" he huffed. "One in math! Ach du lieber Himmel (heavens)! And the other in—"

"Handarbeit (needle work)," I provided gloomily.

"And what could you possibly get wrong in Handarbeit?"

"Sewing. Darning. Knitting. I detest them."

"But they are subjects every girl must know. Part of being a good wife. Your mother is very talented in that department. It was one of the reasons I married her. Do you detest math too?"

"I'm better at writing essays," I admitted, leaning across the desk to draw his attention to the glowing praise Frau Bischof had written in the comment section.

He pulled the report card out of my reach. "I assume you know that math is the most important subject for anyone who wants the *Mittlere Reife?"*

I swallowed timidly. "I may need some help. Ingrid, from across the wheat field, has had math tutors since she was six. I might have made it into the *Oberschule* if someone had given *me* that kind of help. Most kids who do well on the exams get tutored, you see. Mutti said she can't afford it. She said I should ask you to—"

"Ausgeschlossen (out of the question)!" he snapped, slapping his palm on the offending document. "If you don't have it up here the best tutors are useless. Sending girls on to higher education is sheer waste anyway. They all get married and have children. As they should. And if you need a tutor in Handarbeit your Mutti can show you for free."

She'd tried that already. But no matter how patiently she had demonstrated I could not imitate her fine handiwork. My woollen gloves had so many dropped stitches that she finally took them out of my sweaty hands, pulled out row after hopeless row, and reknitted them practically from scratch.

Frau Bischof, who had watched me labor over the crippled things for weeks, suspected as much and gave me a Fiver for the whole project, lowering my yearly grade. For endless months I'd struggled with seams, wooden darning eggs and old practice socks, hoops and embroidery yarn, but the ease my classmates brought to these tasks kept eluding me.

Could it be that somewhere inside I didn't really want to succeed at housewifely skills for fear they'd become a life-sentence?

Vati pushed the sandwich plate at me. "You only ate one. After all the trouble I took to make them."

"The Camembert was very filling."

He glowered at me until I chose another and then watched me eat the whole sandwich before he said, "Your Onkel Franz was right. You have deplorable table manners."

"He's not my uncle!"

The room turned a few degrees cooler. "Do not presume to correct me," he said in a clipped tone. "No wonder he insisted on meeting with me yesterday. You *are* belligerent. Your schooling *has* given you a big head and idle hands—I can see it myself. I must agree with him that it's time you learned a trade. He thinks a rigorous apprenticeship will cure what ails you or at least tire you enough to restore the family's equilibrium."

"He hates me!" I wailed. "He's always trying to get rid of me. I'm surprised he hasn't asked you to take me in."

Startled, Vati said, "I told him that was out of the question, of course. There's no room in my life for a child he himself admits is incorrigible."

"I'm not—"

"Oh? You've run away from home twice. Stayed out all night, doing who knows what. I told him you are your mother's problem, not mine. But I've asked around and have succeeded in finding an apprenticeship just right for you."

I sat rigid, knees pressed together, staring at the trembling camera on my lap and willing my eyes to stay dry. Crying females incurred Vati's instant wrath. "But I'm good at school," I stammered. "I like to learn. I'll do better in math next year. I'll spend the rest of summer vacation practicing word problems . . ."

He tidied away the remains of our lunch and rose. "Your vacation is over. You start next Monday. In a print shop. Just the thing for someone who likes to read. Now pack up and be quick about it. I'll walk you to the streetcar."

I hung my head. "But— aren't you ashamed to be seen with me?"

"I'll force myself." He buttoned his suit jacket and went to the door.

As I stuffed the Leica into my bag the newspaper I'd kept under my arm since walking in fell to the floor, sliding apart. Under his glare I knelt to shuffle the pages together again.

"What kind of paper is that?" He squinted. "Foreign?"

"From London. So I can improve my English vocabulary."

Making a visible effort to stand tall, he said, "But German is all you need, even in Greece and in Egypt. Deutsch ist eine Weltsprache (German is an international language)!"

I stuffed the paper on top of the Leica, added the torn gift wrapping, and trailed after him to the lift where he stepped smoothly onto the moving conveyer, going down. I hopped on stiff-kneed, clutching the wall. At ground level he stepped off with equal ease, glancing at his wrist watch just long enough to miss my grotesque stumble onto the solid lobby floor.

"Really, Marianne," he said as we were walking out of the building together. "Why all the drama? In a few years you'll be married. Hopefully you'll choose someone with a reliable business. I have given the matter some thought—marry a butcher. People will always eat meat."

"A butcher?" I echoed, not trusting my ears.

"Must I repeat everything?"

I begged his forgiveness and walked silently behind him as he sped down the sidewalk. A butcher. White apron splattered with blood. Fingernails caked with it. Carcasses hanging from hooks, upside down, split open, dismembered. All at once I recalled a long-ago Saturday morning in Freidorf. Mutti and I were making a shortcut across the rear of the butcher shop and saw the two butcher brothers alternated swinging their sledge hammers at the pig's head while it gave drawn-out, bone-chilling screams. I said it was murder but Mutti shushed me and pulled me away.

A butcher. For me.

I looked at the man I loved, striding impatiently ahead in his hand-tailored gray suit, rushing me out of his day. As soon as we arrived at the streetcar stop I held out my hand. "Vielen Dank (thanks) for the lunch, Vati, and for your gift. Don't bother to wait with me. I know you want to get back to your work. Auf Wiederseh'n."

He shook, looking relieved, took a few steps away from me, patted his jacket pocket, and returned to stuff a sealed envelope deep into my bag. "The support money," he murmured. "See to it Mutti gets it intact."

I didn't even react to that final insult but couldn't help watching him walk back to his office in the forlorn hope he might turn and wave at least once before he disappeared. I should have known better. For some reason his heart had always been closed against me. Not for the first time, I wished I knew what I had done wrong, and when.

Then I heard his voice inside my head. 'Sie ist ein Fehler (she's a mistake)." That's what I heard him say to a casual acquaintance once when we were riding the streetcar together.

He was talking about me.

CHAPTER 13

MY STREETCAR JERKED TO A STOP at the great tram island on the Karlsplatz, which was bordered and crisscrossed by tracks. Cars buzzed around the traffic circle like a swarm of riled hornets. Drivers tooted their horns, tapped their forehead, and shook fists at each other. Trams, approaching from every direction, clanged shrill warnings. But none of the confusion of sounds and images was fully able to reach me as I wandered from one tram to another and took a seat in the rear carriage, hardly noticing the city noise gradually fading to bearable levels. I caught myself staring off at some infinitesimal point, as I had so often watched Mutti do at our kitchen table when she was taking a smoking break.

"Shell-shocked," she'd say with a laugh when I brought it to her attention. "See?" She'd hold out a hand and together we'd watch her fingers tremble.

And now while the streetcar hummed along its tracks, picking up momentum between stops, I raised my hands from my lap and watched my own fingers tremble—a natural consequence of having been with Vati.

It wasn't just that he didn't love me enough—I'd suspected that for a long time—it was that I finally had to admit to myself that he didn't even *like* me. Some part of me had always known it but I'd lied to myself until I could not lie any more.

Bit by bit I put together snatches of memories and overheard adult conversations containing words like *Hitler* and *Vaterland* until all was plain: It was my father's glad duty as a German citizen to produce sons for the fatherland. Three times he succeeded, and three times Mutti sabotaged his efforts by miscarrying fully formed baby-boys, leaving him to bury his pride and his dreams. Then came the golden-haired daughter fitting Hitler's blueprint for fair Aryan maidens. One day she would grow up to wear gilded braids like a crown, marry a patriot, and produce lusty sons of her own. In the meantime she would be a loving and pliable sister to the boy he was yet determined to create.

At long last Mutti was pregnant again. All was forgiven as he waited for his son to be born. That's when he got me—red, damp and wrinkled—howling to protest my own arrival. The doctor said Mutti must bear no more children. I'd been his last chance at glory and I'd muffed it. It was no wonder he could rarely bring himself to touch me or smile at me—unlike Lucius, who passed out his smiles as if he had an endless supply and was unworried they'd run out if he wasted a few.

Vati believed I had usurped the sacred place reserved for his boy. From my beginnings I sensed his disappointment in me and tried in various ways to be what he wanted. I wore Lederhosen and raced through the village on bare feet, wrestling with boys and climbing to the shaky tops of the highest trees. I even learned to use his hammer and screwdrivers but nothing I did was ever enough. I waited for the day he would look past my unfortunate gender and see how I'd turned myself inside out for him. Fifteen years after my unwelcome arrival I finally had to admit to myself that *my* father would never look at me the way Mutti's had looked at her.

The first thing I did when I got home was to check my Emmenthaler trail. All the pieces a short-legged dog could reach were already gone and the rest had grown hard, sweating oil. Seppi salivated as I checked on each one, hopefully wagging the end of his tail. I got on my knees to peer into his unswerving eyes. They were guileless and gentle as ever. Besides being too fast and too smart to be caught by an overweight dog, Elvis had always had a brotherly bond with Seppi, often curling up in the soft, ample fur on the dog's hip for a quick nap.

"Where's Elvis?" I asked Seppi. "Go find him for me."

He rose courteously and sat by the bathroom door.

"You have to go?" I asked and took him downstairs for a while, glad he was so easy to please. "Elvis?" I said as Seppi sniffed along the side of the wheat field near a cluster of cornflowers so blue they seemed like fringe-petaled bits of condensed summer sky. The wheat grass was already up to my knees. I could barely see to the furrows beneath. If my mouse *was* down there somewhere I'd never find him again, nor would he want to be found.

Back upstairs I stuffed the red dress out of sight, armed myself with the Langenscheidt and a notebook, smoothed the British newspaper out on the kitchen table, and concentrated on the front page. By the end of the first column I knew that "lorry" meant truck, that a bonnet was not always a hat, and that the German word *Benzin* was called "petrol" in England and "gasoline" in America. By five o'clock I had made ten pages of notes.

That's when Anna and Mutti walked in. Anna came from a day at the lake and Mutti from work, loaded with parcels. She was wearing her elegant moss-green suit, her narrow waist cinched tight with a matching belt. She kicked off brown spikes, rubbing her toes. Anna dropped her lumpy beach bag onto the linoleum, untied her straw hat, and tossed it on top of the bag.

"Is your suit still wet?" Mutti asked pointedly.

"Soaked," Anna admitted cheerfully. "The towel, too. I took a quick dip before riding home." Without waiting for further reminders she pulled them out of the bag and carried them to the bathroom, leaving Mutti and me alone in the kitchen.

I held out Vati's envelope. She took it and sighed. "It turns out he could have given it to me himself. He called me at work in the afternoon and insisted I stop by his office on my way home." She filed the envelope away in her purse, releasing the inevitable whiff of Eau de Cologne. For once I hardly noticed, for I was busy staring at her until she grew flustered and turned away to unwrap a block of Neapolitan ice cream. She took three of our best gold-rimmed cake plates from the cupboard, cut the block into three equal cubes, deposited one on each plate, and ringed them with vanilla wafers.

"Let's call this dinner. It's hot out and I'm too tired to cook," she said. Never before had she dished out more than one measly scoop or offered dessert instead of a meal.

Standing in the doorway, Anna sucked in her breath. "Is it my birthday today?" she asked with a quick look at the wall calendar.

But I knew that Mutti was trying to bribe me into accepting my fate. "Did you at least *try* to tell him no?" I said, folding the newspaper and putting it on top of the dictionary.

Mutti twisted her lips into a tired smile. "Who listens to me? Did you?"

"Don't make it my fault," I said, claiming one of the plates and scraping a finger over my stripe of vanilla. "Vati can hardly wait for me to earn my own living so he can cut the support money in half. O.F. just provided a convenient excuse." I licked my finger and opened the report card for her, which had been seriously creased by the Leica. "Five *Einser*, Mutti! And with a little tutoring help I could do much better in math. You know I could."

Anna, who had moved to the silverware drawer to count out three teaspoons, looked from my face to Mutti's. "What are you talking about?"

Mutti concentrated on turning the plates until the three striped cubes matched up precisely, pink to pink, brown to brown, and white to white. "Vati decided that Marianne must leave school to become an apprentice. In a print shop. Starting next week."

The spoons clattered back into the drawer. "And you *let* him?" Anna said, her voice tight.

"I tried to stall him of course. But he insisted that I sign the contract immediately. Apparently the printer called, claiming someone else was interested in the position. You do know that Marianne had a *Zweier* in math?"

Anna gave a sharp laugh. "I have nothing better than Twos on *my* report card, even in art school. Is he going to make me quit too?"

Mutti gasped. "No, no, of course not. Vati would never—" She looked at me, then at the table, brushing at invisible crumbs.

My eyes burned and brimmed. I closed them before she could notice. The only sounds in the room were the ones Anna made, retrieving the spoons, bringing them to the table, and banging them down one by one.

"Our Marianne, a lousy apprentice? She'll die!" she said, throwing herself on her chair.

"She's not a boy, after all," Mutti reminded her. "God forbid she may be married in three or four years. She doesn't need advanced schooling to have babies." She was arguing Vati's point instead of mine or her own.

Anna clicked a spoon against the side of her plate with uncharacteristic vigor. Then she announced, "If they're making her quit, I'm quitting too. I won't go back to the institute in the fall. You'll have to find an apprenticeship for me as well." This was so out of character that I was compelled to peer past my lashes to see what possessed her. Her Aryan eyes glittered as she pressed on. "So if you've already paid my tuition, get a refund. Professional artists come to the school all the time, trying to lure students away to become their assistants. Now that I think of it, one of them gave me his card on the last day of classes. A grafiker. He works mostly for television. Well known in the trade. He could teach me more in a week than the school can in a year."

It was no secret to me that she was bored with her lessons. "Stifling," she called them. I was willing to bet she'd been planning something like this since June. She was not known to make hasty decisions. Like O.F., she'd been waiting for just the right excuse to come along.

The ice cream on our plates was changing to tri-colored sauce. Distracted, Mutti stirred hers into swirls with a wafer. "Anna, bitte, no one is thinking of making you quit.'

"Wait a minute—I'll show you!" Anna jumped up and ran to our room. I shoveled an un-lady-like scoop into my mouth. Mutti frowned but I liked my soups hot and my ice cream brick-hard. "Here," Anna said, returning with a business card. "His name is Horst Obdach. He has a studio in Schwabing and connections in Grünwald. He offered me a small salary when *we* should be paying *him*. Call him. Call him right now."

The telephone rang right on cue. The grafiker, prepared to plead Anna's case? While Mutti rushed to pick up the receiver, Anna sat down to her ice cream, triumphantly shaved off a dainty bit with the tip of her spoon, and licked it clean with great relish. "A print shop," she said smugly. "Smeary black ink. Poor Marianne."

I hissed her quiet so I could listen to Mutti's part of the conversation as it drifted in through the hall.

"Ja. Speaking. What? Our Mariandl? Maria, yes. When was that? My permission to do what? Take pictures of her? *Ach*! I beg your pardon. You do *not* have my permission. Please try to speak clearly." Her irritation seemed to grow with each phrase. "Absolutely not," she snapped. "She's too young. In fact, I'm quite upset that you took pictures of her *before* asking me. The answer is no. I want every print. The negatives, too, or I will go straight to the police. She will fetch them tomorrow. We're decent people. Find your 'models' elsewhere!"

Alarmed, I stuffed a handful of wafers into my pocket and ran to rescue my budding career. "I'm being discovered!" I whispered urgently in her unoccupied ear. "He's a great photographer, Mutti. You must see his work, please. He'll make me famous, I swear it!"

"I'm glad you think she is," she said coldly into the mouthpiece, waving me silent with an impatient swipe of her hand. "So do I. And no, I won't change my mind. Thank you for bringing it to my attention. Good-bye." She slammed down the receiver, scowling at me. "Really, Marianne—the man's a foreigner! A refugee! Doesn't even know how to speak in a full sentence. How *could* you pose for a perfect stranger? Why, anything might have happened!"

"I was *lucky* he picked me! Oh please, come with me tomorrow. He has a studio, just like Anna's grafiker. It's right on the Kurfürstenplatz."

"You know I can't take off from work just for that," she said. Then she shook her head in horror. "You, a model? What would Vati say?"

I corkscrewed a strand of my hair and pulled hard and steady to alleviate the greater pain. "You're just like him and O.F., aren't you? You don't want me to have anything good either. Well, next time I won't even ask." I stormed out of the house to find a private spot in a patch of high weeds where I smoldered, crushing vanilla wafers between frustrated jaws.

*

CROSSING the Kurfürstenplatz the next day, my gait was halting where it had been buoyant before. The gloomy stairs to the studio were steeper than I remembered. More dilapidated, too. It took me a while to gather the courage to knock. The anger in Mutti's half of the conversation still made me cringe.

Herr Kadar opened at once.

"Es tut mir leid (I'm sorry)," I told him.

"I am sorry, also." He stepped aside for me but my feet stuck to the threshold.

"My mother was rude to you. Can you forgive us?"

A smile creased his cheeks as he beckoned me in. "Is mother's job to protect. She not know me, yes? Done from love. I understand. Since yesterday I work fast. Look there."

He did not need to point. Half the wall was covered with a huge enlargement of me. Although it was in black-and-white it seemed to burst with colors. I shone. I sparkled. I was bigger than life. I looked away from it, stunned.

"You and I together, world class, eh?" he said, his voice filled with regret.

A longing to live out our dream surged through me. I dared a second look and clasped my hands together as if in prayer. "It's beautiful!"

"We would win first prize, you see?" Gently, he brushed the cheek on the portrait. "This, I keep. Favorite, always. And this one I make special for you. Gift." He opened a folder. The top picture was a smaller version of the miracle on the wall.

"Yes," I said. "A gift to remember you by. And I will. Thank you." I offered my hands, and he closed the folder and placed it firmly upon them.

"Mother get all of rest," he said, sounding vexed. "She tear up. Throw in trash. Burn. Such pity." He put a friendly hand on my shoulder. "Live," he said. "Feel. Love color. Be Gypsy princess inside. Hear the wild violins. Dance Gypsy dance in your soul. Understand?"

I nodded.

He waggled a lock of my hair, putting it playfully under my nose like a mustache. "Yesterday was very good day. We meet. Today not so good. We part. Is okay. Friends of heart. We not forget."

Afterward at the bus stop I thought how tough it was to live in a place where a child was only allowed to want for herself what the adults wanted for her. And what they wanted most was an obedient quiet girl who would not object to growing up without a will of her own.

They had plotted for me the life they wished me to have. Now they were busy trying to stuff me into it.

It was going to be a bad fit.

*

AT HOME I placed the folder on the kitchen table, unopened. Knowing I would grieve if I saw the rest of the photos I just pulled out the top one, carried it to the bedroom, and propped it onto my pillow. Then I stood back for a long look. The magic of the dress had transformed the face above it. The clear hazel eyes in the picture shone with exuberant joy. A stranger had glanced at me, seen my soul, and rendered it.

My father did not even know I had a soul. O.F. was different. He knew, all right, or else why would he try so hard to crush it? What they had in common was that they believed in my utter lack of value. Somehow they had succeeded in making me believe in it, too.

For one brilliant instant their version of me was suspended while the Hungarian's dazzled my mind's eye. Standing before the wonder of me, I drank it in, deeply. Then I put the portrait in an old math exercise book and slipped it under my mattress, within easy reach should I need a reminder of who I really was.

When I came out of my room Mutti was in the kitchen and the folder was gone. She didn't mention it and I never saw it again.

CHAPTER 14

O N THURSDAY AFTERNOON Anna went to meet Mutti in Schwabing so they could discuss career plans with the grafiker. Seppi and I had the whole house to ourselves. He sprawled on the living room rug while I went through the phone book, writing down the numbers of likely government agencies for some personal research.

My question to the people who answered my call was simple: "I want to give up my German citizenship. How do I go about it?"

I had no idea it would make them so angry. The first bureaucrat I talked to stuttered incoherently and hung up on me. The second screamed, "Eine solche Frechheit (what nerve)!" before disconnecting. The third demanded my name and address. The next one called me a communist. Another threatened to refer me to Haar for a hurried internment in the insane asylum. I was ordered to feel ashamed. A woman snapped, "In Hitler's day you would have been shot for this!"

No one was the least bit helpful. When I ran out of numbers to call I realized it was a lot harder to renounce a citizenship than I thought it would be. Exhausted, I gave it up to move the radio dial to the AFN station. It was in the midst of playing Brenda Lee's 'I'm sorry." I was cheered to discover that I could understand most of the words. I sang along as best I could, but when the announcer came on, emitting a long gush of English, I could make no more sense of it than I did before I embarked on my private lessons.

Keys rattled on the landing. Anna waltzed in and snapped off the radio. "I start in September," she crowed. "Right after summer vacation. Herr Obdach will take me to the TV studio in Grünwald. He knows practically everybody there. And he has a brand new BMW 700 with brown leather seats."

That made him special, all right. Peter's parents had been saving for years for a basic Renault and probably would for many more.

Mutti walked in, looking stunned. "I can't believe I signed that contract without asking Vati first. He'll be so angry!"

"Who cares? It's done," Anna said. "You have custody. We don't need his permission."

I hardly recognized my sister. All her life she'd been the model child. What had gotten into her all of a sudden? She was playing the rebel, which had always been my part, and I was drifting to the opposite pole, the one of quiet desperation and hopeless acquiescence I used to think was only for wimps. "You have custody of me, too," I reminded Mutti.

Her face closed. "What's done is done. You brought it on yourself."

How convenient for her.

On Friday Mutti came home carrying a smelly box with several holes punched through the cardboard. "Any news of Elvis?" she asked. When I said no, she opened the box and pulled out a fancy new cage containing a fat white hamster and a big tread wheel. "Isn't he sweet?" she said, putting the cage on the English paper I'd spread out on the table. It was her way of saying I might as well give up on my mouse, since there wasn't enough space under my bed for two cages. "Something to keep you company," she said with a little laugh. "You can watch him turn the wheel."

Having nothing better to do the little beast climbed inside it at once and started to run in place. Right away I knew it was stupid—you'd never catch Elvis expending his energy on such a useless pursuit.

I moved the cage onto the sports section. "How do you know it's a he?" Once in a pet shop I saw a hamster very much like this one pick up one of her pink babies as if it were a gummi bear and swallow it whole. By the time I managed to drag the attendant to the emergency two more had disappeared.

"I had the clerk check, that's how," Mutti said. "This little guy will be good company for you on the weekends. All Seppi ever does is sleep and eat." It was only because he knew that when O.F. was at home, lying low was the best policy.

Mutti filled the food and water dishes and made me promise to keep hamster and dog in my room for the whole weekend. At six o'clock she gave me a new Bravo magazine and locked us in. I was done reading it by the time O.F. walked into the apartment. Soon chairs scraped in the kitchen. Knives clinked against porcelain. Voices droned. O.F. described a week's worth of sales-triumphs during the meal. From below my open window the sounds of children at play in the gathering dusk provided his only noise competition. Balls bounced, bicycle bells rang, a jump rope thudded against the asphalt.

Seppi took up the lower half of my bed. The hamster's cage sat on a strategic spot on the floor so that the door would shield it from view whenever it opened. The white beast turned from his feeding dish to stare at me out of beady, lusterless eyes, his cheek pouches filled to bursting. Already, his sawdust floor was covered with droppings and moist stains. He ran around his cage, which, proportionately speaking, was the size of my own, climbed into the food dish, and curled up to sleep on a mattress of pellets. At least he knew enough to stay out of the water.

I had less space to maneuver in my jail than he had in his. The beds, end to end, took up one of the long walls. The dresser and the two mahogany wardrobes took up the other. That left a narrow aisle in the middle, stretching from window to door. As the evening dragged on everything seemed to be shrinking. I discovered there was a big difference between me locking the door from the inside and Mutti locking it from the outside. I thought of the days and months I was going to have to spend in this room and knew I could not bear it.

Thank God for Lucius.

After O.F. retired to the TV and his after-dinner cigarette Mutti brought me my supper tray and I told her I had decided to visit a girlfriend from school on Saturday morning and would leave around ten.

She seemed relieved. "Good, good," she said. "I'll be at work, of course, but I'll tell Anna to let you out."

Later, when Anna was ready for bed, Mutti unlocked the door and followed her inside. Fishing in her apron, she brought out two tiny parcels, and gave the smaller to me. It contained a pair of slim, gold-plated hoop earrings. "So you won't have to borrow mine anymore," she said with a an affectionate smile.

I took out the baby-sized pink hearts I usually wore to keep the holes in my lobes from closing. Skillfully, she threaded in the hoops, showing me how to fasten them behind the ear, away from a mirror. I practiced while she handed Anna the larger package. It contained a new key on a long silver chain.

"So you can get in and out of this room by yourself, Anna. Wear it under your blouse and don't leave it lying around."

They exchanged a meaningful glance as my sister slipped it over her lacquered beehive. I understood what they were not saying—my gift was only a bribe but Anna's was priceless and must be kept out of my reach.

"Have fun with your girlfriend," Mutti told me. "Just remember to be home by eight. And if you have someone to visit on Sunday, that's fine, too—only, come home early because Vati wants to take you to the print shop first thing Monday morning." She turned to Anna. "Always relock the door after you let Marianne out. We'll keep Seppi in here for a few weekends. He won't mind. You know how he loves to snooze under her featherbed."

The only lie I'd told so far was to add the word "girl" to the word "friend." It was pure self-preservation. Eine Notlüge (a little white lie), Mutti would have called it, had she been in my place. It would buy me a day of freedom.

*

THE NEXT morning at precisely eleven o'clock I strode briskly along the access road to Henry Kaserne wearing blue jeans and a clinging pastel-green blouse. In my left hand I swung my beach bag stuffed with a sweater, three silver 1 D-Mark pieces painstakingly removed from my saving bank, the Leica, and various picnic items. With my right hand I gripped the curved handle of Lucius's black family umbrella. The rest of it was leaning against my shoulder like a parade rifle, the sharp tip pointing to the rear. It made me feel bold. Only one American dared to stop his car to wave a stick of gum out of the window. He withered under my gaze, hastily retrieved the offer, and drove on.

As soon as I came to the yellow phone booth near the gate Lucius appeared on the other side of the barrier, running around the curve, buoyant and tall. He gave a jubilant wave. I felt my mouth stretch halfway to my ears in response while he showed the guard his pass and then jogged toward me.

"You came!" he said, as if he found it hard to believe.

"So did you." I hadn't been entirely sure that he would. We shook. He held on to my hand.

"Light and dark," he said, raising them higher. "Kind of pretty together, don't you think?"

"Like a picture an artist makes," I improvised, not knowing the English word for Gemälde.

"Entitled 'Fraulein and GI'."

"Fräulein," I corrected. "What means GI?"

"Darned if I know. But whatever it is, I'm afraid I'm it. Hey, you brought the umbrella. Think we'll need it today?" He scanned the sky, where innocent fleece drifted on a slight breeze. "Forget I asked. The weatherman predicted sunshine but what does he know? We could be stuck in a downpour before we reach the next corner and in a blizzard before lunch." He took the umbrella from me and tossed it high in the air, where it hung, momentarily suspended, before twirling back to him.

I pulled out the camera. "For you, Lucius. You said you want to see country. Take photographs like a tourist. A film is inside. You know feet and inches? You keep it. A gift for the food you buy me last Sunday and for the cash."

"For me?" He walked his long, slender fingers over the black box. "It's been a long time since anyone gave me a present. Dankeshane."

"Bitte." I decided to stop correcting his German. That way he might be less inclined to find fault with my English.

"Tell you what." He patted his hip pocket. "I got my pay right in here. Lunch and dinner are on me Heck, the whole day's on me. Where are we going?"

"To Grünwald, to picnic by the Isar river," I said. Anna's future place of business intrigued me more than any print shop could, but not because of the budding TV industry and the movie sets she found so fascinating. I just loved the sound of the word and the images it evoked of sun-dappled forest, rolling hillsides, and the swift, green flow of the Isar. Frau Bischof once took the entire class on a field trip to the ancient castle on top of a rise, overlooking the valley. I still remembered which streetcars took us across town.

"A picnic?" Lucius looked back at the gate. "You want me to run to the PX and buy us a couple of snacks?"

I shook my bag. "I shopped at the kiosk. We have a Baby Ruth. A Butterfinger. Chocolate. Coca Cola for you."

"My kind of day," he said, relieving me of my burden. "Lead on, Maria!"

We matched strides, the sunshine a benediction on our shoulders. For an instant I could hear the metallic screech of a turning key, saw my rectangular bedroom for the mahogany coffin it was, and shook my head to clear away the image. Here and now, there were only Lucius and me, unfettered. At his side, I took the first step of the Gypsy dance, deep in my soul.

On our streetcar ride I listened attentively as he patiently explained the difference between Massachusetts, Maine and Vermont. I barely noticed the other passengers until his nostrils flared like that of a wild mustang who had just discovered he was trapped inside a corral.

"Look," he muttered under his breath. "Everyone on this blessed streetcar is staring at us. Straight on, without blinking. Like a herd of dumb cows. Don't they know how rude that is?"

He was right. The crowd of potential shoppers, sitting elbow to elbow, kept their eyes trained on him, their mouths hanging open in wonder. A couple of weeks ago I might have joined in this unbridled display of fascination—but now I knew better.

"It's best to ignore them," I advised loftily. "Which state is colder, Lucius, Maine or Vermont?"

"Good question," he said, trying to return to our topic. "There's lots of snow in Vermont, but in Maine, see, there's this fierce wind howling in from the ocean. Goes right through your clothes, no matter how many layers of wool you got on, and freezes your bones." Despite his best efforts he allowed himself to be side-tracked by our audience again. "Americans don't stare like that. They might look at you once and then look away. These krauts make me feel like I'm a bug in a jar."

"What means krauts?"

"Your people!"

Was he referring to the fact that Bavarians eat sauerkraut? How would he like it if I called him a hamburger then?

He shook his head. "Sorry, Maria. They're rattling me. Say, can we get off this thing for a while? Isn't it about time we had lunch?"

I spied a little restaurant in the middle of the block we were just passing and quickly pulled the cord to get the driver to stop. We'd sit out the lunch hour in that tranquil harbor until the shopping-crowd thinned. Fortified by a hot meal, Lucius's tolerance level was bound to improve.

I should have been concerned about my own. My troubles started as soon as we walked in the restaurant. The Wirt (proprietor) stood just inside, shaking hands with departing patrons and greeting incoming guests. His well-practiced smile failed him at our entrance. The drowsy murmur of lunch conversation, wrapped in cigarette smoke, came to a halt. All eyes were on us. A young woman wearing a brown linen apron, clearing the remains of a meal from the nearest table, abandoned her washcloth to escape to the kitchen.

The Wirt took my measure and found me beneath his notice. Fastening his wary eyes upon Lucius, he gave a small, courteous bow, saying unctuously, "Good afternoon, sir. This way, please." As he escorted Lucius to the other end of the restaurant he glanced at me just once, black fury in the back of his eyes. He had the talent of making me feel like a barefooted beggar with crusty toes, my head crawling with lice, the stench of spoilt garbage steaming from my clothes.

The diners watched every step of our progress. Two waiters hurried to a vacant table in the darkest corner. One saw to the silverware, the other rearranged a small bunch of red carnations in a glass vase. The proprietor pulled out Lucius's chair. It faced the wall. The plump, youngish waiter with a blonde handlebar mustache laid a menu card in front of Lucius. The proprietor nodded soberly at his employees and returned to his station.

The older, pot-bellied waiter pulled out an ordering pad. Both servers stood at attention behind Lucius's chair while he pretended to study the menu.

"Maria!" He patted the chair to his right and slid the menu card toward it. "Sit here and help me out or I'll be forced to eat wieners and sauerkraut again. They're the only words on here I recognize. Will you read through this thing and order us something more interesting? At four marks to the dollar we don't have to skimp."

I sat and studied the entries. In honor of Kadar Sandor I chose two plates of Hungarian goulash over broad noodles, a salad, and *Kaiser Schmarrn* for dessert, to be accompanied by hot chocolate topped with whipped cream. But although I ordered in articulate high-German the pot-bellied waiter kept his pad blank and his eyes firmly on Lucius while his mustached assistant clasped both hands behind his back and stared vacantly at his own shoes.

After an uncomfortable silence I pushed the menu back toward Lucius and showed him my picks. Unable to pronounce the words on the card, he put a finger over my choices and said, "Svai, bitte." Holding up his index finger, he added slowly, "Und ain Uasser." Two meals and one water.

The elderly waiter disappeared into the kitchen, but the young one stayed a discreet distance behind us, putting a crimp into our table-conversation. The old guy reappeared in record time with our plates and Lucius's water. My plate descended without comment but Lucius's was lovingly arranged, turned this way and that until it sat at just the right angle. Nonetheless, the goulash was excellent, full of zest and paprika, the noodles satisfyingly slippery with sauce, the salad crisp, sprinkled with herbs never seen in Mutti's limited kitchen. And because we were sitting so far from the rest of the patrons with our backs to the room we didn't see anyone stare.

The lighting was low enough so that Lucius's skin tone blended softly with the shadows. If he was bewildered by so much undivided attention he didn't show it. In fact, the pinched look that had come to his face on the streetcar had given way to a broad grin. "Shocked them about the water, didn't I? You-all think it's only good for washing the dishes. Too bad they forgot the ice."

The meat chunks were spicy and tender enough to melt between palate and tongue. At last we finished our leisurely meal. No sooner had Lucius put his fork on the rim of his cleared plate than the Kaiser Schmarrn appeared at his elbow. It came on a heated oval platter and was dusted with a fine coating of powdered sugar. The confection had always been a passion of mine. The accompanying hot chocolate tasted as if the head chef had personally shaved an imported Swiss chocolate bar into cups of hot cream drawn from cows summering on high alpine meadows where they'd fed on nothing but sweet herbs and wildflowers since spring. The dollop of whipped cream on top was laced with brandy and dark chocolate crumbs. Lucius called it a triple decker.

If the Wirt and his waiters thought their obvious disapproval of me would deprive me of my appetite they had miscalculated, for I had plenty of practice sharing O.F.'s table these past few years. The young waiter ran to refill Lucius's water glass at the slightest hint. And when we were done and Lucius left a huge tip to show his appreciation both servers bowed profusely and accompanied him all the way to the exit. I shuffled behind, dabbing at my chocolate-milk mustache with a used tissue. At the door the Wirt shook Lucius's hand in an effusive good-bye, reserving his last glance, iron-hard, for me. And instantly the lice came out of hiding and crawled over my forehead. My clothes smelled like the inside of an unwashed refuse can until we were outdoors.

I was sure I'd never feel clean again but Lucius chuckled, linked my arm through his, and led me away, saying, "That was some high class version of the bum's rush those fine people gave us. Say, let's catch the next streetcar—getting stared at by honest krauts will be an improvement. Maybe we can manage to stare a few of them down, together."

CHAPTER 15

I T WAS A LONG RIDE TO GRÜNWALD. By the time we arrived at our picnic spot on a lush meadow Lucius and I were hungry again. We sat on cushioning grass, the green river below us, the castle, nestled among trees, waiting above. The air was so clear that the Alps seemed a mere two-hour hike away. While we munched on the candy bars I'd bought near Henry I played tour guide, pointing out the various granite peaks I had climbed—some in the summers with both of my parents when I was still small enough to appreciate holding Mutti's hand— some in the winters with Anna and Vati after the wrenching divorce. In the days before ski lifts we'd carried our heavy skis from the valley floor to the top, taking several hours, and skied all the way down again just once.

"The Zupspitze has a restaurant right by the cross," I told Lucius. "You can buy beer, sit on a rock, and see mountains in every direction." Up there, peak after peak of gray and white granite undulated in seemingly endless chains fading to purple, the bottomland swallowed by mist. "Did you climb mountains when you were a boy?"

"On the bay? I went fishing."

"For what?"

"Fish!" He licked melted chocolate from his thumb. "That Butterfinger sure hit the spot. What else you got in there?" He peered in my bag and discovered my red handball. "Hey, can we play?"

At home, that little ball had patiently allowed me to toss it against the stucco wall for hours on end. It came alive the moment I rolled it to Lucius, brightened when he spanned his palms around it, fingertips touching. "Good size," he said, twirling it on his index finger. He let it dance up one arm, down the other to his thigh and his toes, and up again on the opposite leg. He tossed it into the sky where it hung like a red, miniature sun before gravity returned it to our waiting hands.

"Come on, Maria," he said. "Let's teach it to fly."

I ran off a good distance and he pitched the ball to me in a high arc. It quivered with excitement when I caught it. I threw it straight back to Lucius.

"It wants to sail with the birds," he said, whirling it skyward again. Each of our throws took it a bit higher and let it stay there longer but gravity always won in the end. Lucius's final throw made it soar. It shrank to the size of a red dot. I thought I saw it sprout wings. When it started to descend it came at me so fast and so hard that I fumbled the catch. It bounced once on to the grass behind me, then jumped into the river and got stuck in the eddies. Even as Lucius sprinted to retrieve it, it caught a swift current and shot out of his reach to the middle of the stream. There it did a tight good-bye loop and embarked on a solo journey—not a flight, after all, but a swim; it hadn't been wings I'd seen sprouting but fins.

"My ball!" I cried, watching it spiral out of my life.

"Going and gone." Lucius put a supportive arm around my shoulders. "Where do you think it's headed, Maria?"

I called to mind the map in Frau Bischof's classroom. "First through München," I recited from memory, imagining it bob under a stone bridge. "Then from Upper Bavaria to Lower Bavaria, and into the *Donau* . . ."

"The which?"

"The river that goes to *Wien*."

"The Danube? Vienna?"

"Then through *Ungarn*—you know, where they make goulash?"

"Hungary?"

"And through *Jugoslavien*, *Romanien*, into the Black Ocean."

He said, "All the way to the Black Sea? That's quite a trip for such a little ball."

Although it had vanished from sight I could still picture it on the screen of my mind, dancing on green waves and blue, passing white steamers and sailboats, red-roofed villages, dark forests. "Do you think it can do it?"

"Sure," Lucius said with conviction. "Even glass bottles have been known to float farther than that. Your ball's a natural swimmer. I wish it luck."

So did I, but part of me envied it, too, for breaking free in a way I could not.

Lucius began to play with my hair. "What you got shining in there?" He pulled a lock away from my ears. "Little hoops," he said. "Pretty. They look just like wedding bands."

"What is a wedding?"

"You know, when two people get married and turn into husband and wife." Playfully, he put a finger through one of the hoops. "Why don't you wear your hair back, like this, so people can see them? They make you look older."

Mutti had cajoled me into wearing a ponytail once but I'd taken the uncomfortable rubber band out after a few minutes. Exposing my ears had always made me feel vulnerable. "How old do I look?" I asked Lucius.

His mouth twitched. "Oh, eighteen at least. Why don't we lie down for a bit? The grass feels like a carpet."

As we plopped onto our backs, side by side, earnestly staring up to watch the clouds drift, I realized I had never been this close to a man before. Vati would have bristled at the very idea of the implied intimacy and O.F. would have made me retch but lying beside a friendly comrade like Lucius felt just about right.

Once the clouds had finished drifting out of our afternoon Lucius opened the umbrella and we scooted together so we'd both fit inside the circular shade. It gave me my first unabashed close-up of Lucius's face. I marveled at the blue sheen of his brows, the curly lashes. "You have more hairs since last week," I said.

He touched lazy knuckles to his curls. "Grows fast. The CO's always sending me to the barber. Only thing that guy knows to do with my kinks is to shave them all off. Next time you see me I'm liable to be bald." He yawned, shutting his eyes. "That goulash was outstanding. Worth every Pfennig too. Could you make something like that?"

I could boil an egg runny or stone-hard and cook noodles until they disintegrated into goo. "Maybe one day," I said with more optimism than I had any right to. "It is a Rezept (recipe) in my mother's cookbook. Can *you* cook?"

"Barely," he admitted. "Left to myself I eat out of cans."

Wasn't that what had killed my grandfather, in Yonkers? "It is good you have a canteen," I decided. "Is it a restaurant for soldiers?"

He yawned again. "Mmm," he said. "Sure is quiet around here. Except for the rush of the water. Reminds me of . . . home."

He stayed silent so long I risked wiggling closer to study his curls, wondering how they would feel to the touch. I couldn't resist the impulse to try but then Lucius opened one eye, stared at my hovering hand, and tilted away, saying. "Hey! That's not polite."

"What is 'bald'?"

"With any luck you'll find out next week."

"What is 'not polite'?"

"You."

"Is it still a good day?" I asked, wondering at his cool tone. After all, he'd touched *my* hair without asking.

"Guess so," he said. "Only, I wish I had my fishing pole." He shifted closer and I resolved to keep my hands to myself. But that didn't stop me from studying every inch of his features. I was particularly interested in his nose. Moving nearer and nearer I managed to peer up his nostrils, which seemed to be built differently inside than my own. An extra chamber? Of course, I'd never seen mine from that particular angle. Nor anyone else's. There was no doubt about it—seen from below most nostrils looked very odd.

His eyes glinted at me through a screen of lashes. "Anything else you'd like to see while you're at it?"

From the other side of the hill a man's deep voice called, "Hansel, warte (wait)!" just as a flaxen-haired little boy came tearing on to our meadow, giggling and looking over his shoulder. I sat up and Lucius raised himself on to his elbows. The boy took one look at us and gave a piercing scream.

"Kuck, kuck mal, ein Neger (lookit! A Negro)!" he shrieked, unabashedly pointing.

"Yipes," Lucius said as we both jumped to our feet.

The parents dashed into view, the woman a few meters ahead, her plump cheeks flushed with alarm. It gave way to an embarrassed smile as she took in the scene—Lucius hiding behind me, the boy dancing around us like a mosquito, yelling, "Bist du wirklich ein schwarzer Neger (are you really a black Negro)?" He grabbed a brown hand to find out for himself, rubbing the back and then examining the palm. "Das ist aber komisch (that's funny)," he muttered, repeating the process with the other hand.

"Save me from the huns," Lucius pleaded, only half joking, but I had temporarily lost my powers of speech and locomotion and was no help at all. So he decided to speak for himself. "Oh, the color's real, all right," he told the boy. "Guaranteed not to wash off. Here, want some gum?" He pulled an emergency pack from his pocket and held it out with a flourish.

The boy made a grab for it but was immediately checked by the man's stern, "Nein, das tust du nicht (oh no you don't!)" The woman herded Hansel to his father, who imprisoned his small shoulders. "*Verzeihung*," he told Lucius. "Please excuse my son."

Lucius continued to hold out his gum. "It's okay. Fine boy. I am Lucius and this is Maria."

Fascinated with the unusual black man. the parents spared me no glance. Under the thin veneer of their chagrin hid the same burning curiosity that radiated from Hansel.

Lucius wiggled the pack. "Here. Friends."

"*Herr und Frau Steiner*," the man said with a small bow, releasing Hans, who immediately surged forward to snatch up his prize.

"Black." Lucius tapped the back of his hand. Flipping it over, he said, "And white. See? Like magic."

In truth both sides were only different shades of brown but since I seemed to be the only one among us who held that opinion I kept it to myself.

Stuffing the gum away, the boy proceeded to examine Lucius's thumbs.

"Grüss Gott," Hansel's mother said, still somewhat flustered. "Wir machen einen Ausflug auf die Burg. Sie auch?"

I translated for Lucius. "They are going to the castle, also. We could go with them."

"Might as well," he agreed. "Since they're sticking like ticks."

"Ja," I told her. "Geh'n wir gemeinsam (shall we go together?)"

Herr und Frau Steiner looked at each other and nodded. Lucius lifted the boy onto his broad shoulders. Immediately ten pink little fingers raked through his curls. "Sanft (soft)!" Hansel reported. "Wie Wolle (like wool)!"

If things had worked out better for me I would have made that discovery first. Wrestling with her own curiosity, the mother's hand jerked convulsively as I explained to Lucius what Hansel had said. "Does he think I'm a sheep?" he asked, testy. "Actually I feel more like a black poodle right now to tell you the truth."

Losing the contest with her sense of propriety the mother raised her hand toward him and said, "Gestatten (may I) ?"

Lucius understood the question without my translation. His eyes became shuttered. He bent his knees and bowed low for the requested inspection, inadvertently tilting Hansel forward and back and making him laugh. Herr Steiner resisted just long enough to see his wife's delighted smile before he, too, succumbed to the temptation of pawing Lucius's hair.

Watching the quick play of emotions pass over Lucius's face, I remembered an article I'd read. It was about a female British explorer who'd trekked to a sleepy African village submerged in the jungle. All the local children fled upon sighting her. The adults, somewhat more jaded, surrounded her to touch her long nose and thin lips. They rubbed her cheeks to see if she might be wearing a chalk mask and pulled at her pale hair, convinced it was a string wig. Some pitied her freakish appearance while others found it amusing. She laughed right along with them, secure in the knowledge that the features the villagers found repulsive were considered attractive by the males of her own culture.

I suspected that Lucius did not find *these* natives at all funny. I could feel his humiliation and guessed it was not the first time he'd been turned into a black poodle in alien lands—including his own—nor would it be the last. When the boy hung down the side of Lucius's neck to poke a finger into an intricate brown nostril, I decided we'd all had enough.

"Genug (enough)," I told Hansel. "Das ist nicht nett (that's not nice)." I closed the umbrella, picked up my bag, and ambled uphill with my new friends. As soon as we reached the ruins of the castle Lucius lifted Hansel down and helped him explore the dirt floor inside the crumbling tower.

Had I been alone in this place, I would have tuned in to the profound silence we were disturbing. I would have sat with my eyes shut to catch a mental glimpse of the ancient specters I sensed all around us. Once this castle had been full of promise and life. I could feel that time exist next to our own, and was almost convinced that if I reached toward the wall slowly enough I might touch it when it was newly made.

Standing at the stone entrance, I admired the green valley below and listened to the pleasant sounds of goodwill behind me, wondering how Lucius and I, not fitting into our own cultures, might fit each other.

Playtime over, he came to stand beside me. "If you give me the camera I'll snap a picture of you right where you are, for my scrap book."

I took the Leica out of its case. We puzzled over the controls but then, with another small bow, Herr Steiner came to the rescue. He took the Leica and gestured us a few steps farther into daylight. Smiling, Lucius draped a casual arm around me. "Ein feiner Apparat (a fine apparatus)," Hansel's father said, snapping away.

First I posed with my hair hanging loose and then I pulled it away from my face, exposing both of my ears. Once the prints were developed I would soon see which hairstyle made me look more adult.

CHAPTER 16

O N OUR WAY HOME WE HAD TO SWITCH TRAMS at the Theresienwiese. "This is where the Oktoberfest comes in September," I explained. "You know from the Oktoberfest?"
"Never been there."
"We go together, perhaps?" In my mind's eye I skipped right past the beer tents to my favorite ride, the *Achterbahn*, and saw us sitting close together in one of its cars. "What you call the little train goes around the eight?" I demonstrated the high and low curves
"Uh—roller coaster?"
"And the giant round thing. Like what is on a bicycle."
He thought a bit longer about this one and then said, "Ferris wheel?"
"Also we have many good things to eat. Hen. Fish on a stick. Bratwurst."
"Any Coca Cola?"
At a festival dedicated to celebrating beer? Not likely. "Many beers," I said.
"So I've noticed. You like beer?"
"No. I don't like things that *sprudel* in my mouth."
"Strudel?"
"*Sprudel*. Little balls in drink."

He laughed. "Bubbles. Okay—it's a date. Let's shake on it." He took my hand. "I can smuggle in my own Coke if I have to." He looked at our clasped hands. "Don't they look nice when they're together like this? I wish I'd asked Hansel's dad to take a picture of them. I'd frame it and hang it on the wall over my bunk."

That reminded me of the plan I had devised on our ride back to town. "I want to make a test, Lucius. In that big Gasthaus across the street, the Hackerkeller. It is famous for beer."

"What test?"

I unhooked my earrings and gave him one. "You say they look like marriage rings—"

"Wedding bands."

"We put them on our fingers, like we are husband and wife. An American Ehepaar (married couple). I will speak bad German, like you, with a big accent—but good enough to order our food." He stared at me as if I was inviting myself to a free meal he hadn't offered. "Did you not say we have lunch and dinner today?" I reminded him.

"Yeah, sure. But what's with this plan? What's it for?"

I squared my shoulders. "Respect."

"Oh, that," he said with a wry smile.

I slipped the other ring on my finger, muttering, "Ring on right hand means married."

"It goes on the left where I come from."

"Left is for before," I corrected confidently. "When people are promised."

"If you're talking about the engagement ring, I believe it goes on the left hand, too."

"Two rings on the same finger?"

"Yup."

I was sure he must be mistaken. "This test is for people in the Gasthaus. They are German and to them right hand means marriage."

"Unless they've heard that Americans use the left."

Good point. We might as well be authentic with our fake rings. Besides, it would be easier to eat with the right hand free of the little hook, which had already started biting my palm. Solemnly, we both shifted the hoops to our left hands.

"We go to stand in front of the restaurant," I directed. "You take a picture with the Leica. And another at the table we sit. To show we are tourists."

We strolled to the entrance linking arms like a long-married couple and I posed in front of the immense, intricately carved door while Lucius fumbled with the camera. Herr Steiner had given him the same detailed instructions that Vati gave me, with the same results—total incomprehension. Perhaps the fault both times was entirely mine—with Vati, for not listening properly, and with Hansel's father for my inadequate translations. In truth, I was beginning to suspect I wasn't good enough to interpret anything for anybody. To prove the point, I saw that one of Lucius's *Schnürsenkel* had come untied but couldn't think of the English words I needed to convey the message.

Pointing to the affected shoe. "Your things are not right."

He knelt and said, "My laces are undone. I will tie them tight. Like this."

While his nimble fingers went to work, I muttered, "Laces. Undone. Tie. Tight."

"You got it." He got up and took my arm. "Your English is getting better already. Now let's play married."

There was no one inside the door to stop us but before we had a chance to reach the first table a tough-looking waitress came out of nowhere, blocking our way. "*Ja?*" she said sharply. "Womit kann ich dienen (how may I help you)?"

I was ready for her. "Guten Tag," I said haltingly, making my tongue thick in order to lend authenticity to our project. "Su-ai Assain, bittay." I held up two fingers on my left hand to give her a chance to notice the ring.

She did and immediately began to thaw. "*Ja gut,* zwei Essen (two meals)," she repeated, leading us past the central orchestra isle to a window table. As she was about to bustle off for the menus, I held up my fingers again.

"Und su-ai U-assa, bittay."

She looked crestfallen. "Zwei Wasser? Kein Bier (Two waters? No beer)?"

"Nine donkey," I told her, smiling to lessen the sting. Like most locals she probably felt it was a personal insult for tourists to choose plain water over Munich's world-famous beer.

Lucius carefully stuck his legs under the table as if he expected a mousetrap to snap shut on his toe. "Tell her with ice this time."

The waitress turned to him, repeating weakly, "Wasser?" as if she was hoping he'd change his mind.

I repeated firmly, "*Ja.* Su-ai Glas (glasses)."

"With ice!" Lucius insisted.

"Eis (ice cream)?" Confused, the waitress glanced at me for clarification, but I had no more of an idea of what he wanted than she did and waved her away. As soon as she was out of earshot, I explained in a whisper,

"We don't put *Eis* in water here. You want *Eis*, we eat it in a cup after dinner. With a little spoon."

"Ice!" he said. "Not ice-cream. Ice is . . . frozen water."

"You want frozen water in your water?"

"Ice comes in little cubes. To make the water extra cold."

Now I understood. "They do not need ice in cubes in the Hackerkeller because people come here for beer and if you put ice in beer it will melt and make the beer taste thin. Also ice is bad for the stomach." No sooner were the words out of my mouth than I realized I had used Mutti's tedious lecturing tone. It was almost as unpleasant as having her sitting between us.

Meanwhile our waitress had been intercepted by a more militant colleague who was wearing an identical dirndl. She glared at us while she whispered what I assumed were vehement objections to our presence. Before the two women could decide our fate, I snatched up a cardboard coaster engraved with the Hackerkeller emblem, held it up to my cheek, and told Lucius, "Now take that second photo."

He managed to trigger a magnificent flash. It singed temporary holes through my retinas and ended the policy-discussion between the two servers. I was still half-blind when our waitress returned with a tray. She unloaded the customary basket of rolls, two menus, and our water, hesitating as to where to place the tumblers as if unsure what use we had in mind for them.

"Don-kay," I said in the thickest American accent I could fit into two syllables.

"Bitteschön (you're welcome)," she replied with great dignity.

I ordered the *Zwiebelfleisch* dinners and when they came Lucius said they were steaks smothered in onions with mashed potatoes and gravy. Neither of us left a speck on our plates.

"That was good," he said, copying the way I crossed my utensils to signal that I was done. He looked around the vast hall. "We're either too early to be part of the dinner crowd or too late. But even empty, this place feels—what's that famous word?—gemütlich (cozy)."

"Thanks to the rings and the Leica."

"I think you're on to something, Maria. Your people are willing to accept us as a couple as long as they think you're an American. If they find out you're German they'll consider you a traitor to the race. Am I right?" I gave a reluctant nod and he added, "Then we better find us a couple of real rings before our next meal. The one I've got now kept trying to fall in my sauce."

I knew just where to look. "In the place under the roof where you save things?"

"The attic."

"In our attic, we have two boxes with *Fasching*—uh, carnival things. Many play-jewels."

"Perfect. Your plan may not work everywhere but at least we know it'll work here." For a reason I did not understand, he seemed disappointed. It made me wish he hadn't been so good at guessing my motives. He examined the bill, but I was not ready to go yet. First I had to put that sunny smile back on his face—by speaking straight from the heart. As a Bavarian, talking about such fickle stuff as emotions was unnatural to me. In fact, in my family giving compliments was considered a sign of weak-headedness.

"Lucius," I began, fighting tight vocal chords. He tilted toward me and waited. I cleared my throat and hurriedly spilled out an approximation of what I wanted to say. "You are beautiful. Inside and out. Tall like a Watusi prince. Strong like a Masai warrior. Your color glows like Coca Cola in a clear glass. I am happy to be your friend."

A look of incredulity spread over his face. He hid it behind his hands, so that I couldn't guess what he was feeling or how he might answer my foolhardy sentiments. For an endless moment, the only sound I could hear came from the blood pumping through my ears. Then I completed my boggled speech with, "I thank you for this special day."

Some heartbeats later he let out a sigh and peered at me through the fan of his fingers. "You're pretty special yourself." He placed his spread-out palms on the table. "And I can't think of any place I'd rather be right now than here, with you."

I risked a smile. He returned it.

And then the traditional Blechkapelle (brass band) filed in. Elderly men wearing Lederhosen goose-stepped to the orchestra isle, carrying trumpets, tubas, a zither. Because we were the only patrons in the hall they bowed in our direction before tuning their instruments. The zither played a sedate folk tune. When it was over, the brass players shuffled through their notes and raised their horns to pursed lips.

Hastily, Lucius pulled out his wallet. "I hate to eat and run but we better get going if you have to be home by eight sharp." He slid a large bill under his plate. I was sure it included a generous tip.

I picked up the Leica. "One last picture for us American tourists, okay? Stand by the *Musikanten*, please."

"Musikanten?"

I gestured to the band. "How do you say? *Musiker*? Music-makers?" He complied and I began counting off feet and inches. Our waitress tapped on my arm. "Einen Augenblick," she beamed. "Wir machen ein Bild mit uns dreien (one moment...we'll shoot a picture with the three of us)." She tugged at the camera. I yielded it to her and she passed it to her no-longer-so-grim colleague.

"Our waitress wants to be in the picture, too," I explained. "Her friend will take it."

It would be a great memento for Lucius's scrapbook. She, short, round, and jolly; wild-haired Maria, practicing a toothy American smile; the African prince in the middle, towering over us both, his far-reaching arms wrapped around two diverse sets of shoulders, and a bunch of good-natured musicians grinning into the lens from behind us. My experiment was a success. So was the day.

*

ON SUNDAY I languished in bed all day, reading. As much as I liked hunting through the pages for the word "suddenly" and translating whole paragraphs into English, by evening I was determined to spend all my future weekends away from home. With Lucius. It wasn't until Mutti took away my book and doused the light that I remembered the fate awaiting me in the morning.

CHAPTER 17

WHILE ANNA AND O.F. STILL SLEPT Mutti talked me into exchanging my green socks for filmy beige nylons and insisted on replacing my comfortable jeans with a skirt so tight that it all but immobilized my knees. It was in a business-like gray. The blouse tucked into it was white, the matching jacket tailor-made to Mutti's shape instead of my own.

"You'll want to make a good impression on the first day at your job," she explained, trying to kindle my interest in the endeavor with the loan of her prettiest jewelry set: a bracelet, pendant, and two dangling earrings of finest silver with bits of shimmering emerald.

The nylons were too short, stretching the garter straps under the skirt to the point of fatigue. I fingered the ugly rubber-knob bulges on each thigh as I hobbled to the three-way mirror, which showed me more of an apprentice-Mutti than an apprentice-printer. It wasn't until she came at me with bobby pins and combs, wanting to tame my hair, that my "No!" became strong enough to stop all further advances. Even then she managed to slip one of her chic, rectangular little purses on to my arm on my way out with the two magic words, "lunch money."

*

"YOU LOOK presentable for a change, except for that hair," Vati said as I tripped down the streetcar steps at our rendezvous point. To my astonishment, he plucked a silver 1 DM piece out of his pocket, turned it over twice, and pressed it into my hand. "Buy yourself a decent lunch," he ordered, frowning to counterbalance the rare bout of generosity.

At long last he was giving me some sign of approval. I wondered if I could learn to like this new me, or at least make believe that I did. No sooner did he stride ahead, setting a fast pace, than he spoiled my willingness to please. "Now that you are entering the business world I have a word of advice to save you from trouble: Never—" He paused until I caught up, continuing with, "Never trust a Jew. He will cheat you every time."

The words dropped between us like ice shards. I let them lie there, not knowing how to respond. Then I asked cautiously, "Why are you telling me this? Is the printer a Jew?"

"I should hope not," he said. "It's time somebody told you what's what, that's all." He marched on, making me run after him with mincing steps. "You can always recognize a Jew by his fleshy earlobes and hooked nose," he went on when I was beside him again. "And the smell." He held his own, perfectly shaped nose for emphasis. "Garlic. Jews put it in everything they eat. Stay away from people with bad breath."

I listened to the metallic click of my heels and said nothing.

He tried again. "Their hair is usually krausig (frizzy)."

I considered his cap of tight curls. "Like yours?"

He stopped short, touched the top of his head, sputtered, "There's nothing wrong with my hair!" and resumed his march at an increased pace so that I had to raise the hem of my skirt midway up my thighs to give my knees more striding room.

"I don't think I've ever met any Jews," I told him. "Isn't that odd? Where can I find them?"

"*Tja mei*," he said. "Most of them sind nicht mehr da (not here anymore)."

Remembering the skeletons at Dachau I grew furious enough to risk offending him. "I've been meaning to ask you, Vati—where were you in the war?"

His answer came smoothly, leading me to suspect he had rehearsed for the occasion. Could O.F. have warned him about the documentary I'd inadvertently watched the previous week? "At the Russian front," he said. "Until I got crippled with rheumatism of the spine. The Army sent me home with a medical discharge. I can't pretend I was ever in serious combat."

How convenient for him. But was it true? "I didn't know there was something wrong with your back," I said. "I've seen you ski and dance and run, like you're doing now—'

He turned and saw me hitching up my skirt. "Put it down!" he hissed, slowing to give me a chance to catch up. I smoothed it into place, fingered the ugly knobs of the garter belt, and heard the nylons swish as the insides of my knees rubbed together. "Ever since the war," he explained, "I've been taking medicine for the rheumatism. One little pill each morning. It works fine except in damp weather. Every November I make a *Kur,* soaking in hot mineral baths. The *Krankenkasse* (medical insurance) pays for most of the treatments."

"But before they sent you home—what did you do in Russia?"

He raised a hand to squelch my curiosity. "Enough! We are here."

We were in front of a tired brick building smelling of rot. Two windows were blinded by whitewash. The paint on the door between them was peeling. Vati knocked and pushed his way in. I hovered in the doorway until he snatched at my sleeve. The window to the right illuminated a cavernous room. Dusty books spilled from shelves and boxes. Piles of them were heaped on long tables and stacked against the walls. Beneath the second window stood a massive steel desk, and behind this desk sat the stern-faced printer, wiping his hands on a dirty rag as he watched us from under his bushy brows.

Vati went to him, extending his hand.

"No shaking," the man said. "Printer's ink, remember?"

"*Ach ja,* of course," Vati said with a polite bow. "I've brought Marianne for her first day."

"She can't walk by herself?"

"Certainly she can—but since she's unfamiliar with this part of the city her mother insisted. You know how women are."

"I do not," the printer bristled, attempting to scrape dried ink from under a thumb nail with a Swiss pocket knife. "Nor do I care to." He looked fully at me, giving a curt nod.

Who did those deep-set, fanatical eyes hiding under his thick brows remind me of? The parish priest? The salesman who tried to entrap me in his car in a midnight-black forest? But it was broad daylight now, far from the woods, and, according to Mutti, I was good at imagining things.

"This is Herr Hauptmann," Vati told me. "You must do whatever he asks, and no whining, bitte. He'll report your progress at the end of each month. I expect to hear only the best, Marianne!"

The printer looked me up and down. "She's not exactly prepared for physical labor, is she? Oh well, we can only hope. At least she looks strong enough." Judging his hands reasonably clean, he shook good-bye with Vati who glared a silent don't-you-dare-fail-me in my direction as he left.

As soon as the door clicked shut I felt the walls crowd a bit closer. Herr Hauptmann spiraled his hand. "We call this the office but it's more like a storeroom with a desk. The shop's out back. I spend most of my time there, supervising, but today I'm staying in here with you. You may have noticed a certain lack of organization. That's what apprentices are for. I print textbooks. Your job is to dust them off, sort them out, and then pack them into boxes. How's that for a start?"

"Fine."

His gaze lingered on my fitted jacket, the skin-tight skirt, the nylons. "Truthfully, Marianne, I don't think you're dressed for the occasion." He sneered at my pumps. "You look more like the secretary-type to me."

Since it was a secretary who had dressed me it seemed a fair observation.

I gave an apologetic shrug. "My mother thought—"

He waved dismissively. "Women don't think." Indicating the nearest table, he said, "Start right there, where I can see you. Plenty of empty boxes behind the shelves." He shifted some papers on his desk and quickly became absorbed in a ledger.

I put my purse on the flaking seat of a three-legged chair and picked up the first book. After a few minutes the tailored jacket I was wearing grew tight at the shoulders, so I draped it over the chair. Every book I touched was dusty on the outside and dull on the inside. There were no pictures in any of them. No wonder he had so many in stock—nobody wanted to buy them.

Fifteen minutes later my pumps were lined up neatly under the chair and the blouse was no longer tucked in, nor was it as white as it had been when Mutti gave it to me. I fought the urge to unhook the sling-shot garters and peel the stockings off behind the shelves, but by then I was beginning to have the uneasy sensation of being furtively watched.

Whenever I glanced at the desk I saw the printer's eyes jerk away. He'd make a show of rustling a page, become absorbed in some notes, and I'd bend to gather another grimy armful, feeling the skirt ride up in the rear as I stooped to the floor.

Was I making it up or could I really sense his eyes undressing me? Tomorrow I'd wear my blue jeans no matter what Mutti said. I studied the blind windows, wondering if the sun still shone outside while I stood in a box, filling boxes. At home the neighborhood kids were playing cowboys and Indians in the vacant lot across the street right about now, some of them giving war cries, others mimicking the sounds of firing rifles. Wolfi and I had made a see-saw out of an old plank and a short length of log. I could see him sitting on the down-side, spelling out words in the finger alphabet, our newest craze. I pictured Anna at the lake with her Peter, rising out of the water like a nymph. It dripped from the ends of her hair onto milky-white, freckled shoulders as she posed with her chest pushed out to enhance the already well-filled top of her tiger-striped bikini. Proprietary Peter waded toward her and wrapped a towel around her.

While *I* was lost in this netherworld, where the minute hand on the wall clock was made of lead.

I dragged my boxes to the shelves in the dimmest part of the room, hoping to discourage Herr Hauptmann's sly attentions. It didn't work. "Come back where I can see you!" he boomed in a master-to-apprentice tone. "I need to make sure you do everything right!" Reluctantly, I complied. He stared at the front of my blouse and lowered his voice. "You must be getting hot from all the heavy lifting. Go ahead, roll up your sleeves. Undo a few buttons. We're informal here."

Once, while sweeping our kitchen floor, I'd discovered a long-legged house spider high in a corner, sitting motionless on the edge of its jagged web. To save it from Mutti's wrath, I pulled a dishtowel off the oven-door, hoping to gently envelop the spider and carry it to the window sill, where it could choose to climb down the stucco wall toward the Hubers' kitchen, or upward to spin a web high in the eaves. Just as I was getting ready to scoop up the spider, a bug blundered in from the half-open window, buzzed into the middle of the ill-formed web, and got stuck on a sticky strand.

Instantly, the spider exploded into life, threw itself at the insect, and wound a string around it at breath-taking speed while it struggled feebly to escape. I broke the string, freed the bug, carried it to the window in a cupped hand, and watched it zoom away. The spider had already retreated to the outermost strand of its web, motionless as before, waiting for its next victim.

The printer, too, sat motionless, hiding behind papers but watching every move I made, knowing that sooner or later I'd blunder into his range.

What, if anything, was I supposed to do about it?

At last the big and little clock hands met at the twelve and my lunch hour began. I hurriedly slipped on my jacket, wiggled into the shoes, grabbed the purse, and fled to the door. Herr Hauptmann was already there, buttoning his Loden jacket. "Since this is your first day, Marianne, I thought we'd celebrate at a little place I know that serves warm *Leberkaas* with Weissbier (light beer)—or are you the Bockwurst (veal sausage) kind of girl? It'll give us a chance to get better acquainted."

"Oh, no!" I said, unable to keep my dismay from showing. "I can't!" I'd rather eat mud. Fake warmth drained from his eyes, exposing the dangerous glint that had been hiding underneath. "I have errands," I stammered, to appease him. "Shopping. So sorry."

Without bothering to reply he slapped on his hat and strode out. My excuse sounded feeble even to me. There was no doubt in my mind that he'd make me regret the clumsy rebuff. I waited until he'd disappeared around the corner before leaving the office, then limped off in the opposite direction in shoes that were one size too small and had already rubbed my heels raw.

I wanted my mother.

Sequestering myself inside the first phone booth I could find, I dialed her work number. She answered at once. "It's me. I'm on my break," I said. "I'm glad you haven't left for lunch yet. About the print shop? I hate it there. I don't want to go back."

Mutti gave an exasperated sigh. "Nonsense. We signed a binding agreement. If you quit Vati and I will have to pay him a penalty. Whatever it is you don't like, I'd advise you to get used to it."

"It's the printer I don't like," I said in a small voice. "He makes my skin crawl."

She stayed silent overly long. Then she said, with irritation, "These days everything makes your skin crawl."

"But he's always watching me. Like a spider. I'm afraid."

It took her a while to sort through my words. She said, "He's *supposed* to watch you. That's his job."

"His eyes are all over me!"

The third pause was the longest. "Listen, Marianne," she finally replied. "I know you'd rather be at home, playing with your friends. But this isn't something you can wiggle out of, like summer camp. You must do what you're told. Don't mess this up. I have to go. Herr Adler wants me to take some last-minute dictation—"

"Wait!" I cried. "Do I have to do *everything* he says? Mutti, please tell me!"

"Everything!" she shouted. "Genau (exactly)! Just as I have to do whatever Herr Adler wants. And right now he wants me to work through my lunch hour. We'll talk more later, at home . . ."

"No, please." I tightened my hold on the receiver, "Listen—"

The line went dead.

Who else might save me? Vati? Hardly. I was on my own.

CHAPTER 18

W HEN VATI GAVE ME THE HISTORY-MAKING D-Mark, I'd envisioned a grilled Polish sausage for lunch, at a small Wurstbude (sausage-shack). But since I was unfamiliar with the neighborhood I followed my nose to a tiny bake-shop instead where I bought four crisp white rolls along with a pint of buttermilk and then went looking for a bench in the sun.

The sound of rushing water led me to a damp stone bridge spanning the Isar. I walked to its center and leaned over the railing, staring at the swift light-green river below. Two days ago it had playfully whisked the red ball out of my reach. It must have passed right under this bridge on its journey to the Black Sea—unless it got stuck in the brush crowding the bank.

Gripping the edge of the railing, I leaned over farther, searching the green foliage for a spot of red. I couldn't find one, even though I raised my legs off the ground until only my hip bones and hands remained on the stone surface. If I chose to let go, I could easily fall head-first into the chilly water below, which was clear enough for me to see the layer of big white rocks underneath it. I'd probably break my neck so fast, I wouldn't even feel myself die. It seemed a perfect ending not only to this vile day but to my entire insufferable life. But with my luck I'd only wind up injuring my spine and linger in a wheelchair for long, dreary years. And if, by some chance, I inadvertently dropped into deeper waters, I'd be forced to wade ashore in a drenched, knee-tight woollen skirt and sodden nylons—a fate worse than death, especially if I managed to attract a ridiculing crowd. Maybe the printer would elbow his way through it to pull me up the embankment and to the shop by my ear. I'd have to work four more hours with the blouse clinging to my breasts and the steaming wool skirt chafing my thighs.

Nevertheless, I loosened my grip until my entire body teetered on nothing except the two jutting hip bones, waiting to see which way I would tip. Before I could find out for sure, I found myself tightening my hold on the railing and lowering my feet to the surface of the bridge. Color stole back into a world that had momentarily gone gray. The water rushed by with renewed vigor. A bird chirped nearby. A streetcar was clanging a couple of cross-streets away.

On the far side of the bridge, an old stone bench stood in a patch of sunlight. I made my way to it and lowered myself onto the slab, appreciating the warmth radiating up through my skirt. Pulling the first roll out of the paper bag, I ate and pondered my predicament.

The printer was my master now. Or so Vati said. He and Mutti expected me to do whatever Herr Hauptmann wanted. Unless I had a very good reason for quitting I would bring the wrath of the entire grown-up world down upon me if I walked off this job now. Which meant I had to go back to packing those dull books until—what? Till it was too late to break loose? Till the printer crossed some nebulous line I didn't even have a name for?

I stared a hole in the air, absently munching my way through the other three rolls, moistening each bite with a taste of buttermilk a few days past its prime. Then I opened Mutti's purse, looking for something with which I could wipe off my milky mustache. She had tucked a dainty handkerchief into an inside pocket. That bit of lace would do the job nicely. I didn't realize she had soaked it in Eau de Cologne until it was right under my nose. At the first whiff my stomach kicked a well-masticated bite up my esophagus. I re-swallowed it, stuffed the reeking cloth back inside the purse, wiped the mustache on a grimy sleeve, tossed my wrappings into the nearest waste basket, and retraced my path to the print shop.

The door was wide open. I expected to find the printer at his spy-post but saw only a thin young man bending over my boxes and checking numbers off a list.

"Grüss Gott," I said to his back.

He ran an ink-stained hand over his disheveled blonde hair before offering it to me with a friendly smile. "You must be the new apprentice."

"Maria," I said as we shook.

"I'm Dieter—one of the journeymen out back in the shop. I see you've been busy all morning. I'm impressed. Only, now Herr Hauptmann wants Rainhold and me to haul all of your work away. To clear space for the next batch. We've been demoted to delivery boys for the afternoon."

"You'd rather stay here?" I asked, envying his freedom to leave.

With an indifferent shrug he said, "Printing is a solid profession. Isn't that why you've signed on? To one day reach the lofty heights Rainhold and I occupy? Only . . ." He glanced at the door and continued in a low voice. "The girl apprentices don't seem to last long enough to become journeymen." He carried a box out to the sidewalk. I limped after him with another. "Don't strain yourself," he said, setting his load on the concrete in order to help me with mine. "These things are heavy."

"I know. I packed them, remember?" Reluctantly, I relinquished my hold. "What happens to the girl apprentices? Why don't they last?"

He scanned up and down the street before answering. "No one will say. But if Herr Hauptmann drinks beer with his lunch, watch out. He'll come in either too jolly or mean. One minute he's your best friend, the next he's a tyrant with a whip." His pale-blue eyes locked on to mine. "There are limits to what he can ask you to do. And you can always say *Nein, danke!*"

A delivery van pulled up to the boxes. The driver climbed out and opened the rear compartment. Although he appeared to be near Dieter's age he was already inflicted with a good-sized beer belly. He displayed it in profile, then turned toward me, snapped his heels together, and bowed. "Rainhold at your service. You must be the apprentice Hauptmann wants to be alone with this afternoon." He elbowed Dieter and chuckled. "'No need to hurry,' Hauptmann told me, 'I'm closing the shop early today. Breaking in the new apprentice.'" He slapped Dieter on a narrow shoulder. "Come along, fellow sufferer. I see a *Masskrug* (tankard) at the end of our load."

I let them shift the rest of the cartons while I leafed through Dieter's tally sheets. He must have spent most of his lunch hour itemizing. When every filled box had been transferred onto the van Rainhold started the engine and Dieter came for his list. Raising an admonishing finger at me, he whispered, "Nein, danke!" and went out.

No, thank you to what?

It was a relief to be alone in the office. I wouldn't have minded the work half as much if I didn't have to pay such careful attention to how my body moved in Mutti's second-best suit. Hopefully, the printer would linger over his beer and get sleepy enough to stumble home to his easy chair, forgetting all about me until tomorrow. With a burst of fresh energy I cleared an entire aisle, stacking the boxes near the door for easier removal.

I took off the confining jacket and pulled the bottom of the blouse out of the skirt's waist-band, making plans to supplement my Spartan lunch with two scoops of Italian ices at the Kurfürstenplatz on my way home. Lemon and raspberry were my favorites.

As I envisioned a cone topped with two scoops, the printer squinted at me from the front door. "Hard at work, I see," he slurred. "That's my good girl. I *thought* you had possibilities when you came tripping in here this morning. A little over-dressed, a bit formal—but we'll soon put that to rights, won't we, Marianne?"

I replied with an insipid smile, keeping my eyes on my work.

He gave a satisfied burp. "The Leberkaas (liver-cheese) was excellent. Almost as good as the beer."

The four half-digested rolls in my stomach shifted uneasily. That buttermilk definitely had been a bit off.

He tottered to his desk, felt his way along its sides, and eased himself on to the chair. "Must work on the books. Must keep an eye on the apprentice," he muttered. "Master's job."

And so the spider-fly game began anew. If I could keep myself from looking at him I wouldn't notice him stare. Wasn't that the advice I'd given Lucius on our streetcar ride? The trouble was I could *feel* the printer's eyes undressing me.

Soon he stopped bothering to hide behind his papers and leaned back in his chair like a connoisseur, twirling a pencil. "You have a boyfriend, Marianne?" he asked.

I countered with, "Do you have any female journeymen in your shop, Herr Hauptmann?"

"Play your cards right and you'll be the first," he said loudly, and then murmured, "Ever been . . . kissed?" in so low a tone that I had no trouble pretending I hadn't heard.

"When was the last time you *had* an apprentice, Herr Hauptmann?" I asked. His face darkened, so I said, "I was just wondering why there are so many books lying around."

"Not your business to wonder." His voice had grown cool. "Your business is to do what you're told, like your Vati said. Everything you do and don't do goes into a permanent record that will follow you through the rest of your working life. It's more important than any report card you ever got in school, and *I* get to decide what goes in. Only me."

I went behind the shelves to so he would not see the shudder of aversion I could no longer suppress. There must be some way out of this trap. I *could* run away again. Bring a warm coat, a rucksack stuffed with food, a blanket, and wear out my sneakers walking through Austria and over the mountains to the land of my heart. Where the sun always shone. My guess was that it would take several months but after what happened last year I was certainly never getting into a strange car again.

Mutti had hitchhiked with Anna and me once when we were small. A big truck had stopped for us on the Autobahn (freeway) and Mutti helped us climb up into the cab. A few kilometers later the driver said something that went right over our childish heads but tinted Mutti's cheeks red. She insisted he let us off immediately. Scowling, he did—in the fast lane. She fumbled for our hands and led us across to the shoulder. He hurled a few indecipherable words after her and slammed the passenger door shut. She pinched her lips and jerked us toward some less dangerous mode of transportation.

I had remembered that previous hitchhiking episode on the night the untrustworthy salesman gave me a ride. It was why I was sitting with one hand on a suitcase, the other on the door handle, ready to jump out the moment he offered his proposition.

What made me think all Italian fathers were nice to children my age? And what about the Italian men who were *not* fathers? Maybe my salvation didn't lie to the south after all. Even in paradise the best of dreams could turn bad in an instant. Besides, if I ran away now, what would Lucius think when I failed to show for our next rendezvous?

The printer stretched in his chair. "I want you in here where I can see you. How many boxes have you filled since lunch?"

I complied, pointing to the row by the door.

"You're faster than you look. Come over here for a minute." He held out his hand. I clung to the nearest shelf as if it were a life raft.

"Achtung (attention)!" he commanded in a tone that brooked no excuses. "Your father ordered you to obey me. Don't worry, I don't bite—there's something I need to check, is all."

I approached the desk with trepidation.

"Hold out your hands for an inspection."

I did what I was told, hating his touch just as much as I hated O.F.'s. Since infancy, I had been trained to submit to the adult authority figures around me. All the rebellion I could muster on such short notice was of the passive kind. Thus, I turned rigid the instant the printer's hands engulfed mine. He took his time examining each of my fingers, rubbing his thumbs lightly over my palms, ending the exercise at my little fingers. With a polite little pull, I tried to reclaim my hands.

He tightened his hold. "A printer needs dexterous fingers," he lectured. "For detail work. One of my journeymen has hands like yours. That would be Dieter, who plays the piano in some Schwabing nightclub on weekends. He can set up type twice as fast as Rainhold. It's the sole reason I keep him on. He tried to quote guild rules to me when he first came, so I told him I could either ignore him or fire him, whichever he preferred. Rainhold now—he knows when to shut up. Never gives me any trouble. Still, his hands are not nearly as nimble as Dieter's. Or yours." He gave my fingers a squeeze. "*Ja, ja*—you might be the first girl who makes it to journeyman. If you play your cards right."

While I searched for a compelling reason why he should release me from his so-called inspection his eyes wandered from my hands to the front of my skirt. "I've been meaning to ask you—what are those little bumps sticking out on your thighs, there and there?"

Those preposterous garters! I swallowed another buttermilk burp, feeling the blood drain from my face.

"Tired?" he murmured. "You've been on your feet too long. Come, rest here for a minute while I show you my ledger." He patted his knees, pulling me toward them.

I clung to the desk corner. "I can see it just fine from here, Herr Hauptmann."

"You can see the pages, but not the individual numbers. No more excuses. Sit where I'm sitting so you can see what I see. All my apprentices sit there when I show them the books."

The females, maybe. Surely he'd not forced that humiliation on Rainhold and Dieter.

With a quick jerk he pulled me off balance and reeled me in. One of his hands patted me on the back in a comradely fashion. The other snaked to my belly. My stomach quailed. "Nice little numbers," he whispered, accidentally feathering a breast. "How's your math, Marianne? You know your einmal eins (one times one)? Your zweimal zwei (two times two)?" His fingers were pliers, pulling a reluctant nail. "Schau mal her (look here)."

Obediently, I looked to where his zipper had come undone and noticed something peculiar rising from inside it. At last I found my voice and cried, "*Nein danke*, Herr Hauptmann! Nein, danke!"

He breathed stale Weissbier fumes at my face, his slack lips separating just enough to give me a glimpse of decaying teeth, food bits stuck to their ridges. Then my body took charge. In one smooth motion, my stomach turned over and an immense stream of yellowish vomit painted everything around us. He swore and shoved me away, blinking at Mutti, who had suddenly appeared in the doorway, breathless, hat askew, taking in the entire scene.

"Herrgottnochmal (God-almighty), you stupid girl!" he yelped, fumbling with his zipper. "You've ruined my ledger!"

"Mutti?" I whimpered, spewing again.

Spiked heels pounding, she leaped to my side. Her slap left a bruise on his cheek. "Schweinehund (pig-dog)!" she hissed.

Was he ashamed? Not at all. Jumping to his feet, he screamed, "You're as crazy as your daughter. I was only trying to *steady* her. She looked unwell. And this is the thanks I get. My desk! My clothes! The girl is unfähig (untrainable). Something is wrong in her head. She cannot follow the simplest directions. I refuse to continue with this halfwit you've foistered on me no matter how many contracts I signed. Consider them broken. As soon as I saw her I said to myself, 'That girl looks disturbed!' Did you notice how she's dressed? What kind of fool would wear an outfit like that in a print shop? You better take her away before I call the police. She has destroyed irreplaceable papers. I'll sue you for damages, see if I won't!" He stared in horror at the vomit sliding down his pants, waved helplessly at his submerged papers, brushed by me as if I'd become invisible, grabbed his hat, and made for the door.

I coughed up bile. "Mutti—" I began. Then I burst into tears. She raised a hand as if to stay them. The printer's exit was blocked by the solid shape of her boss. I'd met Herr Adler only once but had never forgotten his clear silver-toned eyes. They seemed to take in the whole scene with one glance.

"Frau Hohner, I salute your motherly instincts," he said in a low growl. "Please feel free to call upon me as your witness in court." He stepped aside. The printer scuttled out and away. Mutti gathered my things and helped me to the curb, where Herr Adler's Mercedes waited with its front doors flung wide, the motor idling.

"*Ja mei*," she sighed, tucking me into the rear. "*Ja mei*."

Herr Adler drove us through Munich with all the windows rolled down. I leaned my aching head against a fine leather seat, letting the breeze cool the tears streaming over my cheeks. Although I usually got sick from sitting in the back of a car, this time my stomach had spent its ammunition.

Traffic noises blocked out most of the conversation between Mutti and her boss. I caught only his urgent tone, the words Polizei and Prozess (trial), and the way her placating "Gewiss (certainly)!" changed into a hesitant "Yes, but . . ." and "Maybe." If he thought he was convincing her to stand up for me in front of a bunch of prejudiced black-robed men he was sadly mistaken. I knew her better than that. She would do nothing at all.

The first time I had my period she came to my bedroom for the prescribed chat, silently broadcasting her discomfort. "You know the hole you have . . . down there?" she began promisingly. "The one your pee comes out of?"

"Uh huh."

"Well, that's not the only thing it's for, you see—"

Astonished, I interrupted her with, "What else *could* it be for?"

She swallowed, she swayed, and she fled—never to mention the subject again.

Did Herr Adler really believe *that* kind of mother capable of going to the police about such a delicate subject when she was always warning me not to make a spectacle of myself? The odious printer would relish his part, well-practiced as he was at out-yelling all opposition. He was sure to win, especially since I had no vocabulary with which to describe the event.

What was it that actually happened? I got sick and threw up all over him and his desk. What else? Nothing I cared to recall.

*

MUTTI said I could stay at home until she figured out what to do next. I cocooned myself under my featherbed, Seppi at my feet. He was my sole companion, not counting the smelly white hamster and a stack of old magazines Mutti had thoughtfully provided. Whenever I reached into the cage to make friends with the as yet unnamed little beast it froze and expelled an inordinate amount of droppings. If only Elvis would come back!

Sometimes I went to the wardrobe mirror and stared fixedly into my eyes, wondering if I had finally gone over the edge. Idly leafing through the magazines, I kept seeing a small advertisement I'd never noticed before. "Learn about the facts of life," it said. "Male and female reproductive systems scientifically explained in clear detail. Shipped in plain brown paper wrapping. No tell-tale return-address. Risk free. Just send 5.00 DM to . . ."

I shook six silver coins out of my savings bank, got dressed, and copied the address on a stamped envelope. At the bakery I exchanged five of the coins for paper money and stuffed it into the envelope. With the sixth I bought a *Bienenstich* and two *Negerküsse*, devouring all three pastries on my way to the mail box. I held the letter over the slot, counted to three, and dared to release it, watching it drop out of sight.

The instant I heard the 'plop' of its landing I felt the first small measure of resolve. It was time I found out exactly what was what.

CHAPTER 19

TWO DAYS LATER MUTTI CAME back from her office so pale that the rouge highlighting her cheekbones made her look like a clown. She kicked off her heels without bothering to put them away, slouched into her slippers, fumbled with an apron, and proceeded to peel onions. It wasn't until she'd finished dicing them that she started to cry. "On Monday, when Herr Adler drove us home," she sobbed, the knife slack in her hand, "what do you think went through his mind?"

I recalled his barely hidden dismay as we arrived in the Harthof. It was replaced by a look of pity he couldn't quite conceal when Mutti directed him to stop in front of our bare-bones building. She thanked him profusely, insisting he come up to tea. He politely shrugged off the invitation. "This doesn't seem the appropriate occasion, Frau Hohner. We'll do it next time." He glanced meaningfully in my direction. "Right now Marianne needs your undivided attention. Please think about the options we've discussed. I'll call you in the middle of the week to find out what course of action you intend to pursue."

Now I told her, "I thought it was weird that he said he'd call you when you see him in the office every day."

She put the knife on the scarred cutting board beside the onions and dropped heavily onto a chair. "Herr Adler has always been firm about keeping his business life separate from his personal life. When you called me about the printer at noon it took him an hour to ask why I'd been shouting at you. He either says what he means—or nothing at all."

She dabbed at her eyes with a dish towel. "And he's punctual to a fault. That's how I knew something was wrong when he didn't come to the office yesterday morning. There was a note on my desk instructing me to type up some reports. After lunch personnel called to inform me I was being transferred to another department—on the far of the building. At his request, I'm almost certain! I'm unlikely to run into him again anytime soon."

I tried to recollect the exact expression that had been on his discerning face when I'd climbed out of the car. His momentary dismay had already given way to some quiet internal resolve. "Servus, Marianne," he'd said. "I know you feel terrible right now but I promise you'll be all right soon. A hot bath, a bowl of soup—that will be just the thing. I'm glad I could be of a little help today." His cool gray eyes had studied me a few seconds and studied Mutti a bit longer before she shut the passenger doors. We waved to him as he drove away.

A hot bath on a Monday? Clearly he'd never seen the inside of a cold-water flat.

Mutti went to the stove, dropped a spoonful of lard into her biggest pan, and watched it melt. "Today I got up the courage to sneak to his office and peek through the little window in the door. Another woman was sitting in my chair. I've been replaced! Permanently!" She buried her face in the dishtowel.

I could understand her bewilderment. Perhaps he detested having been dragged into something that might well become a scandal. "What will you do?"

She shook her head, looking discouraged. "Do? That implies a choice, doesn't it?" She scraped the onions into the pan. They started to hiss. "It was he who insisted we rush to the print shop. That's it. I've got it. He's disgusted with me for doubting you." She gave the onions a listless stir. "Of course he's never had any children of his own. He has no idea what they're capable of . . ."

"Neither do you!" I said as a wave of anger rolled through me. Snatching a carrot off the cutting board before she could grate it into the sweet-sour mush she called a carrot salad, I stomped off to the living room to give Ricky Nelson another spin.

I could tell it was Wednesday by the feeling of spaciousness all around me. The room contracted every Friday to the density of cement and only began returning to its natural state on Mondays. In the middle of the week the expansion was at its zenith.

I sat cross-legged before the stereo, biting the tip off the carrot and balancing a notepad on my knee while listening to a full-volume version of "Therlnerbee." When the phone shrilled it had a hard time competing. I snatched up the receiver in the middle of a dissonant ring, dutifully announcing, "Kasperl (clown) Cleaning Supplies!" That little slip of the tongue was my favorite private joke. It could cost O.F. his phone *and* his job, should the caller be his boss, the pompous Herr Kaspar.

But this caller responded with an amused chuckle. "Wie gehts (how are you), Marianne? This is Herr Adler. I've been thinking about you all week. Is that Ricky Nelson I hear?"

"Grüss Gott." I was glad he'd appreciated the joke. "Mutti was just talking about you."

"Really?" He sounded pleased. "What did she say?"

Before I could think of an appropriate reply a glaring O.F. ripped the receiver out of my hand. He stood so close behind me that I could smell fresh air clinging to his trench coat. "How often must I tell you not to answer my phone? This is a *business* line!"

"It's for Mutti," I said, backing away.

He unpinched his mouth to address the mouth-piece. "Hello? Herr Hohner here. Who is this, please? *Ach*, Herr Adler. What is so important that you have to call us in the evening? My wife is busy in the kitchen. What matter? Who told you about Hauptmann?—Marianne, turn off that horrible racket at once or you'll be sorry!"

I rescued my record before O.F. had a chance to get his vile hands on it and hastily withdrew to the kitchen. It seemed almost peaceful in there, filled as it was with the aromatic steam of beef broth and frying onions, the carrot salad gleaming bright orange in Mutt:'s favorite crystal bowl. But then O.F.'s voice became loud enough to be heard through two closed doors.

"Please turn off the radio when you leave the living room!" Mutti said, standing at the hutch and buttering slices of bread. "And next time keep the volume down!"

"It's not the radio," I whispered. "It's O.F."

She squinted at the cuckoo clock. "It couldn't be. It's the middle of the week."

"It's him, all right," I assured her. "He's shouting into the phone at Herr Adler. I believe they're discussing the printer."

"Ach Gott (oh God)!" She put her ear to the door. I joined her, and together we listened to O.F. yelling, "Das geht Sie doch nichts an (That's no business of yours)!"

Mutti squeezed her eyes shut. "On second thought I'm glad I'm working on the opposite end of the building. If I never see Herr Adler again I won't have to die of embarrassment!" Then the living room door opened and she propelled me into my room with surprising strength, ruthlessly turning the key.

"Wait! Seppi is—" I cried, but O.F., stomping through the hall, easily drowned me out.

Shoving the kitchen door against the wall, he yelled, "Lottchen! Why is that insufferable man calling you on matters that are no concern of his? Who encouraged him to tie up my business line with his idle curiosity? What police report? What in heaven's name does he mean?"

"How would I know, since you didn't give me a chance to speak to him?" she yelled back. "And why are you home on a Wednesday? Aren't two days of ugly scenes enough for you anymore?"

He seemed as surprised by her outburst as I was but rallied almost at once. "I'm here because I telephoned your office this morning to find out how things stood at the print shop and the woman who answered said she'd never heard of you!"

Mutti gave a low moan.

"I'm here," he continued, "because when I called Marianne's father he told me that you let her quit! He's washing his hands of the whole affair and refused to discuss it with me any further. I'm here because I've just come from the printer. He says he'll most certainly sue *unless* Marianne apologizes for the damage she caused—and unless you come to scrub out his office. On your knees, he told me."

She stammered, "You have no right to interfere!"

"*And* I'm here to remind you that Marianne is, and always has been, a liar. I hope you haven't let your boss talk you into going to the police about this, Lottchen!"

"Not yet, I haven't," she sputtered. "I thought I should discuss things with you first."

"Excellent! Don't let anyone influence you. Other than me, that is. And don't believe anything Marianne says."

"I *didn't*. I even hung up on her when she called me for help. I sent her back to that monster. Just as I knew you'd have wanted."

I had the nagging suspicion that everybody in the building was listening in. Was the kitchen window open or closed?

"Hauptmann's no more a monster than I am!" O.F. cried. "We're both victims of her deceit. She riles people beyond endurance just to make them look bad-tempered!"

"You have no idea what really happened, Franz. You weren't there. And I'll thank you for not attacking her before you have all the facts. He was forcing her to sit on his lap. He had his . . . his . . . and when he noticed me in the door he started to scream—"

"Was that before or after you slapped him?" he shouted. "You can be sure that if she was on his lap it was because she put herself there! God knows what else she was planning to do before she so conveniently threw up as soon as she realized that you were watching!"

"How dare you!" Mutti yelled. Something heavy, made of glass, broke against the wall. I pictured grated carrots, dressed with oil and vinegar, sliding down toward the floor. Seppi gave a piercing bark that quickly shrank to a whimper. I prayed he'd shut up before he came to O.F.'s attention.

"No matter what else you can say about her you know perfectly well she has no interest in . . . in . . . that!" Mutti went on, lowering her voice toward reasonableness. Perhaps she had finally realized that the window was open. Yes. I could hear her slamming it shut. "How often have you told me it's her one saving grace? That the moment you discover she's become the slut you've so often predicted she'll be you'll get rid of her and nothing can stop you? Oh, I know you've looked high and low for incriminating evidence. Have you even found the slightest hint—"

"Not yet," he admitted. "But you know as well as I do it's only a matter of time. As for now, she must go to the print shop and ask the printer's forgiveness."

"Don't be ridiculous!" Mutti huffed. "As a matter of fact, I'm considering sending her back to school. Let her be a little girl a while longer."

He cackled, pretending to be amused. "You're the one who's being ridiculous. Do you really think anyone in the real world will care that she can quote Goethe or Schiller? School will only spoil her for the kind of work she'll have to do later. And the older she gets the harder it'll be to find her a good apprenticeship. You know most kids start when they're fourteen. If you're planning to indulge her you will force me cut back on your household money. I won't feed a ne'r-do-well!"

Once more, the phone rang. While he went to answer it, Mutti tossed glass shards onto the dust bin, sobbing with rage. Then the front door clicked shut and Anna said, from the hall, "I decided to wait on the stairs for the worst to be over. Sometimes I wonder why I bother coming home at all."

From the living room, O.F. was yelling, "Lottchen, for you—dein erster Gemahl (your first husband)!"

Vati was the only non-business person to whom O.F. allowed telephone access, probably from a sense of guilt at having stolen Mutti away from him in the first place.

"I suppose it's *his* turn to give me an earful," she said. "I don't think I can bear one more cross word. Please, Anna, clean up this mess. We had a little . . . accident. Maybe you could tear some fresh lettuce for a salad?"

As soon as her footsteps receded, I whispered urgently, "Anna, open up. Let Seppi come in."

She did what I asked, blowing her nose. "Just when I think things can't get any worse, they do," she said dejectedly as she locked me back in. I could hear Mutti's low murmurings on the other side of the wall but with two wardrobes blocking it on my side I could find no spot to put my ear to. Perhaps Wolfi's mother, whose ear was no doubt glued to the far side of the opposite wall, was having better luck.

Then Mutti was back in the kitchen. "Careful with the splinters," she told Anna. "Sweep them up with the hand broom. Vati wants you and Marianne to come to dinner on Sunday."

Impossible! Lucius and I had better plans for that day.

"Why?" Anna sounded downright belligerent. "He already gave Marianne the support money for this month. We won't get any more until August. Or does our visit have something to do with what happened at the print shop? What *did* happen there, Mutti? You never explained."

"It seems your father has bigger worries. He claims he's at his wits' end. Gitta just lost her third baby. Another boy, I'm afraid." There was an unconscious gloat in her tone. "She's terribly depressed, as you can imagine. In between crying fits she keeps insisting she must talk to Marianne."

"Then let Marianne go by herself. I've made other—"

"You know what the atmosphere is like at his house!"

"No worse than it's here," Anna muttered.

"She would be caught between Gitta and Vati," Mutti said. "Must I remind you that he can destroy a person with one poisonous look? It's an old talent of his. And Marianne has always rubbed him the wrong way. But he usually cheers up around you. So you must go, of course."

"Of course!" Anna said scathingly. "Just don't expect me to cheer him up past my eighteenth birthday. He'll stop paying for my support then and I won't need to go to his house anymore to collect it. I was at the grafiker's today, Mutti. He's in a flurry of work and wants me to start early. I said I would."

"Your vacation . . ."

"Boring!"

"Peter . . ."

"Boring!"

"Anna! What's happening to you? You seem to have changed overnight. I hardly recognize you anymore."

"What's happening?" Anna said. "For the first time I see a way out of the nightmare we're living. And I'm going to take it!"

A chair scraped as if someone needed to sit. "I only want us to be happy," Mutti sobbed. "That's all I've ever wanted. Don't you know that?"

"I know it," Anna admitted. "It's not your fault, Mutti. Es tut mir leid (I'm sorry)."

She couldn't possibly have been any scarier than I was. But unlike her, I had always been sure that everything wrong with my life—and what wasn't—*was* first and foremost Mutti's fault. Sitting in my narrow cell, I saw her, in my mind's eye, rushing around each morning to get ready for work; saw how carefully she chose the splendidly tailored suits, the matching hats, shoes and purses; how she put lipstick dabs on her finger and rubbed a hint of color on her cheeks so she'd look fresh; the care she took with her eyebrow pencil to get the arches just right; how pleased she was with the results of her labors as she said good-bye and stepped out to embrace the day, her high heels clicking down the stairs and away.

And even though I hated to admit it I was beginning to understand that she, too, felt a need to be elsewhere. She treasured her hours away from home, in an office where she was respected for her finely honed skills, her understated glamour, her quick wit. The dressing up and stepping out, smelling of Eau de Cologne and success, were important to her. So was being someone who mattered, in a place where she could forget about our Marshall Plan existence and all that went with it including two obstinate, almost-grown daughters and a disagreeable husband.

Maybe Herr Adler had quietly admired her for being both elegant and aloof. Those attributes were not her attempts to deceive but a life-saving mechanism, a sort of daily amnesia. It had worked for her until I ruined it. Now, with her carefully wrought illusions shattered between them, sending her away might have been Herr Adler's final act of kindness.

On the other hand—and I liked this idea much better—maybe he had been secretly in love with her for years but kept it to himself because he had always assumed she was happily married. And now that he knew how things really stood he'd had her transferred to avoid office gossip before he started to . . . no, wait, that sounded too much like a plot from the romantic novels that appealed to Frau Keppler. Schade (too bad)!

I cocooned myself under the featherbed and tuned out the world. In the middle of the night I startled awake, remembering that the hamster was still in the bathroom. Yesterday morning Anna had sniffed at her clothes and the ends of her hair. "I'm beginning to smell like the bottom of the hamster cage," she'd complained. "I don't care what anybody says, he's staying in the tub between Mondays and Fridays from now on. I'll set the cage on some newspapers and keep the bathroom window open a crack."

I'd seen no reason to object, considering that I was sleeping right over the rising fumes.

Now I clicked on the light and went to her bed. "Anna," I whispered, trying to shake her awake. "You've got to bring the hamster in here before O.F. sees him!" When she refused to open her eyes I tugged at the chain around her neck that held the key to my freedom. But how could I break my promise to stay put? Without coming fully awake she slapped my hand away, mumbling, "Scheisse (shit)!" It might have been a reminder of the hamster's main problem, a swear-word, or both. But as it turned out it was a prophecy instead.

I plunged the room into darkness and went back to my bed, glad that Seppi was snug under my covers. In the morning the white hamster was floating face-down in the toilet and O.F. was gone.

CHAPTER 20

NNA'S HIGH-PITCHED SCREAM propelled Seppi and me out of bed before dawn. We ran to where she stood in the bathroom, her knuckles pressed to her mouth, her eyes fixed on the toilet bowl. Mutti came rushing out of the living room, clutching a note and tying her robe.

"What is it now?" she asked, a pinched look on her face.

"I killed the hamster!" Anna whispered.

We crowded around her to gape at a waterlogged bit of white pelt in the bowl. Seppi thrust his nose at it for a few short, puzzled inhales.

"It's my fault," Anna insisted. "I was starting to feel sorry for the little guy, always cooped up in that stinky cage, so I left the cage door open yesterday to let him scrabble around on the tub bottom. I had no idea he could climb up the sides."

I tried to imagine him digging his tiny pink claws into the slick tub enamel, crawling all the way up to the rim, fighting for balance, and then leaping down to the floor. "Hamsters don't climb," I informed her. "Nor do they jump." Not even a smart mouse like Elvis could have scaled the outside of the toilet, let alone get on to the seat. Besides, if the hamster had managed all that he could have gotten out of the bowl as easily as he fell in.

"We don't have to whisper," Mutti said. "O.F. left hours ago." She smoothed the note in her hand. "It seems he missed two very important appointments yesterday and has to squeeze them into his schedule today. He says he might not get home again until Saturday morning." She put her arms around us. "No one's to blame for this. Little creatures are fragile and foolish. No use trying to sort it out. Go back to bed. I'll bury the poor thing in the wheat field as soon as it turns light."

I crouched to examine the slick outside curve of the toilet bowl and ran my hand up and down the tub wall. "But how—"

Mutti looked warningly into my eyes. "It was an accident, Marianne!" You must believe me, her eyes said. It's your duty.

Back in my bed, I stared at the ceiling and tried to understand the relationship between belief and logic, concluding there was none. Once, when I was quite small, back in the village of Freidorf, Saint Nicholas appeared in the farm kitchen and asked Anna, Gabriel and me what we wanted for Christmas. I sat on his lap and fingered his white beard while he read from a list of my misdeeds. I noticed that he was wearing my mother's silver and emerald earrings. Saint Nicholas choked on a cough when I brought it to his attention, then asked if I wanted him to add *Unglauben* to the bottom of the list, which was already overly long. That's when I first grew aware that the adults around me expected my unquestioning belief. So I gave it.

And was giving it still.

*

LATER that same morning Seppi and I went for a walk. We passed Frau Huber in the lobby. She answered my polite "Guten Morgen (good morning)," with a curled lip and an audible sniff, cradling her enormous belly as if to shield her unborn from contamination. She'd never held O.F.'s tantrums against me before.

Subdued, I followed Seppi to the wheat field. Neither of us found any freshly turned soil. Afterwards we ambled toward Frau Keppler's end of the building. Frau Stöhrfried and Herr Braun, whispering together on their front stoop, ignored my greeting and looked at me with obvious distaste. By the time I reached Frau Keppler's front door I felt as if some light inside me had been dimmed. Luckily, the smile with which she greeted my knock was as welcoming as ever. I decided to shrug off the slights from the other three neighbors.

"I'm just warming up a square of Zwetschgendatschi (prune-plum pie) for my breakfast," she said. "Shall I add one for you? We'll wash them down with hot Ovaltine."

Seppi and I followed her into the kitchen, which smelled of cinnamon. "Where have you been lately?" she asked, lifting a sheet of waxed paper off a baking pan. "I haven't seen you for over a week. Usually you can't wait to come and pick up your books." She gestured at a carton under the table, overflowing with her latest second-hand finds. I pulled out the box, began skimming first pages, and explained about my short apprenticeship in the print shop.

She stopped cutting the Datschi (pie). "You? An apprentice? You've got to be kidding!"

I liked the outrage in her voice. "My father doesn't want me to go to school anymore," I told her. "He thinks there's no future in it for a girl like me."

"Von wegen (no way)!" she snorted, wielding her knife with unnecessary vigor. "I never met your Vati but if I ever see him I'll give him a piece of my mind." She brought a worn sheepskin rug out of her bedroom and spread it on the floor beside me. "Come, Seppi," she said, invitingly thumping the rug. "The linoleum is too hard for your big bones."

He lost no time making himself comfortable on the fleece, giving a grateful sigh. Frau Keppler ran a hand over his ruff before heaving herself up to add my piece of plum pie to hers in a cast-iron pan. "A handsome dog. There's nothing finer than a German shepherd, unless it's a Dachshund. How fortunate you are to have a piece of both! It makes him twice as loyal as either breed, you know. A truly faithful companion."

I was glad she understood how special he was, but I was only listening with half my attention; the other half was busily scanning novels, building a tower with those that featured reckless young girls and were likely to contain at least one "suddenly" in each chapter. Fleetingly, I asked myself why Frau Keppler would buy herself books that were better suited for a more immature literary appetite.

She put a tray down between us and sank heavily onto her chair. "There are a couple of books of weird stories in the box somewhere. Ghosts and space-monsters. Don't read them before your bedtime, though. They gave me a chill." She poured the hot Ovaltine into our cups, stirring both. My square of Datschi was twice the size of hers. I started to break off a bite for Seppi but she put a restraining hand on my wrist. "I buttered a slice of bread for him. It's much better for his teeth. I assume he doesn't brush?" She laughed at her little joke, fed Seppi his rye, and settled her face into more somber lines. "Your uncle reached a new low last night."

"He's not my uncle," I said, feeling my stomach clench.

"Consider it a blessing. I could hear him from my couch with all the windows shut. Mind you, from what I could make out it's he who should be ashamed, not you."

My morsel of pie had lost its flavor. I pushed it around in my mouth, wondering how much she'd actually heard—and understood. Would she like me less if she had been as close as Frau Huber, who was forced to hear every word? I studied Frau Keppler's kind face. Would that kindness drain out of it if she accidentally saw me with Lucius? Was the girl my neighbors saw when they looked at me the same girl I was inside of myself? Suddenly I felt lost, not sure anymore who I was and who I was becoming. Maybe O.F. and the neighbors were simply seeing some inherent flaws in me of which I was still unaware. Maybe I'd stopped being good and the drowned hamster was divine retribution for my sins.

*

ALONE in our empty apartment, I threw myself whole-heartedly into reading stories for the rest of that day and the next. Consuming books, I forgot to eat food. Friday afternoon was especially delicious because I knew that for once O.F. was not going to spoil my evening. He didn't have to—Mutti did it for him when she came home and told me she had secured another apprenticeship for me. Her eyes actually sparkled with pride as she informed me I'd be an assistant to the secretary of an attorney.

"A splendid opportunity," she exulted. "And this time your supervisor is a mature woman so I know you'll be in good hands. And—oh, yes . . ." She pushed out her chest like a hen who'd just laid an admirable egg. "As part of the deal you'll be attending business school every morning. You'll learn such valuable skills as steno, accounting, and typing. Won't that be fun?"

Drunk on printed words, I could only stare at her in disbelief before diving into the next girlish adventure. Later, lying in bed, I was glad I had at least one thing of my own no one could take from me—for the simple reason that Lucius would always remain my secret. I couldn't be part of his world and he couldn't be part of mine but together we were creating a safe in-between haven just for us.

*

I STEPPED outside on Saturday morning, eager for it and for him. Wolfi was sitting on his metallic blue racer, one foot on the stoop.

"Hey, Marianne," he said. "Where have you been? I haven't seen you in weeks."

"Two, to be exact," I replied, deftly maneuvering around him. "I've been very busy."

He scratched his nose. "Well, are you finished being busy? I'm tired of riding my bike all by myself. Why don't we have a race? Better yet, let's head out to the Baggersee."

"Not today," I said loftily. "I have other plans."

"Oh? Where are you going, then? Can I come too?" Pushing his foot against the side of the stoop, he launched the bike after me.

"I'm afraid not, Wolfi." I groped for a reasonable excuse. "I'm taking the bus to visit a class mate."

"What's her name?" he demanded. "Where does she live?"

I didn't care for his tone. "You've never met her. She lives in the city." I quickened my pace, trying for a businesslike it's-all-settled look.

"You're getting to be as bad as Anna," he said, easily catching up. "She never wants to play anymore, either. What's happening to you?"

I shrugged. "I'm getting older. Girls grow up faster than boys."

"Says who?" He bumped my calf with his front tire. I gasped and stopped to rub at the spot. He said, "We heard the ruckus the other night. Your Uncle Franz wasn't home five minutes before it started. My mother ran from one room to the next so she wouldn't miss a word, but I just wanted to get away on my bike. Anna was sitting on the stairs, hanging onto the banister and crying. What was it about this time?"

"Me," I said shortly. "As usual." I didn't like his nosy questions. The one steady thing about our friendship had always been the silent understanding between us not to mention the embarrassing scenes broadcast from our kitchen window on weekends. Why should this one be different?

"Your hair has grown darker," I said to distract him. "Did you rub shoe polish in it?"

"The color's entirely natural," he boasted. "Yours is getting brown streaks in it. I'm afraid I win."

We had a long-standing bet about whose hair would turn blacker as we grew up.

"They're from the sun," I protested. "They'll be gone by December. My roots are quite dark."

Despite my best efforts he followed me all the way to the bus stop, where a crowd of potential shoppers stood waiting. Pointedly, I rummaged in my pocket for the fare and said, "Pfiat Di (bye), Wolfi. I'll be in town all day and tomorrow I have to visit my father. But maybe we can ride out to the lake on Monday." I had forgotten the unpleasant arrangements Mutti had made for me with the legal secretary.

"Maybe," he said, glancing at the other commuters. Then he moved a bit closer and lowered his voice. "My mother claims she saw you at the

Stachus last Saturday, on one of the traffic isles. She said you weren't alone." His eyes had become watchful.

"I wasn't," I said lightly. I'd been with Lucius, of course. "I was rubbing elbows with a hundred people, at least. All packed together like sardines, waiting for the next streetcar."

"*Ja.* Stossverkehr (rush hour traffic)." He seemed relieved. "That's what I told her. She made a mistake. I'm glad she promised not to mention it to your Mutti. It would only have made her look foolish. Parents can be so embarrassing sometimes."

The bus was approaching. If Wolfi rode away now I would wait until he was out of sight and then cross the street and proceed to Henry Kaserne. But Wolfi stayed put, his feet firmly planted on the ground, watching me to see what I'd do next. I moved to the end of the queue and when the bus arrived I had to get on it.

Two stops later I got off again. Thankfully, the street behind me remained clear. But as I rushed across and zigzagged past a maze of small houses I kept turning around to make sure I wasn't being watched. By the time I finally came out at the Landstrasse near Henry Kaserne I had started to relax. And I forgot my unease entirely as soon as I saw Lucius's brown, beaming face at the gate.

CHAPTER 21

I HADN'T BEEN ABLE TO FIND ANY FAKE RINGS in our carnival trunk, even after I dumped the entire heap of cheap jewelry onto the attic floor. Sifting through nearby boxes, I had discovered a small wooden chest containing faded photographs of Mutti's lost, joyous childhood, long-yellowed documents, and a pink satin pouch. In it were two plain-gold bands. As soon as I slipped on the smaller one I felt embraced by my grandmother's loving presence. I put both rings on a string and wore it under my blouse.

As Lucius and I walked away from the gate together, I slipped off my grandfather's ring and gave it to him. "Just for today," I said. "For the restaurant." I was not surprised to see that Grandfather's ring fit his finger as perfectly as Grandmother's fit mine. When we resumed walking I thought I could feel two friendly spirits waft around us like currents of warm air. Once we arrived at the bus stop they seemed to drift up and away.

The rings must have been as magical as they felt, for the Hackerkeller waitress, who volunteered that her name was Frau Knorr, rushed to make us comfortable as soon as we appeared in the doorway. She gave us the same table we'd occupied the weekend before, patted the wooden slab top, said meaningfully, "Euer Stammtisch (your special table)!" and delivered our standing order of two plates of Zwiebelfleisch (steak and onions). I promised to bring her a print of the snapshot her colleague had taken as soon as the film in the Leica was used up.

Lucius and I lingered over our plates. Then we strolled across the Theresienwiese where I pointed at objects and Lucius succinctly pronounced their English names. The sky was a flawless expanse of blue silk and the air was astir with gentle warm breezes. In fact, the whole afternoon was perfect until I decided to take him to the Schuttberg on our way back to our part of Munich.

"It is the only real hill in the city," I told him when I pointed it out from the Scheidplatz.

"Yeah," he said. "I was surprised to see how flat this town is, considering that it's so close to the Alps."

I promised him a spectacular view.

The Schuttberg was surrounded by wide-open fields but at its foot was a narrow, well-landscaped park with manicured lawns and flowerbeds. Where the ascending path began to get steep Lucius picked a red rosebud and threaded it into my hair, his hands as light as butterfly wings. Then he stepped back to study the effect. "You look like a Spanish dancer," he said. "Not like a regular German girl. That was the first thing I noticed about you."

His words made me feel special.

He kept picking more little flowers as we climbed and when we reached the top of the hill he presented me with a colorful posey. I settled it into the V of my blouse while a hot gust of wind ruffled my hair. The careful landscaping had followed us up; the grass, bushes and casually placed boulders looked utterly tame. Two benches were free. The third, affording the best view, was occupied by an elderly couple who, aided by hiking staffs, heaved themselves to their feet at our approach and headed for the path, calling a cheerful "Grüss Gott!"

"Hello," I replied in my accented German, unobtrusively displaying my ring. "Ein schöner Tag (a gorgeous day)!"

The old man hung a pair of binoculars around his neck and gestured at the nearby granite-topped mountains. "The view is always splendid from up here during a *Föhn*."

He was right—the wind playing with my hair was coming from the south. The two silver-haired hikers, tapping their sticks with every step, were soon out of sight. Lucius and I sprawled on the bench they had vacated. The city stretched out below us, as detailed as any map.

"Look," I said, pointing. "That cathedral over there is the Old Peter, and the one with the twin towers is the Frauenkirche. There are stairs going up all the way to where the bells are. When they ring the sound goes right through you. Let's climb up there next weekend. It'll be fun."

"Why not tomorrow?"

"I have to visit my father."

"I can meet you afterwards. In town. Whenever you say."

I shook my head. "He doesn't live in Munich. The train to his village is very slow. I won't get back until late." I looked for the Ostbahnhof (east train station), from which the little passenger train would puff forth, and then I squinted in the direction of Vati's village. But the distance was too much for my eyes. Still, the air was so clear I had to remind myself that the mountains rising beyond the city were not within walking distance.

Lucius gazed at the peaks, lost in thought. Then he said, "I didn't want to spoil our date today. That's why I was going to wait until tomorrow to tell you that I won't be here next weekend. And the one after that." He brought out a pen and some paper, looking at me soberly. "Do you realize how easily we could lose track of each other the way things stand? One mistake and we might never see each other again. That's why I need you to give me your address and phone number." He unfolded the paper for me and placed it on my knees.

Stunned, I asked, "You are going away? Why?"

He gave a little snort. "My battalion is heading to the boondocks. For maneuvers. One whole month, the CO said. There'll be a river for us to build bridges across and fall into, and damp wool blankets to wrap ourselves in every night." I must have looked puzzled, for he said, "Maneuvers—you know—war games?"

"What is CO? Battalion? Boondocks?"

He composed his face along patient lines and defined the troublesome words. Then he tapped on the paper. "See that mailing address on top? Any letter you send to it will get to me sooner or later. Then I won't have to pretend I don't hear mail call anymore. Once a week would be good. Every day would be even better. And I'll write back first chance I get."

I didn't know what to say so I simply brushed the paper on to the bench between us. At the Scheidplatz, a toy streetcar was winding around a toy track, its warning-bell no more than a whirr.

He cocked his head. "Don't worry—I have no intention of showing up at your doorstep. And letters don't have a color, not even mine. They're white and local. Nothing to give us away." He tried to sound light and amused but failed at both.

"O.F. is usually gone during the week but on Fridays he sometimes gets to the mailbox before I can," I tried to explain. "I am afraid he will open any letter addressed to me."

"Is he the one who made you run away?"

I nodded.

"O.F. stands for Old Fart," Lucius decided.

I asked him to tell me what the word meant. He demonstrated it instead. He was right—it was a good fit.

"I'll write you on Mondays," he said, pressing pen and paper firmly into my hands. "That way the letters will arrive at your house by the middle of the week. He won't be home then."

I made him swear never to call unless it was a dire emergency, and then only on any weekday afternoon before five except Friday. "You sound like an Ami," I said. "What if Mutti answers? Or Anna? Or him?"

"I'll hang up," he said, exasperated. Crossing his legs, he frowned at the Alps. "I don't like this game they're making you play. Far as I know we're just friends. You showing me around and all. We've got nothing to hide."

We didn't. But who would believe us?

His eyes swept the town and got caught on a miniscule red Porsche driving past the Scheidplatz, below. "One of these day I'm going to get me one of those," he vowed. "With black leather seats. Just think how easy it'll be to go sightseeing in something like that." His face took on a fervent glow. "I like foreign cars. Especially little red sports cars." In a dreamy tone, he went on to say, "I can see us now, on the Autobahn. That straight stretch between Munich and Augsburg. I'll floor the pedal. One hundred and forty kilometers per hour. Two hundred. I'll open her up all the way. In the fast lane. And you'll be sitting beside me, your hair waving in the wind."

I caught a glimpse of his shimmering dream but the girl in the passenger seat was blonde, a filter cigarette dangling from her high-gloss lips. "My hair doesn't wave. It flies up and tangles," I said flatly.

Unlike him, I didn't care about cars. Not one bit. What if it turned out I was the wrong girl for him, in the end?

He looked at me sideways. "Never mind your hair. I'll buy you a baseball cap."

I didn't know what that was either but I was tired of exposing my ignorance; I'd look it up in the Langenscheidt later. Filled with trepidation, I scribbled down the information he wanted and gave it to him.

He tore the paper in half, pocketed his part, and held the top half up to my eyes. "I wrote my company's phone number under the mailing address. But don't try to call me till we're back in the barracks. After hours only. Ask for PFC Duncan. Memorize the number. It might come in handy one day."

I folded the paper small and stuffed it away, realizing that I couldn't let anyone find it, not even Mutti. "This place," I said, tapping my foot on the ground. "The Schuttberg. You like it?"

"Yeah. A nice little mountain."

"It is not really a mountain."

"Hill, then," he said.

"It is not really a hill. Not a natural hill."

"What is it?"

I spread my hand over the beautiful city below. "After the war and the bombs there were so many kaputte (broken) buildings that people didn't know where to dump the *Ruinen*."

"Ruins," he said without missing a beat.

"They brought all the broken bits here, made a big pile, covered it with soil, and planted trees and flowers on it. Right under our feet lie the ruins of Munich." Was I just imagining it or was my English improving? Surely I couldn't have conveyed that much information to him two weeks before.

He whistled. "Rubble? Under our feet? How tidy. So . . . German. Don't you think?"

"Why? What would the Amis have done with it?"

He thought it over. "Dumped it all in the ocean, or the nearest lake."

I shuddered. For once, I liked the German way better. I undid the string around my neck and slipped my grandmother's ring on it. Reluctantly he added my grandfather's and I hid them under my blouse. "I bring them again. After you come back," I promised.

He nodded glumly.

I had to agree—a month was a very long time.

*

THE next morning Anna and I sat vis-à-vis on a sooty little train blowing white smoke into an intensely blue sky as the *Föhn* continued. Both of us occupied window seats, pressing our noses to the glass and watching the green countryside roll by. Above us hovered the invisible cloud of Mutti's black rage like a grim blessing. It was the only feeling she had left for Vati since their marriage collapsed.

As the train rolled through lush forest, stopping at every village, I thought about ambitions: Lucius lusted after a car; Anna longed to be famous; Vati yearned for sons; Gitta attempted to succeed where Mutti had failed and give him a houseful; and Mutti just wanted a house. Having lost both family and home at twelve, barely tolerated in her relatives' flat until she escaped into adulthood, she'd eased her loneliness with visions of the perfect little family she'd have one day in a perfect little house on a plot of land that no one could ever take away from her. It was a vision Vati had endorsed and the only one they still shared as their marriage teetered.

To that end they'd saved relentlessly: he by living in that cheerless furnished room in the city near his work and only coming home once a month to save on traveling expenses; she by raising her own produce, gleaning fruit and potatoes, gathering wild berries, mushrooms and hazelnuts. Once we even traveled cross-country to pick hops, sleeping on the dirt floor of a shed until Mutti saw a cat-sized rat jump over Anna's tender white neck in the middle of the night.

We drank watered-down milk long before it became fashionable and ate meat only on Sundays. To save on clothes Mutti sewed our meager wardrobe from scratch and made us wear boys' leather pants from early spring until late fall. We went barefoot in all the months that did not contain an R. As Vati's visits decreased so did the money he brought with him. She grimly made do, knowing that every Mark he withheld from her was going straight into their joint savings account.

And then they divorced and Vati kept it all for himself, buying a hillside the farmer who sold it to him considered totally useless. On that land Vati built their dream house from the blueprints he and Mutti had once drawn up together and presented it to the housebreaker he had married since, thus rewarding her for destroying our family. He also presented her with Mutti's wedding ring, cut down a size for an uneasy fit.

What Mutti minded even more than his betrayal of her trust and her dreams was the fact that he had robbed his two legitimate daughters in favor of theoretical sons. Usually Mutti's rage smoldered quietly and out of sight, like well-banked fire in a wood stove, but once a month it flared up to put us into what she considered to be the right frame of mind for our obligatory visit to the house that should have been ours.

Stop by stop, our sense of dread increased. Anna's chatter faded as she shrank into her seat and her self, while I mutely watched telephone poles flit past alongside the track and conifers stride by at a slower pace in the distance. Scenes of forlorn partings and joyful reunions unrolled on every station platform along our route.

The silence between Anna and me deepened with each kilometer while Mutti's rage-cloud swirled around us and poisoned the atmosphere in the compartment. At last we arrived at our station and walked along a winding path between pastures where brown-and-white cows grazed and plow horses stretched their necks over rustic fences to beg for windfall apples lying out of their reach. Last winter we had come during a cold spell so severe that a crow fell out of a tree and landed at our boots, frozen stiff.

It wasn't until we passed the whitewashed *Bauernhof* (farmhouse) of the farmer who'd sold Vati his hill that Anna said, gesturing at the luminous sky, "You know that the *Föhn* will make certain people more irritable than usual, don't you?"

Immediately siding with Vati, I answered, "It only makes *some* people mean. Others have migraines or get depressed. Maybe Vati will cry."

She gave an incredulous huff. "I don't know who will cry but I do know it won't be him."

Remembering the view from the Schuttberg, I said, "The *Föhn* sure clears the air, though, doesn't it? Blows the clouds and the dirt away and leaves the sky so pure you can see forever."

Our own invisible cloud, impervious to the south wind, sank and settled around our hearts.

CHAPTER 22

I STOPPED AT VATI'S GATE and pretended I was seeing his property for the first time, through Mutti's eyes. A hedge of red roses bordered the path leading to the house, which sat halfway upslope and was framed by vivid splashes of color from Vati's flower garden. I could not see the vegetable beds on the other side of the stone terrace or the orchard he'd planted beside them, but the tall spruce on the veranda was visible not only from my vantage point but from the entire village of Eichensee. Gitta had decorated the tree with white electric bulbs last Christmas. It had been an eye-catching beacon, although the farmers had muttered about wasted electricity.

Behind and above the house was the grove of immense oaks where the farmer's herd used to congregate on hot summer days. Lying content in the shade and chewing their cud, the cows had forced him to regularly climb the rocky incline to fetch them for the evening milking.

The villagers did not socialize with Vati and Gitta. As far as I knew not one of them had ever walked up to the gate. To them, he was the city-fool who didn't know a bad bargain when he saw one. The fact that he didn't have any cows to feed did nothing to alter their opinions.

Vati's splendid hill was an island in a sea of pastures. To this high ground he invited his most hapless colleagues and their wives for tedious

Sunday afternoon teas. During these teas they were required to view endless photo albums of his solo vacations in foreign lands. At a time when most people were desperately trying to build a savings account Vati had managed to travel all over Europe and North Africa on his free yearly rail pass. He brought back a wealth of snapshots to document these trips and insisted on sharing them with anyone who came within range. If they showed sincere interest long enough he rewarded them with homemade egg *Likör*, plum schnapps, or wine. He expected Anna and me to rave over his photographic prowess for free.

I rang the doorbell. Gitta let us in, offering us a tremulous smile that stopped short of her red-rimmed eyes. She was wearing a *hausfrau*ly (homemaker's) apron tied over her still enlarged middle. The dark hallway was like a mineshaft pooling with the unseen but nonetheless palpable gas of Vati's irritation. It needed only a minute spark of his displeasure to explode. Gitta led us to the living room door and glanced in, not sure if she should announce our arrival. If he was already aware of it she risked getting chastised for stating the obvious. If he was not he was sure to hold the omission against her.

He didn't allow her to make either choice. Abruptly looking up from where he was sitting, he snarled, "Gitta! Is that smoke I'm smelling? Don't tell me you are sabotaging our dinner again!"

She gasped and ran to the kitchen. After a brief look at Vati's unwelcoming scowl Anna and I followed, gambling that the polluted kitchen air was sure to be more benign than the atmosphere he was generating on this side of the house.

We found her blinking at black clouds billowing out of the oven. Anna yanked at the French doors leading to the veranda and I opened the window in the opposite wall after pushing aside the numerous candles crowding the sill. Together we watched the draft we'd created chase the billows outdoors.

Gitta stared at the roast she had charred with such obvious horror that Anna took pity on her.

"We can cut off the burnt parts," she said. "You turned the flame up too high. It's probably still raw inside."

While they discussed reconstructive surgery I ogled the misshapen cake on the table. The heavy cream in the whipping-pitcher beside it had not yet begun to go stiff. I took on the job of cranking the handle, watched the steel blades spinning inside, and studied the changes Gitta had made to the kitchen.

A large gruesome crucifix now hung in one corner over a homemade altar. Beneath the nailed and bleeding feet of Jesus stood a bouquet of white lilies, ringed by votive candles quivering in the draft. A gloomy picture of Mary cradling her dead son leaned against the glass vase.

Idly gazing out at the uphill oaks, I saw three mounds near the tree line. Two of the mounds were planted with flowers and surrounded by grasses gone wild. The third was freshly turned. What struck me at once was the miniature size of these graves. A small pile of cut grass lay abandoned before them, along with a scythe, grass shears, a rake, and an upside down wheelbarrow. I was so busy staring that I almost missed the exact moment the whipped cream began to congeal into butter. "Done," I said, pushing the pitcher toward the unfortunate cake. "Do you want me to smear some of this white makeup on the poor thing?"

Gitta grunted from the stove, her shoulders sagging as she tried to stir lumps out of the gravy. Anna, who had started to break lettuce leaves into a bowl, gave me an inconspicuous frown to let me know I hadn't chosen the best possible phrasing.

"Marianne! Why are your hands idle?" Vati asked from the hallway. "Make yourself useful. There's grass to be cut on the hill. I started to do it myself but the sun was too bright. I think I am getting a headache. Gitta, where did you hide the aspirins this time?"

I did what I was told, appreciating the mild, peaceful breeze under the oaks and the shade-dappled ground. Inexpertly, I swung the scythe at knee-high weeds but soon switched to the shears. I knelt and trimmed around the graves, raked up fragrant grasses, and dumped them in the wheelbarrow by the armload.

Then I sat on my heels and watched with delight as a Marienkäfer landed on my arm. Lucius would have called it a lady bug. This round little creature and I were named after the same lady. I counted its spots. Only three. I put a finger in front of it and it crawled on, it's tiny feet tickling my skin. Gently blowing on its beetle-wings, I watched them spread wide. The lady bug whirred into the sunshine, leaving me to wish I could fly away, too.

Vati's gruff voice called me back to earth and to dinner. I sat facing the crucifix. Jesus had an unnervingly green sheen to his skin, except for the wounds, which glowed a bright red. "Why do you have so many candles?" I asked. "Are you having trouble with your electric lights?"

Sawing at the doctored roast, Vati said bitterly, "They are part of Gitta's new craziness." Then he finished cutting four slices and deposited the best one on his plate. Anna's guess had been accurate; the other three cuts were the color of Jesus' wounds.

Normally Gitta cooked almost as well as Mutti although she had the habit of putting sugar in the most unlikely dishes. Her desserts tended to make my teeth ache. Vati could cook better than either of them but rarely did because he preferred being served to serving. After a few listless chews, he judged the roast inedible, the potatoes half-raw, and the as yet uncut cake disguised with thick swirls of whipped goop as grossly deformed. I found it impossible to contradict his sweeping judgments.

"I know your first wife is a much better cook than I am," Gitta said with a rare attempt at spunk. "You've told me so often enough. There's not much point in me trying any more, is there?" Then she dashed from the room. Before long muffled sobs came from the direction of the bathroom. Those of us still at the table pretended not to hear them.

Under Vati's critical gaze and after an eternity of chewing and swallowing, Anna and I managed to clear our plates. When he saw us staring accusingly at his plate, still half full, he said sternly, "I told you, I'm not feeling well."

Anna began to stack the dirty dishes but Vati stopped her. "Leave those to Gitta. I haven't had a chance to show you girls the photos I shot in Greece yet."

For the next half hour we sat beside him on the living room couch, our knees chastely drawn together, our hands folded on our laps, while he slowly turned the pages of his newest album, pointing at exotic snapshots and offering detailed explanations of what we were seeing.

At the end of our ordeal we didn't get a drop of his homemade *Likörs*. Instead, he promised a vigorous after-dinner walk. By then Gitta had restored the kitchen to its usual spotless condition. She joined our march down the lane and through the pretty village. Every front door was hand-carved, every house wall stenciled with intricate designs. Green window boxes filled with red geraniums lined every balcony and window. All the roofs were covered with identical brick-red clay tiles. Vati established a fast pace. I had no trouble keeping up but Anna and Gitta soon lagged behind.

My stride matched his exactly as I revived my role of super child, hoping for his approval. Whenever we encountered a villager Vati forced his face into amiable lines and called out a cheerful greeting, which was always politely returned. It wasn't until we had passed the last building and were heading toward the lake that Vati felt he had enough privacy to vent his anger.

"I heard about the print shop," he growled. "What you claim happened just doesn't make sense. From all reports the printer seems a successful, respected craftsman, well qualified to train apprentices. I told your mother I intend to stay out of the mess you have made. Just keep your ludicrous Uncle Franz away from my door. Next time he comes I won't let him in. I have troubles of my own these days. With Gitta. I don't know why she insisted she had to talk to you today of all days, but you need to hear my account of her irrational behavior first. She seems to have lost her last grip on sanity. That's why I've decided to take her to the asylum in Haar tomorrow."

I made some small sound of dismay, stifling it almost at once.

He looked at me sharply. "Do you know what she did right after she miscarried? She cashed her latest paycheck instead of handing it over as she was supposed to. Then she bought great big boxes of art supplies with the money and had them delivered by truck. Art supplies! The nursery was stuffed full of oil paints, watercolors, canvases, you name it. And she was at the wall, dabbing clouds and angels on with a brush even though she never could draw as much as a straight line. As if the baby hadn't died. All that cash wasted. I told her to pack everything up again and return it to the store but she refused. Refused! What could I do except put her over my knee and spank her like a child, trying to restore her to her senses? And then . . ."

His voice had grown hoarse with emotion. He swallowed and plodded on. "The following morning I got up to go to work and found my entire wardrobe of hand-tailored suits spread out across the room, every sleeve and pant leg hacked off with the scissors. I had nothing left to wear except pajamas and my old leather knickers. I was forced to call in sick and spent the whole day in those knickers, hauling out her purchases and buying myself a new wardrobe. But what do I do next time she decides to pick up those scissors? I made arrangements then and there and told her about it, too. She promised to go quietly if I let you come for a visit today. I suppose she wants to say good-bye to the both of you, although I haven't the faintest idea why she insists that she must see you in particular. So do us all a favor and get it over with. Send Anna forward. I need to have a word with her. I'm sure she already knows why."

Obediently, I dropped back to fall into step with Gitta. "Vati wants to discuss your new apprenticeship with you," I told my sister, feeling sorry for her. Her eyes darted sideways until Vati, watching, gave an imperious wave. Then she went to meet her doom at the same rate of speed with which straight pins are drawn to a magnet.

The grass near the lake was long and thick, interspersed with rushes. Swamp flowers grew in the shade. I went off the path for a closer look at their star-shaped, silvery petals. "Watch out, Marianne," Gitta said. "That's where snakes like to hide. I saw a Kreuzotter (a poisonous snake) near here last week."

I lost no time rejoining her on the trail. She was walking at such a slow pace that my leg muscles twitched with impatience. Way ahead of us, Vati and Anna were disappearing around the bend. Softly, Gitta began to hum an old Bavarian lullaby, which went like this:

> The Heitschi-Bum-Beitschi is kumma
> Und er hot mia mei Buabal wegg'numma
> Er hot's ma wegg'numma und hot's nimma brocht
> Und I winsch meim kloan Buabal a recht guate Nocht
> Aba Heitschi-Bum-Beitschi-Bum-Bum . . .

I wondered if she understood the words to the melody or could even pronounce them since her native tongue was Prussian and the nuances of the Bavarian dialect still eluded her. I could have told her that it was about some scary monster coming in the middle of the night to snatch a little baby boy from his cradle and that he was never seen again. I could have told her but I didn't.

When she was done humming she said, "You know, God has been taking my babies one by one and I've finally realized why. It's because I made you all suffer the way I'm suffering now. I want to fix it, Marianne. So I'm giving your Vati back to you."

I made a sound that was either a moan or a protest or both.

She looked at me, tears gathering in her eyes. "I'm well aware of how much you've resented me from the start. Don't deny it. You've always blamed me. Well, now I am blaming myself. So you can have him back. Everything will be as it was before I came along. Your Mutti can be his wife again. He's always telling me how much better she is at everything I try to do. From the many photographs I've seen of them together I have to admit they were the ideal couple." She had begun to twist Mutti's cut-down wedding ring on her finger. Then she said something even more unexpected. "My brother is coming for me tonight. He's taking me back to our old home in the *Sudetenland*. I'll be gone before morning."

"But your brother fell in the war, Gitta," I said, shocked. "Sixteen years ago."

"He's only been missing in action!" she whispered triumphantly. "They never found his body, did they? I've been putting candles on all the sills and lighting them every night to help him find his way to me. For a while now I've felt him drawing ever nearer. And now the time has come. Here . . ." Giving the ring that seemed to have grown into her flesh one final harsh twist, she pulled it free and held it out to me. "This belongs to your Mutti."

As I stared at the little gold circlet in front of my nose the world and I stopped breathing. Nothing moved anywhere. What did Gitta expect me to do? The ring had been altered, cut down a size. How could it possibly fit Mutti again?

Then Anna screamed and ran out of the rushes, her beehive bouncing dangerously as she brushed past us, still screaming. I grabbed at her skirt and hung on until she slowed to a stop, flailing at me. Vati, parting the reeds, tried unsuccessfully to suppress a satisfied grin.

"Anna almost stepped on a coiled snake hiding in there," he chuckled as he came toward us. "I didn't know she could jump so high!"

Anna narrowed her eyes with dislike but said nothing.

"Who wouldn't jump?" I said coldly. "We better not go to the lake today. Let's walk in the forest."

He began some cutting retort, thought better of it, and stormed toward the tree line. Centuries of fallen leaves and branches had formed a mat of humus so thick that our footsteps made hardly a sound save for the occasional crackling of a dry twig. "Wonderful stuff," Vati said, digging into the mulch with a stick. "See how black it is? I wish I had some of it in my garden. How the flowers would thrive. But the villagers would call it stealing. You know how hallowed the forest is to these people . . ."

"To us, too," I said. "If everyone came to take soil for their garden the trees in this forest would soon—"

"Yes, yes," he said impatiently, tossing the stick aside. "I didn't really mean it. How you do go on!"

At last we were walking together as a group, although we seemed to have nothing left to say to each other. Where the path curved toward the road again, we fell into the same configuration in which we had started the walk. Vati went first, I was a close second, Gitta and Anna lagged behind. That's how we reentered the village and returned to the manse with a view, where Vati asked Gitta and me to prepare our tea and Anna to remove the grass I had cut before dinner.

"No," she said. "I don't want to."

"I beg your pardon?"

"It's not mine," she said. "I don't live here."

I waited for the sky to fall.

"But you must do as I say," Vati prompted, as if she'd grown stupid. "I'm your father."

"You're my father one day a month," she told him. "The rest of the time you couldn't care less. You laughed when that snake hissed at me. I saw you. Cart your own grass. I'll cart Mutti's."

"She has no grass," he said, a crease forming between his brows.

"And whose fault is that?" Anna asked. Then she went through the open French doors out to the terrace and slammed them so hard that one glass pane cracked. He started to go after her. I blocked his path without thinking.

"It's the *Föhn*," I told him. "You know how moody it makes her." He knew no such thing and neither did I but I hoped he would accept the excuse without argument. Secretly, I admired her outburst.

"*Föhn*, nothing," he said. "I was wrong about your sister. She's as crazy as the rest of your tribe. Gitta, where *did* you put the aspirins?"

Pretending to think, she ran a finger along the blade of the cake knife and said, "According to you I'm too stupid to remember anything that important."

He threw up his hands and decided to glue photo corners onto the pages of his new album, slamming the living room door almost as hard as Anna had slammed the French doors.

The water began to simmer in the kettle. The clock ticked hollowly overhead. Gitta held out the knife. "You cut the cake, Marianne. My fingers are trembling. Tell Anna I'll fix everything for her, too. She can have her Vati *every* day of the month." Was there a tinge of relief in her tone? Could it be that she wanted to lose him? That the phrase *every day of the month* was not as appealing to me as I thought it would be?

Carefully scoring the cake, not looking at her, I said, "We can't make it as it used to be, Gitta. Mutti isn't free anymore. O.F. would never let her go, you see. I'm sorry your babies died, and your brother, too. The *Sudetenland* belongs to the Communists now. This is the only home you have." I watched her measure tea into a tea egg, hang it from the rim of the china pot, fill the pot with steaming water.

"I'm sorry," she said, retrieving the ring from a pocket and working it back onto her permanently dented finger. "I wanted to make your dream come true, Marianne. I know how much you long to be part of a happy family."

Startled, I realized she was right. It was the thing I craved most, the thing I'd waited for so long that I'd forgotten what I was waiting for. When had it changed? One night I prayed for my father to come home to us, the next I prayed for someone else to love me. Somewhere in between I'd outgrown the old dream and it died.

We had our tea in the living room. Vati grumbled that the cake was too dry, the frosting too rich, and the peppermint tea too sweet, but I finished my portion in good cheer and dared to tell Gitta out loud that everything tasted delicious, though Vati glared at me for it. Anna was not with us. She had been sitting downhill by the gate, her back to the house, when I tried to fetch her for tea. She refused to come, crying furiously, "I'll not set one foot inside his door again. I'll wait for you at the station."

After I helped Gitta wash up she wrapped the rest of the cake in wax paper and poured tea into a marmalade jar. "For the long train ride," she said. "I'm sorry we never managed to be friends." She hiccupped a sob and groped for a handkerchief while I wrestled with my ambivalence. Who except me could help her now?

"Mutti had three dead boy babies before she had us," I pointed out. Perhaps he never told her. "You'll have your babies, too. I swear it." I didn't promise they'd be sons.

A ray of hope crossed her face as I left to say good-bye to Vati. He was slouching over the album, his elbows on the coffee table, staring dejectedly at three white, powdery tablets lined up along the table edge. I stood before him, dangling Gitta's snack package until he looked up.

"I read somewhere that women who lose their babies sometimes act a bit strange for a while afterward," I said. "I think maybe grief is just like the *Föhn*—it makes some people cry; some get headaches; others just get irritable."

"Irritable? From grief? Imagine that," he said with an inept and rare smile.

I groped for particulars. "Frau Huber, our downstairs neighbor, she lost a baby last year. Her bedroom is right below ours. She used to weep so hard every night that I couldn't sleep. Then she got pregnant again but this time her doctor made her quit her job. He told her to rest more, let her husband do the chores. It worked, too. You should see how big she is now, like a balloon ready to pop. She swears it'll be a boy."

"A boy?" he echoed.

"A strong kicker, she said."

He pushed the aspirin tablets away and closed the album with a decisive snap. "About Anna. She looked so funny, jumping straight up in the air. A meter, at least. Tell her it wasn't a venomous snake." When I turned to go, he cleared his throat and said, "It's your Mutti, isn't it? She put her up to it. Making her choose. Getting you both to hate me. Oh, don't look so surprised that I know. It's written all over your faces when you stand at my door. The we-don't-want-to-be-here look. I know who puts it there. It paralyses me. Every afternoon I spend with two unwilling daughters leaves me exhausted. There's nothing to be done about it, I expect. Maybe once you have grown up you will see there are two sides to these things."

I paused on the threshold, knowing I had spent all the courage I had. "I don't hate you," I said in a tone hardly more than a whimper. "I never will!" Then I ran out. The stretch from the house to the gate took nearly forever. He did not even follow me as far as the stoop. I didn't really expect him to; we both knew that the wrong lips had spoken the right words, which meant that they didn't count.

On the train, Anna and I finished the cake down to the last crumb. And later, when Mutti plied us with cheesecake and hot chocolate in the privacy of our bedroom, hoping for bad news, we ate that, too. Obligingly, Anna recounted every detail she remembered.

Mutti tutted and shook her head, laughing out loud at Gitta's skill with the scissors. "Haar!" she said. "Ach wo (heck no)! Who would clean his house? Who would cook his meals? He couldn't find another woman half the slave. And what did Gitta want with you, Marianne? Why did she ask for you, especially?"

This was my chance to relay Gitta's kind offer. "To say good-bye, I guess," I began. "And . . . to tell you she's sorry she caused you so much pain."

"Oh," she said, taken aback. She rallied almost at once. "I expect she'll still be there the next time you have to visit—on her hands and knees, scrubbing the kitchen floor while he pastes more photo corners into his albums. I could almost feel sorry for her. At least we're not stuck in the middle of nowhere with a tyrannical old crabapple like your father."

"No, we're not," I admitted. "We're stuck in the Harthof with a tyrannical old rooster instead."

She raised one of her magnificently arched eyebrows, then allowed herself an instant of mirth. Stacking the dishes onto the tray, she said, "Isn't it lucky, though, that O.F. is only here on weekends? Gitta has to deal with Vati every single day. And what good is the house to them when they're so unhappy in it?"

I saw that the rage had left her, the lines around her mouth relaxing. "Wouldn't it be nice," she went on, "to have a house and happiness too?"

I couldn't be sure if her dream was finally gone, but the next morning the *Föhn* certainly was. The sky was no longer translucent but gray and opaque and the soft rain, falling, washed away sticky feelings, leaving the air less clear but more clean.

CHAPTER 23

D URING MY FIRST EXAM IN ENGLISH CLASS my
seatmate Eva was anxiously gnawing the polish off her nails.
By then she'd asked to copy my homework so many times
that I no longer bothered to spare her feelings when I refused. I could
overlook her hair, long, straight, and bleached a coquettish near-white. I
could overlook the artlessly applied lipstick, the complexion straight out of
a bottle of makeup, the stiffly caked black on her lashes, and her purple eye
shadow. What I couldn't forgive was the disgusting reek of Eau de Cologne
she had recently begun to add to her arsenal, especially since it was often
mixed with the stink of cigarette smoke after she returned from the
restroom.

She'd sniffed out my aptitude for English on my first day at the
Handelschule (trade school), when the instructor asked me to read a passage
out loud to get an idea of my skill level. On my second day, she was sitting
beside me with plans of her own.

"Please!" she now said in a plaintive whisper, "I have a new lipstick.
Hot pink. You can put some on if you let me look at your test first."

I turned at a slant so that my shoulder blocked her angle of vision. Let
her conjugate her own verbs! I conjugated mine in less than ten minutes,
left Eva to her blank page, and turned my test face down on my desk. Had I

dared, I would have brought Lucius's letter out of my satchel for a thorough rereading, but under Eva's narrow-eyed, increasingly hostile scrutiny I contented myself with recalling the bothersome phrases I'd read while I sat on our toilet last night.

In the three weeks since Lucius left I wrote him eight times and he wrote me twice. The first of his letters had come last Wednesday. I'd pulled the second out of our mailbox yesterday, which was a Thursday. It was pure luck that I got to it before Mutti did, because we'd walked home from the bus stop together. When we reached Frau Keppler's end of our building I told Mutti I was in a hurry to go pee and put on a burst of speed. It gave me the time I needed to snatch his letter from the box and stuff it away before she caught up and gathered the rest of the mail.

I tore open the envelope with my toothbrush handle and tried to decipher his words while sitting on the commode with the bathroom door locked. It was the one room in the apartment where I was least likely to be disturbed. I could make little sense of his short note except that he seemed to be having a very bad day. What gave me the most trouble was the second half, which said,

> . . . then I got chewed out in front of the whole division at noon. I went from feeling mortified to being mad in ten seconds, was a bit slow with the yes-sir-routine, and lost my stripe over it. Now it's near dark so I can hardly see what I'm writing. I'm soaked from falling in the river all day and am rushing to put this on the truck before it pulls out with the mail-sack. Sorry about the chicken scratch. I hope you got my other two letters all right.
>
> —Your *Private* Lucius

What other *two* letters? There had only been one! I should have known something would go wrong. He'd kept his promise about using plain white envelopes, but they were of a size and shape that could not be bought at a German stationer's and were stamped with a queer seal that looked suspiciously foreign. Lucius's handwriting on them looked foreign, too. True, the letters inside were utterly harmless—but it was one thing to get conspicuous letters from the other side of the world, and quite another to get them in odd-sized envelopes, mailed locally. And worst—I couldn't decipher half of his words.

Ignoring Eva's mute final appeal, I put my test face-down on Herr Neuhof's desk. It was the first one there.

"What? Already?" he asked. "Are you sure?"

When I told him I was, guarded appreciation bloomed in his eyes. It gave me the courage to ask, "What does the word 'mortified' mean?"

He gave me an odd look. "You didn't get that word out of our textbook!"

"I was reading a foreign newspaper last night." I didn't say I had found it there and he didn't ask.

"Hmm. Let me see," he said, focusing on a spot on the back wall to indicate deep thought and scratching at the brown tufts of frizz growing around his bald spot, which was the size and shape of a pink bathing cap.

Eventually, he murmured, "Ah, yes. Mortified." To demonstrate, he hunched up as if he'd developed sudden stomach cramps. "It means *schrecklich peinlich.*"

Horribly embarrassed? Lucius's letter was beginning to make sense! I mumbled my thanks and Herr Neuhof sat up straight and jerked his chin at the door. I took a step and stopped, wishing I could get him to translate the rest of the letter. Then a sense of self-preservation took over and I went out wiser by only one word. In the schoolyard I hunched to cradle my own stomach and muttered, "He was horribly embarrassed. It made him mad." It was a good start, though I never did find out where that chicken scratched Lucius or why.

The snack table in the shade of the Linden tree was laid out with pastries and drinks. I paid for a bear claw and a brown-glass pint bottle of milk and sat on my heels with my back leaning on rough bark, ready to eat. But the fact that Lucius had written me three letters and I received only two was impeding my appetite. What if the missing one showed up today and O.F. got to it first? I needed to go home to rescue my mail!

I had a typing class yet to get through. It required me to sit at a typewriter for forty-five minutes with my back straight and my head turned to the left while my fingers copied such nonsensical words as *fas* and *daf* out of an exercise book. Yesterday Fräulein Ufholz, in a frustrated tone, told me loud enough for the whole class to hear that after three weeks of practice my progress was still imperceptible. If I cut her class I would be doing us both a big favor. No doubt she would be relieved to find my seat vacant today. Adding up travel time and making allowances for possible glitches I estimated that I could arrive at the law offices of Rechtsanwalt (attorney) Möller punctually at one o'clock. It would confound his secretary, Frau Zimmer, who felt compelled to list every one of my shortcomings in the little black notebook she kept in the top drawer of her desk.

I ran all the way to the bus, fighting for breath, but had recovered it by the time I got off across from the little bakery shack. Then I lost it again as I sprinted for home, the leather school satchel thudding against my spine. Unfortunately, the hoped-for letter was not in our mail box, after all. But my instinct of self-preservation had been sound—for what I found instead was a book-sized package addressed to me, wrapped in brown packing paper. No tell-tale return address. Risk free. I stuffed it into my satchel and reversed course.

As soon as I was on the next bus heading into Munich, I tore at the wrapping for a glimpse at the sex manual I'd so carelessly sent for. I started to leaf through the pages until I noticed the *Hausfrau* sitting next to me was squinting nearsightedly at the first illustration. Slamming the book shut before her eyes could properly focus I hastily whisked it out of sight.

After I transferred onto a streetcar I tried for a second look but gave it up when the man sitting behind me started to breathe excitedly on the back of my neck. I decided to smuggle my new reading material into Herr Möller's sanctuary in my cleaning-caddy.

Yes—after three weeks of apprenticeship I had become an expert duster of Herr Möller's endless gallery of diplomas. On my first working day Frau Zimmer had given me a short letter to type. Two hours and five misspent attempts later she had retrieved the original with a fixed smile and led me to the file cabinets where a basket of documents waited to be returned to their folders. I sat in that corner for hours, humming the alphabet song the whole while to enhance my shockingly bad filing skills.

*

BEFORE that first day was over Frau Zimmer had developed a permanent crease on her forehead along with a sure-fire plan to get rid of me long enough every afternoon to recover her equilibrium. It involved vinegar spray, dust cloths, Herr Möller's empty inner office, and one hapless apprentice.

In the beginning of my new career I'd imagined an interesting clientele of shifty-eyed hoodlums and the bandaged victims of assaults and divorce proceedings. Herr Möller practiced a much duller but infinitely more rewarding kind of law. His occasional clients were fat businessmen smoking cigars. They usually came in bunches. Sometimes I could hear their clandestine murmurs through the thick connecting door, each discreet syllable dripping with money.

Frau Zimmer always kept her ears keenly tuned to every nuance of sound seeping through that solid door until she was sure everyone on the other side, including Herr Möller, had departed through his private exit straight to the hall. Then she'd give a cautious knock, take a quick look inside, and send me in to throw open the windows and commence the job of wiping cigar smoke from every available surface. Since she never came in to check up on me it made the sanctum a more private spot than the bathroom at home and perfect for my first unhurried look at what my five D-Mark had bought me.

After running at my top speed from the streetcar all the way to the office I burst into Frau Zimmer's domain less than a minute past one. The black notebook was already on the desk, topped with her fountain pen. I hung my jacket on its assigned peg on the coat tree, slid my satchel toward the supply-cabinet, and pried sweat-glued bangs from my forehead. Pinch-mouthed, she made a short entry in the notebook and then, for one pained second, allowed her gaze to stray to my bare knees. Although she'd made several attempts to lecture me about the importance of good grooming I refused to wear anything more fancy than last year's school clothes—pleated wool skirts and white blouses that buttoned up to the chin, white knee socks and freshly polished brown leather walking shoes of the kind old ladies favored for afternoon strolls.

If Herr Möller was anything to go by those old school clothes made me invisible to men. He was portly and middle-aged with a receding hairline, an unfashionable mustache, and no facial expression whatsoever. Yesterday he'd made a rare excursion to our anteroom to check Frau Zimmer's version of the appointment calendar. As she trailed him into his sanctum with her calendar in hand, I heard him ask who I was and why I was there. Three weeks after I started!

I remembered filing her original typewritten request for an apprentice, on to which he'd scribbled his stiff initials permitting the expense of an advertisement. It seemed having an assistant was a new status symbol among the building's secretaries. Frau Zimmer was not to be left out of this trend. Unfortunately for us both it became quickly apparent that Mutti's glowing description of my multiple talents had been somewhat exaggerated. After I failed the initial typing exam I'd shyly offered my equally dismal shorthand skills. Frau Zimmer had pursed her lips and murmured, "Perhaps you are aiming too high."

By the second week I'd realized that the last thing she wanted was someone with adequate shorthand skills who'd crowd in on her job. And now, at the end of the third week, I knew her favorite routine perfectly. It never failed.

It did not fail now. Promptly at one-fifteen Herr Möller buzzed. Frau Zimmer's parched middle-aged hands flew to her hair, fluffing here, smoothing there. Pulling out her pencil drawer, she snapped open the compact within to powder her nose and examine the state of her lipstick.

Then she stood up and tugged at her too-tight suit. Grabbing a handful of sharp pencils along with her steno pad, she marched purposefully to the connecting door and opened it just wide enough to squeeze her ample hips through. At that point she snatched off her horn-rimmed glasses, her expression becoming worshipful even before she turned to close the door firmly behind her. The odd half hour of taking dictation was sacred to her.

I lifted the caddy out of the cabinet, hid my new book under the rags, and waited for Herr Sonntag to come for his usual visit. It wasn't long before he stuck his head in from the corridor to make sure I was alone. Then he ambled in with a mug of black coffee and said, "What! Are you still working in Iceland? Careful or your knees will turn purple!" He was the highlight of my afternoons. Loosely speaking, he was a colleague of Herr Möller. Other than that they had nothing in common.

Herr Sonntag was craggily handsome in an antique sort of way. He had a bush of gleaming white hair and bright eyes like blue suns raying laugh lines in every direction. "Business is slow," he said cheerfully. "If it were not I'd have rescued you from this morgue on your very first day. Tell me, can you still smile?"

He claimed Frau Zimmer had lost that capacity long ago as one of the hazards of working in this office. He encouraged his own secretary to actually joke with him. Once their door had been ajar when I walked by and I heard them both chuckling. At the same time! No wonder everyone else in the building was scandalized and looking forward to his imminent retirement.

"Most lawyers, like most doctors, take themselves far too seriously," he went on, twirling in Frau Zimmer's revolving chair. "If they have more than a couple of diplomas on the wall they think they've become divine. There ought to be a law against the display of such vulgarity. I'd be the first to press charges. Guess against whom." He fished a couple of cookies out of his jacket pocket and held one out to me even though he knew as well as I did that leaving a single crumb in Frau Zimmer's office was a punishable offense.

To my regret his visit was cut short when his secretary, who wore her auburn hair in a bun and favored comfortable, good quality dresses, beckoned to him from the hallway. "I believe you might have a chance to snag an innocent passerby as a client if you get to hobbling," she said. "That is, if you're still playing at being an attorney."

He heaved himself to his feet. "Sounds promising. Maybe we can hire Marianne away from Möller with the advance."

She rolled her eyes at me. "Don't believe anything that comes out of the mouth of a lawyer," she said with a grin. "They are notorious liars. No,

Herr Chef (boss), what it means is that you might be able to pay the sole employee you've got for a change. If the man is still waiting."

I heard their footsteps recede down the corridor. He must have made one of his little jokes because she was laughing. I hoped she wouldn't be arrested for that unforgivable misdemeanor.

I'd disposed of the last cookie crumb on my lap and the last carbon in my basket when Frau Zimmer reentered the room. Glowing with pride, she seated herself carefully behind her desk, leaned toward me confidentially and whispered, "Herr Möller has a most important court case this afternoon. He needs to sign the letters he dictated to me before he leaves. Please do nothing to disturb me until I am done."

She assumed the classic typing position—stiff-backed, her face turned to the left while her fingers flew miraculously all over the keyboard. Every few minutes she'd zip out one flawless letter and insert a fresh multi-level sandwich of sheets and carbon paper. In record speed she created a stack of immaculate documents, addressed the envelopes that went with them, and proofed all her work. It was entirely possible—and I don't say this lightly—that she was even more skilled in the occupation than my mother, although she could compare neither in looks nor in charm.

In the end Frau Zimmer placed the unsigned letters in a crisp new folder, knocked on the connecting door, and went in to present her accomplishments. The virtuoso performance left me with the deep and abiding conviction that I would never reach her lofty professional heights even if I took a thousand typing classes.

A minute later she was back looking fulfilled. She folded the letters, inserted them into their envelopes, sealed them, attached stamps, and handed me all the copies. "File these before you start your dusting. He is gone for the rest of the day. I've already opened the windows." She walked to the front door and smiled beatifically up at the ceiling. "Such an important case! He's sure to be noticed." Then she jingled her keys. "I'm going for a quick bite after I mail these. I'll just lock the door from the outside. That way you won't be disturbed." It was her tactful way of saying I would be useless should a client walk in while she was absent.

Right after I dispatched the carbons I took the cleaning caddy into the sanctuary, placed it on the conference table, and polished everything in the already spotless room until it was entirely sterile. Only then did I permit myself to uncover the book and browse through the pages.

Soon I was glad that I had followed my impulse to run home for the mail. This manual would surely have gotten me into worse trouble than any letter Lucius could have sent, even if it had only been Mutti who discovered the package. I never saw anything like it. It answered questions

I didn't know could be asked, in clinical and very detailed terms. By the time I finished the first paragraph Herr Möller's office disappeared along with the legs I was standing on.

The information poured straight through my wide-open eyes into vast as yet unclaimed regions of my brain. There were frequent illustrations and several full-page ink drawings to stun the mind. One was labeled "The Mission Pose." A few pages farther was a second, tagged "The Dog Pose." I stared at that one with my eyes wide open, hardly understanding what was in front of my eyes. Then I noticed a definite cooling trend in the air.

Glancing over my shoulder I saw Herr Möller standing directly behind me, studying the picture with a fascination as great as my own. He tore his attention away from the drawing to look at me fully for the first and last time. For a small eternity those iron-cold eyes pierced through me like a sword and held me transfixed. Then he picked up a file folder he must have forgotten the first time he left, stuffed it into his bulging briefcase, and walked out of his private door as quietly as he had entered it. That's when I hunched over to clutch at my impaled stomach, finally understanding the entire meaning of "mortified." It wasn't just horrible and embarrassing; it had something of death in it.

That night I waited until I was alone in the bedroom before I took the book out of my satchel and climbed into bed with it. While Anna was busy removing her makeup in the bathroom I studied the two scientifically correct drawings again. When the telephone shrieked I snapped the book shut and tossed it under my covers as if it had grown too hot to touch, for I knew at once the call was about me. It was from the law office, Anna informed me when she came to say Mutti wanted me in the living room right away.

It seemed Frau Zimmer had called on Herr Möller's behalf to tell Mutti that I was just not working out. My skills were too poor. She suggested I be enrolled full time at the trade school until they improved. I was extremely grateful that she did not mention anything about the book. Mutti decided that Frau Zimmer's advice was sound. Tomorrow she'd get in touch with the school to ask if I could be admitted as a full time business student. Vati would have to share the expenses.

"My old school was free," I pointed out.

"And look where it got you," she said, dismissing both me and my argument with a wave of her hand. "You better scoot. I think I hear O.F. coming up the stairs."

I found Anna sitting up in her bed, her back pressed against the headboard and my book on her knees. She didn't even hear me come in. Her cheeks were aflame and her eyes lit with an ungodly gleam. There was no way of getting the manual away from her now. The light stayed on long after I tossed myself into a fitful doze. Every now and then I surfaced long enough to hear two voices on the other side of the wall. They wove in and out of a shrill opera broadcast and finally lowered to become almost indistinguishable from the squeaking springs of the unfolded couch bed. My mother, in the mission pose, pressed to the sheet.

The light was still on when I heard the church bell strike midnight. My sister slept curled on her pillow, one arm draped over the closed book. I eased it loose, found my place in it, and read it through to the end. The merciless eyes of Herr Möller stared back from every page, damping my enthusiasm for the material. When I was done I buried it under a jumble of old textbooks at the bottom of my wardrobe, wishing I could bury Lucius's missing letter alongside. My wardrobe bottom was a place where not even I ever found anything I wanted and where I hoped the manual would remain perpetually undiscovered.

CHAPTER 24

F OR THE REST OF THE NIGHT I dreamed I could fly. Without wings. All I had to think was "up!" and I would soar far above the ground. Slowly, gravity would reclaim me and I'd touch down for an instant in a flat field or on a slope, set my aim high, and off I'd bounce again. Every person I encountered was a friend. I was surrounded by smiling faces, laughter, and the warming rays of love, and knew with great certainty that I could do anything and go anywhere entirely unfettered.

On Saturday morning I awoke without the usual sense of dread. I stretched luxuriously, not remembering until my feet encountered Seppi that we were prisoners together, hiding from a powerful enemy who seemed to have full control over our lives. It was the start of another weekend without Lucius but I had good excuses to leave home on both days.

Anna had invited me to the grafiker's studio for tea on Sunday and today Wolfi was finally getting his wish—Mutti had given me permission to ride out to the Baggersee with him for a picnic and a swim. She even gave me the room key after extracting a solemn promise that I would lock Seppi in when I was ready to leave. Since O.F. would be home by himself most of the day he only needed to heat enough water for his own bath and no doubt intended to spend the rest of day in the living room smoking and brooding about my immediate future. In fact, sitting up, I could hear typewriter keys pecking away.

I got dressed and sprawled on my bed, reading old magazines until I heard him descend to the basement for the first boxful of pine cones. Then I tiptoed downstairs. Wolfi was already revving his blue racer back and forth at the stoop. True to her word, Mutti had carried my bike up from the cellar and parked it behind the garbage shed for an easy getaway, all the picnic supplies strapped to the luggage rack behind the seat.

Halfway to the lake Wolfi, in a magnanimous mood, offered to switch bikes with me. He seemed content to pump the remaining kilometers on my green plow horse, giving me a good lead. As it turned out, riding the racer had a couple of minor drawbacks. I didn't much like how the curve of its handlebars forced me to lean most of my weight onto my arms, nor how high I had to lift my leg in order to mount and dismount. But without a doubt I looked impressive coasting to the lake shore in style.

Dredged from a gravel pit after its contents were removed for the rebuilding effort, the Baggersee was no natural lake. It was laid out in a precise rectangle with a uniform slope from rim to lake bottom. Beach sand was sparse. A few trees struggled valiantly out of the poor rocky ground. The grass over which I spread our blanket was no more than a mat of stunted weeds but there was a good inlet and the water was fresh.

Wolfi reclaimed his bike. Together we rounded the perimeter of the lake a couple of times. Growing bored, we decided to ride straight into the shallows at an angle, cutting our wheels across the sharp corners, getting in a bit deeper with each try until it became a challenge to remain upright on the steep submerged slope. We strained, jerking the handlebars away from their natural inclination, which was to follow the grade toward the bottom. It worked fine on the plow horse but the racer was bred for level roads and did not maneuver well over rough, sodden terrain.

That was no doubt why Wolfi insisted on reclaiming my bike after we'd successfully navigated the first two corners. I did not realize how much trouble I'd have with the racer's steering until I was riding in water up past the pedals. Forcing the bars toward the upcoming corner, I could not shift the front wheel, which was determined to stay in a descending groove. Furiously jerking the recalcitrant handles and pumping the pedals, bike and rider sank as one. I was so dumbfounded at the speed of my mishap that I was still pedaling after the sky disappeared from sight and a roof of water caved in on me. Right to the point of losing my breath I kept trying to pull the metal lump back to the surface with me. It proved too unwieldy. At last, utterly spent, I sacrificed the bike in order to save my own life. I stumbled ashore spewing water every which way. As I collapsed onto my knees, I saw Wolfi sitting on my bike with both feet on the ground, his eyes and mouth wide with shock.

"My mother will kill me!" he said, so pale I could see a spattering of freckles under his tan.

With my hair and clothes dripping I stumbled to my feet and said valiantly, "Don't worry—I'm going back in. We won't leave for home without it."

We dove until we were too exhausted to move. Neither of us had fins or goggles or a reasonable plan, and the bike was painted the exact shade of lake water. We found nothing bigger than coins and sunglasses and keys until at last, making one last heroic effort, I thought I saw a length of chrome gleaming in the murky blue gloom. Soon I managed to touch the handlebars and shot straight up from my find to signal Wolfi. Together we prodded and pulled and heaved until our treasure lay on shore, water flowing from both handles as if they were faucets.

Too spent to mount, we walked the bikes to our blankets. There I collapsed onto my back and watched Wolfi set the racer tenderly upside down, hoping to empty its waterlogged innards. Then he spread-eagled with a long sigh of relief.

For some time all I could hear was the sound of our panting. The next thing I knew we were both laughing, perhaps from prolonged oxygen starvation. I tried to describe how I had felt as his bike was dragging me down to the bottom. He said I'd looked so absurd sinking along with the ship that he was convinced it was all a bad dream. We decided to go into the diving business the following year. For Christmas, we'd both ask for goggles and fins and next summer we'd collect enough drowned coins to fill a couple of sacks. We'd be rich.

Then, without the least warning, he snatched up my nearest foot and started to tickle the arch. The initially pleasant sensation soon became irritating, but some bodily reflex forced me to go on giggling long after there was nothing left to giggle about. Then I told him sharply to let go. He did stop for a second, during which our eyes met as if for the first time and I knew without the shadow of doubt that the foot he was holding was connected to my leg, which was connected to something neither one of us had ever bothered to think about. Wolfi knew it, too.

Instead of releasing my foot, he pressed it tight against him and tickled me even harder, an odd, driven expression on his face. "Let go!" I cried, suddenly furious. When he didn't I kicked my other foot straight at his solar plexus by sheer instinct. He clutched at his middle and rolled around on the weeds, mouth gaping, until he finally managed to suck in a lungful of air.

"What'd you do that for?" he wheezed, looking stunned.

"I told you to let go!"

"I was just having fun!"

"Well, I wasn't!"

`We glared at each other and then he shook his head. "I don't know what's gotten into you lately," he said. His glance went to where my wet blouse clung, revealing the fact that I was not wearing a bathing suit under the thin cotton material. I sat up, turned away from him, and surreptitiously pulled the fabric loose from my skin. It was too late. We had already discovered that our bodies contained at least a couple of parts of which we had been blissfully unaware. That's when I knew we'd never play Cowboys and Indians again.

*

THE NEXT day Anna left early to help the grafiker put the finishing touches on a joint project of theirs. It occurred to me that he had become a replacement for Peter who had simply ceased to exist now that his usefulness to Anna was over. Seppi and I had a leisurely morning of reading and daydreaming until O.F., in a bid to reestablish his hold on Mutti's emotions, invited her to the Gasthaus near church for Mittagessen *(lunch)*.

I watched from my window as she complacently walked off arm-in-arm with her oppressor, both wearing Sunday finery. For some reason the sight enraged me. I glared at myself in the mirror, fighting the impulse to shatter the glass with a well-aimed hairbrush. It wasn't until I took Seppi for a quick stroll that I formed a reckless plan involving the new secretary outfit Mutti had proudly shown me before Herr Adler banished her from his office. The stylish dress was an unfortunate, almost flesh-colored beige, with matching jacket and full accessories. No doubt she'd been planning to bedazzle her old boss with the clinging material while taking dictation.

It had languished in her closet ever since. What if I broke it in for her now? It might emphasize my blossoming maturity to Anna, the grafiker, and the rest of this town. Since Mutti had already forced me to wear some of her cast-offs I coldly assumed nothing in her closet was out of bounds. As I slipped on the dress she'd modeled for me I wondered which of us looked prettier in it. To my pleasant surprise, the beige didn't seem as boring on me as it had been on her. It fit differently, too. My legs were longer, making the dress appear shorter. My waist was narrower than hers but I easily fixed that by ruthlessly punching an extra hole through her leather belt. What spare room there was at the chest was taken up by my wide shoulders. After adding the matching jacket, medium-high heels, gloves and a purse, I was sure I belonged on a magazine cover. I brushed my hair all to one side for extra chic, decided to appropriate a beige hat from her wardrobe's top shelf, and enhanced the stunning effect by adding her emerald jewelry set, including the long-coveted dangling emerald-and-silver earrings once worn by St. Nicholas. When I emerged from the apartment I could feel myself glow.

Downstairs, I could see Wolfi drooping out on the stoop. I swept through the lobby like a high-fashion model negotiating the runway, compelling him to sit at rapt attention. With a gracious nod, I brushed past him, informing him airily that I had an engagement in Schwabing for afternoon tea.

Frau Keppler, who sat reading the Sunday paper at her kitchen window, wiggled her hand in the French way and said, "U-la-la!" as I sashayed to the corner. I rewarded her with a small curtsy. Other neighbors did double takes as we passed on the street, and the small crowd arrayed at the bus stop watched my leisurely approach with something like wonder.

I got on, claimed a window seat, and watched the bus pull into traffic. Then I saw something quite strange. A little black man was racing alongside, rapping on my window and yelling, "Halt! Halt!"

The driver, forbidden to insult members of the occupying forces, grudgingly complied. The little man leaped on and stood fighting for balance as the bus lurched viciously forward again to make up for lost time. It wasn't until the new passenger worked his way toward me that I noticed his unspeakably old-fashioned black derby, set at a rakish angle, his dark shades, and an ebony walking stick hooked over an arm. Without so much as a "May I?" he plopped in the seat next to mine, gasping, "Maria! Didn't you hear me yell? It's me. Duncan's friend. Spider." He slid the shades to the tip of his nose and I recognized the degenerate I'd last seen standing under a wet tree in the dark, sticking a hand up the skirts of his lady.

"Hello, Spider," I said, forcing myself to keep my dislike from showing. "How do you do?"

"Getting better every day, thank you," he replied.

I nodded with disinterest.

"See, I got sick the night before the battalion pulled out," he went on, gloating. "An appendix attack hurts like heck and can be life-threatening if it's ignored."

"Appendix?"

He patted the right side of his belly.

"Blinddarm," I guessed. I could appreciate the danger involved, having heard several gruesome tales about kids complaining to their indifferent parents about bellyaches but were shushed until it was too late to save them. Of course, the reason kids were shushed in the first place was that appendix attacks were a favorite ploy of shirkers. The same bit of reasoning told me that Spider could not have chased down a bus unless he was fully mended—or had been faking the malady in order to get out of the war games. "And now that you are all better you go to the maneuver?" I asked, thinking that Lucius was carrying a double load because of the likes of this man.

"I'm not that well yet," he grinned. "In fact, the doc wants me to stay put so he can keep an eye on me. No surgeon in the boonies, you see. The battalion will have to get on without me. I'm sure Duncan will tell me all the good stuff I'm missing." He scooted closer, his bony knee stabbing my beige thigh. "Where you going, Maria?"

"To a meeting," I said shortly, inching away.

He considered my outfit. "Must be some meeting," he said. "You sure don't look like a school girl today. In fact, you seem years older than last time we met. Them past few weeks you spent with Duncan done aged you." He slapped his knee and laughed heartily, revealing his gold tooth. "Thought we could step out together, on account we both so fancy and all. I buy."

"You buy what?"

"Lunch."

When he saw my reluctance, he added, "It'll give us plenty of time to talk about our common friend Duncan."

The only thing I liked about Spider was that he knew Lucius. The only thing I didn't like about Lucius was that he knew Spider. It hardly seemed a good reason to talk. "I cannot. So sorry." Watching his grin fade, I grew vaguely aware that he reminded me of someone, though I couldn't think who. He must have been lurking at the Alabama Bar in broad daylight, amidst glass shards and cast-off cigarette butts. How smoothly he'd crossed from his world to mine!

"Next time then." He spoke with an air of certainty that made me uneasy. "When we meet up again."

"Why should we meet again?"

"Because," he said with a lame shrug. Then his face brightened. "Because Duncan's been telling me how you're showing him around. Cat used to sit in the barracks every weekend and now all he's talking about is castles and mountains and such. You being a good tour guide and all, I'm hoping maybe you can show *me* a castle or two."

I'd rather stay locked inside my room! "This I do only for . . ." I hesitated, remembering that 'Lucius' was a secret name, and finished with, " . . . Duncan. And no other."

"Aw—Duncan won't mind. He'll be glad to find out we're getting along, both of us being his friends and all . . ."

"He will?"

"Sure 'nuff!"

"I ask him first."

Spider gave a triumphant smile. "But he's not here."

"I write him a letter."

The smile disappeared. "You do that," he said. "Better yet— I tell you what. I'll call him on the company phone. How's that? And then I'll tell you exactly what he said." He tipped his hat, pulled the cord, and worked his way to the exit.

I made a point of averting my eyes until the bus was well on its way again. And then I saw that every face on the bus was glaring at me. How could I explain to these judgmental Germans that I didn't trust Spider any more than they did? That I had done nothing to encourage him to burst onto the scene? Whoever it was he reminded me of, it couldn't have been anyone nice.

An even stranger thing happened when I transferred to the streetcar that would take me into the heart of Schwabing. I boarded just as the warning bell clanged. There was a shout and then a young man came barreling across the square. Elbowing onto my carriage just as the doors swung shut, he soon stood panting before me. He looked a bit like Lucius, with the same open, friendly smile, although he was somewhat shorter. "I saw your shine," he said. "And I just couldn't let you ride out of my life." He held out his hand. "I'm Terrence Williams, from Detroit, and I want to take you out."

While we shook I tried to make sense of his words. "You want to take me out of what?" I finally asked. "The streetcar?"

"That, too," he said. "I thought we could get a couple of sodas somewhere so we can talk. I'd like us to be friends."

The other passengers were watching us as if we were performing a stage play, but with none of the hostility the previous crowd had shown toward Spider. What was it about me that was attracting males all of a sudden? It had to be more than the dress. I was almost sorry to turn him down. "I am on my way to a meeting," I said with an apologetic smile. "And I already have a friend."

He thought it over. "Boy or girl?"

Well, Lucius was hardly a girl. "Someone like you," I explained.

"A serviceman? Colored?"

I stared.

"A soldier? Dark, like me?"

I nodded.

That seemed to please and grieve him at the same time. "I wish it *was* me," he said, reaching a pocket for some paper. "Look, things change. If it doesn't work out between you and your friend why not give me a call? I'm ready to fill the vacancy any time you say." He began patting himself down for a pen, but I stopped him by gently shaking my head.

"Thank you for your interest," I said. "But no."

His face fell. "At least give me the next ten minutes," he tried again. "Just enough time to share a bottle of Cola."

"It would make me late and I don't like Cola. I'm sorry. I have to go now." I disembarked and moved briskly away on the sidewalk, waving at him as the streetcar passed by. Then I decided to walk the remaining few blocks to the grafiker's studio. It would give me a good look at Schwabing, the infamous quarter inhabited by university students, dropouts, artists, and other misfits. The sun on my shoulders made me feel glad. A breeze lovingly caressed my face, whispering that I would rise with the updraft if only I could spread my arms wide enough. Remembering yesterday's flying-dream, I said, "Up!" half-convinced I was already lifting. Then, making do with what I had, I did my best to bounce along the sidewalk in Mutti's medium-sized heels.

CHAPTER 25

I T WAS ANNA WHO OPENED the grafiker's door. Her eyebrows shot up as she took in my stunning outfit. "There's hope for you yet," she whispered. "I'm impressed—although this is hardly the place for your unexpected conversion." Turning, she called out, "It's only my sister, coming to tea."

The grafiker strode into the hall with outstretched hands. "Hello, Marianne. I've heard so much about you. The water's on the boil." He was a delicate man the size of Spider but while Spider kept his eyes hidden behind dark glasses the grafiker's were wholly forthright. Anna introduced him as Horst Obdach. His sandy hair was thinning and he wore an old plaid shirt with the sleeves rolled up past the elbows. When she had invited me over she bragged that her Chef was very informal. After my own experience with bosses I had not believed her. Now I saw she'd been right; his frayed, baggy jeans made me feel hopelessly overdressed.

I whipped off my fancy gloves. We shook. His finely-made hands were smudged with charcoal but the nails were remarkably clean. "So you are the tomboy," he said with a chuckle. "Anna, when was the last time you took a good look at your 'little' sister?"

"I said younger, not little," she protested while I piled my accessories onto a chair heaped with magazines. Taking a second look at my outfit, she told him, "I'm just as surprised as you are. Until now her favorite clothes have been grungy jeans and old shirts, much like those you've got on now."

"I'm sure if she'd known how dusty my place is she would have worn them today, too," he said. Pushing a pile of rags from the couch, he cautioned, "Watch what you lean against, Marianne. Beige shows dirt fast. I'd say this couch would be your safest bet. Stay away from . . . everything else." He looked around with a rueful grin.

The studio was one large, well-lighted room with a big skylight. Canvases, mats, paints, and drawing pads lay every which way. "Mutti came *here* to discuss the apprenticeship agreement?" I couldn't help asking.

Herr Obdach threw back his head and laughed. "Anna advised against it. For that occasion I hired a house-cleaner to sort things out at my apartment. I do it once a year anyway, usually in early spring. Your Mutti appreciated the effort but I haven't been able to find anything since. Now relax while I brew our tea."

In all my life I'd never seen a couch so decrepit, except maybe in the Hilde's kitchen, in Freidorf. I lowered myself gingerly onto the frayed blanket, which did an inadequate job of hiding bulges, holes, and worn springs. Stuffing protruded from where the blanket had slipped off the armrests. The coffee table I bumped my knees against was layered with odds and ends, all of them laden with dust. Two sturdy drafting tables made up the rest of Herr Obdach's studio furniture. The odd chair, here and there, was evidently part of an eccentric filing system. None of it mattered, for the walls were full of glossy oils and misty washes. Thriving houseplants stood in the corners.

I caught a blurred glimpse of my elegant self in a wall mirror and realized that my hat was still upon my head. Suspecting my hair was squashed flat underneath it by now, anyway, I resolved to leave the hat on. That was what fine ladies usually did when they visited someone for tea. While Herr Obdach busied himself at the hotplate I studied my fascinating reflection, experimentally crossing and recrossing my stockinged, slim legs.

Then Anna showed me the illustrations for a toothpaste commercial they were working on. "They're due tomorrow," she said, elated. "Horst is taking me to Grünwald with him, in the BMW. Straight to a real TV studio. Wouldn't it be funny if I accidentally wandered in front of the cameras? Everyone would see me, all over Bavaria."

"Anna wants to be discovered," the grafiker said, pushing aside the coffee-table clutter to make room for a tray holding three gilded cups. "One second on screen," he grinned, "and who knows, next week she'll be the weather girl and I'll have to find a new assistant." The cups were chipped, their flower patterns mismatched. The tea he poured was the bitter black kind I wasn't allowed to drink. I dropped three sugar cubes into mine and stirred in a liberal amount of condensed milk straight from the can.

If Anna was too dumb to know how lucky she was to work here maybe there was a chance he'd hire me next. She would rather die than admit it but I was every bit as artistic as she was—except that, so far, I had drawn mostly for my own pleasure.

Anna blushed. "You're making fun of me, Horst. So what if they hire to be the next weather girl? It won't interfere with this job, since one is in the evenings, the other during the day."

Horst? She called her new boss by his first name? I wondered how Mutti would feel about that. I pictured her sitting beside me, mentally cataloguing all the things that were wrong with this room. How she would wince at the condensed milk served from a can caked with yellowed residual drips.

The grafiker unceremoniously ripped open a package of butter cookies and strewed them onto the tray. I started to sketch Lucius's head onto a notecard sized patch of the dust-laden table. In profile. Using the tip of my little finger, I feathered in his tight curls. "Hey, this is good," Herr Obdach said. "I didn't know you were an artist, too. Is it someone you know?"

"Oh," said Anna dismissively, "she's always doodling African heads. She can't seem to draw anything else. Not like me."

"Even if you're right," he said placatingly, "I won't clean the table again for a month!" At that, all three of us burst into fits of side-splitting laughter, since it was obvious it had been at least a year since he'd last wielded a dust cloth. He pointed at the wide-open front window. "Welcome to Schwabing, where dust is considered a wholesome bit of the outdoors blowing in with the breeze. No different from the stuff under the lawns of the English Garden where Sunday picnickers sit with their potato salads and cold Schnitzels. The dirt in here is the same dirt that makes flowers grow there."

When we'd finished the last cookie and drained the teapot dry he filled my hand with sugar cubes. "I saw how you looked at them. I used to love to suck on them, too, when I was a boy." Then he asked me to call him Horst. "It's only fair," he said, "since I get to call you by your first name. We're quite informal in Schwabing. Restrictions and art don't mix. Come again. Any time."

Anna walked me to the vestibule and said in a low voice, "You should see him in Grünwald. He wears Italian suits to the TV studio and carries his drawings in a fancy leather portfolio." I didn't want to squelch her fervor, but his jeans and frayed shirt impressed me far more.

On my way to the streetcar I saw two barefooted women with unbound hair and long dresses walking arm in arm. Three bearded young men dressed in identical black turtleneck sweaters stood at a corner, discussing Goethe's color theory. At the next corner a vagabond played his guitar, singing the latest American hit, an upended hat at his feet, its bottom covered with coins. Halfway down the block an old woman with a cloud of soot-black hair sat at a rickety card table, offering to read the tarot. The adjoining sidewalk café buzzed with conversation and laughter.

Horst's breeze, wafting from the direction of the English Gardens and the Isar beyond, seemed sweeter than any I'd smelled in my part of town. I sucked on my sugar cubes and took care not to step on the cracks in the sidewalk. A merry gaggle of small children came toward me on hand-me-down tricycles. One of them stopped at a child-sized shiny red bike leaning against a building, impulsively abandoned his tricycle in favor of the two-wheeler, and began to ride shakily away from his friends. Unable to reach the seat, the little boy stood on the pedals, his glee quickly giving way to alarm as he discovered that although he could keep some sort of uneasy balance he was moving ever faster toward the busy street and didn't know how to stop.

"Step on the brake!" I cried, and when he didn't respond, "Pedal backward!" Already, I'd kicked off my heels and was running, reaching for the luggage rack behind him. The front tire had rolled off the curb by the time my fingers closed on the rack. I pulled him to a stop.

He got off, white-faced, cried "I want my tricycle!" and ran to his friends, leaving me with the borrowed red bike.

I heard the clanging of an approaching streetcar, most likely mine, and hastened to lean the abandoned bicycle against the nearest wall hoping its owner would find it. Then I recovered Mutti's shoes and slipped them on in front of the tram shelter. Directly across the street from me, at an identical stop, stood a brown-eyed young gentleman with well-cut dark, curly hair. He wore a fine white linen suit, a crisp handkerchief peeping from the breast pocket. He looked at me and I looked at him, and then both our streetcars approached at the same time, his from my right, mine from my left, their long blue-and-white-painted sides blocking our view.

I boarded, moving from one strap to another until I'd worked my way to the rear of the carriage. No sooner did I sit than another passenger slid on to the adjoining seat, so close that our thighs grazed. It was the young man from the opposite curb.

"You got on the wrong streetcar," I said, dumbfounded.

"*Nein*, Chérie, yours is the right one for me," he said in German with a musical French accent.

I tilted sideways to break bodily contact, overwhelmed by the perfume of his aftershave.

"Sprichst Du Französich (you speak French)?" he asked, one eyebrow raised in private amusement.

Politely, I replied, "Not French; just English."

"Ah—this is good," he said, switching to that language but taking the accent with him. "It is a fine day, is it not? The air is fresh, the city is gorgeous—and so are you. Come, let us get off at the next sidewalk café. I wish to buy you a cup of espresso."

Impulsively I craned my neck toward the upcoming little tables, highlighted by sunshine. How fine we would look sitting vis-à-vis, him in his handsome white suit and me in Mutti's priceless ensemble. But—shouldn't he have realized by now that I wasn't quite old enough to enjoy coffee? "No, thank you," I said blandly. As the streetcar slowed and stopped right beside the café, I moved to another part of the tram to discourage further conversation.

He was not so easily dissuaded. Shadowing me to my new seat, he put his mouth to my ear, blowing warm air at it with each of his words. "I am a stranger in your lovely city. Perhaps you can show me interesting places to go. Like a—how do you say—tour guide?"

I swiveled my head toward him in surprise. He was the second man today to ask me that question. Was it some kind of lure to attract do-good adolescent girls wanting to feel special? If so, where did it leave Lucius, who had seemed entirely sincere when we first met? "I am sorry," I said with growing apprehension. "I do not have the time. You must ask another girl." And then, before he could come up with a brilliant response, I darted out of the closing doors just before the streetcar prepared to move on. Equally fast, I leaped into the second carriage, making my way to its very end in order to put as much distance between him and me as I possibly could.

My predicament was the fault of the borrowed clothes, of course. They made me look too grown up. Surely the Frenchman would have been uninterested in a fifteen-year-old wearing baggy old trousers. Hopefully he would now leave me be and discover a more mature guide better at being assertive. But when we reached the end of the line and I raced to the waiting bus along with a dozen other passengers, the one who sat down next to me—in the last vacant seat—was the very same Frenchman.

Inadvertently I inhaled a few enticing molecules of aftershave with my next breath, amazed at the heat radiating from his body. His hands were resting calmly on his white linen slacks but when the bus began to move, so did he, until the small space between us was gone. I was boxed in. Even though our arms and thighs were just touching lightly it felt like an embrace. I pressed myself against the window, gaining a couple of centimeters of privacy, and decided to stare out until we came to the Harthof, pretending he was not there.

"Chérie," he said, his breath feathering my neck, "there is such a thing as love at first sight. At least in Paris there is. From the long moment during which our eyes first met I could do nothing but come to you. Why are you afraid? I do not bite. Love between a man and a woman is a wonderful thing. You will see." With the next bump the bus made my seatmate's hip leaned heavily against mine.

Still looking away, I protested meekly, "You have made a mistake, you see. I am no woman. I am only a child, barely fifteen." In case this was not enough to deter him I added, "And my mother does not allow me to talk to strange men."

He made a low whistling sound and, putting a finger under my chin, turned it toward him. "An enchanting fifteen, Chérie. Hardly a child. And your mother . . . is not here." His eyes were so very tender, the fingertip under my chin so gently supportive that I could think of no further response. What *could* I say? Such repartee was not taught in school, nor did my mother educate me on how to say no with the proper degree of genteel rejection.

Meanwhile we were drawing ever nearer to my stop. What would I do if he followed me off the bus? Followed me home? "We are strangers," I repeated, trying to push his finger aside but succeeding only in feeling it worm itself into my palm. "You must leave me alone."

His smile was a shade too guileless. "I am Lauren," he said, adding the other four fingers to the worm for an unwelcome handshake, "and I am bewitched. Forget the espresso. Forget our tour. We will simply go for a short afternoon stroll, yes, to get better acquainted. My mother would be delighted to meet you. She lives in Paris, only minutes away from my own apartment. She met my father when *she* was fifteen. It is a magical age. It was love at first sight for them too."

It occurred to me that he was indulging in some sort of game he had played many times before, one that delighted him anew each time he played it. Hastily withdrawing my hand, I said, "I already have a friend." Why not? It had worked with Terrence Williams, of Detroit.

"He has kissed you, this friend?"

The man would leave no stone unturned. I said nothing. He seemed to think my silence was answer enough.

"Chérie, what I saw in that first moment between us was a mouth as yet unkissed. It is too sad. But you are in good hands." Somehow, he contrived to cup mine firmly in his. "I will show you the fun of it."

Mesmerized, I focused on his generous mouth, still stretched in a smile, his strong, even teeth parting as the tip of a pink tongue appeared to slowly moisten his lips. He put one of my hands to his pounding heart, the other to his knee, pressing it discreetly, releasing, and pressing again, soliciting involuntary responses I didn't know enough about to be guarded against. All this in broad daylight on an ordinary, rather noisy bus where we were surrounded by the kind of passengers who had so cruelly inspected and unnerved Lucius. They were not bothering to scrutinize Lauren and me although they did offer fleeting, encouraging smiles.

And then I realized that I was like the toddler who had exchanged his reliable tricycle for a bike capable of more speed than he was ready for. The clothes I had so carelessly slipped on had put me in a fast lane toward adulthood without supplying the controls I needed for velocity or direction. It also occurred to me that the only reason Lauren had so quickly switched our conversation from German to English was because that way he could be sure that no one else would comprehend him. Did I have the nerve, at this late date, to switch back to a language the other passengers understood? I did not.

And now his finger was doing strange things to my palm. A shaft of heat swept through me like a contamination, leaving me limp. Then I saw the bakery approaching. Before I could pull the cord a stiff-jointed elderly man, already heaving himself to his feet, signaled that he wanted to get off. The bus stopped. Sighing with each creaky step, the man began to disembark. I shot up just as the doors began to shut, scrambled over Lauren's knees, and dove outside, landing hard on the sidewalk behind the feeble oldster who seemed to be waiting for enough energy to make his next move. Recovering my balance almost at once, I skirted around the back end of the bus, dashed across the street on my toes because I dared not pause to remove the cursed heels, and heard Lauren's voice behind me, calling me by the name that wasn't mine.

Prey that I was, I ran blindly around the side of the bakery, hoping to find some niche in which I could hide. But there was none. Then I fled to the Alabama Bar, raced to the rear of the shack, and was astonished to find a huge green bullet-shaped car parked from corner to corner—with Spider, lazily smoking a cigarette, leaning against the open passenger door. In my confused state I remembered only that he was Lucius's friend and that *Lucius* meant *safe*.

When Spider said, "Hey, Maria—" I was already diving past him to cower on the floor mat in front of the passenger seat. Without missing a beat he closed the door, shutting me in.

CHAPTER 26

I WAS TRYING TO MAKE MYSELF SMALLER. Through the open passenger window, I heard Spider say reflectively, "All good things come to them that wait." Somebody's footsteps were hurrying closer then stopping next to the car. Lauren's silken voice asked in English,

"Pardon, please, have you seen my young Miss? She wears a beige ensemble with a saucy little hat."

My heart bludgeoned my ribcage. I imagined Spider taking a long drag on his cigarette. Then he said coolly, "She ran through the field. That-away." Lauren thanked him and rushed on. I dared to take a ragged breath. My slip was sweat-soaked. My ears were starting to buzz.

Spider made himself comfortable in the driver's seat. "Your friend's standing in the middle of the field, looking in every direction," he reported. "He's bound to figure things out in a minute. What do you say we roll out of here?"

Why not? Right then and there Spider seemed the lesser of two evils.

"If you will let me out down the street," I conceded.

He grunted an unintelligible reply. The big car pulled away from the shack like a stately cruise ship moving from its pier out to sea. "I'm not even going to ask what that was all about," he said, driving across

Schleissheimerstrasse. "But I believe you owe me a favor. Seeing that I lied for you and all."

"I am grateful," I stammered. "That man followed me all the way from town and would not leave me alone." A quick peek showed me we were just passing the stationary shop. Feeling a bit more at ease, I scrambled on to the passenger seat. This seemed to trigger more buzzing in my ears, accompanied by spots dancing in front of my eyes.

"Spider's face stayed impassive behind the perpetual shades, but he looked at me twice before saying, "You're whiter than—white. You're not going to be sick in this car, are you?" He slowed as if expecting the worst.

"Everything's spinning," I confessed, my head lolling against the backrest. But this was not a good time to give in to weakness so I gritted my teeth against the odd light-headedness and said bravely, "I think I can walk home from here."

He stopped the car and looked hard at me. "When's the last time you ate?"

"An hour ago. I had cookies and—" I shuddered at the memory—"a handful of sugar cubes."

He whistled through his teeth. "You got the sugar-blues, girl! Hold out your hands." My fingers trembled. Spider nodded sagely. "Yup. You ought to stay put till you feel better but if it's that important to you to stand on your own two feet, go right ahead. Walk. I'm willing to bet your knees will buckle in a minute. Or less."

He was right. As soon as I climbed out daylight dimmed and the buzz in my ears became a loud, ceaseless ringing. I clutched at the car, shaking my head to clear it. Then I saw Wolfi's mother come out of the stationery shop, busily attending to her purse, which seemed to have a stuck zipper.

"Looks to me like you're not ready to go anywhere just yet," Spider said kindly. "You better sit unless you want to fall down. If we don't fix you up real fast you'll pass out on me. Lucky for you I got the proper cure." He groped under his seat.

Ducking behind the car, I watched Wolfi's mother raise her head, sniffing suspiciously with her raptor-like nose. I crept on to the passenger seat, quietly closed the car-door, buried my face in my hands and flattened myself, hoping she couldn't see me. Over the past couple of years I'd occasionally felt faint upon getting out of a chair. Mutti claimed it was a normal part of what she called 'growing pains' and no cause for concern. But this spell felt different; it reminded me of a long-ago late afternoon, on the farm.

*

I MUST have been three or four that summer. I had just climbed the ladder to the hayloft looking for Gabriel and Anna but they were not there. My legs had seemed heavier with each rung. I had to rest on top of the ladder before crawling on to the loft floor. From there I collapsed on a loose pile of hay and watched a sunbeam stab through the barn's only window high in the narrow west wall. The beam rayed the whole length of the dusky, cavernous space until it touched the great double-doors in the east wall. On this celestial highway, countless dust motes shimmered and danced without cease. The longer I beheld this beautiful sight the dizzier I felt. Soon I couldn't have moved if I had tried—and lost all interest in trying. Teeth chattering, limbs trembling with cold, I felt my conscious mind dip to some nebulous place.

I stayed in the grip of this strange paralysis for what seemed like hours. Finally I heard someone on the ladder. It was Hilde, come to feed her cows. She climbed off the top rung to raise the square little trap door in the middle of the loft floor. Then she looked through the hole into the stable, lifted a pitchfork off the wall and began to toss hay down to the feeding-cribs. From below, I smelled the familiar, comforting aroma of warm dung and heard soft rustling and mooing. Hilde didn't see me until she had rehung the pitchfork and was in the process of lowering the trap door. That's when she gasped and let it slip from her fingers.

"How long have you been here?" she asked. I put all my effort into an intense, pleading stare. She came closer, tilting to study my face, and gingerly touched my forehead. Then she quickly descended the ladder. Soon she was back with a bottle and a metal schnapps tumbler, pulled me to a sitting position, and forced a golden-brown liquid into my mouth. "Swallow it," she commanded. "It'll do you good." I did. It scorched my throat and rolled into my stomach like a fireball, heating my insides. With a satisfied nod, she tapped the label with a work-worn finger and said, "Cognac!" She had always been a woman of few words.

*

"THE CURE is called 'Cognac'," Spider told me more than a decade later, holding a similar bottle in front of my fifteen-year-old face. "It never fails." He filled a shot glass and held it to my lips. "Drink this. It'll put you right in a hurry." I did. Within seconds my fingers stopped trembling and my ears cleared—but now I was unbearably hungry.

Watching me from behind his dark glasses like any spider bent on catching a fly, he said, "I know a nice little place that makes great Schnitzel with noodles. In fact, I was planning to drive there for dinner in a couple of hours. But now that you're in need—well, look here, Maria—a man doesn't like to eat alone. You could use a good meal and I could use the company. Don't shake your head. You do owe me a favor."

My stomach was a bottomless pit. Wolfi's mom was still on the opposite sidewalk, rummaging in her purse and stealing sly glances at the out-of-place American car in the hopes of collecting a tidbit of gossip. Even if I waited until she decided to give up her quest my walk home seemed impossibly long. At the end of it I'd have to contend with O.F., who was most likely sitting in the kitchen, supervising every detail of Mutti's meal preparations.

I couldn't imagine steeling myself for the strenuous task of walking past him even with Mutti in the same room. Nor did I have the heart for a confrontation just now, especially considering whose clothes I was wearing. Besides, the only food I could expect at home before my solitary dinner in bed was a dry slice of bread.

"Like I told you before, I'm just trying to do Duncan a favor," Spider said, capping the bottle and shoving it under his seat. "He'd want me to take care of you, don't you think? Him and me being buddies and all. I'll make him pay for your dinner soon as he gets back from the boonies."

Spending a couple of hours in a restaurant would insure that I arrived home after O. F. was safely installed in front of the TV watching the evening programs. Meanwhile, what could go wrong? It was the middle of the afternoon. It wasn't as if I was going to be alone with Spider. And I did owe him that favor.

"All right," I said grudgingly. Wolfi's mom had begun to chat with an acquaintance, positioning herself so that she could keep the car under observation. Not for the first time, I was glad she was not *my* mother. I was relieved when the car started to move away from her and out of my neighborhood.

Spider turned left onto the Landstrasse, passing all three Kasernen. I assumed he was heading for the inn near Warner, where Lucius and I got acquainted. But he drove on toward the forest. My hand flew to the door handle. He chuckled. "It's all right. There's a restaurant in there."

He was correct. In the middle of the woods, surrounded by conifers, oaks, and a variety of other deciduous trees, we came to a small but respectable-looking inn. Two cars were parked in the lot, which seemed just about the right amount for the dead hours between lunch and dinner. "What time do they start to serve?" I asked nervously.

"Any time I show up," Spider bragged. "The waitress is a friend of mine."

The dining room was scented with pipe tobacco and diminishing lunch odors. Two of the long tables were occupied by a group of pensioners. Judging from the walking staffs leaning against the nearby wall I guessed the men belonged to some sort of hiking club and were enjoying a respite of beer, smokes, and congenial conversation. It stopped when Spider entered, wearing his silly derby and tapping his fancy ebony cane along the floor, leading me to a secluded table. I sat facing away from the crowd and tried my best to look inconspicuous.

"Trudi," Spider told the red-haired waitress who greeted him profusely when she brought our menus. "I got a favor to ask." He beckoned her closer until she stood with her ear to his mouth. Then he murmured something too low and fast for me to understand.

She sucked in her breath, looked at me, and gave him a playful shove. "Go on! You wouldn't!" Her English was better than mine but I suspected she had not learned a single word of it in a classroom. Spider whispered again. She laughed and shook a finger at him. "You're too much. They ought to lock you up and throw away the key." He caught her arm; something passed from his hand to hers. "No skin off my nose," she said, stuffing whatever it was into her apron.

"Ain't that the truth!" Spider stretched his mouth into a lazy smile. "Now quit your gossiping, Trudi. My friend here is hungry. We want two Wiener Schnitzels. How long do you think it'll take?"

With a lazy shrug, she said, "You know we don't usually do dinners till five. The cook will have to make everything from scratch for you. It'll be half an hour, at least. Why don't you drink a couple of beers while you wait?"

"Not for me," I blurted. "I want a glass of milk, please."

She giggled and jabbed Spider's arm with her elbow as if I'd said something funny.

"They don't have any of that junk here. Sorry," he said firmly. "Tell you what—Trudi will bring you a *dark* beer. Tastes like malt and is very nutritious. It's the light beer that tastes sour." He started to wave her away.

"If there is no milk, bring me some water," I insisted.

They looked aghast. Trudi forced out a laugh. "You don't come to a Gasthaus to drink water. Water's free. The creek outside is full of it. Here we're in the business of selling beer."

Spider slapped the table with glee. "Atta girl, Trudi. Two *Mass*. One dark, one light."

She nodded, appeased, leaving us for her errand.

"Hey," Spider said, leaning back in his chair. "What's the big deal, Maria? From what I hear your people feed it to their babies by the spoonful. Nothing better for you than Bavarian beer." After a casual look around, he pulled the cognac bottle out of his jacket, along with two brass shot glasses. "This is an old trick I learned," he said, filling both. "Drinking a little cognac ahead of your beer will make it taste much smoother."

Trudi returned with the two *Mass* and set them before us. The light beer looked golden and the dark was a transparent, mysterious brown. They came in thick glass mugs that had round indents, like thumb prints, all along the outsides. I matched my thumb to the hollows, wiping off the condensation.

Trudi shook her head at the cognac, sighing theatrically. "I see you're leaving nothing to chance. Spider, you're too much. You kill me!"

"Not today, Trudi," he said. "Go help the cook shell our peas, why don't you."

When she was gone Spider pushed my portion of cognac at me. "Let's just follow my plan," he said. "*Prosit*!" He picked up his tumbler and waited until I picked up mine. We drained them at the same time. I was barely able to suppress a shudder as liquid fire spread through me. In contrast the beer was pleasantly cool and thirst-quenching. Before I knew it I had emptied my entire *Mass* (tankard). Wiping the foam from my lips, I asked companionably, "Do you come from Maryland, like Duncan?"

He finished his mugful, smacked his lips, and said, "No, I'm from California. After we get out of the service I'm gonna help him get settled in my home town."

"Los Angeles?" I guessed.

"Almost. I grew up in a sweet little place called Compton."

"Is it by the ocean? Do you have palms and oranges growing on trees?"

"We got palms," he said, "but the beach is one town over. Long Beach, it's called. I'm sure there are some orange groves around there somewhere." He refilled my shot glass and pushed it against my hand.

"You live near a long beach?" I asked. "Do you go fishing?"

He stared at me, then said, "Sometimes I catch me a good one. It takes patience." He nodded at the shot glass and the two fresh mugs of beer Trudi was lowering between us.

She picked up the empties, announcing, "It won't be long now. The Schnitzels are sizzling in the pan as we speak." She winked at Spider and left me to his plan.

"How about a race, Maria?" he asked. "Let's see who can finish faster. We'll drink to the long beach." We clicked our tumblers together, emptied them, and tackled our second mugs of beer. Mine went down even more smoothly than the first one had. I slammed my glass onto the table empty. I had won. Spider's was still half-full.

"You beat me! Hot Dog!" he cried, shaking his head in exasperation. "You got room for one more *Mass*?"

Maybe he thought I'd be tipsy by now, but I was made of stronger stuff than most. In fact, I had to marvel at my own clear-mindedness. I seemed to be getting more alert with each beer. "But of course," I said grandly. "If I visit the WC first."

He jerked his thumb toward the hall. "Ladies' room's that-away."

I nodded gravely and stood up. My head seemed to be much farther from the floor than it had been when we arrived. Spider's half-smile became fixed. Leaning forward, he slid his shades to the tip of his nose. I let go of the table to take my first tentative step. And then the room grew still as the chatting men paused to watch me as I carefully placed my second foot onto a floor that seemed to be sliding away.

If they expected I would slide right along with it they were about to be disappointed. I imagined a straight line between me and the hall and concentrated on gliding toward it with incredible poise, chin high, back straight. Whatever kind of test this was I was determined to pass it. Mustn't let on that the room was tilting. Mustn't let Spider see how vulnerable I had become. At last I reached the hall and trailed my hand along its steadying wall. Behind me, conversations resumed, interspersed with guffaws.

Still carefully balancing one foot in front of the other, I passed a big door that was slightly ajar. I pushed at it just enough to see the cook and Trudi sitting at a worktable between two ranges and a sink, newspaper sections spread before them. They were not shelling peas. The stovetops were immaculate—and empty. Neither pot nor pan sizzled upon them. With my newfound clarity I understood what had passed from Spider's hand to Trudi's and why.

I did not owe Spider any favors. He had lied *for* me as easily as he had lied *to* me. His sole reason for bringing me to this out-of-the-way place was to get me dead-drunk. Well, he would not succeed. I negotiated the rest of the hall with renewed vigor. At last my hand found the door to the WC. Quietly, I let myself in, locking the door from the inside. I realized all at once who Spider reminded me off—Sporting Life, the bad little man who took Bess away from Porgy. Mutti and I had seen the movie together last summer. I had been enchanted by Sidney Poitier.

I would not go back to the table. The window above the toilet was a bit high but I was a good climber, especially on an empty bladder. I sat on the commode and listened to an endless stream of urine passing into the bowl. Somewhere in the middle of the exercise I closed my eyes and could not open them again. Try as I might, my lids remained stuck firmly together. Every now and then I listed to one side or another, slipping toward the floor. Each time I managed to haul myself upright again, telling myself sternly that it was time to proceed.

Then a loud rap brought me to my senses. Trudi called, "You in there! Are you all right? You been on the toilet a long time."

"I am fine, thank you," I replied with great dignity. "I will be done in a minute."

But when the minute was up I was still glued to the seat.

There was another rap. Spider said, "Maria, your Schnitzel's getting cold. You best come on out now."

"Certainly. I will be right there," I told him, taking care to pronounce each word distinctly.

Trying to listen to their muttered conversation, I heard ". . . falling asleep. . ." and "Go get the key."

The proposed outrage to my privacy motivated me to rearrange my attire, slip off Mutti's heels, climb onto the toilet, and drop the shoes out of the window. I pulled myself up to the sill, painstakingly turned around, and lowered myself to the outside, feet first.

When the door handle rattled and a key scraped in the lock, I was already retrieving the heels. Clutching them tightly, I ran around the nearest corner and made straight for the woods, not stopping until the occasional noise from a car passing on the Landstrasse was no more than a hum. Only then did I notice that I was bareheaded. I'd lost Mutti's hat somewhere behind me but there was no way I was going back to retrieve it.

CHAPTER 27

I FOUND A CLUSTER OF BUSHES IN THE MIDDLE of the forest and crawled to its center, falling asleep before I could properly lie down. Waking hours later I stuck my head in the creek until the world stopped revolving around me. I stumbled on, brambles tearing my stockings to shreds. I peeled them off and tossed them under a bush. After I stepped on several sharp objects I put on the accursed heels, but only until I found my way out of the woods. Then I took them off for the last time and vowed never to wear them again. My hair dried on the long walk home. It was late when I finally made it to our building. The light was still on in the kitchen and the lobby door was unlocked. Plodding upstairs, I gathered the courage to ring our bell.

Mutti opened the door so fast I suspected she'd been waiting behind it. Her face underwent several unpleasant changes as she slowly registered my disheveled appearance. In my sincere effort to rinse a grass stain off the dress hem I had smeared on mud from the creek bank. Both smudges lingered. She skipped right past where-were-you and why-are-you-so-late to the important stuff. "You're wearing my new dress! My God, you've ruined it! And my heels are all scuffed!"

"I went for a walk in the woods," I said lamely. "I got lost."

She yanked me into the apartment. Regrettably, O.F. was sitting at the kitchen table and watched her shove me into the bedroom, but not before I'd seen the wine bottle and two long-stemmed glasses on the table before him.

"Anna's later than me," I pointed out when I realized the bedroom was empty.

"You leave her out of it," Mutti said. "She's still at the studio. Herr Obdach is driving her home in his BMW when they're done. Now give me my things. At once!"

Without another word I divested myself of the jacket, undid the belt, and stepped out of the dress. Then I took off her pretty emerald jewelry, glad the earrings had strong fasteners, and put the whole set in her cupped hand. Since she didn't know I had also borrowed her favorite hat I thought it unwise to mention I'd lost it.

As I stood exposed to her fury in my thin slip Seppi growled on the other side of the door. Mutti opened it abruptly to find O.F.'s eyes at keyhole level. "This does not concern you," she told him coldly. "Please wait for me in the living room."

He straightened at once. "I just wanted to make sure you give her the punishment she deserves. You've made an admirable start."

She slammed the door in his face and hung the jacket over the handle. "There are leaves in your hair!" she muttered, brushing them off. "Your cheeks are scratched. So are your shins. We were about to call the police when you deigned to arrive. Your sister is working hard to meet a business deadline and you smell of beer and get lost in the woods." She pinched my ear and propelled me in front of the mirror. "Take a good look at what you've become!"

I glimpsed a shifty-eyed stranger crowned with a bird's nest of frizz interwoven with twigs. If I told her now I had done nothing wrong even I'd be hard-pressed to believe it.

"You. . ." she said, pointing at my sorry image, ". . . are running wild. Thank God you start a full school day tomorrow. Judging from Frau Zimmer's report you are a deplorable typist. From now on I want you to practice on my typewriter for two hours when you get home. Every day. Then you'll spend an hour on shorthand and another on math. That's what I did before I applied for my job. It is true that practice makes perfect. And now I'd advise you to lie down without saying peep. I may recover my temper by morning."

I was under my covers before she could finish closing the door behind her. Unfortunately, the room spun worse once I was in the horizontal position.

"Is that how you're punishing her? By letting her go back to school?" O.F. asked incredulously on the other side of the door. "You should have let me call the police. One look at her and they would have hauled her off to the Anstalt (institution)."

"For ruining a dress? I think not!" she replied. "In any case, please remember that my daughters are my responsibility." She paused to wrestle with her temper, and continued more cordially with, "And now I must ask you to unlock your closet door long enough to bring out the typewriter. You may still use it on weekends but Marianne needs to practice her basics during the week."

"That's out of the question," he told her. "I can't have her grubby fingers all over the keys. She'll break it on the first day. You know how clumsy she is."

"No, I do not," she said. "And I'm afraid I must insist. It is *my* typewriter. I decide what to do with it. She will practice here at the kitchen table so I can keep my eyes on her while I cook."

"No," O.F. said.

"No, what?" she asked in a dangerous tone.

"I'm keeping the typewriter for myself." He sounded uncommonly rational. "If your wayward daughter needs to practice you'll have to make other arrangements."

Something big crashed against the wall. Seppi yowled and began to bark shrilly. There was the sound of a brief scuffle and then Mutti shoved him through the bedroom door. "Take care of your dog!" she shouted at me. "He's getting on my nerves!"

This time she locked me in.

"He's beginning to be a real nuisance," O.F. agreed sweetly. "Did you hear him growling at me? Soon he'll bite, never doubt it. It's time we did something about him."

"I told you before—he stays!" she cried. "What dog wouldn't growl with all the discord around here?"

"Do stop shouting, Lottchen," he said with the air of someone who is tired of asking. "Please remember—as head of this household I don't need your permission for anything I decide. And as far as your delinquent daughter is concerned, you must allow me to share in her discipline for as long as she is resides under this roof. Basta (case closed)! Now be so good as to clean up the wine before it leaves a permanent stain on the wall." With uncharacteristic restraint, he marched from the room.

In vain I waited for her to break down and weep over her dustpan. Instead she muttered darkly to herself, slamming chairs left and right, searching for shards. Something odd was happening to the household dynamics. It was almost as if she and O.F. had reversed positions. Except, of course, that his sweetness was not genuine. I sensed something dangerous lurking beneath it— as if he'd concocted some kind of scheme and nothing she said or did would dissuade him. Her reaction was even stranger. Was it the wine? Her doctor had prescribed a glass of red with dinner at night to relieve excessive anxiety. In my opinion it was working too well.

*

MUTTI LEFT for work early the next morning. Herr Obdach swung by to take Anna to Grünwald. He offered me a ride into town. That left O.F. alone in the apartment, a fact that made me faintly uneasy. But I'd given Seppi a quick walk and he was blissfully installed on my bed by the time Anna locked the door and we left. I had to be in school early to sign up for additional classes. The only one I was looking forward to was German because I had always excelled in the subject. The advisor insisted I also take bookkeeping, business math, and economics even though I disliked anything to do with numbers. They left no room for my imagination.

The economics teacher was the same drab, unappealing woman I had for stenography. She had an impatient streak but appeared generally mild. It wasn't until she walked up to a tall, gangly boy named Rudi, who was sprawling in the front row, that I realized she had a dark side. He muttered something I couldn't quite hear. Then, without any warning, she slapped him across the face so hard her hand left a white imprint. It quickly turned red. He started to leap at her but thought better of it and slouched, rubbing his cheek. "One more remark like that and you are expelled," she told him calmly, crimson with rage. "And I don't have to remind you it will be for the last time."

I wondered what he could have said to bring on such wrath. Maybe she had found his lazy posture offensive. In case she was looking for additional victims, I shrank down in my seat, hoping to escape her notice.

Eva was in my German class, too. The instructor, Herr Schreiner, asked me to sit in the vacant desk to her right. He was a tall, brown-haired young man wearing a corduroy jacket with elbow patches—an almost impossible feat in a school where every male, regardless of age, was expected to dress in a formal suit and tie, and every female was required to don secretarial garb. Herr Schreiner wrote *How I spent my Summer Holidays* on the blackboard. It brought on a class-wide groan but after the vacation I'd been through I thought it a brilliant essay topic. The method we were supposed to employ was compare and contrast. With great pleasure I chose my two failed apprenticeships and spent the next hour deliriously happy as my fountain pen flew from line to line and page to page. When the class was over I floated reluctantly back down to earth.

I had just as much fun in the English class. Herr Neuhof asked me to read a page of text out loud to the class and I did so with great aplomb and pleasure. During mid-morning break I sat on my heels under the Linden tree. Eva joined me, introducing an over-dressed classmate who was as dark as Eva was light. Gisela immediately launched into a long discussion about her voluptuous divorced mother who was a real Italian and was giving her makeup lessons at home. "You should see her vanity table," she boasted. "Bottles upon bottles of liquid makeup for every skin tone. Lipstick colors of every shade. Her perfumes come in tiny little bottles and are so potent they can only be applied one drop at a time. All gifts from her many admirers."

Eva took out a cigarette and moved to the far side of the tree so she would not be visible from the rest of the yard, offering Gisela an occasional drag. "So," Eva said after a couple of minutes. "What did you get on your English quiz, Marianne?"

"I did okay," I said modestly.

"You got a One," she said flatly. "And I got a Five. Because you wouldn't let me copy."

"Because you didn't study for the test, you mean."

"If you'd let me copy I wouldn't have to study for tests," she said.

"But then you wouldn't actually learn anything."

"If I wanted to learn English I'd go to a translator school. You want to know why I'm here? Why most of us are here?"

"Why?"

"Because our parents don't know what to do with us, that's why. This so-called school is just a place to drop off unruly offspring too old for the sitter. Me, I've got my own plans. They include Herr Schreiner or Rudi—I haven't decided which, yet. They're both tall and have more spunk than the rest of the idiots in this place."

"Make it Rudi," Gisela said. "I hear he's quite forward. Herr Schreiner likes the Latin type. He's always looking at me when he thinks I won't notice."

"That's how much you know! He borrowed a cigarette from me outside the lady's room last week," Eva bragged. "I gave him the one I was just lighting. It had a lipstick stain on it. He looked deep into my eyes when he thanked me. I can hardly wait until he pays it back. We'll have to arrange our tête-à-tête off-campus, of course. The administration has strict rules about that."

Gisela glared, grinding Eva's spent cigarette under her heel. Then she gave an acquiescing shrug. "I suppose I could go for the new bookkeeping teacher. He's a bit short but he's a much spiffier dresser than the other two. I'll ask my mother to arrange for tutoring sessions. After regular school hours."

I reached behind me to rub my fingers over the rough bark of the Linden tree. It was the most real thing in the yard. I was still touching it when Gisela looked me over and said, "Hey, why don't we go to my house for lunch? I could do wonders with your face. I admit the rest of you is beyond me." Her eyes razed my childish school skirt, knee socks and flat leather shoes, then lingered on my tent-like blouse. "Myself, I'm wearing two bras," she went on. "It really helps the contours until nature takes over."

The bell rang, saving me from having to think of an appropriate response. For once I was glad I could escape to the typing class. I sat in front of my machine, back erect, head to the left, copying *geh* and *hase* on alternate lines of the page and wondering if Mutti had managed to get her typewriter away from O.F.

The rest of the day passed in a blur of numbers and DM signs. On the way to the bus stop I had a brief bout of envying Anna who didn't have to learn any of this. All she had to do was pick up something to draw with and then draw it. It hardly seemed fair. The idea that I had to spend identically boring days five times a week over the next two years was depressing. I was tired when I got home. The first thing I did when I entered the living room was throw open the balcony doors to get rid of accumulated O.F. smells. Mutti had won; the typewriter was sitting on the oaken desk. There was a sheet of paper inserted into the roller.

```
    Marianne!
    I must insist that you do not snack before
or during your lessons. Please wipe each key with
a damp rag every night, especially on Fridays. If
your next report card contains anything below a
Two, I will make sure you quit school and enter
into another apprenticeship. I will choose where.
    —Franz Hohner.
    P.S.:  It  is  time  you  learned  about
consequences. Therefore, I have disposed of
your dog. The decision is final.
```

The bedroom door was unlocked. Seppi's indent was still on my featherbed, along with some stray bits of shepherd-gray fur. But he was no longer there. Since I had seen Anna lock the door with my own eyes, O.F.

had either picked the lock or found another spare key. Even though logic told me that Seppi was not waiting for me at the stoop I bolted downstairs anyway and spent a futile half hour calling his name along the trail we usually took together. At the end, I knocked on Frau Keppler's door.

She didn't seem as glad to see me as she usually did, especially after I asked if she'd seen Seppi. "Your stepfather went off with his briefcase, the way he always does on Mondays," she said, averting her eyes as if she could not bear to look at me. "But then he drove the VW to the curb and went up to your apartment. A few minutes later he came out pulling Seppi along on a rope. The poor dog was resisting as hard as he could but it did him no good. Frau Huber saw the whole thing from her bedroom window. She leaned out and cried, 'For God's sake, Herr Hohner, you are strangling the dog!' When he shoved Seppi into the back-seat, the poor thing bawled as if—as if—" She took a shaky breath. "As if he knew he was never coming home again. Frau Huber was so upset that she started her labor. Her husband came straight from the office in a taxi to take her to the birth-clinic."

I stared at her. "Is she all right?"

"She *was* almost due. And it usually takes a long time for the first one," she said.

"Where do you think O.F. took Seppi?"

Helplessly, she shook her head. "It could be anywhere. He might have asked a vet to put him to sleep, or dumped him in some lonely woods. At least that way there would be some tiny hope . . ." She dabbed at her eyes with a handkerchief and said, "He was such a good fellow, too. Never did anything wrong. Pure spite, that's what it is."

I ran all the way back to the apartment and called Mutti at the office, forgetting that she no longer worked for Herr Adler. "She never gave me her new phone number," I told him when he answered. "And this *is* an emergency."

Herr Adler cleared his throat and said, "I happen to know she's gone for the day, Marianne. I saw her walk to the tram stop at five o'clock sharp. Is there anything I can do? I'm good in emergencies."

I hesitated, not wanting to expose our sordid private lives, but decided Seppi was more important than any notion of dignity. "O.F. dragged my dog off somewhere when the rest of us were gone. He left me a note saying he has disposed of him. Maybe Mutti knows what he means." I remembered the little exchange they had during their argument last night before she threw the wine bottle at the wall.

I heard a sharp intake of breath. Then Herr Adler said, "The first place to look is the pound. That's where a cheapskate like him would take a dog.

A regular vet costs money, you see. But I'm afraid it's closed for the night, Marianne. Look here—I have a dog of my own. A wonderful black-and-silver German shepherd. We dog-lovers must stick together. Tell your mother to call me as soon as she walks in the door. I'll drive you both to the pound in the morning. If we're lucky we'll get there in time."

"In time for what?"

"For a happy ending, dear girl. I like happy endings."

What an odd thing for him to say. Happy endings belonged in American movies.

CHAPTER 28

B ut Mutti insisted that Herr Adler was wrong. "O.F. wanted me to take Seppi to the pound for adoption. When I refused he decided to do it himself, is all. We'll just tell them we changed our minds. Don't worry, Seppi will still be there. An old dog doesn't get adopted that fast. One night at the pound isn't so bad. He'll forget all about it by the end of the week."

Still, she seemed glad Herr Adler was taking an interest, and grateful that he had offered to drive us there. She took the morning off and called my school to tell them I would be late. We were ready for Herr Adler long before he came.

At first Mutti was ill at ease with the boss who had so abruptly caused her to be transferred out of his office. But he chatted amiably with me about Ricky Nelson and told us about his Alex, who brought him his slippers at night and gently awoke him before the alarm clock rang every morning. "I'm not sure if he's taken on the job to please me or himself," he said. "He hates loud noises and my alarm is particularly shrill. I much prefer his method, though—a soft doggish nose blowing warm air at my cheek."

On that wet, overcast morning, the pound seemed a dismal place. The high wire fence surrounding it looked like a mantle of gloom. Mutti argued with the officer at the desk, who claimed he could not release Seppi because O.F. had insisted he was a dangerous biter and should be put down at once. He was awaiting execution on death row; they were not in the habit of issuing pardons. Mutti had to reveal personal details she obviously found embarrassing, especially in front of Herr Adler.

"There is nothing whatsoever wrong with Seppi," she said. "He's always done everything he is supposed to. He belongs to Marianne, not to my husband. He and I had a quarrel and he brought him to you in pure spite. Seppi has never bitten anyone. He just doesn't have it in him."

The officer asked a guard to escort us to the prisoner. Seppi was at the end of a long corridor, locked in a stinking cage so narrow he could not turn around. There was no blanket on the wire, nor was there so much as a bowl of water. His cage was in the third tier of a stack. Most of the dogs flattened themselves to their crate floors when we approached. Seppi was shivering uncontrollably.

The guard hauled him out like a sausage, tail end first. Seppi cowered at his feet. I knelt to put my arms around him. "Seppi, it's me," I sobbed. "I've come to take you home." But when he looked up his pupils were fixed; he didn't seem to recognize me. After we snapped on his leash and walked him out into daylight Herr Adler suggested we take him for a short stroll so he could stretch a bit and breathe in fresh air. Seppi lapped greedily at the first puddle we came to. His tongue was swollen and blue. "Why didn't they give him some water? I don't think he's had anything to drink in two days!" I said.

Mutti and Herr Adler looked at each other. "You see," he said, "if the dogs don't drink they won't need to empty their bladders. It's more convenient that way."

This time when Herr Adler dropped us off he agreed to come upstairs for the offered tea. He sat on the couch, appreciatively nibbling on a piece of Mutti's rich pound cake. Seppi put his full weight across my feet, shivering so hard that the floor vibrated. He must have known exactly what his jailers were planning for him the whole time he was stuck in that cage.

As Herr Adler casually looked around the living room I began to think it had been a bad idea for Mutti to invite her old boss. For all at once I saw flaws wherever I looked. The room was so small that each piece of furniture butted the next. The mahogany double-wardrobe, taking up most of one wall, loomed over us as if O.F. was hiding inside, spying on our little gathering. When I went to the bathroom I became acutely aware that the toilet was right next to the tub and the sink right next to the toilet. I prayed Herr Adler would not ask to use the facilities.

Mutti decided I should stay at home for the rest of the day to help Seppi readjust. Before she accepted a ride in Herr Adler's Mercedes she called a locksmith and asked him to replace the bedroom-door lock. While she was scheduling the work I saw Herr Adler looking at me with my peripheral vision, his face full of outrage and pity. Keeping my face blank, I thanked him stiffly for all the help he had given. I watched them drive off together, almost at ease with each other as they chatted. I hoped he would not come here again. It was no fun to see the apartment through his well-to-do eyes.

I gave Seppi a good brushing and a massage, and then I took him downstairs for a leisurely walk around the wheat field. At the end, we knocked on Frau Keppler's door.

"*Ach*!" she said, clapping her hands together, "You've found him! Wonderful! Do bring him in. He's looking somewhat subdued but we'll soon fix that." She offered Seppi a soup bone, which he sniffed at politely before turning it down. I explained where he had been. Placing her hand on his forehead as if conferring a blessing, she asked, "What are you going to do when your stepfather comes home on Friday?"

I shrugged. "Mutti is having the lock on my bedroom door changed. He won't be able to get in there again."

She nodded without comment and hand-fed Seppi small bits of cooked liver until he stopped shivering. Then she looked fully at me and said gently, "Do you really think you can keep Seppi safe?"

I assured her I could, and I believed what I said until O.F. arrived earlier than expected on Friday afternoon. I was practicing on the typewriter at one end of the kitchen table while Mutti chopped, mixed and grated at the other. Seppi was snoozing on his blanket. Somehow, we all missed the jingling of keys. The moment O.F. saw Seppi lying where he belonged he paled as if seeing a ghost.

"Marianne, why don't you take Seppi to your room," Mutti said, her voice shaky. "Franz and I have some things to discuss in private."

She lowered the flame under the boiling soup stock and preceded O.F. to the living room. He followed without saying a word. As soon as they were gone I took a glass tumbler out of the cupboard and locked Seppi and me in the bedroom. He crept under my covers while I took the drawers out of the dresser. I deposited all six of them on Anna's bed and then yanked the heavy piece of furniture aside just enough so that I could cup the tumbler to the wall.

Unfortunately, the conversation on the other side started out low. For a while it appeared as if Mutti had the upper hand. He actually stammered an apology for "misunderstanding her wishes" about Seppi, adding he had simply wanted to spare her feelings by taking matters into his own hands. But then she mentioned something about a mouse, a hamster, and the commode. O.F. raised his voice until I could hear him just fine without the tumbler, shouting, "If it doesn't hurt, it isn't punishment. Nothing you have tried is the least bit effective. If it had been up to me I would have made her watch the dog die. It would have cured what ails her real fast."

Behind me, Seppi gave a desperate moan. I went to reassure him and found him entirely rigid. Then he peed all over the mattress. I sat down beside him and had a mental glimpse of something tiny and white with a long, pink tail being tossed into the toilet bowl. Unlike the hamster, Elvis was small enough to be flushed without leaving a trace.

Clearly, O.F. was determined to take away from me everything that I loved. I had no doubt that before long he would finish Seppi off permanently, even if he had to call a locksmith to get at him—and that Seppi knew it as well as I did. I ran my hands over his terrified back, wishing I could massage all the love I had into him. Then I snapped on his leash and led him out of the apartment.

He dragged his feet like a cripple on our way downstairs, his tail tucked between his legs. It wasn't until we rang Frau Keppler's bell that it came out of hiding. She opened her door. I placed the leash in her hand and said, "I couldn't bear to give him up to anyone but you. You were right—I can't keep him safe anymore. He'll be much happier here. Will you do me the honor of taking my dog?"

*

THEN I scrubbed my mattress, changed the sheets, lay down and did not move for the rest of the day. I left the food Mutti brought me untouched. When she asked what was wrong I told her that I had given Seppi away. She looked relieved. Now she and O.F. would have one less thing to fight about.

Once she was gone I whispered three terrible words: "Elvis ist tot (is dead)." He was not happily gnawing on roots in the wheat field, free to go his own way as I had envisioned—but at least he'd died fast, unlike the hamster, who'd scrabbled for a foothold in the commode until he tired and slipped under. How long did O.F. stand there and watch? If Herr Adler hadn't interfered Seppi would be dead by now, too. But that wasn't the worst of it. Mutti had suspected what O.F. had done and had nevertheless pretended all was well. Pretended to me or to herself?

*

THE TELEPHONE started to shrill early on Saturday morning. Anna and I were both reading in bed. We counted six rings. Then she said, "O.F. must be in the cellar getting pinecones. I bet it's Horst." She leaped up and fumbled with the key. The phone rang two more times before she got our bedroom door open. I squeezed out ahead of her and dashed to the living room. There was something insistent about the rings, drawing me on. I managed to grab the receiver before Anna could, clutched it firmly to my ear when she tried to wrestle it away, and announced, "Kaspar's Scheuer-Tücher (scrub-clothes)."

For a few seconds the line remained silent and then Lucius asked, "Maria? Is that you? Can you talk?"

"Nein," I said, forcing myself to sound neutral.

Anna eyed me suspiciously.

"I just got back from maneuvers," he went on. "Dumped all my stuff on my bunk and ran straight for the phone. Can I see you today? For three hours. That's all the time the CO is willing to give me. He and I are on the outs."

"Ja, doch (sure)," I said, struggling to come up with some German phrase Lucius might recognize that did not give me away to my sister.

"How about right now? Bring your bike. I'll wait for you at the gate. We'll go riding together. Okay?"

"*Fein,*" I said.

"Fine?"

"*Ja, gut. Also, ich komme dann sofort mit dem Fahrrad. Ich freue mich schon. Tschüs!* (Okay, then, I'm coming on my bike right away. I'm looking forward to it.)"

He laughed. "Is that a 'yes'? I hope I'm not getting you into trouble. I was going to hang up if someone else answered. But after four weeks I couldn't wait one more minute. See you soon."

I hung up and casually told Anna, "It was a classmate, from the Handelschule."

"*That* was a girl's voice?" she scoffed, her eyes wary.

"She smokes. It makes her sound husky." It might well have been Eva, who was obviously heading in that direction. "We're going to ride our bicycles for a couple of hours. Want to come?" I was reasonably sure she had something else planned for today and would decline. I watched her struggling to believe me. Then she relaxed and shook her head.

"Horst is picking me up in an hour. I'm hoping O.F. will let me have the first bath."

"Good luck. If he says no you can always have my turn." I felt numb one second for telling lies and grateful the next simply for being alive. I dressed in a big hurry and waited impatiently until we heard O.F. bump into the apartment with his box. While Anna talked to him in the bathroom I tiptoed through the hall and flitted down to the basement for my bike.

*

LUCIUS beamed as he watched me ride up to the gate. "You're the first real female I've seen for weeks," he said, mounting his blue racer. "And you're even prettier than I remembered."

He seemed different to me. More gaunt, perhaps. Less polished. In fact, he looked as if he needed a nap and a good soaking, in that order. All at once I felt shy. After four weeks of being apart we were strangers again. I was glad we were riding along the Landstrasse single file so that I could study him from the rear, unabashed. We passed Henry, Williams, and the storage sheds with the one open door and the motorcycle. As we drew level with the Gasthaus on the other side of Warner Kaserne Lucius stopped to look at the big chestnut tree we'd sat under for our first meal.

"That day will always be special to me," he said wistfully. "I don't have any cash on me today, so I brought these." He indicated the brown paper bag squeezed onto his luggage rack. "C-rations I saved from maneuvers. There's another Gasthaus halfway through the woods. Maybe we could get some sodas there later. To wash down the cake."

It was the inn where Spider had tried to entrap me, but I was not about to mention that misguided adventure.

Once we got to the forest, we leaned our bikes against a tree and hiked to the brook. We took off our shoes and socks, rolled the bottoms of our pants to the knees, and splashed upstream.

The last time I'd been here I'd followed the flow of the water, hoping to find the rim of the forest before Spider found me. Somewhere nearby I had snaked down the bank and immersed my head in cold water to clear away the mental fog brought on by his scheme. Was Mutti's beige hat still on my head at that point? I'd pushed the empty hat stand to the back of her closet shelf the next day, rearranging things to fill the gap its absence created. I fervently wished I could find the hat on this outing. I'd have it cleaned and back in its place before she knew it was lost.

I kept scanning the banks while Lucius sang, "Michael, row the boat ashore, hallelujah . . ." His voice was as lovely as it had been on our first date, with the same silvery treble I had found so delightful when we walked through the rain under his black family-sized umbrella. Then I recalled how unpleasantly that night had turned out.

At the end of each verse of the Michael song he skimmed a flat stone over the brook's surface. Reluctantly, I began to hum along. "Good, now we can sing round robin," he said. Next to his voice mine sounded decidedly childish but if he didn't mind, neither would I. We sloshed and sang until, looking up, I saw the whitewashed wall of the inn through the trees.

"Strange place for a Gasthaus. What kind of business can they get, way in the middle of nowhere?" Lucius wondered.

I told him it was not a nice place. Nonetheless, I led the way to the parking lot and then to the bathroom window but the hat was not there.

Lucius rummaged for change. "Cokes?"

"I don't like Coke," I reminded him. How could he have forgotten so soon? "In the restaurants you always ask for a glass of water. Here is a brook full with it. Free." We reversed directions, settling on a mossy spot on the bank long after the Gasthaus was out of sight. Lucius took four unlabeled gray cans out of his bag. He opened two, tipped them, and rapped sharply on the sealed ends. Two moist yellow cylinders popped out. He gave me one.

"Pound cake. Our main course," he said.

The cake's color reminded me of a particularly obnoxious shade of plastic, unlike the rich tint Mutti imparted to hers with egg-yolks and butter. The canned version's overpowering sweetness seemed to cover less pleasant flavors but I was more than hungry enough to ignore those minor faults.

"Ready for dessert?" Lucius asked when I was done. He opened the other two cans, which contained rock-hard blocks of cocoa-mix. "If you add boiling water, these are supposed to make delicious hot chocolate," he said, sounding doubtful. "But I like to gnaw on the blocks. Gives your teeth something to do. Providing they don't crack." We sat in companionable silence, finished our portions, and waded back into the stream to rinse our mouths and make cold chocolate milk in our stomachs. Then we sat on the bank, keeping our feet in the water. "This is nice. Peaceful, like," Lucius sighed. "Much better than crawling around on the forest floor with a rifle. Thanks for your letters. Every time they shouted my name at mail call I felt like a star. Sorry I only squeezed out three. I'm not a fast writer, especially after dark. Did you get them all right?"

"The second one never came." I wished I had listened to my intuition when we were sitting on top of the Schuttberg and he'd promised to time his letters so they would arrive on a Wednesday and would never ever call me on a weekend. After a few hang-ups Mutti would start to wonder.

"Can Old Fart read English?" he asked.

"Not a word."

"Then he won't understand a thing, even if he does open the envelope. Nothing in there to be ashamed of, anyway." Lucius stretched and lay down, putting his head on my lap, more like a small boy needing to cuddle than a man taking liberties. I held still, trying to get used to the nearness of him. After a couple of minutes I dared to touch his wooly curls, grown long in the month he spent away from his barber. He did not object. Up close, his skin shone like black tea in a clear glass held up to the light. His ears, as brown as the rest of him, were fragile shells. But my favorite parts of his head were still the thin, flawlessly arched blue-black eyebrows and the matching curled lashes beneath.

In the filtered light his irises looked so black that I could not tell them apart from his pupils as he put a hand behind my neck and slowly pulled me close. "Can I kiss you?" he murmured. Immediately, I stopped stroking his hair and whipped out my hand. He blocked it and then cradled it between his. "All right," he said. "All right."

I recalled two of the illustrations from the sex manual, overlain with Herr Möller's censoring eyes, and burned with shame. "We are friends," I said sternly. "I am a Catholic girl. We do not kiss before we marry. It is the rule."

"Heck," he said. "I'll marry you. Tomorrow. Just say the word."

"I am too young."

"How old do you have to be?"

"Sixteen when parents say yes."

"Fat chance," he said, releasing my hand. "We *could* go to Gretna Green. I heard anybody can get married there, no questions asked."

I didn't understand what he meant, nor did I care to. Clearly the head resting on my lap was less boyish than I had imagined. I shifted until it slipped to the ground and tried to make up for the rebuff by picking pine needles out of his hair.

"Gretna Green's a little town in Scotland," he explained, warding me off. "If I was married I could live off-base. In an apartment. With you. The Army would be like a regular job. Wouldn't need to ask for a pass anymore. I'd be free."

He made it sound like a business proposal. "You have money for this trip?" I asked. "For the apartment?"

"Not exactly. Besides, my CO would have me shot for going AWOL. And I have the funny feeling I'm supposed to get the Army's permission before I get hitched. I told you—they treat me like a child." Even though he managed to sound casual, even glib, his eyes were alert to every nuance of my response.

I said, "I knew it would be a bad idea to give you my phone number. I want it back. I will keep yours. From now on, I will call you."

He grunted something that might have been reluctant assent, opened his wallet, and dropped a crumpled piece of paper on my lap. I wadded it up and tossed it into the creek. We watched it float away.

"Now what?" he asked, no longer smiling.

"Now we begin again," I said. "Both of us older and wiser."

He was silent for what seemed like a long time. Then he chuckled. "You know, Maria, I think your English has really improved. Who's been helping you while I was gone?"

I laughed, relieved by his good-natured reaction. "The AFN. London newspapers. My English textbook. But I still don't understand all the words to Ricky Nelson's song."

"Which one?"

I hummed the melody.

"Ah! *There'll never be*," he said with a broad grin. "I know every verse. Listen up." He started to sing the lyrics with his soft silvery voice, every word clear and easy to understand and just right for us except for that one line about kissing. The whole time he sang his eyes locked with mine, and when he had finished the last verse I recognized the Lucius he had been before he went away to the war-games. And I understood exactly what I would gain if we lived together in our own place. I would never have to go back home anymore because *he* would be my home for the rest of my life.

I couldn't imagine a better ending.

He held out his hand. I placed mine in it. We looked at the dark and light skins, complementing each other.

"They belong together, don't they?" he asked, making an effort to be casual. I nodded. "And if we make up our minds that nothing in the world will come between us," he went on, "we can overcome anything. Together. Right?" His eyes locked with mine.

I held his gaze, feeling fearless. "Right."

"Let's make a pact." He raised our hands toward the sky like an offering. "With a little help from up there we'll be married as soon as you turn sixteen. And nothing and no one can stop it. What do you say?"

I thought of Mutti's disapproving, pained face, O.F.'s ill-disguised hatred, Anna's indifference, and Vati's frozen heart and permanent absence. I would have to fight through all the obstacles they would place in our path.

"Why?" I asked, looking into Lucius's eyes. Surely there were easier ways of defying authority figures. "Get married why?"

He put my hand against his cheek. "Didn't I say it?"

I shook my head.

"Because we lo . . . lo . . . love each other."

The forest grew very silent. So did my heart. I said, "Yes. We do."

These words were worth fighting for.

I had no doubt we would win in the end.

CHAPTER 29

ON OUR RIDE BACK TO HENRY KASERNE I BEGAN TO suspect that we had only been indulging in a bit of wishful thinking. With each turn of my pedals the sky seemed to shrink a bit more, dimming the afternoon light. It was as if a heavy curtain was drawing shut between me and the world. At home there was no book left to read, no dream left to dream, and no dog to keep me company. Even Lucius, cruising his French racer, grew hazy in front of my eyes. "Why must you go back to your barracks so soon?" I asked when he stopped at the access road leading to Henry. "What is the reason?"

He played with his gear shaft. "Only that the CO ordered me to scrub down our company's bathrooms with a toothbrush. On my hands and knees. To teach me a lesson I'm not willing to learn."

"What is the lesson?"

"That he is God," he said with a morose smile.

"Will you be done with the bathrooms by tomorrow afternoon?" I asked heartlessly. "The Oktoberfest is starting and you promised we go there together. To ride the big wheel. What do you call it again?"

"Ferris wheel."

"From its you can see everything. There is a parade tomorrow, too. Costumes from near and far. Very interesting to watch."

"No," he said. "I don't like parades. Next thing you know all those people watching it will turn around and watch me. But if I scrub real hard the CO might let me get on the big wheel with you."

"And the *Achterbahn*!" I drew a figure eight in the air, having forgotten the equivalent English word.

"Roller-coaster," he reminded me. "What the heck. One way or another I'll be gone this time next year. This is my last chance at the famous Oktoberfest. If you show me what you like about it I'm bound to like it too."

I undid the string from around my neck and gave him Grandfather's ring so he could wear it to our date the next afternoon. We arranged to meet in front of the Hackerkeller and walk across to the festivities together. Then Lucius rode on to the gate without me, turned for one final wave, and disappeared around the bend.

Riding home I felt as if my feet were pumping up a steady incline. Briefly I considered staying out until dark but there was nowhere for me to go. When I came to our building I followed an impulse and knocked on Frau Keppler's door to ask for new reading material. She was glad to see me and invited me to browse through her bookshelves. Seppi was lying on her only upholstered chair, his front legs draped elegantly over an armrest.

"He took me on two long walks today already," Frau Keppler laughed, slapping her ample hips. "I can actually feel the fat melting away. He makes the apartment feel full—when it was always so empty before. And the neighbors have begun to be a bit friendlier. I can't thank you enough. By the way, Frau Huber had a healthy baby boy. Her husband said he's quite small but the doctor thinks he'll be strong enough to come home with her in two weeks when her confinement is over."

I chose a novel about Nefertiti, solely on the appeal of its cover. Seppi accompanied me to the door but showed no desire to follow me out. Not that I blamed him. In fact, right then, I wished I could stay with Frau Keppler, too.

I was glad to have something new to read even though I'd never considered the long-ago life of a giraffe-necked Egyptian queen riveting before. For the rest of the day I sat up in bed, turning pages. O.F. stayed quietly in the living room. At dusk I heard him switch on the TV. Mutti didn't come home till nine. Her face was glowing in a way it hadn't for a long time. "What took you so long?" I asked when she walked into my room. "I was afraid he'd start something. He would have, too, if he had known I don't have any way of locking the door."

Her smile seemed too bright for my cramped and dreary space. "One of my colleagues invited me to tea," she said, her cheeks turning pink. "We found so much to talk about that tea became supper." She gave me a plate with a couple of belegte Brötchen (finger sandwiches), covered with exotic, thinly sliced cheeses, and a generous dollop of Wurstsalat (sausage salad). "Made by the cook. I told her she was good enough to open her own restaurant. She was so pleased with the compliment that she would have given me all of the leftovers if I'd let her."

When I asked permission to go to the Oktoberfest, she said, "But the first Sunday is always so crowded! People sit elbow-to-elbow in every beer-tent. Why don't you wait until Anna's birthday next weekend? By then things will be a bit calmer. We'll go on all her favorite rides. It'll be like old times."

"Okay," I said. "But can't I go tomorrow too? Being alone in the house with O.F. gives me the creeps, now that I know what really happened to Elvis and the hamster."

She blanched. "You heard? Last night?"

I nodded. "The walls are like cardboard."

"Ja, so (oh)" Guiltily, she cast her eyes to the floor. Then she gave me ten whole *Mark* for the midway and casually mentioned that she had accepted her colleague's invitation to go on an afternoon stroll the next day. "I'm looking forward to it. And since O.F. dislikes hiking I guess he'll have the house all to himself while we're gone. No doubt he'll want to catch up on his typing."

"And snooping," I added. She did not rebuke me.

While I ate the best cheese sandwiches of my life and delved into Nefertiti's secrets, Mutti stripped the kitchen linoleum and applied a new coat of paste-wax. She was busy running the heavy polisher over it when Anna came home.

Long after my sister and I were in bed Mutti was still hard at work, relining shelves and washing down walls. A couple of times O.F. came to fetch her. She told him she was too busy. Once I peered through the keyhole wondering why things were so quiet on the other side and saw her sitting at the table, vaguely staring at recipes in her cookbook. The kitchen light stayed on even after O.F. had turned off the TV and converted the couch. The next time I looked her head had sunk to the tabletop and she was asleep.

Instead of going to Mass the next morning, I finished spying on the Egyptian queen and, on the spur of the moment, decided to ride the bus into town early so I could watch the parade before meeting Lucius. Maybe the enthusiastic cheering and clapping of the other onlookers would be catching, lifting my mood.

The streets were already lined five rows deep when I arrived. Just last year gracious mothers and fathers had moved aside to let me sit on the curb with their kids. They didn't budge for me this time. Luckily I had grown tall enough to look over the heads and shoulders of most of the adults standing in front. Everyone around me seemed to be part of some enviable social group—happy families were clustered together and singles joked and laughed with their best friends and next-door-neighbors.

Because I stood alone I was an easy target for Italian guest workers bent on making a sport of pinching young girls. Whenever I got nabbed I turned around quickly to discover the culprit but found all the sloe-eyed, raven-haired young men within slapping distance focusing innocently on the passing parade.

Then I got smart and wedged myself into a group of four local boys wearing identical white shirts, Alpine hats and leather pants. "*Ach*, those cheeky foreigners!" said a tall one the other three called Otto. "Someday one of them will pinch the wrong girl and her sweetheart's going to teach him a lesson." They made room for me but soon got distracted, eying a nearby gaggle of girls. Dressed in identical blue dirndls, the young ladies alternated between flirting with the boys and ignoring them.

I'd forgotten how outrageous some of the marchers' costumes could be. Each little village had its own Tracht (regional costume)variations. Whole clans of them, dressed alike, played brass instruments and waved gay banners as they passed before us. Today I mostly noticed ludicrous hats.

"Hey—these women have black flowerpots stuck on their heads!" Otto shouted. "Filled with red balls!"

I smiled in appreciation of his wit, thinking that *Otto* was one of those magical names that looked the same from both ends. He had nice dimples but his voice was a bit loud, as if he'd begun celebrating the Oktoberfest with a liquid breakfast made from hops, wheat, and barley. But why should I mind? As long as I remained at his side I could watch the parade without getting pinched. Together, we admired hats as tall as smokestacks and as flat as pie plates, with every possible shape in between.

Some of the marchers had decorated their hats with the beard of a mountain goat or elaborate bird feathers; others had stuck dried sheaves of grain, spruce twigs, and fresh-picked flowers in their hatbands. Every man wore leather pants, which came in an array of colors and lengths with unique, regional decorations on belts and suspenders.

Magnificent teams of draft horses were pulling festive brewery wagons stacked with flower-decorated beer barrels. A lot of the marchers belonged to *Schützen-Vereine,* associations of volunteer marksmen who watched over our irregular, mountainous borders.

The female participants consisted of stately proud matrons, eager young girls, and sparkling brides. Some wore ankle-length dirndls, others dared to reveal their calves. There were countless styles of puff-sleeved, low-cut blouses, chokers, pendants, shawls, vests, and jackets. And these were only the Bavarian entries. The delegates from Süd-Tirol (southern Tyrol), Austria and Switzerland were even more inventively turned out. The crowd had come to see a feast for the eyes and they were not disappointed. "I heard this parade is five kilometers long!" Otto shouted in my ear.

When it was finally over my hands were numb with clapping. As the music faded in the distance the onlookers began to amble toward the Oktoberfest grounds. What happened next was so repulsive to me that I vowed afterwards never to participate in anything like it ever again.

Some stealthy, invisible shadow-dragon moved through the cobblestoned street like a giant millipede, sucking up the souls of every young person nearby. I watched their faces grow dark and smelled sulphur. Then the dragon came for me.

One instant I was fully myself, slightly awkward and ill at ease. The next I was infected by a strange excitement that made me part of a frenzied army bent on mischief and destruction. Yelling and laughing, we turned over trashcans, smashed bottles, and pried stones from flowerbeds, throwing them at shop windows. Running beside a much altered Otto and his circle of friends I screeched mindlessly along with the rest of the millipede's rioting segments.

When my individual consciousness resurfaced I found myself in the middle of a mob that was trying to rock a streetcar off its tracks. Otto kept shouting, "One-two-three-go!" The rest of us put our shoulders to the carriage and heaved, determined to push it over onto its side, though none of us knew why. Looking up I saw the face of a dignified white-haired woman in the streetcar window above. She was staring straight ahead as if pretending we weren't there would make it come true.

Then police whistles blew and a squad of mounted officers rode us down. Their horses reared and kicked, pushing us away from the tracks. Some of the officers aimed a wide-open fire-hose at our ring-leaders, knocking them off their feet with a powerful spray. "Disperse!" the officers yelled. "Go have your fun at the Wies'n (Oktoberfest)!" Above me, the old woman continued to ignore us. Her strategy was working. We were beginning to drift apart.

The phantom that had stolen our souls now shook us out of itself and whooshed away. Otto scrambled up off the sidewalk, drenched and dazed, not knowing where he was or what he had done. He pulled his clinging shirt away from his chest and helped his friends to their feet. The girls, no longer giggling, were already trotting off, looking confused and ashamed. A subdued Otto ran after them, followed by his buddies. I headed in the same direction but at a more leisurely pace, as alone as I had been at the start of the parade and glad of it.

The nearer I came to the Theresienwiese the denser the crowd grew. I saw Lucius long before he saw me. He was standing stock-still in front of the Hackerkeller, looking ill at ease in his tan camelhair coat, pretending not to see people staring at him as if he were part of some African side-show. One of his coat pockets was bulging, and I remembered his intention of smuggling in a bottle of Coke. I waved when he glanced in my direction. He began to cross the street toward me with tentative steps as if expecting an ambush. Locals in a holiday mood, emerging from streetcars and busses, were streaming around him. The more well-heeled revelers climbed out of black taxis that were inching through the choked street in fits and starts.

"Are you hungry yet?" I asked when he was finally standing before me. "There are lots of good things to eat." I indicated the nearest stall, decorated with gigantic *Bretzen*. Another sold chocolate hearts wrapped in red cellophane and looped with red ribbons, and oversized *Lebkuchen* hearts on strings. I showed him one covered with a flourish of white frosting that said: *I hob di gean.* "It means 'I really like you' in Bavarian,' I told him. He was not impressed.

At the next booth, a vendor was turning *Bratwürste* on a grill. My mouth was watering. "You want a fried sausage?" I asked Lucius eagerly. "Or a roasted hen? Better yet, how about a fish-on-a-stick? Unless you'd rather have some of that ox stuck on that that spit over there!" I pulled him toward the gory spectacle and was puzzled to find him unresponsive. "Are you all right?" I asked. "You look sick."

"As a matter of fact, I *feel* sick," he said. "Is there someplace to sit?"

This was my chance to show him the inside of a beer tent, as any good tour guide would. "Of course," I said, slipping my arm through his, "Come with me." He resisted only briefly before he let me drag him through the crowd. The people in front of us divided to make room for a brewery team pulling a garlanded wagon. "Look," I told Lucius, "are the horses not beautiful?"

The huge draft-animals were bred and devotedly groomed for this job. Headdresses covered their ears, white fringes swept down to their eyes, great saddle-horns swayed on their backs. Their muscular necks and chests were bedecked with silver chains, buckles, and Bavarian banners featuring a blue and white diamond pattern. I pointed out their hooves, polished and shod with silver shoes.

I recognized the blue Löwenbräu tower nearby. In it sat a huge lion. "Watch!" I cried as the lion lifted a giant Masskrug (tankard) to his mouth, sipped, and then roared, "Mmmm! Löwenbräu!"

Lucius remained apathetic but I would soon fix that. "Come," I said, "I'll show you a piece of our Bavarian heaven! '

I pulled him into the Hackerbräu tent. It was massive inside, filled wall-to-wall with long tables and benches, all of them overflowing with laughing, yelling, and singing people who sipped from foaming glass mugs. A waitress rushed by, carrying ten of the mugs at once, five in each hand, some filled with dunkles (dark) beer, some filled with helles (light).

The middle of the tent floor was given over to a raised platform complete with a cheerful brass band, every musician wearing his Bavarian costume. In the web of green wreaths above their heads danced life-sized statues of coopers wearing the red uniforms of their guild, and above *them* stretched the tent top, cleverly transformed into a vast Bavarian sky complete with white fleecy clouds and huge golden stars. The tent walls were covered with giant cut-out replicas of iconic city buildings, including the twin-towered Frauenkirche.

"See the balcony up there?" I asked, pointing. "From it we can see everything!" I tried to draw him to the stairs but he wouldn't budge. Following the direction of his horrified gaze, I saw a man lean over the upstairs railing and puke an impressive stream on to the table directly below him. People shrieked and scattered, laughing hysterically. An overheated young woman climbed on the adjacent table, swaying to the music while she unbuttoned her blouse and then coquettishly lifted her skirt, showing off her dimpled knees.

Otto and his friends were sitting near the entrance, across from the four blonde, blue-dirndled girls. They had emptied every beer mug standing between them. Otto was banging his shoe on the tabletop to signal the waitress for refills. Then he recognized me and started to wave but stopped to stare past me at Lucius. He elbowed his buddies until they, too, stared at Lucius, their lips parting in awe. "Schau mal (look)!" Otto was yelling. "Ein richtiger Neger (a real Negro)!"

More and more eyes found us. This morning I would have called this a friendly and curious crowd, but that was before my experience with the mind-altering dragon. Lucius backtracked to the entrance without me, waiting just outside the door, one hand on his bulging coat pocket. I hurried to catch up.

"I meant someplace to sit where it's *quiet!*" he muttered, his lips etched in white.

I doubted there was a quiet corner anyplace at the Oktoberfest, especially on the first Sunday afternoon. But on impulse I led him around the side of the tent to where the hawkers had parked their transport trucks and trailers. I spotted a picnic table occupied by a harried mother and her three offspring. She was shaving a beer-radish into spirals to accompany the pork-leg specials she had bought for them. The kids squealed at our approach. Lucius groaned softly and rushed past them to the rear of the tent. And there was the only private spot on the whole Wies'n—one lone beat-up picnic table as yet undiscovered by the multitudes mingling in front, from which the lion was again roaring, "Mmmm! Löwenbräu!!!"

I sat down. "What is it, Lucius? What's wrong?"

"This!" He pulled a bundle out of his coat pocket and tossed it onto the table. It unfolded, becoming a hat. Mutti's beige hat. "Spider stopped me when I was leaving the barracks," Lucius said. "He asked was I meeting you and would I mind giving back the hat you left on the backseat of his car."

Dumbly, I said, "But I was never on the backseat."

His eyes flashed. "I was hoping you'd say it isn't your hat!"

"It isn't. It's my mother's."

He paled. "Then you're not denying you went out with Spider? In his car? While I was away?"

Words failed me. I picked up the hat, rubbed at a dried mud stain that surely had not been there before I lost it, and said reluctantly, "It's a long story."

He stopped me with a sweep of his hand. "I don't want to hear it. Truth is, Maria, it dawned on me on the way over here that I don't know you at all. I mean, I'm not even sure if you lie for a reason or just because you enjoy messing with my mind."

"I don't lie—" I began indignantly. But it was no longer true. Since I met him that part of my nature, so unflagging before, had become lost in a maze of trying to make things come out right for him and me while following everyone else's rules. I was smart enough to understand that an omission was also a lie; I had neglected to mention my adventure with Spider.

"There was nothing to tell . . ." I tried again, choking on my own words.

"Fact is," Lucius said, "you and I don't have anything in common. You're a sneak, and I like being straight. Can't call you at home, can't come to your door. Makes me feel worthless. And if I wanted to lie, I'd be a Spec 5 by now with the rest of the battalion's brown-noses. It's been nice and all but I've had enough. From now on I'd just as soon keep to myself. You want to eat a butchered ox? A dead hen? Here, be my guest. Buy yourself a souvenir while you're at it. One of those hollow chocolate hearts will be just the thing." He held out a clump of change, opened his hand, and let the coins spill to the ground.

Behind us the midway beckoned with its booths and freak shows. Carnival music cascaded enticingly from every ride. From inside the beer tents myriad voices shouted drinking songs over the blare of various horns. Then my ears ceased to interpret all sounds.

"You're wrong about me!" I said, the words dissolving into nothingness as soon as they came out of my mouth. Lucius reached into his other pocket, pulled out my grandfather's wedding ring, carefully laid it on the picnic table, and walked away. I stared at the spilled coins, the gold ring, and his receding back, unable to understand the finality of his gestures.

At last I started to chase after him, determined to offer a more detailed explanation of the hat incident. But he was already getting into one of those crawling black cabs. It crept off before I could reach it, the crowd swirling to close the gap it left behind. I stood watching it negotiate a corner. Lucius was riding out of my life. And then he was gone.

*

THE MINUTE I got home I tossed Mutti's hat into the darkest corner of my wardrobe, threw myself on my bed, and sobbed into my pillow. There I stayed, crying until Mutti found me. Clearly she'd had a better day than me, for once again she was glowing from somewhere within, smelling of pine sap and fresh forest air. "Marianne! What's wrong?" she asked, putting a hand on my heaving back. And then I spilled my terrible secret.

"I have a new friend," I confessed. "A black American soldier. He wants to meet you. *His* mother is dead. Can I invite him to tea?"

"There now, there now," she murmured, awkwardly patting my back. "Of course you can invite him. Of course you can." I sobbed on for a few minutes after she left the room. Then her words started to sink in. I repeated them to myself in wonder. Did she really mean them?

Without giving a thought to O.F. I burst into the living room. He was not there, but Mutti was standing at her wardrobe, changing out of the pretty silk dirndl I hadn't seen her wear since we lived in the village. Smiling absentmindedly, she pulled off one white knee sock after the other.

"Did you just say I can invite him?" I asked, uncomfortably aware of how sexy she looked in her lacy, flesh-colored slip.

"Huh? Oh sure," she replied, temporarily surfacing from some private fantasy.

"Can I call him right now and tell him?"

"Uh-huh."

I dialed the number I'd memorized from Lucius's scribbled note, counting four rings until a man answered the phone. "Private Duncan, please," I said. He dropped the receiver and called down an echoing corridor, "Duncan! Duncan! For you!" I heard a murmur of voices and was almost sure one of them belonged to Lucius. Then the man picked up the receiver and said, "Sorry, miss, he's not here."

When I looked at Mutti again she was rubbing lipstick from her mouth with a tissue.

"He's not there," I told her.

"Hmmh?" She turned sideways, studying her flat stomach in the mirror, pulling back her shoulders in an effort to improve her already sublime silhouette. Obviously she'd given me all the attention she was capable of. It was enough.

I went to sit on my bed, automatically feeling around for Seppi until I remembered he was no longer here. I'd call Lucius again tomorrow when he was sure to be in a more reasonable mood.

But why call him at all now that I could give him what he'd always wanted? I still had his address. Rummaging through Anna's art supplies, I fashioned a card. With black and gold ink and her two best calligraphy pens I proudly issued Lucius a formal invitation to tea.

CHAPTER 30

I COULDN'T UNDERSTAND WHY MUTTI DID not ask me any questions about my proposed tea guest. It was almost as if our short conversation about Lucius had never taken place. I was afraid to remind her of it in case I had imagined it all. Maybe I did. Why else would the phone stay silent in the week after I mailed off the card? Every day, I kept all the doors in the apartment open so I could make an unimpeded dash for it at the first ring.

Meanwhile I brushed and dabbed at Mutti's hat until it was almost as good as new. Then I put it on its stand, pushed it far into the recesses of her hat shelf, and hoped the beige felt would recover its jaunty shape in the dark. By Friday I realized it was easier to mend a hat than a friendship.

The only thing I had left of Lucius was the gold band he'd so carefully placed on the picnic table behind the beer tent. During bouts of despair I slipped my hand into my pocket to hold it tight, comforted by the fact that something that had touched him was now touching me. For a while I considered wearing both rings on the same finger, as was the custom for widows. But I was afraid Mutti would recognize the two unimposing gold bands that had belonged to her parents and which she assumed were still tucked away in the attic. In the end I threaded my grandfather's ring back onto the same string that held my grandmother's, hung them around my neck just over my heart, and took them with me wherever I went. During a particularly trying steno class or after an hour of typing nonsensical syllables I'd touch the comforting relics through my crisp linen blouse.

On Friday afternoon Mutti wondered out loud why the front of my blouse was so dirty. "These look like grease stains, Marianne," she complained. "Please wash your hands before you touch the buttons. This was your last clean blouse. I've been too busy this week to take care of the laundry. I'm going to have to do our laundry tomorrow evening, since we'll go the Wies'n the next day. It means I'll be spending half the night scrubbing clothes down in the washroom and most of Sunday morning at the ironing board."

The only part of her speech that penetrated was that I was getting a second chance at the Oktoberfest. I still had my itinerary memorized from the aborted visit with Lucius. I'd left his insulting handful of coins on the ground for some lucky child to find but I had saved the ten *Mark* Mutti had given me for rides.

She came home late on Saturday afternoon even though she was only supposed to be in the office until twelve. As soon as I tasted the potato salad she brought to my room in lieu of dinner I knew it was made by her colleague's professional cook. After she returned to the kitchen I alternated forkfuls of the salad with bites of salami, my eyes never leaving the page I was reading.

"You haven't said a dozen words to me since I came home yesterday," O.F. grumbled on the other side of the door. "And now you're serving me picnic food when I want a decent hot meal."

"I don't have time to cook supper tonight," she told him. "I'm going to do our wash. The girls need some clean clothes to wear to the Wies'n tomorrow."

"They're old enough to scrub their own clothes!"

"And you're old enough to scrub yours. If you come help me down in the cellar we'll have plenty of time to talk."

He coughed and muttered something I couldn't quite hear.

"Marianne's got enough on her mind trying to keep up with her schoolwork," she said in response. "The principal tells me she's doing well in German and English but needs to pick up her typing and shorthand speeds. That's why I'm making her practice at home."

He gave a loud sniff. "She's wearing the typewriter out. One of the keys is starting to stick."

"I'm thinking of taking an evening course in accounting at her school," Mutti went on without acknowledging his interruption. "It would help me get another promotion. In fact, that's what I want to talk to you about. I need a car of my own. Oh, nothing fancy—don't look so upset, it won't cost you a Pfennig. I found an old, reasonable VW in excellent condition. I'll pay for it out of my raise. If I don't have to depend on streetcars and busses I'll have far less traveling time to worry about. The car's current owner has offered to hold it for me until I can get my license. I want you to teach me to drive."

My mouth hung open, I suspected O.F.'s did, too. Then he sputtered, "Ausgeschlossen (out of the question)! Whoever heard of two cars in one family? We only need my VW and one licensed driver. Everyone knows that women can't learn to drive properly. You're much better off using public transportation. As for your raise, I've been meaning to tell you—it has to go into our savings account along with the rest of your salary."

"Never mind my raise," she said, her voice tight. "Did I hear you correctly? You're refusing to teach me to drive?"

"Precisely!"

"All right then. I know someone who will." She pushed her chair away from the table. "Will you at least wash the dishes for me?"

"Don't ask me to do women's work! Let Marianne do it."

"She can't. Thanks to you she's confined to her room every night," Mutti said on her way to the hall.

I stifled a giggle.

After she clattered down the stairs he said in a dangerously bland voice, his mouth at the crack of my door, "I see you're starting to turn her against me. It's only a matter of time before I catch you doing something wrong, you know. Then I'll be the one laughing!"

My only answer was to hang a scarf over the door-handle to block his view through the keyhole, but I couldn't block the hate-waves penetrating the wood.

*

ON SUNDAY morning Mutti was in the kitchen before it got light. Drifting in and out of slumber, I heard the iron hiss, the way it did when she was pressing damp blouses and shirts. Then O.F. gave a pitiful moan from the living room, crying, "Lottchen! Lottchen!" She dropped the iron and hurried to his side. Anna unlocked the bedroom door, put the sputtering iron onto its heel, and stood waiting until Mutti came to gather aspirins, a thermometer, and a wet washcloth.

"What's wrong?" Anna whispered.

From my bed, I watched Mutti's shoulders sag. "He says his heart hurts," she said. "His head, too. Maybe the aspirins will help."

While she ministered to his needs Anna opened her makeup bag in front of our dresser, redrew her eyebrows, smoothed the outermost layer of her beehive, and said, "I'll bet your next Wurstbrot (sausage sandwich) she'll cancel my birthday-trip to the Wies'n. He'll stay in bed all day groaning just to make sure. Tomorrow he'll drive off in high spirits knowing he's ruined the weekend for us."

The same thought had occurred to me. "But—he's never done this before," I replied. With a prickle of leftover guilt I remembered the morning I'd swallowed my entire supply of vitamin pills hoping the resulting bout of nausea would convince Mutti to let me play hooky. The only tangible thing I had gotten out of my theatrics was an unripe banana, but no doubt O.F. would fare better than me at the invalid-game.

An hour after his first whimper it was obvious that Mutti felt obliged to stay home and practice her rusty nursing skills.

"*Wurstbrot*!" Anna said, slipping on her best dress with a vengeance and stepping into matching pumps. "I'm desperate to get out of this house! I only wish I could stay gone forever!" I followed her to the kitchen, where she told Mutti, "Don't bother preparing a birthday dinner for me. I'm spending the evening at the atelier."

Still busy at the ironing board, Mutti tried to ignore all but O.F.'s most dire groans. The table was covered with stacks of freshly pressed blouses, shirts, handkerchiefs, towels and pillow cases. "Es ist zum heulen (I feel like screaming)!" she said, pressing the sizzling iron over a linen sheet. "I'm so sorry—but what can I do when he whimpers like that? Why don't we plan a little birthday celebration for you here at home tomorrow night, after he's gone? We can go to Oktoberfest next year. The fact is, I can't leave him alone today. Maybe with all the extra attention he's getting he will be well enough to drive off on schedule tomorrow morning."

"My guess is he'll make a miraculous recovery overnight," Anna snapped. "And don't bother trying to put together a birthday dinner on my account. I've got plans of my own!"

I ran to my wardrobe and extracted the bar of Swiss chocolate I'd gift-wrapped for her. "It's filled with *Likörs*," I whispered, handing it over. "Happy Birthday!"

Her eyes misted, though her lips remained pinched. "Here's another prediction for you," she said, stuffing it in her bag. "I bet your little present is ten times better than anything Vati's willing to part with for the occasion. I seem to be the only one around here who thinks turning eighteen is a big deal. But don't worry—tonight I'm giving my own self a present. All I can say is don't bother to wait up!" She slammed the hall door *and* the front door on her way out. Promptly, O.F. gave another moan. I thought it was filled with poorly disguised elation.

"He's making so much noise I can't even read," I complained as I listened to Anna stomp down the stairs. "If you don't mind, I'm getting out of here too."

Mutti gave a resigned shrug. "This isn't my fault. If you can catch up with your sister remind her I tried." She showed me her chafed hands. "Why do you think I stayed up half the night scrubbing?"

Not for the first time I realized that her life was more confining than mine. Unlike her I'd get to walk away from this family one day. She needed O.F.'s permission to get a divorce and he would never give it. Nor would he vacate the Marshall Plan apartment he'd married into.

I didn't see any sign of Anna when I got outside but Wolfi was sitting on the stoop picking at an elbow scab. "What's wrong with your uncle, anyway?" he asked, his voice glum. "He's driving my mom insane. She's about to drag Papa and me to two consecutive Masses just to get away from all that groaning. Maybe in the end I'll remember when to kneel and when to stand. Want to come with us?"

I pointed to my jeans. "Do these look like church clothes to you? I've got other plans for today."

He narrowed his eyes. "You better watch it. My mother is beginning to notice that you stopped going to church. Don't you know it's a mortal—"

I snorted.

"She won't let me play with you anymore if you're planning to become a serious sinner," he warned. "Besides, it's going to rain."

I looked at the dark clouds and said, "Good. I hope I get soaked."

*

I JOGGED to the phone booth that was standing outside the neighborhood grocery store. If Lucius would not call me I'd call him. The least he could do was to decline the invitation I'd sent. I counted sixteen forlorn rings before I hung up. Touching the two wedding bands through my shirt, I recollected his dejected silhouette at the entrance of the beer tent; his hand opening to spill the coins; the black taxi crawling from sight. Then I recalled him singing and wading in the brock; the way he'd so trustingly put his head in my lap afterwards; how much he'd always loved the vision of our contrasting hands clasped in an unspoken promise. Until recently I'd meant something to him. I was determined to remind him of it.

Wearing the same matching denim shoes, pants and jacket I'd chosen for our afternoon at the Oktoberfest midway, I headed for the forbidden zone. I stuffed all my hair under my cap before I got to the Landstrasse. On approaching Henry Kaserne I was sure I could pass for a boy.

Somehow Lucius was bound to realize I was nearby. All I had to do was wait the few minutes it took for him to put on his shoes, get a pass, and start running toward me. Meanwhile I lurked beside the yellow telephone booth and studied the soldiers trickling out of the gate. Few of them walked, preferring to hail cabs. None rode bikes. The occasional black GI was always the wrong shape, the wrong height, the wrong shade.

Then it started to rain. A chilling fog stole over the land. I sought shelter inside the booth. Waiting for Lucius to follow the call of his heart, I leaned against the glass wall, dozed, and startled awake to find myself clutching the receiver. I eased it onto its cradle and went out into the rain, pacing back and forth along the whitewashed retaining wall between booth and gate. When the sentry began to stare at me from inside his cozy security cubicle, I knew it was time to move on.

I backtracked toward the Landstrasse then took the faint trail dissecting the ragged field that served as a buffer between base and highway. The trail and I stopped at a chain-link barrier in front of a row of three barracks facing me through the wire. Was Lucius behind one of those windows? The center building called to me most. I stood facing it, weaving my fingers through the mesh, and waited for him to come out. Nothing and no one stirred.

The day I first met Lucius there had been a bunch of men dressed in olive-green Army fatigues on the grass beyond the fence, playing some sort of game. But now the lawn was bare and wet. The sealed barracks windows looked despondent, reflecting an inhospitable sky. I paced along the fence for a long time, looking for some sign of habitation. Tiring, I sat on the ground across from the center building like a dog at the grave of his master. When I felt a howl coming on I decided it was time to go home.

I tried again the next Sunday. The fog had thickened and the barracks looked as abandoned as I felt. But the third time I went I could tell from the Landstrasse that they harbored life once more. I was just about to step onto the footpath when someone called my name. It was Spider, tapping his cane smartly toward me from the access road. He wore the same fancy clothes I'd seen him in the last time we met. I gave a half-hearted wave without slowing.

He called, "Wait up!" So I did. "Girl, what you doing here?" he said when we stood face-to-face. "Only hookers parade along that fence. You don't watch out every man in there think you one."

I smoothed a hand over my denim outfit and then checked to make sure the cap was firmly in place. "I'm dressed like a boy. How did you guess who I was?"

He grinned. "No one else walk like you. Now, let me take you away from this sorry place."

"No, thank you. I'm here to see L—Duncan."

"You guys broke up," he reminded me in a self-satisfied tone.

"Because you lied to him."

"Because you skipped out on me and left me with two plates of Schnitzel. I was just trying to make him pay for yours. That was our deal."

He obviously didn't realize that I had seen the empty restaurant stove. But why argue with him? "Goodbye, Spider," I said curtly, walking away.

He wasn't that easy to get rid of. "Hey—what you want him for, anyway?" he asked, keeping pace. "He's in deep shit with the CO. Room arrest. Almost as bad as jail."

I stopped again, wondering if I could believe anything that came out of his gold-plated mouth. "Why?"

He spread his gloved hands. "He was in a fight and sent a white guy to the hospital. See, what you've got to realize is that Duncan's none too bright. That's why he's always in trouble. Somebody put *me* down, I smile, easy like. Get them back when they least expect it. Dude calls *me* a name, I just laugh in his face, like this." He threw his head back to give me a clear view of his golden canine and every silver bit in his molars. He looked so much like a serpent poised to strike that I took an involuntary step backward.

When he was done laughing at me I asked, "In which building is his room? What window?"

He stared at me from behind his dark shades, considering. "I'm on my way to that restaurant over there." He pointed into the fog. "Warm and clean. Good soup. Come with me. My treat."

"I'm here to see Duncan," I repeated.

His smile became a frown, then turned into a grin. "You a hard case, Maria. Middle building, second window from the left. But I told you, he can't come out."

"Thank you, Spider," I said, inclining my head to signal the interview was over. "Guten Appetit (good appetite)."

I took off the cap when I arrived at the fence and shook my hair down over my shoulders to help Lucius recognize me. Inside the mesh six soldiers in work uniforms were playing with an oddly shaped ball. One of them tossed it. Another caught it, and then three more, built like delivery trucks, threw themselves on top of him and buried him under their bulky bodies. He fought his way free and passed the ball to a friend who disappeared under a new heap of flesh. I could make no sense of the game.

Then the soldier with a tow-haired crew cut, on top of the heap, broke away from his buddies and came to the inside of the fence. "Hello, Fraulein," he said, curling his fingers through the mesh.

"Hello," I replied.

"My name's Jim. Care for some lovely pink bubblegum?"

"No, thank you."

He wiped at the sweat beading his forehead. That's when I noticed he had a bruised eye that had faded to a sickly yellowish green. "Are you here for some fun?" he asked, looking me over.

"I am waiting for Private Cho Duncan."

He gave a short, nasty laugh. "Then you'll have a very long wait." He went back to the others. They huddled and then sent another interrogator, indistinguishable from Jim except that his crew cut was a shade darker. This one had a bruise on his cheek bone. It was a wonder they were still in one piece considering the fool-hardy game they were playing.

"What do you want with Private Low Class Duncan?" he asked sternly.

"I have a question for him."

He scowled. "Don't you know you're trespassing? This here is U.S. Government property. No loitering allowed. Jim's about to call the Polizei to come and haul you away. You better leave while you still can." He jerked his head, whereupon Jim dashed toward the building. His friends guffawed.

I retreated into the field, making sure to stay aligned with the second window from the left. Jim had rejoined his buddies. I sat on the ground, touched the comforting rings through my jacket, ignored the men pretending to ignore me, and focused firmly on my goal. Today I could feel Lucius inside those walls. Sooner or later he would feel me.

Fifteen minutes passed before a lone figure plodded around the corner. His hair was the same texture of Lucius's but a dull brown and his fleshy, yellowish face was crowded with dime-sized sepia freckles. He brought a small paper sack and a metal cup to the fence. "Your name Maria?"

I started to rise. "Yes?"

"I'm Washington. Duncan sent me. Come on over here a minute." He glanced nervously at the white soldiers involved in their game, then sidled along the inside of the fence until he came to a break in the weave that was so insignificant that a casual observer would have missed it. He put bag and cup down, twisted a wire to widen the gap, and passed them both through to me. Following the zigzag line of the break I saw that it could be made big enough to allow a full-grown man to climb through and that the faint trail I was on stopped directly beneath it. "Hope you like hot cocoa," he murmured. "Duncan made me go to the clubroom for it. The donuts, too. He said you were sure to be hungry."

I thanked him and asked, "Is he okay?"

"Almost. The cracked rib's slow to heal and his lip's still split. But the swelling's way down."

I couldn't imagine Lucius fighting. His eyes were too kind. "Can he come out?"

"He's confined to his room. In bed, mostly, with nothing to do." Washington pulled out a folded note and offered it through the gap. "He wanted me to give you this."

I unfolded the scrap and read,

M.—I got something to say to you. Come to the gate in two weeks, on Sunday. I'd call you first to make sure, but I lost your pretty card and your number. —L.

Washington handed me a pencil stub. I wrote O.F.'s phone number on the back of the note and returned it to him along with the pencil. While I sipped and chewed, Washington uneasily shifted his weight from one foot to the other, frequently glancing behind him. "That's my mess cup you got there. There weren't any paper cups in the clubroom. Duncan says you better go home when you're done eating. Nice girls don't come here, you see. He'll be all right if he just keeps his mouth shut long enough to give the CO a chance to forget about him."

The players abandoned their wobbly ball and came to form a half-circle around Washington. Square-jawed, thick-necked and bulky, they looked like six versions of a bull waiting for a red cloth to unfurl. I handed back the empty cup and helped him adjust the weave until the gap disappeared. He turned reluctantly, his head bowed, and stepped between two of the soldiers. One of them stumbled, accidentally bumping against Washington's shoulder and bringing a boot heel down on Washington's toes, drawling "Excuuuse me!" Washington's only response was to limp away, keeping his shoulders hunched until he was at the corner.

"You better stick to your own kind," Jim said, his eyes hard with dislike. "We don't hold with this mixing shit. That's what got Duncan in trouble in the first place. He was warned to keep to his side of the fence. You better keep to yours."

I brushed off my pants, said, "Sorry. I not speak English so *gut*," and walked off.

"Cunt!" Jim yelled after me. Something about the way his friends hooted told me I wouldn't find the word in my Langenscheidt. In my opinion, men who played absurd games with a perverted, lopsided ball had nothing to hoot about.

*

THAT evening I made a two-week calendar and tacked it over my bed right beside Ricky Nelson. I crossed out a square every night. Lucius called when I got to the twelfth. It was a Friday afternoon. I was home alone. O.F. had not yet returned from his sales route but I was keeping a vigilant ear tuned to any footfalls that might be coming up to the landing. There was no reason for me not to answer the phone when it rang. Just the same I felt compelled to stretch the cord until I had a good view of the street through the balcony doors. The tarmac was empty except for Wolfi who was coming from the direction of Heinz's apartment, dribbling his see-through plastic ball.

"Maria?" Lucius whispered into my ear. "I'm out."

A bolt of joy shot through me. Looking around to make sure I was still alone, I asked, "Where are you?"

"They got me back to peeling potatoes and scrubbing latrines with my toothbrush. I'd tell the CO what to do with the toothbrush but then he wouldn't give me that lousy two-hour conditional pass he promised for Sunday. He made me volunteer to wash the mess hall dishes all of next week to pay for it. There's got to be some kind of law he's breaking, treating me like a slave. Can you be here on Sunday at six-thirty? I know a little place where we can have dinner and talk."

Through the sparkling glass of the balcony doors I could see O.F. advancing from the garages, wearing his tan trench coat and a black hat, importantly swinging his briefcase.

"Yes, Lucius, at six-thirty," I murmured hastily before I hung up. Then I ran to the bedroom window to measure O.F.'s progress. He'd stopped just below at the corner and was pinning a fidgeting Wolfi to the stucco wall, overwhelming him with a barrage of low, vehement words. Wolfi listened unenthusiastically, shaking his head. O.F. spoke again and pulled out his wallet, showing Wolfi a blue ten-*Mark* bill. Wolfi considered the crisp note and nodded just once. Then both their faces turned at the same time to look up at my window.

I moved away from the curtain even though I was almost sure they couldn't see inside the darkening room and wondered what kind of deal they had struck.

CHAPTER 31

O N SUNDAY I LEFT THE HOUSE AT FIVE-THIRTY. Wolfi was coasting his bike up and down the street, his face blue with cold. I was afraid he'd try to follow me again and was relieved when he merely gave a disinterested wave before riding around the corner. The air was full of a drizzle so fine I could hardly see it. It soon settled on my curls, weighing them down. The roads were empty all the way to the Landstrasse. Then a boy about Wolfi's age pedaled by me several times, drawing his chin into his collar for warmth.

I pulled up my own collar before crossing the wet highway. Long before I got near the gate I could see that Lucius was not there yet. The guard in the cubicle watched my approach with undisguised displeasure. I waited for half an hour, walking up and down the sidewalk, feeling conspicuous and ill at ease.

At last Lucius appeared at the bend, the black umbrella hooked to his arm. When he presented his pass, the guard scrutinized it thoroughly. Then it slipped out of his fingers and landed in a puddle. Quickly, Lucius retrieved it, drying it on his sleeve. I called his name. His face lit with a smile. "You're soaked," he said, quickly walking toward me. "Don't you have one of these?" He opened the umbrella.

I shook an excess of raindrops out of my hair before I joined him under its shelter and said earnestly, "You're late. Is something wrong?"

With an uneasy glance at the gate Lucius said, "Let's get out of here," took my arm, and slanted the umbrella to the rear, blocking us from the guard's view. It wasn't until we had reached the highway that he stopped to carefully wrap his arms around me. I leaned into him and closed my eyes, barely registering his low moan. As I savored the welcoming warmth emanating from his body something inside of me that had been soundlessly weeping for weeks finally uttered one last sob and stilled.

"I've been a fool," he said, rocking me to and fro. "I want to get that out of the way real fast. You still speak English?"

I laughed, gently touching his swollen lip and the bruise under his eye.

"It's nothing," he said, letting go of me to squint at the opposite sidewalk, where the boy who'd passed me on the way here was now crouching over his bike, wrench in hand. "Is that someone you know? He was staring hard at us a second ago—till he saw that I noticed."

The boy looked as cold and miserable as I felt. I said, "He's fixing a flat." Already, he was upending his bike, rotating the rear wheel.

"Poor kid. I'd help him if we weren't so late already." Lucius indicated a group of shops behind billowing mist. "There's a secure little restaurant over there. Spider put me on to it."

Startled, I said, "Spider? He lied about me, Lucius. I don't think he's a good friend."

He didn't agree. "I trust him like a brother. He said the bar I took you to would be safe, didn't he? The one that turned out to be such a dive? And he was right. No MPs, no Polizei. If we hurry we'll have enough time for a hot meal and a good talk." He pulled up his sleeve to glance at his wrist. "Oh yeah, I took off my watch before I started in on the dishes. Reason I'm late. They made me scrub every pot twice just to rile me." Frowning, he looked at my watch. "After seven already? Oh, well—we'll have almost an hour if I send you home in a taxi."

We began to walk at a fast pace. "I want to tell you what really happened the day I lost Mutti's hat—" I said, but he cut me off with a brisk flip of his wrist.

"Hey, no need. I'm over it. Max nix (I don't care). All right? Besides, I've got plenty to tell you soon as we get out of this fog. Ah—here's the place. I almost walked past it. Blends right in, doesn't it?"

The restaurant was squeezed between a shoe store and a greengrocer's, both shut. As we studied the menu posted in the glass case by the restaurant's entrance the boy rode past us, staring straight ahead, his chin tucked into his collar again. I wondered at the speed with which he'd repaired his flat. Then I translated the special for Lucius. "Oxtail soup. Just right for this weather."

He grimaced. "Which end of the tail, do you think?"

We entered the dry, well-lighted inn. It smelled of soap and tangy beef broth. Except for two men wearing business suits who were just finishing their meal it was empty of customers. The floor and tabletops were of bare, well-scrubbed wood. We went to the far wall to sit in front of a radiator.

Lucius pulled off his scarf. "Your hair's dripping. Here, rub it with this." I did, then took off my jacket and draped it over the back of a chair, pushing it close to the hot metal. Lucius eased out of his coat and sat across from me, wearing a port-colored shirt with a pattern of green swirls. The colors looked good against his brown skin.

"You broke a rib?" I asked, seeing how cautiously he settled himself.

He fingered his chest. "Just a hairline fracture. It's healing already. Tender, is all." He looked around for a waitress but there was none to be hailed. Wearing a sober expression, he leaned closer. "I told you I've got things to say. If I'm talking too fast or if you don't know a word I'm using, stop me. Okay? And tell me when it gets to be a quarter to eight."

I nodded.

"When I was under room arrest I had lots of time to think," he began. "About the weekends we spent together. The castle. Those earrings of yours, on our fingers. Our steaks at the Hackerkeller, where you called me an African prince. Lying on my hard bunk day and night, I tried to recall every word you said to me that day. And I saw how dumb I was for breaking us up." He put a hand over mine. His palm was pleasantly warm. "I never mentioned it but people have been hassling me about us since the get-go. Everybody from Spider to the guard at the gate. The honkies in the barracks—"

A sallow-faced waitress stood before us, wearing a washed out gray apron over a faded dirndl. She looked from him to me without the smallest vestige of a smile.

"You order," he said.

"Zwei Ochsenschwanzsuppen (two oxtail soups)," I told her. Turning to Lucius, I asked, "Anything else?"

"Sandwiches?" he suggested.

"*Kalte Platte*," I translated. She nodded silently, not writing anything down. It wasn't until she disappeared that I realized she had not brought us the customary breadbasket covered with a starched towel. Cutting corners? I put my second hand on top of Lucius's first. "What are honkies?"

"Nasty white guys. They did some ugly talking. I ignored it as best I could but it settled inside of me, anyway. It's dangerous for a Negro to be noticed by them."

"Why?"

His gaze went to some distant place and time. "My mom tried to explain it to me when I got old enough to ask some serious questions. She never could get me to understand the idea of barriers and colors and what my place ought to be. Guys like Spider, they're born knowing how America works and how to make the best of things. They learn to maneuver." He studied my helpless expression. "You don't have a clue, either. I noticed that the minute we met. When I smiled at you and you smiled back. There was no curtain behind your eyes, slamming shut. There was nothing inside of you, flinching away. People like us, we can't learn what those honkies and Spider know. That doesn't make us wrong or stupid—no matter what they say."

"No?" I felt slow-witted enough just trying to make sense of his words.

"No!" he said firmly, giving my hands a squeeze. "When I left you at the Oktoberfest I had a cab drive me all the way to Henry. Cost me a fortune even with four marks to the dollar. I was too wound up to go inside and I didn't like the way the sentry was looking at me. Same guy who was there today. A buddy of Jim's." He sighed, shaking his head. "So I decided to let off steam by walking along the highway toward the woods. For a while I was too mad to notice anything. That yellow convertible full of white guys must have passed me a couple of times before they got brave enough to jump the shoulder and cut me off. Jim was the first one to swing at me. Told me he'd seen you and me going around together, didn't like it, and now him and his buddies were going to put me in my proper place."

"Proper place?" I echoed.

He chuckled drily, staring in amazement at the soup plate steaming under his nose. "When did that get here?" he said, gingerly testing the broth with a finger. "It's still boiling hot."

I hadn't noticed our unfriendly waitress either. She still hadn't brought our breadbasket or napkins. Cheap.

He played with his spoon for a few seconds and then continued. "I never could stand it when people called me names. Even when it was my own father I'd see red. Best thing he ever did for me, he taught me boxing. I never told you but I'm a regular Cassius Clay. Lucky for me the honkies didn't know it either—or else they'd have brought along some bottles or knives. They made the mistake of thinking five to one were good odds." He grimaced, touching the back of his head. "When the MPs pulled us apart I was on automatic. Fighting blind with blood in my eyes. Accidentally took a punch at a cop. They clubbed me, took me to Second Field Hospital, and put me in the psycho-ward for observation."

The broth was a rich dark brown, smelling delicious. Already, it was losing heat, but I was working too hard on mentally trying to interpret his rapid speech to think about eating.

"The CO called me a troublemaker with dangerous tendencies," Lucius went on. "He and the battalion went off to play some more war games and when the doctor let me out I was put under house arrest with another outfit. Soon as the CO came back he added more time to my sentence, but in my own room, in our barracks. Which was a good thing, really. Because by then Jim had turned every white guy in the battalion against me. For a while I was scared to go out into the hall. When you showed up I knew you were giving me a second chance and I took it."

He frowned at me. "We're not letting anyone or anything stop us this time, you hear?" He must have seen how his story upset me, for he playfully turned my hand over and tickled my palm until I jerked it away. He laughed. "Still the same old Maria, aren't you? Well, I wouldn't have it any other way."

Embarrassed, I ran my fingers through my hair. It was drying fast. Already, the curls were starting to spring back. "I had no idea from any of this," I said. "None!"

He dipped his spoon, stirred briefly, and abandoned it in the broth to announce, "I hope you're still listening because I've got more to say."

"Yes?" I leaned over my plate so I wouldn't miss a single word.

"You and me, we belong together," he slowly went on. "The day we picnicked in the woods we weren't really serious about getting married. But I'm serious now. Next July I go back to the States. Will you come with me?"

"How, when you need permission from the Army, and I from my mother?"

He grinned. "We have a while to figure it out. Did your mother really invite me to come over?"

"Really," I said. In a weak moment, weeks ago. Did it still count? "It's not the same as giving permission to—"

"It's a start," he said with a pleased grin. Then he looked thoughtful. "In the movies, when parents try to keep a boy and his girl apart, soon as the girl says she's pregnant, the parents marry her off in a hurry."

"Pregnant?"

He patted my flat belly. "Having a baby."

He had no idea how much that particular lie would hurt my pride. Or Mutti's.

"So what do you think?"

Flustered, I asked, "About what?"

He sobered, shaking his head. "I didn't do that right, either. I didn't ask proper. So here it goes." He took on a ceremonial posture, spine erect. "Maria, I want to marry you. Will you be my wife?"

Marry? Wife? Those were ponderous words when all I wanted was to be with someone who'd laugh with me, play ball with me, and occasionally treat me to a good restaurant meal. Then I remembered the day I'd been determined to renounce my citizenship. Actually, flying from the land of mass murderers to that of saviors seemed a good alternate plan. Moving from a small, locked room to a spacious apartment I might share with Lucius was equally appealing. If I got married I'd join the ranks of grown-ups, and no one—not even Mutti—could tell me what to do anymore. Still, being a wife seemed much too final when my most ardent goals, until recently, were to be allowed back into Frau Bischof's class and have two parents who loved each other. But those things would never be again. And there was nothing else.

"Yes. I'll marry you," I heard myself say. "I will." I watched tension draining from his face. He dimpled, cradling my hands. Something inside of me lurched and released. In all the world there was nothing I loved better than those almond-shaped eyes, that radiant smile. Did that mean I loved him?

Impatiently he pushed his plate aside. "Okay," he said. "Okay. Now we're engaged. You still have those rings? The whole time I was in trouble I wished I'd kept mine. Or do you want me to buy some fancy, brand-new ones—"

"No, no." I moved my plate out of the way too, startled to see the grease on the surface was already congealing. Then I slipped the string holding our beloved rings over my head. "We keep these. They are special." I undid the knot and laid the two simple gold bands on the table between us. He slipped the smaller one on my left finger. I took it off again and said, "For now, it must be a secret engaging. I wear your ring around my neck and you wear mine."

"Good thinking" He slipped off the beaded metal chain holding his ID and snapped it open to thread on my grandfather's ring. Then we solemnly tucked our jewelry out of sight. The exchange was almost as impressive as becoming blood brothers. That was a rite Wolfi and I had performed with the dull blade of a pocketknife in our cowboy-and-Indian days, sheltering behind a mass of king's thistles. We must have gotten it wrong, somehow, or else he would never have accepted a ten-*Mark* bill from my worst enemy.

"What's the German word for fiancé?" Lucius asked.

"*Verlobter*. We are *verlobt*."

"And we don't need anybody's permission for that!" he said.

We gazed into each other's eyes, unblinking, clasping hands. Then he picked up his spoon and I picked up mine, wondering briefly why the waitress hadn't bothered to bring us the rest of our meal. We were still holding hands when two policemen came into the restaurant and headed straight for us. Too late, I glanced at my watch. It was one minute to eight.

"Entschuldigen Sie, Sir (excuse us)," the older, dark-haired one told Lucius. Then, looking down at me, he said, keeping his face perfectly blank, "Ausweiss, bitte!"

No one had ever asked me for an ID before; I didn't even know what an Ausweiss looked like. I hardly noticed that Lucius had let go of my hand and was scanning the room, no doubt for MPs. There were none; unlike me, he would be free to go. The younger, blonde officer gravely stared at the wall clock over the entrance. Neither Lucius nor I had known it was there. It wasn't until the minute hand swept to the twelve that he moved close, as if to keep me from bolting. Even if I did have an ID it would make no difference tonight; I'd still be fifteen, in the forbidden zone, consorting with an Ami soldier.

But then they didn't know what I knew. "We are verlobt," I explained, sure that important bit of information would solve everything. Quite reasonably, I pulled the ring out of my blouse to prove it. Neither officer seemed impressed. They signaled to each other over the top of my head. Then both moved closer still.

"You are under arrest," the senior officer said, gripping my arm. "Please get up and come with us at once."

Lucius and I locked eyes. I could feel us careening down the dizzying loop of an invisible roller coaster. Straining against gravity, I rose onto my shaky feet and waited for my speechless fiancé to make some brilliant remark that would put everything right—but he continued to look as stunned as I felt. My eyes burned, causing my vision to become defective; where a minute ago the world had expanded with promise it was now shrinking past my understanding, taking Lucius with it so that he seemed as remote as a star.

"Remember," he mouthed in a voice no louder than the whir of a beetle's wings, "worst comes to worst, tell 'em you're pregnant."

Then the officers led me away.

*

THE heavy-jowled desk sergeant smirked knowingly when the officers escorted me into the precinct station. He ordered me to take the only vacant seat left behind a gate while he finished interviewing the last of his "catch." My bench-mates consisted of three heavily made up women in too-tight dresses and too-high heels who sat at their ease, one filing her nails, another chewing a wad of bubblegum, the third taking a drag on an American cigarette.

"They're starting young these days," the smoker said, giving me the once-over. I sat on my hands to stabilize ten trembling fingers and looked at the young woman sitting across from the sergeant. Wearing her hair in a simple, mousy-brown chignon, navy-blue walking shoes, and a matching cardigan, she looked as out of place as I felt.

"Your registration, please," he ordered, pecking at a typewriter. She rifled through a plain navy-blue purse, an apologetic smile on her unadorned face.

"I thought so," he said, typing another word onto the form. "You're not even registered, are you, Ingrid? That'll cost you. Go sit over there with your friends until the transport gets here."

The young woman's eyes glistened as she complied. The sergeant beckoned me to the chair she'd vacated and rolled a blank form into the typewriter. He pecked my name and address without comment but laughed when I said I was fifteen. He laughed again when I told him I'd been arrested while eating dinner with my fiancé. Then he asked for my current health certificate.

"I've never even seen it," I said, my voice strained. "Does everybody get one? Maybe my mother is keeping it with our papers."

The women on the bench tittered while he said, grinning, "You do the school-girl act quite well. You ought to team up with Ingrid. She's playing a teacher tonight." His face turned grim as he nodded to the waiting policemen. "These officers will take you to the address you provided, in the squad car. If no one there will vouch for you, you'll get to ride in the van with these fine . . . ladies."

The woman filing her nails said without looking up, "Don't hurry, Kleine (little girl). We don't mind waiting a while."

The sergeant handed the dark-haired officer a slip of paper, and he and his partner led me back to their patrol car. My mind stayed frozen the whole time we were driving through increasingly familiar streets. When we arrived at our building I was glad that it was dark and that our apartment was at the corner. With any luck the neighbors would keep their drapes drawn against the winter chill and stay oblivious of my shameful return.

Walking me to the stoop, the policemen stayed so close to my sides that I kept bumping into one or the other. The lobby door was still unlocked. Going upstairs, the young officer glanced at me with obvious pity. The steps seemed narrower than they had when I left a few hours ago. They also seemed scruffier. Our landing smelled of fried onions and greasy potatoes. The senior officer pushed our bell, then backed off and nodded to his young partner, who immediately took his place. I prayed that Mutti would answer but it was O.F. who opened the door just wide enough to stick out his nose. He showed no surprise at the sight of my uniformed escorts.

The junior officer asked awkwardly, "Do you know this girl?"

O.F. hesitated as if he needed to think about it. Then he answered, "Unfortunately, yes."

"What is her name?"

"Marianne Edel."

"Age?"

"Fifteen."

"Is this where she lives?"

"At the moment," O.F. admitted, adding, "but not for much longer!"

The young officer looked helplessly at his partner, who gestured impatiently. It prodded the young policeman to recite rapidly, "Then I must tell you, Herr Edel, that she was arrested in a restaurant at twenty hundred hours for violating curfew."

I waited for him to mention who I had been with but he didn't, perhaps because O.F. was rushing to correct him. "My name is not Edel," he said. "I am only her stepfather. And I always knew she would come to this. She's a bad one."

The young officer stayed mute and stared until his partner gave a discreet cough. Then he said in a contemptuous tone, "Since she appears to have no criminal record we are required to release her into your custody. Next time we pick her up we won't bring her home."

Grudgingly, O.F. opened the door a bit wider, exposing the claustrophobic hallway behind him. "There won't be a next time, officer. I'll make certain of it." He forced his face into what he seemed to think was a smile and stepped aside. "Come in, Marianne. We've been waiting for you."

If I hadn't known him so well I would have thought I was being invited for Kaffee und Kuchen. The older policeman went downstairs, but the young one stayed to the finish, watching me gather the courage I needed to go in. When I looked at him one last time, he jerked his hand as if he meant to shake good-bye. The overhead light on the landing illuminated his eyes, soft with involuntary compassion. A guilty blush crept over his cheeks. Then O.F. closed the door on his face.

I took a measuring step through the dark hall, like a tightrope walker unsure of the strength of his cord. Despite the sound of O.F.'s too close, rapid breathing, the house was unnaturally quiet. The living room door was ajar. I inched toward it, touching the ring hiding under my blouse to steady myself.

CHAPTER 32

MUTTI AND ANNA WERE SITTING ON THE COUCH under the green overhead lampshade, watching my entrance as if it were the main event in a horror show. The green-tinged air was thick with judgment, condemnation, and second-hand smoke.

O.F. went to the balcony door to peer through a gap in the drapes and said, "They're leaving. Good." When I made a move to sit in the armchair, he barked, "Keep standing! Perhaps you'll think better on your feet. We have some questions for you. We want the right answers."

Mutti dabbed at her red-rimmed eyes with a sodden handkerchief. Avoiding my gaze, Anna stared at the heavy crystal ashtray on the mahogany coffee table, full of crushed cigarette stubs. One, lipstick stained and still half-alive, was sending a weak smoke signal toward the ceiling.

O.F. sat down beside Anna, whereupon she scooted closer to Mutti. I tried to control my trembling thighs. He lit a new cigarette, took a drag, looked up at me and said, "Question One—what were you doing in a restaurant at the Landstrasse at eight o'clock at night?"

I had my answer all ready. "I was cold and I noticed they had a special on Ochsenschwanzsuppe. The waitress was slow bringing it. And then it was boiling hot so it took me a long time to finish the bowl."

Anna looked at me with obvious disbelief, trying to convey an unspoken message I could not decipher. Mutti picked up the smoldering stub, raised it to her lips, stared at it with distaste, and ground it onto the crystal. O. F. placed freckled hands on his knees, squeezing his cigarette between two hairy fingers. "By yourself?"

"A couple of men were just finishing their meal. They left right after I got there." So far every word I said was the absolute truth. Hopefully I'd be able to keep it that way.

He looked at Mutti. "Lottchen, do you see what she's doing? Do you finally see?" He leaned back, crossed an ankle over one knee, wiggled his foot luxuriously, and said mildly, "We know all about you now, Marianne. The deceit. The lies. . ." And then he told me how, no more than half an hour ago, Frau Forster had rung the doorbell. With Wolfi in tow, she had asked if they could come in for a minute to impart some information that might be of interest. "She saw you on the Stachus a few months ago, standing next to a very tall Neger (negro). Wolfi convinced her it was by chance. But tonight a friend of his saw you with einem Schwarzen (a black man) that looked very much like him. You let this . . . Ami . . . put his arms around you. Right on the street! And then you went into a restaurant with him. Holding hands!"

So that's what my blood brother Wolfi had done with the money—he'd opened a temporary detective agency, hired an aspiring Nick Knackerton, and had me tailed. Splitting the fee fifty-fifty?

O.F. chewed on his cigarette. "Question Two. Anna said you took a call on my business line. You told her it was from a girlfriend but she could plainly hear a man's voice. Foreign. How many Amis did you give my number to? For what purpose?"

Mutti gasped. Anna hung her head. I dug my fingernails into my arms, reeling from my sister's betrayal. O.F. was obviously enjoying the inquisitor role; he did not need a reply. "I knew you were up to something way back in August. When that letter came for you. In English. With a local stamp on it. I put it in the wardrobe for safekeeping."

Mutti looked taken aback. "You never told me about a letter, Franz!"

"It slipped my mind until now. Perhaps you can translate it for me."

"Who was it addressed to?"

"Her."

"I don't read other people's mail," she said, delicately blowing her nose.

He sniffed. "Parents must be vigilant at all times. Besides, children don't have the same rights as adults. He signed his name. It's Luzifer."

Stung, I cried, "No it's not! It's Lucius! We are engaged! He wants to marry me!"

Mutti wailed, accidentally slapping her snotty handkerchief against Anna's nose, who tipped her head back to avoid further contact. "Ach, das sagen sie doch alle !" Mutti cried. "That's what they all say, to get their own way!"

A smile of sheer joy was spreading over O.F.'s face. "How long have you been seeing this . . . black devil, behind our backs?"

"But Mutti knows about him! She invited him over!"

Two heads swiveled in her direction.

"I did not!" Mutti protested like a child caught out.

"Yes, you did," I said. "Remember the day I came home crying last month? I told you I had a black American friend who wanted to meet you and you said I could bring him for tea." Looking straight into her eyes, I saw the memory surface before she deliberately submerged it again.

"She's making it up!" she hastened to tell O.F. "Every word! I don't remember a thing about it!"

It was a full-out lie, which meant that the only person I could still trust was Lucius. There was no way I would let them take him away from me. "This time next year I'm flying to America with him," I vowed, making my voice hard. "You'll never see me again."

To which she replied, "Ach, hör doch auf mit den Lügen (stop lying)!" But she was mistaken. Unlike her, so far I'd managed to stick to the truth.

"The question is this, Lottchen," O.F. said reasonably. "Now that you know your daughter is everything I said she was—a liar, a sneak, and a whore—what are you prepared to do about it? She can't stay here anymore. Neewahr (don't you see)?"

Mutti's recent efforts to assert herself against him crumpled under the pressure. "I always knew living so close to the Kasernen would be a mistake," she murmured. "It's a bad environment for an impressionable child. Let Vati take her on for a while! She can ride into town with him in the mornings, go to school, and ride home with him after work. I just paid a whole year's tuition, Franz—non-refundable!"

It took all my concentration to keep a feeling of relief from flooding my face. At least I'd be able to stay in touch with Lucius by phone—until we could work out a more satisfactory arrangement.

O.F. rubbed his knees, pretending to think. "How can we find out if her Vati is willing to take her on?" he asked. "He has no telephone—and I want her gone in the morning."

"Really, Franz! Your car, of course. And don't quote company regulations, ich bitte dich (if you please). This is an exception." She loaded the coal stove with briquettes. That's when I noticed my suitcase nearby. From the way the sides were bulging I could tell Mutti had stuffed at least half of my clothes into it. They meant to be rid of me one way or another.

*

ON THE long ride through Munich and the thirty-odd kilometers beyond, I sat wedged on the backseat behind O.F., a mute Anna beside me. As always, the car reeked of raw gasoline. While I fought an ever-increasing nausea the headlights sliced through black mist; the wipers squeaked from side to side; scrawny red plastic wings flapped in and out between the doors and the back windows at every turn.

When we reached Vati's village O.F. found his way effortlessly across pitch-black fields and down the lane past the old farmhouse. Obviously *he* had been here on at least one previous occasion, but when the VW's bright bug eyes lit the outside of Vati's wrought iron gate I realized Mutti was getting her first look at the dream house she'd saved for so diligently. Her gaze followed the headlight beams to the rose hedge leading up to the house, taking in every visible detail.

There were enough fallen leaves on the ground to keep a girl busy with a rake for days. And the garden covering the front slope needed to be tucked in for the winter. Silently, I vowed Vati would find me unendingly useful.

O.F. set the emergency brake. "Here you are, Lottchen. Just follow the path. I'll leave the beams on for you."

There was a tremor in her voice when she said, "No. I'll not set foot on his land. You go." This was bad news, for had not Vati told me that next time O.F. came to his door he would not let him in?

With a put-upon sigh O.F. climbed out, coached Mutti to get in the driver's seat to thwart any escape attempts, and advised Anna to keep me in the back of the car by any means necessary. As he ascended the driveway the beams shining on the back of his trench coat illuminated every wrinkle the drive had pressed into it and cast a long shadow before him. He passed the first giant oak; it was nearly bare.

Uphill, the outline of the house was almost undistinguishable from the dark sky. Only the kitchen window was lit. The VW's motor shuddered, paused, and ran on. O. F.'s shadow merged with the night. I offered my final prayer to God. It was simply, *make Vati hear me*. And then I hurled this thought toward my father's apathetic heart: *I have always loved you more than her. Now that I need you please take me in.*

The night air was heavy with the perfume of the last overblown roses. When the porch light came on it silvered O.F.'s thinning gray strands and bronzed Vati's shock of dark curls as he stood blocking the doorway. O.F.

gestured and talked. Vati listened and shook his head. O.F. talked some more, beating his chest the way he often did when he got excited. Vati shook his head more emphatically.

He had never liked O.F. Perhaps it would make him immune to the lies O.F. was surely spewing. If forced to choose sides Vati was bound to choose mine. He'd be amazed to discover the goodness in me. I'd even be an asset to Gitta in the kitchen, much as I hated housework. With my help she could have all the babies she craved.

Why was he so quick to refuse?

Of course, it was possible they weren't even discussing me. Knowing we could not overhear the conversation, O.F. might be asking for a cash loan. That would account for Vati's horrified expression. O.F. was calculating enough to do anything that would make Vati look bad in Mutti's eyes.

For her eyes were on both of her husbands, comparing, contrasting.

In the midst of O.F.'s escalating breast-beating display Vati shook his head one last time, stepped inside, and slammed the door. I had to admire his courage to be so openly rude. If Mutti had shut the door in O.F.'s face the first time he came to look us up in the city we wouldn't be here now.

The porch lamp blinked off. For an instant it seemed as if O.F. had ceased to exist. And then the headlights picked up his ghostly form walking down toward to the car. Mutti's breath sounded like a deflating balloon. Then, realizing this was her only chance to see what all those years of deferred gratification helped buy, she craned her head left and right, letting her gaze sweep hungrily over the night-shadowed slope.

Shielding his face against the VW's blinding beams, O.F. opened the driver's door and told Mutti, "He doesn't want her either. But maybe you can change his mind, Lottchen. Get Gitta to help you persuade him . . ."

How clever of him to mention her old rival's name. Immediately, Mutti pressed her lips together, shaking her head every bit as emphatically as Vati had done and saying, "The man has a stone for a heart. I shouldn't have asked you to come."

My insides lumped.

The drive home was slowed considerably by the still thickening fog, icing the windshield. The reek of gasoline became ever stronger. And then my stomach churned, tipped, and rolled over. "Let me out!" I gurgled desperately, "I have to throw up!"

"And watch you disappear? I think not," O.F. said, refusing to slow.

Wringing her hands, Mutti advised me to stick my head out of the window. As we retraced our route to and through Munich, I emptied the entire contents of my stomach onto the outside of the car, hoping the acidic vomit would eat a hole through the white paint. We were all glad when we reached home.

O.F. parked at the curb and told Mutti to leave the suitcase under the hood. After he whispered instructions Anna climbed out to lean against the passenger door. When I emerged from the sour-smelling driver's side Mutti was already standing next to O.F. Each of them clutched one of my arms and held on tight. Together, they dragged me upstairs to the apartment. Submissive and pale, Anna locked the front door behind us. O.F. held his hand out for the key, slipped it into his pocket, and gestured me to the living room.

"I'll call her school first thing in the morning," Mutti said, collapsing on to the couch. "It has a branch in Augsburg. With boarding facilities. I'll have them bill Vati for the tuition increase. That way she'll at least be able to keep up with her typing, Franz. And in a couple of years, when she's more reasonable . . ."

The thought of never seeing Lucius again was too hard for me to bear. "I won't go," I declared. "I told you I'm getting married. You can call Lucius and ask. Talk to him, Mutti. You'll like him, I know you will."

"Nonsense," O.F. said. "I've seen his kind around the Alabama Bar, drinking and fighting. She must forget about—"

"Lucius isn't like that," I broke in. "And I won't forget about him. I'll go with him no matter what you do."

Mutti opened the stove door, adding briquettes. The coals painted a red glow on her cheeks. "You'll go where I say when I say!" she snapped, wiping her hands on a rag.

"I'll run away. Even if it is almost winter!"

She sagged, giving O.F. a helpless look.

"She needs to be locked up," he prompted. "Under continual surveillance. For her own good."

Mutti stared at the coals, undecided.

Luckily I knew just how to tip the scale. "You *must* let us get married. I'm going to have his baby," I announced, adding under my breath, "Someday."

The ensuing silence was deafening. Even O.F. needed time to digest the complication. Anna grimaced and blushed.

Mutti clutched at her head and began to keen. "A baby! Ach Gott! Diese Schande! (A baby! Oh God! The shame of it!) What will the neighbors say?"

And then came O.F.'s finest moment. "They don't have to know anything about it, Lottchen," he said gently. "That's precisely what the Erziehungsheim (reformatory) is for. In fact, you can tell everybody she's gone to the boarding school in Augsburg. Basta (and that's that)."

She gave an acquiescing sigh. He had won.

Locking me into the bedroom, Mutti said, "Don't try anything foolish!"

Such as what, I wanted to ask, needing ideas.

The three of them continued the family conference without me.

*

I SAT on the dresser, shivering in my coat. After a while I quietly opened the window to measure the distance between it and the Hubers' window directly below. If I climbed out backward, clung with my fingers to the edge of the sill and let the rest of me slide down the rough stucco wall, would my toes find their sill—or would my hands, already rigid with cold, slip before I found that first crucial foothold? If I broke a leg, would they still lock me away? Leaning out, I examined the nearby metal drainpipe. A nimble person could shimmy it down to the ground. I stretched, giving it a hard yank. It came loose, scraped down the wall, and crashed on to the grass. Quickly re-shutting the window, I went to sit on my bed.

From there I looked around the whole room. A sheet-rope? Where would I go? It was way too late to call the barracks for Lucius's help. And as an experienced runaway I knew how cold even a rainy summer day could be. A dank, late November night spent curled in a soaked mossy hollow under a bare tree would gain me the freedom of hypothermia. At last I was old enough to understand that I had no place to run to.

I caught a glimpse of myself in the dresser mirror. There was rime in my hair, giving it a grayish tint. Were my cheeks starting to sag? In my gaunt reflection, I saw the old woman I would become. And then I remembered the Hungarian's photo portrait, tucked under my mattress for safekeeping. I groped for the exercise book, extracted the portrait, and leaned it against the mirror to study both images. The girl in the photo looked like a younger, prettier sister of the hag in the mirror. Could there be a warp in the reflective glass I had not noticed before?

I held the studio portrait up to the light. Those guileless, clear eyes; that expectant smile; the vibrant face. That's who I was. Not ugly. Not old. And certainly not bad. Tenderly, I traced every feature, growing more and more certain it was not a face that belonged behind bars. Then I returned the photo to the book and wedged it into its hiding place.

Too cold to sit up any longer, I slid under my featherbed, coat, shoes and all. And then I escaped the only way I still could—into sleep.

A stealthy sound startled me awake sometime later. Cautiously, I peered through my lashes to discover Mutti crouched over my wardrobe shelves, which were overflowing with books. With the aid of a weak flashlight beam, she systematically went through each stack and each shelf, ending with the bottom, where she dug around until her hand closed on the hidden sex manual. In the interest of family solidarity, Anna had given up the last of my secrets.

As Mutti looked furtively at me to make sure I was still sleeping, the diffuse beam brushed her cheek with unpleasant results—thrusting forward her strong chin, lengthening her nose and recessing her glittering eyes. In the vague light, her back appeared humped from the side. She pulled the book out, leafed through several pages, stifled a hiss of alarm. Then she slithered through the doorway and closed the door so quietly behind her that I, lying two feet away, could not hear the moment it shut and almost missed the sound of the lock clicking twice.

Closing my eyes I envisioned what Mutti was compelled to do next— slide aside the burner plate atop the coal stove, tear the book page by page, careful not to glance at the enlightening drawings, and feed them to the coals one by one, where they would flare briefly, like rejected ideas, before turning to ashes and soot.

CHAPTER 33

L AST WINTER AFTER A DEEP SNOW a flock of huge black birds collected in the wheat field near our trashcans, desperately searching for food. Mutti, shaking out a dust cloth at the kitchen window, was fascinated by their wild beauty. "These crows must be from the Ukraine," she told me. "They're bigger than our own. They fly south for the winter. The storm must have detoured them."

She cut up a couple of shriveled apples, gathered vegetable peelings and old bread, and we trudged through the unbroken snow to lay down our offerings. The hungry birds rapidly snatched them up and cocked their heads to stare at us sideways with piercing yellow eyes. "Isn't this better than throwing our garbage in the bin? It'll give them the strength to fly on," Mutti said with a glad smile. Then she addressed them directly. "This place is hardly an improvement over Russia. It's Italy you want. Thataway." She pointed south and they looked off in that direction.

Elated to have been of help, we retraced our steps. Herr Braun, who lived in the apartment two lobby doors over and often sat at his window with a pair of binoculars, waited for us at our stoop with his hands on his hips. "Sie Schwein (you pig)!" he said to my mother. "How dare you feed those awful birds! Don't you know they eat spoilt flesh?"

"Ja, und?" she retorted, matching his tone. "Isn't that better than eating something still living?"

"Giving them food will only encourage them to stay. We don't want their kind around here. I'm warning you—if you feed them again, werde ich Sie anzeigen (I'll turn you in)."

Mutti huffed, pulled me into our foyer, and slammed the glass door behind us, but did not dare to go near the birds again.

Anzeigen was a national sport, a game anybody could play, for Germany was bursting at the seams with rules and regulations. You didn't even have to look one up. If it occurred to you that something ought to be against the law it most likely already was.

The morning after he'd passed judgment on me O.F. wore the smug anzeigen look as he dragged me to the car by the sturdy rope he'd fastened around my waist. The streets were still empty but I could feel eyes on my back from every window behind us. One pair was surely Anna's, who had so recently denounced me.

Mutti, walking on O.F.'s other side, carried two bulging briefcases stuffed with what he considered incriminating evidence against me. He planned to present it to the Youth Authority within the hour.

As we drove away from the Marshall Plan quarter I sat by myself in the backseat playing the *if* game. If I hadn't vomited all over the outside of the car O.F. wouldn't have carried a bucket of soapy water downstairs in the middle of the night. If he hadn't gone downstairs he would not have stumbled over the drainpipe lying across the walkway. If he hadn't stumbled over the drainpipe he would not have found it necessary to put a rope on me and drag me to the VW the way he'd dragged Seppi the month before. And if I hadn't been trussed up I'd surely have found an opportunity to break loose before he could shove me into the car. I'd be on my way to Lucius right now, who, as things stood, would never know what happened to me.

In the city O.F. parked in front of an anonymous gray building. Inside was a labyrinth of vast corridors containing evenly spaced, numbered doors. He stopped in front of one and rapped, still clutching the rope. A stern-featured woman answered, her severe gaze taking in the three of us to the smallest detail.

"I am Herr Hohner," he told her. "I've written to you and talked to you on the telephone."

A veil of dread passed over her face. With a peevish glance first at the rope and then at my face, she asked, "This is the girl?"

"Ja," he said eagerly. "My wife now agrees we can no longer discipline her at home. If I may have a few moments . . ." He gestured at her office. Unenthusiastically, she invited him in. He exchanged the loose end of the rope for the two briefcases Mutti was still holding. "You wait out here," he crowed as he scuttled around the woman and into the room.

She stared after him and the overflowing briefcases, appearing bereft. Then she pulled the rope from Mutti's slack hands and offered it to me, saying, "If you run we'll have a city-wide alert out for you. The police are very helpful in cases like this." Inclining her head at Mutti, who tried to reply with a polite smile that failed miserably, the woman shut us out to listen to O.F. present his side of the story.

He'd found his way to the right office as easily as he'd found his way to Vati's garden gate. I pictured him haunting these halls over the years so that his every move would be perfect when the time was ripe.

Mutti sat on one end of a wooden bench, staring straight ahead. I sat down at the other. "Mutti," I tried. "If only you'd—"

"Hush! Not one word. It's too late for that now."

The whole time O.F. spent in the room Mutti and I stayed at our ends of the bench, she dabbing at swollen lids with a cologne-scented lace handkerchief, me coiling and uncoiling the rope in my hands. The corridor remained empty. None of the anonymous doors ever opened.

I waited for Mutti to look in my direction but she seemed determined not to. For most of my life she'd been the one person I could always count on, the one who'd made it okay for me to be who I was. I could feel her cutting the invisible bond between us to set me adrift, could feel her shutting me out of her heart.

While I shrank out in the hall, O.F. seemed to have expanded inside. He emerged beaming, squeezed Mutti's shoulder, and said, "You're next," sounding thoroughly mollified. She went in and he sat down so close beside me that I could smell the reek of his hair oil. His pale eyes glinted. Most likely he was envisioning our apartment cleansed of my presence. I slid away from him until half of me hung off my side of the bench and then I got up to sit on the next one. He never noticed. I made knots with the rope, and loops, but did not attempt to untie the other end from my waist. I had no doubt the woman meant exactly what she said. I'd not escape her and her kind.

I expected Mutti to come out with her eyes red and wet and she did. I had no illusions about my part in the proceedings. We were interviewed in order of importance; after the other two had made certain the woman, who seemed to hold all the power they lacked, was firmly on their side, it was my turn to step in.

The first thing she did when I walked up to her desk was to ask me to show her my hands. She peered at my fingernails, flipped one hand over to study the palm and pulled my hair away from my face, exposing my ears and my neck. Then she pointed at a worn brown leather chair. We sat.

Pen poised over a form, she asked, "Full name?"

"Marianne," I said. "Marianne Edel."

"Edel what?"

I stared. "Bitte?"

"Edelstein? Edelmann? Edelsohn?"

Confused, I said, "Just Edel. Like my father."

"Yes, well . . ." She scrutinized my features, paying close attention to my nose. "Be that as it may—do you know why you're here?"

I was sure she was a Nazi interrogator fallen on hard times, snatching at fragments of power wherever she could. I suspected the whole country was full of them, hibernating in niches like these. Waiting.

"You were seen with a black Ami. A soldier. Is that right?" she began.

"Lucius. We are engaged."

Her eyes probed my ring finger. If I showed her the slim gold band under my sweater she'd probably take it away. I needed it now more than ever.

"You are too young to be engaged," she said. Then she leaned over the desk. "Tell me, how does it feel?"

"What?"

She glanced to both sides before speaking again. "To go against your own people. To be a traitor to the German race."

We sat, measuring each other.

She looked away first, shifting papers. "You are pregnant?"

"No!—Yes."

"How do you know?"

I groped for an answer. Then I remembered a chapter of the defunct sex manual. Though I'd found it tedious reading now I was glad to recall every word. "A urine test. At the pharmacy. It has something to do with frogs or rabbits, I think."

"Which pharmacy?"

She had me there. Thinking fast, I named the largest in Munich, most likely to be inundated with such tests. Promptly, she opened the telephone directory and dialed.

"Was it under your name?" she asked, cupping a hand over the mouthpiece.

I weighed my options. The trouble was, I couldn't be sure which was more likely to save me—being pregnant or being a virgin. If she knew I was a virgin what was to stop her from tearing me away from Lucius? For my own good? If I convinced her that I was pregnant she'd have to deal him in somehow, although, so far, not even she had bothered to ask his last name.

"Well?" she demanded.

"I believe that's confidential information," I murmured humbly. It sounded better than, "I don't have to tell you," or "It's none of your business," though it meant the same thing.

She pursed her lips to reply but took her hand off the mouthpiece instead. "May I speak to your head pharmacist?" She swiveled her chair sideways to give herself privacy. "*Ja*. Grüss Gott. Ich bin die Frau Berger. Jugendamt. (I am Frau Berger. Youth Authority). I am interviewing a young girl who claims she came to you for a urine pregnancy test. Her name is . . . oh. Even though she's a minor? Shouldn't her parents be informed? Strictly confidential . . . I see. Can't you make an exception in this case, for the state? A lot depends on it . . . Yes, of course. I'm sorry, too." She hung up, chewed her lip, and swiveled toward me again "It would be wise to tell me the truth. For your own sake. But we have other ways. Please ask your mother to come in. Not him. He doesn't even have custody."

O.F.'s face fell when he realized he was to be excluded from final negotiations. "Now, Lottchen," he said sternly as she rose once more from the bench. "You know what must be done."

In her discomfort she did not reply but followed me in quickly, sitting in the chair beside mine and dragging it closer to the massive desk.

"*Ja*, Frau Hohner," the woman said. "Your case has long been familiar to us. We have received almost weekly complaints from your husband for years. We've stopped reading them long ago. It seems he has created a situation that bears him out at last. You agree? '

Mutti swallowed, looking stricken.

Putting her elbows on the desktop, the woman made a fist, curled the other hand around it, and rested her chin on the edifice. "Frau Hohner, has your husband convinced you that Marianne is unmanageable and must be made a ward of the state?"

Mutti pressed her hands to her cheeks and sobbed, "I'm at my wit's end!"

"Frau Hohner—I've been at this job since the end of the war. I've had to deal with many wayward girls. In my opinion your daughter does not yet fit into that category, even if—and I say if—she's pregnant. You may take her home."

Mutti sat stunned, trying to digest the last sentence. "But Franz! The neighbors! Die Schande (the shame)!" she stammered, trying to think.

While she wiped her nose, a hard voice I barely recognized as coming from me said coldly, "You let O.F. stay with us before you got properly divorced or remarried. The whole neighborhood was talking. They used to call Anna and me names. Why weren't you ashamed then if you care so much about what the neighbors say?"

Mutti blushed beet-red. Frau Berger shuffled the various forms spread before her into one pile, which she thumped on the desk until the pages lined up precisely.

"You see how she talks to me?" Mutti cried. "My husband is right, she is unmanageable. She's destroying me and my marriage, and driving my Anna away from home because of the constant battles she instigates with her stepfather. No, no, we've decided. Where do I sign?"

*

THE ANSTALT (institution) was in a peaceful, affluent neighborhood where every lawn was impeccably manicured and the shrubbery was trimmed until each leaf knew its place. As O.F. lifted my suitcase out of the trunk the last shred of morning fog lifted and the sun shone on the façade of the old mansion before us, making the windows sparkle.

"Are you sure this is the right address?" Mutti asked. "I didn't think it would look so nice."

He pulled out Frau Berger's directions. "I'm sure," he said, comparing house numbers. "Frau Berger called ahead. The abbess is expecting us."

On a branch of the symmetrical spruce near a wide-open downstairs window a hidden bird sang his joy. The solid entry-door opened. A black-habited nun smiled from the threshold. "Frau Hohner? Marianne? Welcome. Please come in. The Mother is waiting. It's going to be a beautiful day."

Uninvited, O.F. stayed behind on the path.

The abbess's office was large and remarkably uncluttered, as was her desk. There was a faint smell of beeswax and turpentine. The oak floor gleamed. A sunbeam, pushing through the open window, found a bouquet of end-of-the-season red roses on the desk and brightened it. The abbess's shrewd blue eyes brightened, too. Graciously, she invited us to sit. "Just leave the suitcase by the door, Marianne," she said congenially. "This is our time to get acquainted."

Mutti glanced at me with obvious relief. That was because she didn't know her nuns. When they got syrupy sweet it was time to watch out.

"I believe Marianne will stay with us for a while. Is that right, Frau Hohner?"

"Well . . . yes."

"Not to worry. We'll take good care of her. She will be quite safe, I promise. We are in the habit of reclaiming lost souls."

"My soul is not lost!" said the same hard voice that had gotten me in trouble in Frau Berger's office.

The abbess's smile was serene. "Here children speak only after they are spoken to. That is one of the first things we teach young girls who have forgotten their manners. My dear Frau Hohner, I am glad we can be of assistance. I understand Marianne has had a good Catholic upbringing. You are to be commended. I'm sure she's still reachable. Aren't you, Marianne?"

Now that she had given me permission to speak I could find nothing to say.

"Leave everything to us, Frau Hohner. Let your faith sustain you. We will add our prayers to yours."

"Yes. Thank you," Mutti stammered, shy as a schoolgirl. " . . . M-M-Mother."

"She never prays," the hard voice said clearly. "She doesn't even go to Mass anymore since she's been excommunicated!"

The abbess and Mutti gasped in the same instant and looked away from each other. For the second time that morning Mutti blushed a bright red. "You see how she is," she muttered, twisting her handkerchief.

"Yes, yes indeed," the abbess agreed. "I can see the evil in her. You are right to bring her to us. Rest assured we know how to deal with her sort. It's our vocation." Addressing me, she said, "I promise we'll make you thoroughly ashamed. Now say your good-byes. I'll have my assistants escort you to the dayroom." She opened a side drawer and withdrew a finely wrought silver bell. It rang a high, pure note. The door behind her swung wide to admit two burly nuns. The abbess nodded.

While the bird in the spruce trilled into the sunshine again, I looked at Mutti and tried to grasp the idea that she had signed me away and did not wish to correct the mistake. Surely divine intervention would pluck me out of this place while it still could.

My mother and I stared at each other across the chasm between us. Speechless, I offered my soul in my eyes. It was our last chance.

"*Ja, mei,*" she said as if to a small child. "Just try to be good."

But I *was* good. How could she not know it? How could she not see? She leaned across the chasm to offer a damp Judas kiss. I tilted my face out of her reach.

"Is that the best you can do for your mother?" the abbess asked sharply.

She was wrong; I no longer had a mother. Mine had thrown me away. Discarded me like garbage, casting my pieces to these black-habited crows with their vigilant faces who looked at me as if I were a due morsel. I said in a tight voice, "What does she expect?" and went to the door, stuffing the rope end into my coat pocket.

Behind my back Mutti wailed her sorrow.

The child in me wept along with every fiber of her being. Pinching myself on the arm to keep the tears from spilling I chanted silently, *I will not cry; I will not cry for her; I will never cry again.*

I did not look back. The husky look-alikes fell into step beside me, one on each side, their black sleeves brushing my arms. The suitcase stayed. I could hear the door being shut softly behind me, no doubt by the abbess's well-bred hands. Before me loomed a second door, made of steel.

The nun on my right jingled a big metal ring crowded with keys, easily finding the right one. Her voice was ice. "You are a wicked child to treat your mother so. After everything she's done for you."

"We'll teach you respect," the other one added.

"Ja, und?" I answered. It was my last phrase of open defiance in the world of the free. The steel door, swinging wide, showed me another. Before me lay a bare corridor. To the right was a row of shut, unnumbered doors. High on the wall to the left were matching windows, heavily barred, through which the sun refused to shine.

One of the nuns pushed me into the shadowless hall. The metal door behind me slammed with a shout, hurling its echo down the long narrow space to bounce against the door at the opposite end, announcing my arrival. Then the echo returned, losing strength until it became a forlorn whimper and died at my feet.

CHAPTER 34

MY VISION BLURRED AS THE NUN with the keys unlocked the door to the dayroom. Stepping inside I stumbled onto a landing. When the key grated behind me I whirled and stared at the shut door, which seemed to be covered with a blizzard of white dots. Then the coiled end of the rope slipped out of my coat pocket and landed on the floor with a dull thud.

"She has a tail!" a girl with long, wavy black hair said from one of the tables below. "Is she a cow or a pig—or maybe the devil?"

Most of the other girls staring up at me laughed. A moon-faced nun sitting behind a desk facing the girls chuckled along although her hand stayed within easy reach of the telephone. Her charges sat in groups of four on bright orange plastic chairs around small square tables. Two baskets stood on the center of each, containing dark, limp masses of something I couldn't make out.

The nun clapped for attention. "Girls, this is Marianne, here to join us." She beckoned to me with a friendly smile and I clumped down the stairs, gripping the banister and dragging my tail behind me. In front of the Sister I worked on loosening the rope at my waist but O.F. had made the knots too tight for my tense fingers to unravel.

The nun rose. "Let me." Her fingers were stiffer than mine; the knots defeated her too. In the background, girls tittered. "Hush!" she cried, to no effect. Flustered, she pulled the rope and me to a metal box, which she unlocked with a key fastened around her belt by a thin chain. Taking out a pair of giant-sized scissors, she sawed at the rope until it fell off. I picked up the pieces and stuffed them into my pockets. The nun held out her hand. "You can't keep those!"

"Why not? It's my rope." I'd certainly earned it.

"Because it's against the rules," she replied.

"Because you could hang yourself with it," the black-haired girl shouted gaily.

"Because you could use it to escape," giggled her neighbor.

"Because you could tie up the guardian of the keys with it. Then we'd all escape!" shouted a frizzy-haired girl at the same table. Almost everyone laughed.

"No, she couldn't, Helga," said the black-haired girl bluntly. "Not anymore. Because of you, they've doubled up."

"Oh, sheeeat, Liese. Halt's Maul (shut up)," Helga bit back.

I wished they'd all shut up, and so did the nun, whose voice rose to an almost unladylike pitch. "I want silence!" she said. "Immediately." Her cheeks flushed an ominous pink.

Ignoring the nun, Liese cried, "She *must* be the devil. See how she's leading us into temptation?" She picked up something round and began to tap the tabletop with it. Her friends copied her. In a moment, the whole dayroom reverberated with the sounds of their tapping. "Pfui Teufel (yucky devil)!" Liese cried.

"Pfui Teufel!" echoed the others, except for three quiet girls I'd noticed from the landing, who sat at a side table, their eyes downcast. As if aware of my gaze, the one with short, rust-red hair looked briefly my way. There was something medieval about her features.

The nun put her hand on the receiver. "Shall I call the Mother?" she asked shrilly, evoking instant silence. "Put down your darning eggs and get back to your work. Now."

They did.

The nun scowled at me. "Do you always make such a loud entrance?"

"I didn't do anything."

"You were disruptive. I'll start a demerit sheet on you at once. You've earned your first one. We practiced order in this room."

"Es tut mir leid (I'm sorry)," I said, handing over both parts of the rope.

She took them, looking appeased. "I'm Sister Gertrude." She put her mouth to my ear and murmured, "Has anyone informed you that you are not to volunteer what brought you here? The girls are bound to ask. They always do. Ignore the questions. Understand?"

I nodded although I did not.

"You see," she said, her eyes kind. "It doesn't matter what any one of you did before you came. In this room you're all treated alike. A fresh start."

"Yes, Sister."

"Now take off your coat and follow me. I'll show you what to do."

But what had been a coat outside was needed armor in here. In full view of uncounted hostile girlish eyes I could not bring myself to relinquish my thin layer of protection. "I'm still cold," I protested.

"No coats inside," Sister Gertrude said, her round face tensing. "It is a rule. Or must I add another demerit?"

I slipped it off and watched her paw through the pockets before she hung it on a hook among the rest. Then she led me to the only empty chair. It belonged to the table at which the three girls who hadn't tapped along with the crowd were seated. "This is our work," she said, picking up a dark, limp object from inside each of the two baskets. They were black socks. The one she held out first had a gaping hole in its heel. "These socks come from our monasteries, to be repaired." Showing me the other, which was darned, she beamed, "As we mend, so are we mended. Do you know how to sew?"

"Theoretically," I said.

She took that for a yes and supplied me with a wooden darning egg of my own, along with a spindle of black yarn, a blunt needle, and round-tipped baby-scissors. Soon I was sitting erect, the egg in the heel of my first damaged sock, concentrating on threading my needle. Pleased with my progress, Sister Gertrude nodded her approval. She said, "The monks are ever so grateful," and waddled away.

The owner of this sock wouldn't be. I could guarantee it. He'd get a blister. On second thought, he'd probably be grateful for that, too, since suffering was considered to be good for Catholic souls. I tied a knot at the end of my thread, clumsily stabbed through the sock, and whispered, "God! Is this what you do all day long?"

"Yep," the girl with the rusty hair said. "The monks consider it a fine arrangement. The Mother thinks it teaches us humility. In her opinion a girl can never be too humble."

"Maxi!" Sister Gertrude said from the desk. "No talking, please."

I allowed myself to look at the chastised girl, noting again her outlandish face. It was naked, having no eyebrows or lashes.

"I chopped them off yesterday," Maxi whispered, catching me stare. "With my good-for-nothing-else baby scissors. To protest my imprisonment. I considered whacking off my hair, too, but it's more startling this way, don't you think?"

I nodded. "I'm glad you left your hair. It's pretty." Short and straight, it was the color of sunset.

She flashed me a quick smile. "Pay no attention to the rough girls. They like to scare newcomers. If you ignore them they'll soon pick on somebody else."

In the wall facing me were four low, thickly barred windows. Those in the opposite wall was much closer to the ceiling, but nonetheless more inviting. One of them was open to provide crisp late-autumn air. Beyond it lay freedom. I studied the bars, concluding they were mostly decorative. The gaps between them seemed wide enough for a slender, unobserved girl to squeeze through.

"What are you in for?" Maxi asked.

I shrugged. "My mother didn't want me anymore."

Maxi pinched her lips but said nothing.

"Mine didn't want me either," the girl on my other side volunteered, trying in vain to tuck a recalcitrant strand of bright hair behind a shapely ear. "I'm Johanna. Liese and her cronies were hard on me on my first day too. I've only been here a month."

"Two," Maxi corrected.

Johanna gave a languid shrug. "Because I fell in love with a Gastarbeiter (guest-worker)." Released from the tight ponytail, her hair would spill over her back like a golden waterfall.

"With several," Maxi corrected. "At the same time."

Johanna grinned. "So I'm crazy about Latin types. I grew up eating cabbage soup. Can I help it if I like spaghetti better? Or that Italian men find me irresistible?"

"Slut," Maxi muttered amiably.

"Delinquent!" Johanna whispered back.

The third girl at the table, who had been practicing a beatific smile since I sat down, removed the darning egg from her sock, snipped off an excess of thread, and dropped the sock into the second basket. "God doesn't want us to squabble," she said mildly in the high, thin voice of a child. Her swollen features belonged to a ten-year-old. Eleven, at most. What could she have done to land her behind bars? My gaze slipped to the bulging apron she wore, and I knew.

Tears welled in my eyes. I concentrated on staring at the open window until they cleared, brushing a sleeve over my cheeks to make sure they had remained dry. Then my head grew so heavy that I had to rest my chin on both hands. Closing my eyes, I met a blackness within that was darker than monkish socks, crows, or habits. The whirling hole at its bottom reminded me of a bathtub drain. I spiraled toward it until Liese called from across the room,

"Sister, der schwarze Teufel (the black devil) stopped working already. She's a lazy devil."

"She is too working!" Maxi shouted back.

"That will be a demerit for Maxi," Sister Gertrude said, arriving at my elbow. "What's the problem here?"

"I don't know," I mumbled. "I feel faint. Is there a place to lie down?"

"Not in this room." She put a concerned hand on my forehead. Why was that always the first thing women did? I longed to shake off her fake-motherly touch but forced myself to hold still as she asked, "When was the last time you ate?"

I couldn't remember.

"In half an hour it'll be lunch time. Can you wait?"

I could do nothing else. In every second ticking away I was waiting for the phone to ring from the abbess's office explaining to Sister Gertrude that a mistake had been made and I could go home now. Every minute, my gaze strayed to the locked door, expecting the renewed rattling of keys as the burly guards, holding my unwieldy suitcase between them, returned to escort me outside to an idling cab. Contrary to recent evidence I had to believe my mother still loved me. And a mother who loves you does not give you away. It was not possible; therefore, what happened to me couldn't be true.

"A mistake," I muttered, but Sister Gertrude had already abandoned me to return to her post. "I don't belong here," I told Maxi. "Frau Berger said so."

Maxi and Johanna looked at each other and snickered.

"Girls!" the Sister threatened, pen poised

The pregnant little girl opposite me put down her needle, rethreaded with black yarn. "Don't tease her," she whispered. "It's not nice."

"Yes, Sister Klara," Maxi laughed. "We all know it pays to be nice. If you can get through a whole day without a single demerit you're allowed to knit for half an hour after supper."

"That's my idea of hell," I said, forgetting to whisper.

"Maxi! Marianne! One demerit each. We must have quiet in here."

"Why?" I wondered out loud. "This isn't a classroom. Why can't we talk?"

"Third demerit for Marianne."

"Thank you, God!" I said, earning a fourth.

*

AT THE end of the day I was as exhausted as if I'd climbed to the cross on top of the Zugspitze. Great chunks of time passed during which I was nowhere. I didn't remember lunch or dinner, or much of anything in between except for an endless supply of black socks. When I became aware of my surroundings once more I was lying on a strange bed covered by two leaden blankets instead of my plump and soft featherbed. There was an intense ache in my chest.

Somebody said, "Can you believe it? She's snoring! Devil, will you shut up?"

I found myself staring dry-eyed at the dim shapes of four cots aligned with the opposite wall. Next to my bed were three more just like it. The ninth bed stood behind the door, which was ajar, allowing a faint glow to seep in from the hall. Then the snoring started again, loud and near. Someone threw a shoe. It hit my thigh and bounced to the floor. The snoring stopped.

"Good shot, Helga," the voice said. "Go on, what happened next?"

"So, anyway," Helga murmured. "The first time I escaped I wound up in Hamburg at the Reeperbahn. Where the carnival rides are? It was all very efficient. There was this long wooden hut. It had little cubicles in it, see, each the size of a cot, with a door at its foot. The sailors lined up at a booth outside to buy numbered tickets. And we lay on the cots, blankets over our heads, legs spread wide and ready. Bang-bang it went. Fast as they could get it up. Never even had to talk to any of them, or bat an eye. No touching. No kissing. They bought a five-minute hole and we were it. It's easier when you don't have to see their faces . . ."

Hamburg. Vati took us there once. I remembered the thick, freezing fog outside the restaurant window, at the harbor. He'd broken his own rule and bought us a tureen of hot split pea soup with great chunks of ham. We had been tenting in the dunes on the island of Sylt, subsisting on his infamous cheese sandwiches, when the weather changed for the worse. Even on good days the wind was forever pelting us with pebble-sized sand. When the storm got serious we hunkered down in our miserable pup tent until Vati woke us in the middle of the night and took us down to the beach with him.

The waves were like dark towers and when they crashed on to the sand they made mountains of luminous foam. With each breaking tower the ground shook beneath us, though we stayed well out of the way. I learned the awesome power of water that night. In the morning the storm blew itself out but it rained so hard that the canvas got soaked and we shivered awake wrapped in wet blankets. With uncharacteristic pity—his teeth were chattering too—Vati called the vacation short. We were still numb by the time the train pulled into Hamburg. Thus the soup. Once my insides thawed I dared to bring up the Reeperbahn, which I imagined to be like the midway at the Oktoberfest. "In this fog?" he snapped. "Don't be absurd!"

Now I was glad we didn't get to go. We might have seen Helga the moment the child in her died.

Someone was snoring again.

"Make her shut up!" a voice hissed.

A shoe hit my chest, crushing something fragile inside. Losing my last hold on shifting reality, I became entirely insubstantial and spiraled down the black drain hole of my worst fears to be flung into the murky bowels of a grinding and alien universe.

The next time I opened my eyes an angel stood over me, its wings spread wide, a faint glow all around it. It put a finger to its lips and beckoned me to get up and follow. I rose at once, knowing it was going to show me a way to get out.

In the lighted hallway the angel assumed Maxi's shape. She led me to the bathroom, wearing a wide-sleeved beach robe over a tattered flannel gown. We stood on icy blue tiles. There were a couple of sinks on the far wall and a row of toilet stalls along the side.

"You were crying in your sleep," she whispered. "So I woke you."

"I don't cry."

"No? All right. Then you were moaning, I guess." She looked at my bare feet. "Where are your slippers?"

"At home. Under my bed. My mother was in such a hurry to get rid of me that she forgot to pack them."

She nodded. "My mother got rid of me too. Listen, I've been meaning to talk to you alone. It's an impossible feat during the day. Someone's always spying." She opened each stall to make sure it was empty. Then she stood facing the door and asked, still in a whisper, "You want to know how to get out?"

"Yes!"

"There are two plans that might work for you. This place is escape proof so you'll have to run away from somewhere else. First Plan A. You ever had appendicitis? A pain in your right side so bad you can't move. Even doctors have a hard time diagnosing it. But they can't risk ignoring you, see, because if an appendix bursts the patient usually dies. So pretend you can't get out of bed in the morning. Complain of a terrible stabbing pain. You can't bear to be touched. The nuns will get scared and call an ambulance. There are no bars on hospital windows. No locked doors either. And since you're too sick to even sit up, no goons waiting out in the hall. By the time the busy doctor comes to examine you your bed is empty and you're long gone. Get it?"

What a dumb idea. True, the appendicitis scheme had worked for Spider, but then he hadn't tried to flee from a hospital room in a flimsy nightgown.

"Okay, okay," Maxi whispered, registering my lack of enthusiasm. "There's always Plan B. It's a bit more—" Smoothly, she segued into a loud yawn and stretched. "Boy, am I tired. Helga's jabbering kept me awake too long. Hello, Elfriede!"

The door moved. A girl came in, gave us an indifferent glance, and went to the nearest sink to wash her hands. In the middle of the night? Without going to the toilet first? Her eyes found us in the mirror. I could practically see her ears rotate toward us.

"Really, you ought to get your slippers sent," Maxi told me, yawning again. "There's a rule against wearing shoes in the dormitories. We better get back to sleep. They wake us at five, for chapel."

*

THE LIGHTS came on promptly at five. "Good morning! Everybody up!" a nun shouted at our bedroom door before moving on to the next. My nose, the only part of me sticking out of the blankets, was numb with cold. The girl at the next bed picked up the pitcher standing on her nightstand and held it over a big porcelain bowl. Nothing happened. "It froze again!" she muttered, jabbing the handle of her hairbrush into the pitcher. I heard ice cracking and when she poured chunks of it plopped into the bowl with the water. She dipped in her wash mitt, rubbed it vigorously over face, neck, and underarms, and dried herself with a small towel.

Shivering, I got dressed as fast as I could.

"You didn't wash. I'll tell!" the girl said, pointing to my towel and mitt, still folded laundry-fresh on my nightstand. She watched me break ice, pour, dunk in the cloth, and dab it over my face. I gave my neck a swipe and turned away, pretending to wash my tender-skinned armpits. After I rubbed myself hard with the towel I looked as clean as she did.

Satisfied, she went to the four beds at the opposite wall, pulling the blankets off each. Three of the sleepers roused enough to sit up. Helga, the fourth, uttered a curse that would have made a North Sea sailor blush, retrieved her covers, and drew them over her head. The girl ran to the door and whispered urgently, "The Sister's coming down this way. Get up or we'll all get a demerit!" Instantly, the four laggards jumped to their feet.

With their hair tangled and their musty flannel gowns furrowed, Helga and her three devoted disciples reminded me of lumpy, unwashed potatoes.

"All right," Helga groaned, struggling into her clothes. "Thanks for the warning, Grete." She was busy combing her hair when the nun stuck her head into the room again.

"Line up. Let's go!" the Sister cried.

The girls shuffled out in their slippers while I was still working on lacing my sneakers. I got my fifth demerit for wearing shoes in a bedroom and the sixth for being the last one in line.

We knelt in the pews by wavering candlelight. Shadows danced across the white altar cloth, occasionally illuminating the dark cross above, where the Heiland (savior) writhed under His crown of thorns. To the right of the altar stood a life-sized statue of the Virgin Maria wrapped in a painted-on blue shawl.

With great dignity a long line of nuns slowly filed down the center aisle chanting in unearthly tones. They looked so much alike in the near dark I couldn't even pick out the refined abbess or plump Sister Gertrude. The procession of habited silhouettes passed one by one to the altar where each nun bowed low, as to a king, crossed herself, and entered a front pew to kneel and cross herself once more. When the last nun was on her knees they sang endless Latin prayers in high eerie voices. Eventually the stained glass windows on each side of the altar began to shimmer with first light.

I chose that hopeful moment to steeple my hands and connect with God. I found Him nearby, chortling at my mortal pain. I tried to reach Jesus next but He continued to hang on His cross, speechless and engrossed in His own suffering. The Holy Ghost, Whose identity had always been unclear to me, did not answer my call either. It occurred to me that all three were the kind of male Gods who were not likely to be on my side about anything—especially if O.F. had gotten to Them first.

That left me with kind-hearted, humane Lucius, so I sent my mind in his direction, mentally calling his name. I heard him sing, "There'll never be anyone else . . ."

"Lucius!" I called across space and time. "Lucius!" And then I was back in the woods with his head on my lap, his almond eyes smiling at me. My voice, high as a lark's, joined his. We sang the rest of the vow together. Some violins began to accompany us, and a trumpet. Soon the rest of the orchestra joined in. The melody grew louder and louder until it felt as if all of Munich's church bells were ringing at once. I vibrated along until, at last, every sound but one faded away. It came from a piano, striking divinely pure notes. Each was like a sparkling, glorious flake, gently falling on me until musical snow covered me like a white gown. Then I told Lucius, "I *will* go with you. Nothing and no one can stop us. I promise you, I *will* get out!"

When chapel was over we returned to the dorms for morning chores. I made my bed and swept the floor, but only my body was there. The rest of me still soared.

CHAPTER 35

BEFORE WE LEFT THE DORMS I got my seventh demerit for arguing with a young nun who demanded I take off my jeans in favor of a drafty wool skirt. The nun won. After breakfast we all filed into the dayroom for another aeon of mending our souls. At ten o'clock, the phone rang. Sister Gertrude answered it, her faded eyes soon seeking mine. She hung up and summoned me to the desk, her blue-veined hand still rested on the receiver as she murmured, "The doctor is here. He comes every Tuesday morning. You are to have an examination."

"But I'm not sick," I said.

She rose laboriously, gently cupped my shoulders, and whispered, "Be brave."

Was it pity I saw in her filmy old eyes? I couldn't imagine what it was for.

Then my escorts came to fetch me. They led me silently upstairs to a room all in white. The unsmiling nurse who stood waiting for me at a low table wore a white butcher's apron almost as long as the habit underneath. The apron was stiffly starched with crisp, ironed-in creases.

"Marianne Hohner?" she said, leafing through some papers.

"Edel!"

"Yes, right. I'll leave you alone so you can get undressed. Take off everything and then wrap yourself in this sheet." She indicated the one lying folded on the curiously shaped table.

Shocked, I asked, "Why?" The rare times I'd seen a doctor he shone a flashlight down my throat and hit my knee with a rubber hammer.

"You are a tedious child. Just follow my instructions if you please. When you've covered yourself with the sheet sit on the examining table and wait. I'll be right back."

As a heavily indoctrinated Catholic girl I'd never had my clothes off in front of anyone except my mother and the last time I undressed for her I was still learning to undo my own buttons. Although Anna and I shared a room we stepped behind our wardrobe doors to disrobe. Neither the parish priest in his twice-weekly lessons nor the supposedly explicit sex manual had prepared me for what came next.

A cold-eyed, chisel-faced stranger, wearing a white doctor's coat, walked in and asked me to lie down on my back and open my legs. Outraged and frightened, I looked at the nurse for help. None came, so I clutched the thin sheet with a vice-grip and continued to sit, my spine rigid.

"The doctor said to lie down!" the nurse said harshly from behind me. When I didn't comply she heaved at my shoulders without warning until I lay flat, legs and teeth clenched.

He stepped to the bottom of the bed. "Scoot lower and bend your knees. Put your heels in these," he ordered in an emotionless voice. I squirmed toward the top edge of the table, where the Sister's hands gripped my head, pushing me back toward him.

He pried at my feet. They remained locked. "Listen here—" he said, glancing at my chart. "—Marianne. You girls make me sick. You spread your legs for everything in pants and then act coy with me. I have neither the time nor the patience for it." He scowled at the nun. "Sister!" he commanded as I slid toward the top once more.

She pushed me toward him, hissing, "You must obey!"

He yanked at the sheet. I yanked back. Quickly grabbing my hips, he jerked them to the bottom edge and said harshly, "Fine. If you insist on being difficult I will call the guards in to tie you down so I can get on with my job."

I desisted. He jammed my heels into steel contraptions and lifted the sheet. I had a mental glimpse of Helga's cubicle at the Reeperbahn, knew I was no better than she, and squeezed my lids tight, shutting out the doctor the only way I still could. As his fingers probed at the part of me even I was forbidden to touch the nun pressed her hands to my shoulders, pinning me down. Briefly, I wondered why, with all the laws in the country, there was none against this, and then I deliberately turned off my feelings and forced myself to submit, doing my best to ignore the contempt in his voice when he told the nun, "Tell the Mother she is not pregnant. She couldn't be."

I watched him turn away to scrub his hands at the sink as if touching me had contaminated them. And then he left the room. Once the door closed the nun released me, not meeting my eyes. "Call me as soon as you're dressed," she said, trailing him out.

I lay there defeated, wondering what crazy rule they were practicing that said they must not see me undress and redress but could violate me in-between. It wasn't until the guards walked me downstairs that I remembered the pity on Sister Gertrude's face. Did anybody ever make her . . . I refused to complete the picture forming in my mind's eye.

In the corridor leading to the dayroom the guards unlocked a new door for me and motioned me in. It was a schoolroom, a real schoolroom, complete with a wall blackboard and sticks of white chalk. A lay-teacher sat at the only full-sized desk, a book open before her. On the slanted, old-fashioned pupils' desks, spaced evenly throughout the room, ten big girls sat in ten little chairs, bending over identical books, their index fingers marking the word they'd been on before they'd looked up to watch me come in.

Consulting a form, the teacher asked, "Marianne Hohner?"

"Edel!"

She nodded, crossed out a word, and asked me to sit on an empty seat at the back, flanked by a scowling Liese on one side and a flustered Maxi on the other. "Continue, Maxi, if you please," the teacher said. Maxi, twisting a red strand of hair with one freckled hand, moved the other to the next word, laboriously sounding it out. And I discovered a staggering fact—my sharp-tongued new friend, the most quick-witted and articulate among the inmates, could barely read. She stuttered from one syllable to the next, ignoring commas and full stops. It was such an excruciating performance that I soon felt ashamed for her.

I should have felt ashamed of myself, for when she was finally done with her assigned paragraph, the teacher came to me, put an open book on my desk, and asked me to read the next segment. Overcoming a fleeting sense of loyalty, I took pride in my superior skills and read rapidly, correctly, and with feeling, while the scowl on Liese's face grew more pronounced with each sentence. But what did that matter to me when the teacher smiled warmly and said, "Thank you, Marianne. Good work."

Then it was Liese's turn. Her performance was worse than Maxi's. As was Helga's, whom the teacher called on next. The streetwise girl could not decipher any word made up of more than three letters. I sat through the rest of the lesson in a daze, unable to understand how these girls, my age and older, could read so poorly. The teacher called on Maxi twice more but did not ask me to repeat my glowing performance.

Arithmetic was worse. The teacher wrote one-digit subtraction problems on the board. Even Helga managed to get them right, but when the teacher began to pair numbers, Helga stammered and failed, unable to comprehend the idea of placeholders. Maxi wasn't much better at it. And even though we spent ten minutes reciting the multiplication table together out loud, not one girl except me, reciting alone, could get to the end of the sixes.

Wiping the blackboard clean, the teacher wrote a set of long divisions across it, called on me, and handed me the chalk. Shamelessly and speedily I solved every problem, taking the mental shortcuts I'd learned years ago. I was hoping to show off my talent for composition next but the teacher had had enough of me.

"You better go now. Tell the nuns you don't belong in here," she said, pressing a button behind her desk. And I, preferring even this dunce class to monkish socks, was escorted back to the dayroom, where I gave Sister Gertrude the teacher's message.

"Don't you have a more advanced class I can go to?" I asked. "I like school."

"I can see you do," she said, sounding impressed. "But no, there is no advanced class. Not in this place there isn't."

I took my usual seat across from little Klara, picked up the sock I'd been in the process of ruining before I was escorted upstairs, and got so busy trying to solve the puzzle of the schoolroom that I almost forgot my recent humiliation. "Where's Johanna?" I asked, finally realizing that her chair was empty.

"They took her to see the doctor," Klara said. "I have to go too, sometimes, but not today, God be praised."

I couldn't resist asking the question I thought each time I looked at her childish face. "Klara, do you know why you're here?"

She paused in her work and smiled shyly. "Because my uncle was nice to me." I could make no sense of her answer until she added, "That's why I'm getting fat, the Mother said. Because he was nice to me."

I considered her swollen features, letting my gaze pass over the soft rise of her belly, and asked, "Where is your 'uncle' now?"

She looked surprised. "At home with my mother, silly. Where else would he be?"

Focusing on my blighted sock, I tried to decide if Klara was simply slow-witted or just naturally naïve. "Are you . . . a Catholic?" I finally asked.

Again, she was surprised. "Of course I am. Sister Gertrude said if I work hard at being good I can be a novice one day. Then she'll be my big sister, you see, and the Mother Abbess will be my real mother." A blissful smile lit her face as she leaned closer to whisper, "I'll be the bride of Jesus and I'll never have to go home again."

"Yes, but," I began, breaking off my protest as soon as I realized that I was pretty slow-witted myself. Why should she want what I wanted? What should she want? What should I? The answer to the last sentence came quickly and silently. Out of here. By any means that might present themselves. Looking at Sister Gertrude, content at her post now that the worst girls were busy elsewhere, I decided to be bold and went to her chair.

"Sister," I said, keeping my voice down. "My mother forgot to pack my slippers. The floor in the dorms is icy. Especially in the bathroom. I already got a demerit for wearing street shoes on the bedroom floor."

"Yes, we keep the dormitories unheated all winter. Crisp air is good for the health." She pulled out the demerit sheet and started counting. "You better watch out. The girls who have less than ten demerits for the whole week get to listen to an hour of radio music on Saturday. Those who have more than ten must go to the schoolroom during that time to practice their reading."

That wouldn't be so bad. I was already hungry for books. "What kind of music?" No doubt, it was something uplifting, such as Mozart or hymns.

She smiled. "The girls prefer the 'hit parade', on the American station."

Ricky Nelson? Elvis Presley? Brenda Lee? I missed them even more than I missed reading. At once, I decided on a course of abject humility. Piously folding my hands and casting my eyes to the floor at my feet, I murmured, "Please, Sister, I don't want to collect additional demerits, but as long as I'm forced to wear street shoes in the dorms, I can't avoid getting more. I wonder, would it be possible for me to call my mother and ask her to bring my slippers?"

She seemed to enjoy the new me. After thinking it over she said with a generous smile, "I don't see why not as long as you promise not to talk about anything else. Remember, she is no longer responsible for you. We do not wish to disturb her."

"No indeed," I said. "Thank you, Sister. I'll keep it short."

The telephone was a magic invention. You picked it up, heard a flat dial tone, dialed a number, and when it rang at the other end part of you went with it back into the world now denied you.

When Mutti answered, "Hohner hier (here)," it was almost like standing at our blonde oak desk beside her.

Until I said, "Mutti?"

I heard a jagged, almost hostile intake of breath. A long pause. A cautious, "Hello?"

"Mutti, I've been allowed to call you to ask for my slippers. They are required in the dorms. The floors are quite cold."

"I see." Another long silence.

"Can you . . . bring them to me?" I asked, hoping the suggestion wasn't too bold.

The earpiece hummed. Then she said, "I'll mail them. In the meantime keep your socks on."

Bad advice. Most likely there was a rule against that too.

I'd been listening around her words, behind them. What wasn't she saying? What would she have liked to? And even though Sister Gertrude stood right at my elbow I decided to risk offending them both. "Mutti," I whispered. "I saw a doctor today. He says I'm not pregnant."

"That'll do," Sister Gertrude snapped. "You better hang up now."

I turned my back on her. "Did you hear me?" I mouthed into the receiver. "Are you still there?"

"*Ja*," she said. Nothing more.

I spelled it out for her. "It means you don't have to be ashamed of me after all. In front of the neighbors I mean. Please—" Sister Gertrude snatched the receiver from me, murmured an apology into the mouthpiece, and hung up. As she worked her faded brows into a frown, I dipped into a curtsy and took myself off before she could choose between lecture and demerit.

*

ONCE more, it was dark. Someone snored loudly nearby.

"There she goes again!" The girl who'd broken the ice in her pitcher rapped her hairbrush against the metal frame of my bed. The snoring stopped.

Helga said, "Maxi, what are you doing?"

"Nothing."

"You took out your wedge! I'm telling! Sister! Sister!"

The crack in the door widened, admitting the black shape of a nun. "Yes?"

"Maxi pulled out her wedge and pushed it under her bed." Helga said with great agitation.

"Stupid snitch!" Maxi exploded. "I'm used to lying on a flat mattress! I can't go to sleep with my head raised!"

"You must put it back in," the nun said firmly.

"But then I can't sleep on my stomach."

"Good. That's an entirely unnatural position and bad for your posture. Besides, the wedges are permanent parts of our beds. Put yours back, now."

Maxi sobbed once, in fury, then got out of bed, retrieved it, and restored it to its rightful place under the mattress.

"Good," the nun said. "Let us hear no more about it. I want quiet in here—or I'll have to report the whole room."

For a while Helga was satisfied, Maxi resigned, the rest of us chastised into obedience. Then the nun's footsteps receded, a faraway door opened and shut, and Helga took up the saga she'd started the night before. "After they found me and brought me back here, I was desperate," she murmured. "I couldn't stand being locked up any more. But I knew that all the easy ways of breaking out had already been tried. At first I thought I'd put on a burst of speed on the path connecting the front building to the dorms. Plunge through the living walls the nuns form on each side of it every morning and evening, before we're allowed on the path. It seemed an okay place to make a run for it. I mean, how could the nuns ever catch up? In their bulky gear? But then I noticed those giant whistles around their necks. The second they blow them someone's on the phone to the police. Five minutes later the whole neighborhood's swarming with them. I figured the best way to escape would be from somewhere no one expected. When there were no witnesses."

"Like Liese," her bunk neighbor whispered. "She almost made it."

"Might have," Helga conceded. "If she hadn't underestimated the size of her ass and got herself stuck. I had a better idea. One Tuesday, I found a bottle in the infirmary, see? I hid it under my jacket. When the guard led me back downstairs, I smashed it upside her head. She keeled over like a felled tree. Glass all over the place. Luckily, nobody heard a thing. I took her keys and let myself out. Would still be out, too, if I hadn't been stupid enough to go home on my way through our town. Just for a few hours, I thought. My mom called the police the minute I fell asleep. So take my advice—don't trust nobody, ever—especially your mother."

*

IN THE middle of the night I followed Maxi to the bathroom again. "You saw the doctor today. Were you sick?" she whispered.

"No."

"So he examined you to find out if you're pregnant."

"I'm not."

"And now you think they'll let you out?"

"They have to."

"Don't be stupid. The abbess never lets any girls out until they're eighteen. Even then they have to go off to work and come back in the evenings. I call them the broken girls. They live downstairs. They don't need to have their windows barred anymore, see, because they've forgotten how to fly. So, what do you think about Plan A?"

"If it's so easy why haven't you done it? Don't you want to run away?"

"I don't have to," she said. "My father's getting me out any day now. If I run he won't be able to find me."

"Huh?"

"My mother had a fight with him. She made him leave. And then she signed me away. He doesn't even know I'm gone yet. The instant he does, he'll come for me. And not even the abbess will be able to stop him. He didn't sign any papers. Never would, 'cause he loves me. All I have to do is wait. A couple more weeks, at the most."

"How long have you been here?"

"Long enough," she said quickly. "Let's talk about Plan B. You know how the teacher said you're too smart for our class?"

"She didn't actually—"

"Who cares?" she hissed, continuing more calmly, "Tell them you want to improve yourself. There are other Anstalts (institutions), you know. Can you type?"

"Well, yes, but—"

"Good. There's one in Würzburg for smart alecks like you. Ask the nuns for a transfer. How can they say no? They like it when you show an interest in your future. There's less security in that place. It'll be easy to get out. All you have to do is climb a tall fence."

"How do you know?"

"I grew up around there. Only, my mother wanted me as far away from her as possible. Besides, I'm not interested in schoolwork. I already know things. Things that count." She glared at me with her unlashed, medieval eyes.

"You could be right," I conceded. "It might work."

"I know it will."

"Only—I thought maybe I could escape through one of the dayroom windows. I noticed the bars are kind of far apart . . ."

Maxi grinned. "Liese tried that already. One day when we were lining up to go eat lunch she hid in a cupboard. Sister Gertrude messed up the head count and didn't realize she'd disappeared After we were gone Liese stacked three tables on top of each other, climbed them, and squeezed herself through two of the iron bars. The more she wiggled and waggled and pulled, the tighter she wedged herself between them. It took the fire department an hour to get her unstuck. Everybody thought it was a big joke. Even the abbess laughed for days. So you can see why Liese would like to make you the butt of a new joke, real fast. But that's not the only reason she hates you—"

She broke off before the door started moving. Skinny Elfriede came in and busied herself at the sink. "Sundays are special," Maxi continued evenly, with no perceptible pause. "We get to have a lovely Mass, with a real priest and altar boys. We look forward to it all week, don't we, Elfriede?"

"Huh?" the girl said, looking at us in the mirror. "Oh, yes. The altar boys are nice."

Maxi jerked her chin at me. We left at the same time. Maxi whispered, "She's caught on. We can't meet here anymore. She'll tell on us in a minute. Then they'll watch us like hawks. You don't want them to do that, do you?"

I definitely did not. In our bedroom, in the faint light from the hallway, I saw Maxi pull the wedge out from under her mattress, raise it triumphantly high over her head, and shove it under her bed.

*

LONG after Maxi fell asleep I lay awake and counted my tribulations. The doctor's scorn. The nurse's harsh hands. Mutti's latest rejection. The way O.F. sniffed loudly before speaking. The way he insisted on calling Mutti "Lottchen" as if she were a child, when everyone else called her "Lotte." The disgusting net he wore as a nightcap. The rancid smell of his hair oil. His whining Prussian dialect. The awful, attention-grabbing bluish-white paint on his car.

The list grew longer and longer but Vati's name was nowhere on it. He wasn't to blame for what happened after we drove away from his house. He had no idea where his "no" had landed me. One day I'd have a chance to tell him. His eyes would soften and he'd say, "I'm so sorry. If only I'd known." And I'd forgive him—even if it wasn't his fault. Then I thought of him slamming the door in O.F.s face and almost laughed out loud with glee.

The thrill of my newfound hatreds saw me through the rest of the week. Every time I stabbed the darning needle through a sock and pulled the yarn extra tight, buckling the weave, I envisioned some monk's bleeding blister. More and more, my eyes were drawn to the open window, the bars, the occasional sunbeam that never quite managed to make it to the inside. And the smoldering coals in my gut grew hotter with each passing day.

My slippers arrived on Thursday. When Sister Gertrude gave them to me I examined them surreptitiously for some private sign that Mutti still cared for me—a short, friendly note stuffed in the toe part, say, or a clandestine piece of candy. There was nothing, though. She had clearly severed the last link between us.

It was time to execute Plan B.

CHAPTER 36

W ITH A SAD SIGH, I HUGGED the old-familiar slippers to my chest. "Sister Gertrude," I said, keeping my eyes downcast, "I worry about all the class-time I'm missing. My mother sacrificed a lot so I could become a secretary. I was getting quite good at it, too. Isn't there some place I can practice? I'm afraid I'll forget everything I've learned!"

"That would be a shame!" she exclaimed, perking at my contrite tone. "A mother's sacrifice should not go unrewarded. We do have an Anstalt in Würzburg where you could continue your typing and such. I'm glad you're taking an interest. I tell you what—I'll speak to the Mother about it."

I made my face light up with hope. "Oh thank you," I said. "I'll be ever so grateful."

She studied me, then said impulsively, "Look here. You have worked so hard on improving your attitude, I want you to have first pick at our new shipment of wool-yarn. Christmas is coming. Surely you're eager to start a present for your dear mother? To show her how much you appreciate all she has done for you? What color would you like?"

I shut my eyes to hide a quick flare of anger. "White!" I said, fine-tuning a high degree of ardor. "I'll knit her a scarf! With long fringes!"

Sister Gertrude clapped, delighted. "An excellent idea. We'll start with a couple of skeins."

I never thought I'd be so desperate to get away from darning that I'd take up knitting instead. But I was. And a scarf would be simple to make, even for me. One row right, one row left. Too bad I wouldn't be around long enough to finish the project.

*

SOMETHING new was in the dayroom when we filed in on Saturday morning. Centered in front of the desk stood a low, square table with wheels, and on it sat a big television, already plugged in. Having lived with a set until the week before, I went to my usual table. But the other girls rushed to surround it, poking and prodding. While I listened to them exclaim over the TV I shaped a cozy nest on our table out of monks' socks and lovingly laid our clutch of four darning eggs in its center.

Then Sister Gertrude clapped her hands and told everyone to be seated. Once the last chair had scraped into place she announced, "A very kind women's group has lent us this apparatus on a trial basis. If there are no demerits today it will replace our usual Saturday afternoon radio-hour. The Mother has already picked out an appropriate program for us."

If the Mother had asked our preference I would have voted for the AFN radio station. I'd been seriously looking forward to American voices and American songs. But in this I was alone.

"I've never watched TV before," Johanna whispered in awe. "Will it be like the movies? I like the movies."

Even Maxi seemed impressed. "Well, it *is* an old set they're palming off on us. But still . . ."

Klara's eyes shone as if Sister Gertrude had promised us an early Christmas. She looked up at the ceiling and mouthed a prayer of thanks.

It turned out that discipline was relaxed on Saturdays. Talking was permitted as long as the tone remained calm but since most of the girls were used to whispering they kept on doing it anyway. And although every hand must continue to be occupied productively, it was not necessarily with socks. Various ongoing projects appeared, along with crocheting hooks, embroidery frames and knitting needles.

Johanna helped me wind my loops of white wool into balls of sweet-smelling yarn and I managed to knit about three centimeters of scarf—but what with dropped stitches and uneven rows, I had to unravel it twice and begin again. On my third try the wool was no longer as white as it had been and I was already wishing I had chosen a more stain-resistant shade. It wasn't until I saw Elfriede come out of the storage room with damp hair, flushed cheeks and a limp towel that I realized Saturday, here too, was bath-time.

"Is there a tub in that room?" I asked Johanna.

"There is," she murmured, "and I'm next on the list. I always have to go after that pig."

"What about me?" I whispered. "Will I get a turn?" It wasn't a question that rolled easily off my tongue but after a week of cursory dabbings with freezing water, an ice-cold bedroom, and complete lack of privacy, my skin felt itchy and dry.

Johanna nodded toward Sister Gertrude. "Talk to her. She makes up the list."

I went to the desk, taking my knitting along. The Sister was furtively sucking on a peppermint candy and working four needles at once, a half completed black stocking dangling below them. "Sister, can I have a bath, too?" I asked.

Astonished, she said, "You, a bath? But according to your record, you never—" She bestowed an approving smile upon me. "Commendable progress! But unfortunately we only have one tub, you see. And we must be frugal with our hot water. It's a challenge to provide enough for every girl." She ran her finger down the sheet of paper in front of her. "Your turn is not until *next* Saturday, I'm afraid." She glanced at the smudged piece I was knitting and said gently. "You know, Marianne, that bit of scarf, dirty and twisted all out of shape, is just like your soul—which we will slowly clean and repair, with God's help."

When her words sank in I wished I had a bottle to smash into her well-meaning face. Instead, I willed myself to say calmly, "Yes, Sister. Thank you, Sister," before I removed myself from her presence.

"Does every girl get fresh water?" I asked Maxi when I was seated again.

"Every other one. That's why Johanna's mad at Elfriede, who's famous for picking her nose and then wiping her finger on whatever is near. But even if you do get first crack, there won't be enough in the tub to get your knees wet."

"At home there were always six of us sharing the same water in our tin basin," Klara said. "Mama made us wash at the sink first to keep the precious hot water clean."

On the other side of the room Helga was indulging her fans with another one of her travel adventures. Every now and then they tittered approvingly and Liese said, "Sheee-at!"

"The dumb cow ends practically every sentence with that word," Johanna muttered. "It's tough being in the same dorm with her. She talks all night and gets mad when I start to doze while she's still speaking. They should put all the nasty girls in the same room, don't you think?"

"They'd explode, like dynamite," Maxi said. "Which is why the abbess spaces them so carefully in the first place."

"But Liese definitely has the dirtiest mouth," Johanna insisted. "She makes me feel filthy just listening. How about you, Klara? You're in the bed next to hers."

Klara shrugged. "I put my pillow over my face and pray until I fall asleep. God will protect us if only we ask." She was knitting herself a washrag out of white cotton. Even though it was almost a complete square already, there wasn't a hint of gray in it.

"Sheee-at!" Liese said, right on cue, scowling at me from her chair. "What are you looking at, devil? Keep your eyes to yourself!"

I focused on my scarf, promptly dropping another stitch.

"Liese—just one demerit will keep the television silent today!" Sister Gertrude called cheerfully, pleased with her new power. Immediately, Helga hissed at Liese, who sent one last hateful look at me before turning away.

"I can't figure out why she doesn't like me," I complained. "She doesn't even know me. What could I possibly have done to offend her?"

"You showed up," Johanna murmured.

"Bath-time, Johanna," Sister Gertrude sang out. "Did you bring your things?"

"In my cubby, Sister." Johanna folded the sampler she was stitching and stretched. "Fifteen whole minutes alone in the storage room. The highlight of my week," she murmured, wildly fluttering her lashes.

"*Tja*," Maxi said. "Don't rub yourself raw. There's always a next time."

Shielding her face from the Sister, Johanna stuck her tongue out at Maxi and left.

"But not for you," I whispered to Maxi. "Your dad will surely come any day now. You'll get to spend Christmas with him."

Her face began to glow. "At his house. I'm never setting foot in my mother's again. Not even if she begs me. You want to know why Liese hates you?"

"Yes, why?"

"Because you look like her, only better."

Across the table, Klara nodded agreement, but as far as I could determine Liese and I looked nothing alike. Nothing I wanted to claim, anyway.

"Don't you see?" Maxi said. "You're both the Gypsy type. Long, black, curly hair. Dark skin. Only on you it looks better. That's why she hates you."

I shook my head, unconvinced.

"Okay, okay," Maxi said. "Take away her pimples, cut a couple of centimeters off her nose, whack a few pounds off her butt, and what have you got?"

"A skinny Liese with a snub-nose and acne scars?" I guessed.

Klara giggled. Liese, sensing our appraising stares, shot a killer look in our direction. Fortified by Maxi's explanation, I risked a peace-making smile.

"Sheee-at!" she replied.

"Actually, it's s-h-i-t," I said mildly. "There's no 'a' in it."

"Marianne!" Sister Gertrude cried. "What's this? Are you using a bad word?"

"No, Sister. I'm only helping Liese with the pronunciation of hers."

Maxi sputtered and Sister Gertrude frowned, trying to find a pertinent rule to quote. She said, "We speak only German in here. Save your English words for the schoolroom."

"Which schoolroom?" I asked innocently.

She chose not to reply.

By lunchtime she'd only had to mention the word "demerit" twice. As soon as we came back from eating our potato soup she turned off the overhead lights. Helga and Liese volunteered to draw the curtains, plunging the room into twilight. Sister Gertrude clicked on the set. The girls carried their chairs closer. Some sat on the floor right in front of the screen. The TV droned, then a black-and-white picture took shape. All conversation stopped, even though no sound was coming out of the set.

I saw a street. An ordinary street. A car passed. A toddler rode a tricycle along the sidewalk. On top of the fence behind him a striped cat sat washing itself. Behind it a tree shivered slightly in the breeze. One autumn leaf floated leisurely in a widening spiral toward a black Spitz. The little dog, trotting past the tricycle, was followed by two laughing girls who walked in a straight line down the straight sidewalk, uninterrupted, to where the street ended.

I shuddered, realizing how limited my movements had become since I arrived in this place. My world had shrunk to the size of a room while these two fortunate girls could walk on for miles should they so choose.

Where the street ended they crossed a rugged dirt road and entered a field. Ahead of them stood a mostly bare oak. A squirrel sat on the ground under the tree, sorting through fallen leaves for usable acorns. The Spitz made a dash for it. The squirrel leaped to the trunk and scurried up the bark, its bushy tail undulating behind it.

The set still droned. "Where's the sound?" Helga said. "Sister, please turn up the sound."

Now the camera panned to a third girl, waving from the far side of the field. As she ran closer her skirt rippled and her long hair flowed out behind her. The camera brought the background into clearer focus. A wild duck flapped toward a fluffy white cloud. Behind it the Alps pushed their granite peaks into the sky, dark conifers generously covering steep slopes. I recognized the chain of summits Lucius and I had admired from the Schuttberg on the day we watched the Föhn clear the air. The same mountains had stood steadfast at Freidorf's horizon. My parents had started taking me to explore their heights as soon as I was old enough to walk on my own.

And then I was ambushed by conflicting urges. I wanted to weep, to scream my rage at being locked away, to plead for mercy from someone willing to hear me. But I couldn't think who it might be. So I locked my throat against rising sorrow and my legs against an unbearable itch to walk a long and straight line, plucked my darning egg from its nest, and squeezed its solid ovoid shape between my palms.

A communal sigh drifted across the room from mouth to mouth; the imprisoned girls, shifting in their seats, seemed to envision their shadow-selves running and playing with the three laughing girls on the screen. Maybe the inmates were beginning to feel the stark contrast between where they wanted to be and where they were. Klara, white-faced, wiped at her eyes with the immaculate washrag and whimpered.

"The sound!" Helga ranted. "What's wrong with the sound?"

Sister Gertrude peered myopically at the controls, blocking the screen. A roomful of girls shouted, "Move! Move!" as if their lives depended on it. The nun tried a few knobs, without success, and hastily retreated.

I saw that the vista of mountains had disappeared. There were only the three girls meeting in the meadow and skipping back to the street. They passed the tree from which the squirrel, now safe on a high branch, cursed at the dog. On the sidewalk, an old woman dressed in black, a kerchief tied under her chin, rode a sturdy bike, her groceries fastened to the luggage rack. In the apartment building behind her one of the upstairs windows opened and a motherly hand appeared, shaking out the same kind of fuzzy flannel dust cloth Mutti always used.

"The sound, dammit, the sound!" Liese shrieked, and Helga hugged herself, swayed to and fro, and cried, "God-oh-God!" Then the entire upper half of the motherly figure leaned out to beckon the girls. A low moaning began on the far end of the dayroom, rapidly sweeping across. There were the three lucky girls, skipping to the stoop. And there was the plump mother inviting them in, maybe for Zwieback and hot, creamy cocoa.

The communal sigh grew pitched. I felt an invisible electric force crackling through the air, and smelled a hint of . . . sulphur? The downy hairs on my forearms rose as I remembered where I'd smelled that odor before. Crouching low in my orange plastic chair, I waited for what was sure to come next.

"I need to go home!" Liese howled an instant later.

"Home!" Grete echoed, plunging a finger into her nose.

"Mama!" wailed Klara, rubbing her eyes with her fists. "Mama, please!"

"Goddamn it to hell. The sound! The fucking sound!" Helga yelled, beside herself with fury. A chair fell, and another. And then the same insatiable shadow-dragon who'd played pied piper at the Oktoberfest parade invaded every girlish mind in the room except mine. It gave me a wide berth only because it knew it couldn't capture me twice. All at once, the air was full of missiles—knitting needles, balls of yarn, baby-scissors, a shoe. A basket thumped against the screen, spilling black socks in every direction.

"Girls!" cried Sister Gertrude. "If you don't stop at once—"

What would she do? Threaten us with another demerit?

With a shrill laugh Liese slammed three tables on top of each other at one of the high windows and climbed them toward the bars. A chair skidded in Sister Gertrude's direction, colliding with her robes. She hopped backwards, then ran to her station and picked up the phone. Somewhere in the building a bell clanged just as three darning eggs, made of solid wood, sped through the air in rapid succession, hitting the screen. There was an odd little 'pop' and a trace of ozone as glass bits exploded onto the girls still sitting on the floor. They dodged, screamed, and scrambled out of range.

I sat in the calm eye of the storm, gently putting my darning egg back into the nest I'd made on the table. It was the only one left. Beside me, Maxi's hand was still extended from flinging the others. Johanna was helping Elfriede throw chairs and upend tables. Liese shook the bars she still could not fit through. Klara ran to the door, clawed it, slid to the threshold and curled into a sobbing ball of misery against the wall.

Then the door slammed open. A flock of nuns streamed in, veils aflutter, black sleeves flapping in the charged air. I closed my eyes to shut out the invasion and thought I heard the muffled beating of wings among a chorus of high, childish keening. Then came a protesting hiss, announcing the dragon's departure.

The next time I looked the nuns were everywhere, picking up tables, chairs, baskets. Two of them escorted a trembling Klara back to her seat, a damp spot on the back of her dress distinctly smelling of pee. Two more helped Liese down to the floor. Every glass shard was brushed up before the flock swooped from the room, lugging the TV and wheeled table between them. The guards remained motionless inside the door. And Sister Gertrude, who had been hiding among the winter coats, fingering a rosary, broke through her stupor of fear and limped to her station just as the telephone rang.

She murmured into the receiver, nodded, hung up, unlocked a cabinet, and brought out a radio. With shaking hands she plugged in the cord, turned a knob, and tuned not to a chamber music concert, not to Stub'nmusi (parlor-music), but to the coveted AFN station where Ferlin Husky sang, "On the wings of a snow white dove/ He sends his pure sweet love . . ."

The last time I had heard that song I was wearing Mutti's beige outfit, swinging my hips in front of the mahogany wardrobe, practicing feminine wiles.

Next, Hank Locklin wailed, "Please help me, I'm falling . . ."

Enthralled, the girls leaned back in their chairs and allowed themselves to be lulled into passivity. Their hands, trained to stay busy, sought needles and crocheting hooks. An hour later Liese was once more peppering her sentences with "Sheee-at!" and I understood why Sister Gertrude never called her on it—the word was nothing more than a comforting sort of hiccup keeping Liese content.

Once the radio was snapped off and locked away again the hit parade was replaced with cautious giggles and light gossip and the guards finally walked out and locked the door behind them. I continued to sit absolutely still, hands folded on my lap, stunned by the vision lingering within—of Alpine peaks, now in full color, and of a solitary red autumn leaf spiraling on the light breeze, forever falling.

CHAPTER 37

I STAYED IN MY CHAIR until dinner time, so motionless that I was too stiff to rise when Sister Gertrude asked us to queue at the door. She came hobbling up to my chair, put her mouth to my ear, and whispered, "I noticed you weren't swayed by Satan's assault on our poor girls." Taking my hand, she heaved me to my feet, adding, "I won't forget."

I shuffled to the dining room on feeble legs and sat staring at my plate until Klara asked shyly if she could have my bread. Maxi helped herself to my bowl of stew, and Johanna took the canned pears. The rest of the day was a blur. I didn't come fully alive until the middle of the night, when I found myself in a dream.

It glowed with glorious late afternoon colors. I stood in a meadow, ankle-deep in spring grasses crowded with flowers of every hue, and whispered the magical phrase I'd loved since I was a toddler: *Kunterbunte Blumen*. Flowers in a riot of colors. Low-slanting sunlight transformed each petal into tinted church glass. Where the forest began the space between trees was already growing dark. Lucius stepped from the dusk into a gilded evening, his pants legs rolled, his bare calves long and slim. He moved like a deer, step, stop, step, stop, looking along the ground. What did he lose? "There'll never be anyone else—" he sang to himself.

I waved both arms wildly, crying his name and running toward him. He looked up, startled. Our eyes locked. Then his changed subtly from human eyes to those of a deer and he shifted onto four slender legs and leaped back into the safety of the darkening forest.

I ran and ran but got no closer to him. Then he was gone. A bird called my name. I looked up and saw a distant black crow no bigger than a pencil scrawl. Swiftly, I rose, flying high, the cool wind brushing my hair. Looking down, I saw a patchwork of flower-crowned meadows. Horses galloped in summer-green fields and plump brown-and-white cows congregated in pastures. Acres of black freshly turned soil bordered a village of whitewashed farm houses. Their walls were artfully stenciled, their window boxes filled with a profusion of red geraniums.

I hovered over a sea of unfamiliar red-tiled roofs until I recognized a little hill off to the side. It was like an island, the village church on top. Small, simple and slate-gray, the church had a distinct, bulbous steeple and a walled graveyard. Once, a procession of children had wound up the path to celebrate their first communion, one of them me. I had worn a white dress, a white blossom-wreath in my hair, my white-gloved hands balancing a long, magnificently white candle, decorated with gold.

And now, poised over the steeple's high metal cross, I began to search for my birthplace—Hilde's farm. As I looked, the sky paled and a thick layer of snow hid all the landmarks so that I had to circle each snow-laden farm-roof until at last I found the familiar shape of Hilde's house, plainer than the rest, its old walls unstencilled. Stretching my arms toward it, I was swiftly surrounded by a vast cloud of crows. They cursed loudly and dive-bombed at me. Falling, falling, I spread what I thought were my wings and flapped them, expecting to rise again. But the wings degenerated into useless, thin arms, flailing the air, and I dropped headfirst from the sky. The whole bed shook when I landed.

I jerked awake and sat upright, not knowing where I was and in what time. From one eye-blink to the next I glimpsed a Christmas tree lit with slim beeswax candles and sparklers. Underneath it stood the two small doll houses that Vati, commissioned by the Christ-Child himself, had hastily hammered together. The nearby table was covered with festive holiday platters filled with Mutti's best Christmas cookies, fruitcakes, and white-powdered Stollen (a semi-sweet Christmas bread).

Then the image was gone and I knew I was lying on a cold hard bed in the dorm, covered by two scratchy blankets. Something gave way inside my chest. I stifled the first moan as it rose, transmuting it into a breathy sigh unlikely to disturb the sleepers around me. I muffled every moan that followed with my pillow. Pain ran through me in the same long waves I imagined a woman in labor had to endure. I knew this illness well; it had stalked me for half of my life and was my most shameful secret. The word "homesickness" could not begin to describe the torment.

My skin yearned for the stroke of a gentle hand. I ached to be held, wrapped tight in a soft blanket. I longed to mold myself against a warm, loving presence, was hungry for a crooning voice, for a smile from bottle-green eyes. Once, Mutti had held me like that, her eyes on the clock, waiting to show me to Vati for the first time. But when he came he brought frost to the middle of May. Mutti slumped, put me down in the drawer disguised as a bassinet, and left me to cry myself to sleep, a double waif.

I suffered the malady through the remains of that miserable night. At last the door shivered, a hand reached in to turn on the light, and a Sister called, "Time to get ready for chapel!"

The pain withdrew to linger somewhere within. Bone-weary, I dragged myself down the long corridor behind the other girls, holding on to the wall for balance. I descended the stairs like a toddler or crone, resting both feet on each step. Gripping the rail, I had a mental glimpse of losing my hold and pitching head-first to the landing below, saw myself splayed, neck twisted, dead. It was a tempting outcome; I filed it away, just in case.

I found my spot in the pews and adjusted my eyes to flickering light. Kneeling, I welcomed the sting of hard wood against uncushioned knee caps. When the nuns filed in, keening their lonesome song, I thought there were less of them than before. They spread out in the front pews, careful to leave no gaps between them. Their dull, shadowy forms were a poor contrast to the priest at the candlelit altar. He was attired in brilliant reds and whites and flanked by two altar boys less grandly robed, though with the same two colors. One of them held a vessel in which stood what looked remarkably like a toilet brush. The other swung a metal basket suspended by long chains. It contained the coals of Holy Smoke which, encouraged by the to-and-fro motion, soon filled the chapel with the noxious fumes of smoldering myrrh.

While everyone else rose to stand, sit, and stand again, I stayed down, welcoming the gnawing pain in my knees. My elbows stabbed the top of the pew, my hands forming a steeple, my chin trembling on unsteady thumbs. I avoided looking above the altar where Jesus sagged palely on His cross. Turning to the dark corner at His right I fastened my gaze upon the Virgin Maria whose lips were parted slightly in a sorrowful smile.

Because she was a mere woman, O.F., who had successfully turned the Trinity against me, would not deign to pray to her. Therefore, the Holy Virgin, wrapped in sky-blue veils, acclaimed patroness of Bavaria, was mine for the asking. Had she not been near my age when her troubles began? I imagined her raising her face to look straight back at me, her smile now patient and kind as she waited for me to address her. So I did.

Heilige Maria (holy Mary), I thought at her. *Are you inside that statue? Can you hear me?* When I sensed a sharpening focus, I continued with, *Holy Mother, help me get free. Guide me to Lucius, whose real name, as you well know, is Joseph, too. Let us be joined together forever. Amen.* Solemnly, I crossed myself. Then I remembered that supplicants were supposed to offer something in return. What did I have left to give?

If you help me, I will . . . I began, faltering until the right vow presented itself, *. . . take your name truly as my own and answer to no other. From now on.* Now I could I feel her full attention. But she was still waiting. What else could I offer? *And I will always wear something blue in honor of you and this moment. Amen.*

There. That did it. Her smile widened. "It is given," she said without speaking actual words. "Expect the unfolding. You shall know the signs. But tell me . . ." She seemed to lean closer. "Are you sure you truly want what you've asked for?"

Puzzled, I replied, "There is nothing else *to* want!"

She leaned closer still. "Then consider it done. But remember this— you can always change your mind." Right after her smile and the blue garments faded back into the corner shadows, the Holy Smoke billowed into my face, taking my breath away. My ears buzzed. And then the chapel disappeared.

*

SOMEONE was slapping my cheeks. The smell of ammonia made me gasp and open my eyes. "Oh good!" the nun bending over me said with satisfaction, capping a vial. "You were out a long time!"

"Gave us quite a scare," a second nun added from the foot of my bed, where she was pulling one of the stiff blankets up over my legs..

I laid my hands on my chest to search for the wedding ring. It was still on the string.

"How do you feel, Marianne?" the nun with the vial said. "Where does it hurt?"

It was my moment of truth. Looking squarely at her, I said, "The Virgin Mother came to me in a vision and asked me to take her name. I promised I would. From now on I will answer only to 'Maria'."

Stricken, the nuns looked at each other, then at my hands resting piously over my heart. "You may stay here until chapel is over," the nun near my head said, crossing herself. As she followed the other one out the door, she murmured, "Did you notice her eyes?"

Lying still, I listened to the buzz inside my ears until it dissolved. When my roommates returned from Mass, Maxi came to stare down at me, whispering, "Well, that's better. For a while there your face was as white as paper. I thought you had died, wedged in that pew. Disrupted the entire service." She grinned. "Nuns running in every direction. It took four of them to carry you out. Too bad you couldn't have faked it a bit longer. You'd be on your way to the hospital for sure."

"I didn't fake it at all," I told her. "It must have been all that vile Holy smoke. I never could stand the smell. Listen . . ." I sat up. "Take a look inside my clothes closet. Have you ever seen so many shades of green? I'm longing for something different. Blue, I think. Do you have anything blue you might want to trade?"

Maxi walked her fingers over my things. "Only my mom's stupid silk scarf. It was the last thing I swiped on my way out. What'll you give me for it?" Her hand stopped on the thick moss-green knee socks Mutti presented to me last Christmas.

"Take them," I said. "They're as warm as snow-boots, you'll see." But unbearably itchy; I hoped she was not sensitive to wool.

Later, in the dayroom, I draped the silk square over my shoulders like a cape, tucking the ends into my collar. I felt as if I were wrapped in a piece of the sky. For the rest of the morning I had no wish to move. Safe in my shawl, I sat with my eyes cast down, my hands clasped in my lap, letting the usual dayroom sounds swirl around me. Although the girls gaped and gossiped about my odd affliction, not even Liese mentioned my idle hands. Sister Gertrude's old eyes kept straying in my direction. She seemed worried. I was not, for I was waiting for the unfolding my namesake had promised.

Late in the afternoon I was still sitting in the same position when Sister Gertrude bent over me, shaking my arms to get my attention.

"Marianne?" she said.

"Maria!" I corrected at once.

"But in our paperwork . . ." she began. I stared at her. She swallowed and looked away. "Can you walk?" she asked. "Frau Neumann is here with her flute to help us practice our Christmas carols. Today is the first Advent. Do you want to join the group who is making our Adventskranz (advent wreath), or our singers?"

But I would not sing in a cage, nor decorate it.

Half of the girls stood around a well-dressed matron who was holding a recorder and leafing through a leather-bound book on her music stand. The others occupied three tables, pushed together and heaped with spruce boughs, wire, candles, and red ribbon. Once the advent wreath was completed, it would be suspended from the ceiling by four long red ribbons and hold four fat red candles, evenly spaced. The first one would be lit tonight to the sound of joyously raised voices practicing Christmas *Lieder*. Next Sunday the second candle would be lit along with the first. I was so certain that I would be gone by then there seemed no point in taking part in the activities.

"Thank you, Sister. I believe I'd better just sit and listen. I'm still feeling weird."

Sister Gertrude nodded. "I suspected as much. I can tell by your eyes. They are unnaturally bright. Almost . . . penetrating. I hope you're not coming down with that nasty flu that's going around the order. Why, half the Sisters are already—" She cleared her throat, no doubt only just recalling the Mother's strict instructions not to let the girls know how understaffed their jailers were becoming.

I pulled a chair to a heavily barred window between the group of crafters and the aspiring singers and sat gazing out at the walled court yard. Sister Gertrude, who had always forbidden that particular inaction, solicitously opened one of the panes just a crack, supplying me with fresh air.

"Let's see now," Frau Neumann said. "Do you all know Ihr Kinderlein kommet (come, little children)?" After a few murmurs of assent she blew a high note on her pitch-pipe, nodded encouragingly, and accompanied the girls on her recorder as they started the first verse.

"*Ihr Kinderlein kommet/o kommet doch all . . .*"

Frau Neumann removed the flute tip from her lips. "More jubilation," she said. "Let's try again."

*

THREE evenings later, in half-hour increments, the girls were still trying but never quite reaching acceptable levels of joy; I was still watching for the signs the other Maria had promised. Closing my eyes, I let the sounds of Frau Neumann's Blockflöte (recorder) wash through me. The notes it produced were almost as pure as a songbird's. Then a house-fly collided with the closed side of the window I'd adopted as my semi-permanent resting-place. His transparent green wings whirred straight up the glass as he tried to get out, not knowing that freedom lay only a hand's breadth away.

"Not quite what I had in mind," Frau Neumann said after the girls had muttered their way amiably through the first verse yet again. "But we must move on to the other three verses. Here, let me demonstrate the second—" She blew a note and lowered the recorder to sing with great feeling, "*O seht in der Krippe/im nachtlichen Stall* (oh see in the manger in the dark stable) . . . "

I watched the fly drop to the sill, gather his strength, and crash into the closed side of the window again, butting against it from bottom to top. The next time he fell I touched him with a fingertip, trying to steer him toward his freedom. He did not get the hint. Just as he started to throw himself at the pane once more, I cupped my hand over him, closing my fingers like bars of flesh, and felt vibrating wings tickle my palm.

"And the third goes like this," Frau Neumann continued ardently, "*Da liegt es/ihr Kinder/auf Heu und auf Stroh/Maria und Joseph* . . . (here it lies, on hay and on straw/ . . .)"

At first I thought she was calling my name but she was only modeling boundless enthusiasm for her thick-tongued singers. I stuck my hand between two of the iron bars, uncurled my fingers, and watched the fly lift off. He zoomed to a nearby twig. A bit of weak December sun shone on him, making his whole body sparkle. From a stately cedar growing in the middle of the yard, the same unseen bird who'd fooled Mutti and me on our arrival—was it only a week ago?—repeated his intricate tune, making Frau Neumann's voice appear flat by comparison. Downy red feathers flashed from the cedar's innermost branches. I flexed my hand between the bars and wondered at what exact point confinement ended and freedom began.

Then the fly took off from the twig and, to my horror, headed straight back to the open window. Quicker than thought I slammed it shut; I couldn't bear to watch him get trapped all over again. He brushed lightly against the glass then veered and corkscrewed away.

A heavy hand fell on my shoulder. "It will die out there, you know," Sister Gertrude murmured.

Maybe not. He could just as easily find his way to the kitchen, where the window was kept ajar most of the day, and where he could find crumbs for the rest of the winter.

"The Mother just phoned. Didn't you hear me calling your name?" the Sister asked. I hadn't even heard the telephone ring. "I mentioned your concern to her last Thursday," she explained. "The Mother thought it was valid." She stretched her mouth into an unsisterly grin. "She's been in touch with the school in Würzburg. Arrangements have been made. Tomorrow two of our nuns will escort you there on the train. Now go with the guards to get your suitcase out of the basement. Push it under your bed and don't mention it to the other girls. Envy is a deadly sin and we don't want to be its cause. In the morning, after everyone has left for chapel, you must stay behind and pack everything you brought with you. The guards will take you straight to the Mother's office as soon as you're done." Her smile grew wistful. "I wish you a good trip and a good life."

My insides quivered as I reined in a triumphant shout. When I could trust myself to speak meekly, I said, "Thank you, Sister. I'm ready." Then I got up and walked across the whole room, feeling every eye in it upon my back. Frau Neumann launched into the fourth verse. I couldn't agree with it more: I, too, wanted to bend my knees, raise my hands in thanks, and rejoice with the angels.

The two guards were already waiting for me at the door—both smiling! at me!—and moving aside to let me pass.

CHAPTER 38

JOHANNA SHOOK ME AWAKE in the middle of the night, then she put a finger to her lips and signaled for me to rise. I got out of bed at once, not bothering to step into my slippers until we were both in the hall. She led the way to the bathroom, where she, like Maxi, checked every stall before easing the door shut. Then she asked, "Is it true you're leaving for Würzburg this morning?"

"It's supposed to be a secret. Or so Sister Gertrude said."

Johanna grinned. "These walls have ears. Maybe the abbess thinks if we all knew where you're going we'd give you advice that might do you some good. So listen up." Standing in a white flannel gown that reached to her ankles, her hair unbound, she looked like a film star. Dim light lent the blonde hair cascading down her back a reddish sheen and darkened her blue eyes to violet. "*Why* are you going to Würzburg?" she asked.

"Maxi told me it will be easier to escape from there."

Johanna tossed her head, causing her hair to ripple over its entire length. "Maxi? She's full of it. That place is where I started out. Their abbess runs it like a military command post. No kindhearted Sister Gertrude, either. The place is walled *and* barb-wired. The girls are smarter there—and so are the nuns."

"But Maxi said—"

"Maxi is an incredible liar. You know how she's always saying her father will come for her any day now?"

I nodded.

"It was her father who brought her here."

At first I couldn't take in the words. Then I asked, "Did you see?"

"Everybody knows. The day before you came Sister Gertrude made the mistake of reminding her of it. In front of the whole dayroom. Maxi got so upset she cut off her eyebrows and lashes. If the scissors had been any sharper God knows what she would have done with them."

But the unexpected information only compelled me to like Maxi better. If she found it hard to believe that the person she loved most had betrayed her she was not alone.

"If you want to escape you'll have to do it before the train gets to Würzburg," Johanna said. "It's a speed-train. Only makes two stops, in Augsburg and Nürnberg. Once those tough nuns come to pick you up at the station it'll be too late."

"But a couple of our nuns will be traveling with me. They'll watch me like hawks."

She shrugged. "You'll have to discover their weak points. Maybe they'll doze. Maybe one of them will go to the restroom and then you can catch the other one unawares. Here—" She handed me a scrap of paper.. "Just in case you do get away—go to my house, in Nürnberg. My mother will hide you."

"But she turned *you* in!"

She hugged herself against the cold. "The social worker told her if I came home and she didn't report it at once she'd go to jail. Even though she has three little kids to take care of. Not much of a choice, was it?"

The door swung open, admitting Elfriede, the spy.

"Good luck!" Johanna whispered, carelessly bumping against the girl on her way out.

The nose-picker went to the sink and began her hand-washing ritual, her eyes tracking me in the mirror. But she no longer scared me; I had more important things on my mind, all of them whirling around inside my skull in a dizzying rush. In my confusion I locked myself into the nearest stall, where I sat on the cold toilet seat, staring at the shiny tile floor and trying to make sense of everything I'd just heard. Who was right, Maxi or Johanna? And if Maxi was wrong, why couldn't Johanna be, too? I pulled the blue scarf out from under my nightdress and draped it over my head. It settled over my face like a caress.

"All right," I told the Virgin. "I suppose this muddle makes more sense to you than it does to me. Tell me—what am I supposed to do next?"

*

THE SUITCASE Mutti had given me was our ugliest piece of luggage but it seemed exquisitely beautiful to me as I packed it in the quiet of the empty dorms. When it was closed and securely strapped I wrote a brief note to Maxi: "Thanks for everything. You were a great friend. I wish you well. Maria." I folded it and slipped it under her pillow. In the general predawn rush to get ready for chapel I'd been unable to find even one second of privacy with her.

No sooner had I stripped my bed than the two guards appeared to take me back the way I had come eleven days before. As our steps echoed from the corridor walls, I asked, "Are you taking me all the way to Würzburg?" I could think of nothing worse.

"And who'd watch over our little lambs while we were gone?" the heftier one said.

The other added, "The Mother couldn't get along without us for a minute, especially now."

"I've noticed you're very good at your work," I agreed. So—my escorts would be two other nuns, hopefully less fierce than these.

*

THE FIRST thing the abbess told me when I entered her office was that she'd sacrificed morning chapel for me. Nonetheless, she managed to look quite pleased with herself. "Ah, Maria," she said from her desk. "Put down your suitcase and be seated. I have some things to discuss with you."

I'd been right to assume the nuns would report every word they heard me utter. With great pleasure, I placed the suitcase in the very spot it had been standing the last time I was in the Mother's presence and sat in the same chair, remembering to fold my hands demurely on my lap.

She studied me thoughtfully and said, "I am delighted with your progress. Your attitude is much improved."

"Yes, Mother. Thank you," I murmured with a respectful half-smile. It was getting easier to give the nuns what they were after; who would have thought those miserable summer-camp months in the care of Sisters would have prepared me for such intricate maneuvers? I'd learned my nuns, all right. In fact, I knew them better than they knew me. If Helga understood them half as well she wouldn't be hitting them over the head with glass bottles.

"I agree with the teacher and Sister Gertrude—our girls are too coarse for you," the abbess confided, folding her aristocratic hands in a relaxed fashion upon the desk. "You have a fine mind and, basically, a steady disposition. You'll do well in our Würzburg school. It will prepare you for life outside—perhaps better than the business school you attended before you joined us. In three years you can be a secretary, just like your mother."

I composed my face into lines of awed gratitude. "She'll be so pleased."

"In fact, Sister Gertrude feels some of our more volatile girls might be a bad influence on you. It's why I've decided to act at once. But—" She shifted in her chair. "There has been a change in plans . . ."

During the uneasy pause that followed, I sat as still as my namesake, not letting on that I was afraid of what the soft-spoken tyrant before me might say next.

She cleared her throat. "Everything was perfectly arranged, you see, but then this morning the two Sisters who were to travel with you came down with the flu. They couldn't even get out of bed. And we are so short-handed already I cannot spare anyone else."

"Oh," I said with a sinking feeling. "I'm sorry to hear it."

"Yes," she said. "I was in a little predicament, but then I prayed to the Holy Virgin about it, and all at once I felt inspired to call your mother. At four in the morning! She assured me she is an early riser."

"She is."

"It occurred to me that with the proper instructions she and your sister—who is eighteen, after all—could stand in as escorts. Your gracious mother agreed at once. She's waiting outside, in a taxi. Please be so kind as to ask her to come in while your sister watches over you in the cab." She held out her hand. I wasn't sure if I was expected to kiss it or merely shake it. Her grip was surprisingly flaccid. "Behüt dich Gott (may God protect you)," she said, reaching for her bell. Its peal reminded me of the sound Mutti's Christmas bell made on Holy Eve, signaling to Anna and me that the Christ Child had finished dropping off our presents and we could come out of our room.

As the two Sisters delivered me to the black taxi idling at the curb, Mutti emerged from the passenger side and opened her arms for a tearful reunion. But I couldn't bear the idea of being engulfed by hot tears and wet kisses and quickly turned to say good-bye to my guards. Then, struggling to appear polite, I greeted the woman who had discarded me so easily, informing her that the Mother was waiting for her in the office.

Bravely ignoring my rebuff, she nodded and stumbled up the driveway. That's when I realized that there was over a foot of snow on the ground and that the fluffy things landing on my hair were snowflakes.

"You won't get far in those," the hefty nun said, jerking her chin at my sneakers. "But luckily you don't have much walking to do. Now get in the rear with your sister while we have a quick word with the driver."

I scooted next to the dark form on the backseat. The driver briefly climbed out to listen to the nuns' murmured instructions. Big flakes dotted their habits as they watched him put my suitcase into the trunk and squeeze himself behind the steering wheel again. Then they inclined their heads in my direction and went to the house, their backs powdered in white. I almost regretted giving my woollen knee socks away; the thin cotton socks I was wearing were already damp, conducting the cold.

"Grüss dich, Marianne," Anna said with artificial cheerfulness as soon as the guards had disappeared inside. "What a miserable morning for traveling. Hope you're dressed for it."

"My name is Maria!" I told her vehemently. "And any fool can see I'm *not* dressed for this weather." For some reason, just looking at the complacent outline of my pampered sister upset me.

"Why are you so angry?" she asked, startled at my hostile tone.

"I've spent almost two weeks locked up behind bars," I said, grinding my teeth. "How do you expect me to sound?"

The driver twisted toward Anna. "She has every right to be angry. This is a terrible place. What awful thing has she done to wind up here?"

Anna looked at him, at me, and at the dark, silent façade of the old mansion. "Nothing," she admitted in a hoarse whisper, rubbing at the pale blur of her throat. "She's done nothing at all."

He grunted something to himself and said, "I know it looks harmless from this angle, but it has a reputation. Inside, it's a prison."

"A—*Ach*," Anna stammered with what seemed to be genuine shock. "Really?"

"Yes, really," I growled. "And *you* helped put me there." It was a good thing the abbess couldn't hear me now; she might wonder at the depth of my sincerity.

"I'm sorry," Anna said. "O.F. pressured me into it. How can I make it up to you?"

"I'll think of something," I replied.

But I already had.

*

THE JOURNEY began with admirable precision. Our cab got us to the already bustling Hauptbahnhof fifteen minutes before our departure time. The abbess had given Mutti three tickets. Shortly after we found the right *Schnellzug* and the proper compartment the conductor blew his whistle and the train pulled out of the station. I slid the compartment door shut, noted with relief that we were the only passengers inside, and hefted the suitcase onto an overhead rack before sitting to face my guileless rescuers.

"It's so good to see you!" Mutti tried again.

"Is it?" I snapped. The treacherously soothing movement of the long-distance train made me sound even harsher than I'd intended. I reminded myself that it made only two stops; the first would come too soon but the second was an opportunity I couldn't afford to miss.

"You look a bit pale," Mutti continued, subdued. "Do you feel ill? Maybe you're coming down with that—"

"I'm quite well, thank you!" I leaned against my luxurious backrest, crossed my arms, and smoldered while she bit her lips and gazed at our reflections in the window. Perhaps she thought staring at mine was less dangerous than looking me straight in the eyes.

"I tried to get you out, you know," she said to it softly. "After Lucius came to tea."

"Lucius came to tea?" I echoed, interested in spite of myself.

"He sure did. The phone rang every evening and when I said hello no one would answer even though I could hear someone breathing. Finally I asked, 'Are you Lucius?' and he said, 'Yes.' He's very nice. Anna and I both like him. Not at all what we expected."

"I told you he was nice before all this started!"

She blinked back tears. "I know, I know. I should have listened to you. But I was afraid."

"You're always afraid!" The nerve of the three of them, getting acquainted without me. While I was being fractured and reformed, they had been laughing together, Mutti practicing her rusty English, Lucius trying to impress her with his few bits of German. Maybe he didn't even care that I wasn't there with them. "What did you find to talk about?" I couldn't resist asking.

"He said he wants to marry you. In fact, he brought a stack of papers for me to fill out. Over thirty pages. He's started to petition the U.S. Army. It'll take a long time because the American military doesn't like its soldiers to marry foreigners."

"I don't understand. If you're letting us get married why are we on this train, going to Würzburg?"

"Because . . . apparently I lost all custody rights when I signed you away. At least that's what Frau Berger told me when I called her to say I changed my mind. She informed me that you'll be a ward of the state until you are eighteen. But maybe if you show them your best behavior they'll reconsider—"

"Let me get this straight," I interrupted. "You like Lucius, just as I promised you would."

"Well, yes."

"But you're still volunteering to take me to another jail?"

"It's a school, not a jail. A very fine school. The abbess said so."

"A prison!" I insisted, gripping the upholstered arms of my seat. "Like the one I just came from, only worse. Iron bars, locked doors, high walls with barbed wire on top. Until I'm an adult. And for what?"

She gave a nervous little laugh. "Oh, Marianne, you exaggerate, as usual—"

"Shit!" I cried. "Why don't you ever listen to me? I told you on my last birthday that I changed my name to Maria. Even the abbess called me that at the end." There was no way I could let Mutti get away with ignoring the change anymore. I wasn't about to break my promise to the Virgin. My future depended on it.

"She's telling the truth," Anna chimed in. "The taxi driver said the same thing. He said it only looks nice from the front."

Tears swimming in her eyes, Mutti reached inside her bag for one of her dreadful, scented handkerchiefs. "You don't understand. The abbess demanded I give her my word." She blew her nose in the dainty way I'd always hated and fluttered her hand. "She mentioned dire consequences if I break it. Arrest. Court. Prison." She began to tremble in anticipation of the horrors awaiting her should she dare to defy the nun's wishes. Then she looked fully at me for the first time since our relationship was so hurriedly restored without being repaired. "Besides, you can never live at home again. I couldn't hide you from O.F. And the first thing the police would do is search the apartment." Weeping into her handkerchief, she added, "Don't you see? There *is* no alternative!"

Inside myself, I disagreed. The abbess might have choreographed this entire maneuver to the smallest detail—even taking into account Mutti's unfailing fear of authority—but she'd neglected to understand just how desperate I was.

CHAPTER 39

MUTTI BROUGHT OUT THE BREAKFAST she had so hastily packed while waiting for the cab the abbess had arranged for her. It consisted of a thermos full of hot cocoa and a few hefty squares of her dependably delicious Apfelstrudel, tasting of cinnamon and thick cream even when cold. She had taken the trouble of bringing a corner piece for me to give me an extra dose of sweet-soggy crust. Even in my stressed state the appetite I'd lost in captivity revived instantly. I ate with such gusto, that she, who had only been picking at her portion, pushed it onto my plate, saying,

"I can always get something in the Würzburg train-station, after—"

That little reminder ended the temporary truce between us. I licked sticky juice from my fingers, ignored the napkin she hastily thrust at me, and snapped, "Can't you be on *my* side for a change?"

"I only want what's best for you!"

"Correction—you want what's most convenient for *you*, not what's best for *me*."

Her lips trembled. "This is hardly convenient!"

"Is that why you want me to pay for it with three years of my life?"

She groped in her purse for her silver-plated *Etui*, releasing a whiff of *4711*. I watched her pick out a filtered cigarette and fumble with matches.

"If you're going to smoke that in here I'll throw up," I warned, merciless.

Her eyes filled as she rose and wrestled with the compartment door. It wasn't until she was out in the narrow corridor, standing with her back to us at a gapped window, that I realized I'd been doing a credible imitation of the way Vati had always treated her. Funny how she brought out the worst in some people. Her shoulders shook; it was a good thing she was still clutching her handkerchief.

Soon the train slowed to enter the Augsburg station. Carriage doors slammed; on the platform, hurrying porters banged carts into posts and benches. Footsteps dashed to and fro, some of them running. She fumbled with matches that kept going out each time a traveler, wrapped in a thick overcoat, squeezed past her.

Anna gave a genteel cough, as was her habit whenever she thought she had something important to say. "She'll always be afraid, even if she can see you're right. You know how she is."

I did know. I just kept hoping I could shake her out of it. "Do *you* think I should be locked away?"

"I've done worse things than you," she said, blushing.

I was surprised at the voluntary confession and curious about the titillating facts hiding behind it. One day, I might ask her for details, but at the moment, I had more important things on my mind. Looking through the glass-door of the compartment at Mutti, who had finally succeeded in lighting her cigarette and was releasing the first puff of smoke out the carriage window, I said in my well-practiced whisper, "Listen—you wanted to know how you can make it up to me. I need your help getting off this train. Before we arrive in Würzburg. It's my last chance."

Anna slumped, bewildered, her eyes seeking Mutti as if for advice or approval. Then she looked inward, sat up, and said with resolve. "Okay. What do you want me to do?"

I scooped up every morsel of Apfelstrudel left on the plates, wrapped them in the wax paper they'd come in, stuffed the bundle into my coat pocket, and told her.

*

WHEN the train left Augsburg Mutti stayed at the open window, letting the draft ravage her hair. She smoked the cigarette to a stub, flung it out at the snow, and lit another. Then she stuck her head in to tell us she was going to the WC. "Will you be all right?" she asked Anna.

Anna laughed. "You mean, alone with our dangerous prisoner? On a moving train?"

While Mutti was gone I made Anna repeat every part of our plan. Then she reached behind her neck and unclasped a silver chain, pulling it out of her blouse. From its bottom dangled her St. Christopher medallion, blessed by the Cardinal. It had been Mutti's confirmation present to her. For my confirmation she gave me a rhinestone studded silver cross, which, though blessed by the same Cardinal, languished in its original box in the back of my closet. I'd wanted a medallion too.

"Take it. For luck," my sister said, fastening it around my neck. The disc, depicting a giant carrying a small child on his shoulder, was still warm from resting against her skin. "St. Christopher is the protector of children. Even those who aren't crossing a river. Give it back to me on your wedding day."

Touched by the gesture and by her belief in the medallion's power, I stuffed it past the blue scarf into my collar. It clinked softly against the ring. Mutti came in, looking calmer. We managed a polite conversation.

She told me again how much she'd liked Lucius. "He has a warm smile. And nice eyes. That's the first thing I noticed about him. Those eyes." Soon I had her reminiscing about Yonkers and the odd and remarkable people she had met during her year in America.

As we neared Nürnberg I gave Anna the smallest of nods. A minute later she stretched and said, "I have to go to the WC. Maria, what about you?"

Mutti winced at the name but said nothing.

"Me, too," I said.

"Shall we *all* go?" Anna asked brightly.

Mutti looked at the coats, her traveling bag, my suitcase. "I'll stay and watch our things. Don't be too long!" She was already reaching for her purse when we rose. I was sure she'd light up the instant we were out the door.

The train began to slow as Anna and I passed every WC we came to on our way to the last carriage. There, we locked ourselves into a cramped restroom, squeezing between steel sink and steel toilet. She pulled out a glossy new wallet, contemplated it for a moment, and then, with a sigh, counted out 60 DM. "It's all I have. Good thing I just got paid."

I folded the bills and stuffed them away. Over the noise of squealing brakes and protesting iron rails, I said, "It's only a loan. Now remember to stay here until the train is well on its way again. She'll be too embarrassed to pull the emergency cord. Tell her you tried to hold on to me but I got away. That way you can't be blamed."

"I'll do no such thing," she said firmly. "I'll tell her I helped you because it was right. Will you call me tomorrow morning, just to let me know you're okay? I won't leave home until you do. I'll fill you in about our arrival in Würzburg."

A quick phone call from a pay booth surely couldn't be traced. "I will," I said, modifying the promise with, "if I'm able."

The whistle blew. The train jerked and began to roll. She went out to stand in the corridor while I used the commode, then we traded places. We hadn't been lying—both of us really did have to go. She opened the WC door just a crack, still on the seat. "Good luck! I'll stay in here so I won't have to look."

It was a relief. Any audience might have made me clumsy. I went to the rear of the carriage and opened the final door. When the train was out of the station and just beginning to pick up speed, I looked down at the soft cushion of new snow and jumped.

*

JOHANNA'S penciled map was easy to read. Her apartment was within walking distance of the station, in one of those medieval *Fachwerk* houses with oversized gables that are pictured on postcards and in tourist guides. The house number hung from a cast-iron triangle over the front door. I pushed down the handle, but could not make myself go in until I'd walked twice across a cobblestone square and around a whole block of look-alike buildings, all of them massive and unwieldy, to give myself time to gather some courage. It was only when my feet began to go numb that my resolve finally firmed. I *had* to ask Johanna's mother for asylum; I had nowhere else to go and needed to find a hiding place fast.

The foyer's walls were dingy with poverty and age, and dank from being subjected to centuries of base household smells. The stairs I climbed sagged in the middle. Though well-scrubbed, they lacked the high gloss finish Mutti and Frau Forster imparted to theirs every week. I found the door numbered 2-C, put my finger on the bell-button, and was unexpectedly drenched in sweat. What if Johanna's mother refused to take me in? Could I really trust the optimistic offer Johanna had stayed up half the night to make? For her sake, I ignored my protesting heart and pushed the button. When the bell shrilled I jumped.

Somewhere inside small children began to screech a quarrel. A woman's voice scolded. The screeching stopped and I heard the shuffle of footsteps. The door, scrubbed down to bare wood around the handle, opened just wide enough for a woman's head to squeeze through, her face a worn-out version of Johanna's, golden hair dimmed and pulled back into a tight bun from which long strands had escaped to hang limp. The eyes, surely once as deep blue as Johanna's, had dulled and were ringed with dark shadows. Instead of thinking that, just a few years before, this woman had been as vibrant as her daughter, I thought that a few years hence Johanna would fade to look like her mother.

The odor of mildew and cabbage soup wafted out as an unseen child began to wail loudly. The woman looked from me toward the sound, and at me again, harassed and impatient. "*Ja?*"

"I—I'm a friend of Johanna's," I began.

"Sorry. She's not here," she said and abruptly closed the door in my face, leaving me to stare at the bare patch near the handle.

"I—I—" I stammered, unable to comprehend her rudeness. Then I blushed, feeling foolish and ashamed. Shaking the smell of cabbage gas out of my hair, I reached for the bell-button again. And reconsidered. Most likely her welcome would be no friendlier on my second try. Obviously, she did not care for Johanna's friends. Nor, perhaps, for Johanna. Odd, how wrong some kids could be about their parents. Despite Johanna's insistence, her mother was not looking for an addition to her crowded household. And to be honest, I didn't want her to take me in. For one thing, I couldn't stand the smell inside. For another, she *had* turned in her own daughter. Why should she hesitate to do the same thing to me?

What was I doing in Nürnberg? Logic told me that as soon as Mutti reported my escape the Würzburg nuns would call down the line, warning the clerk behind this town's ticket counter to expect a runaway. Racing back to the station, I stopped just long enough to wait for a bumbling, dirty-white streetcar to clear an intersection. I longed to be where streetcars were a familiar, two-toned fresh white-and-blue, longed to warm myself in the radiance of Lucius's smile.

The ticket clerk, bored now that the morning rush was over, hardly looked up as he took my money and handed me a ticket. The train to Munich screamed into the station a couple of minutes after I found the right platform, proving that the Holy Virgin was still on my side.

*

NOT knowing what to expect, I was cautious upon arriving in Munich. Instead of exiting onto the platform with the other travelers I elected to skirt the last carriage, crossing a river of tracks until I found a deserted back-route out of the station. The temperature had dropped since I left the abbess. After a couple of blocks the thin, green corduroy coat I was wearing gave up the last vestige of my body-heat to let in the cold. I couldn't call Lucius until he was off-duty. In the meantime I needed a hole to curl up in where I could unclench my jaws and thaw out. I passed several hotels until I found one I thought I could afford.

Since I'd never rented a hotel room or seen anyone go through the process I felt a bit timid, stepping up to the counter. Willing my teeth to stop chattering, I asked for a small room. The sharp-nosed, balding clerk, dressed in a fine navy suit, looked at the spot to the right of my feet and asked where my luggage was.

"Uhm," I stammered, trying to think. "Still at the station?"

His lip curled. "I see!" he said with as much discourtesy as he could stuff into two words. "We don't normally give our rooms to people without luggage. May I have an ID?"

"ID?" I repeated dully. "What kind of ID?"

His shrug was colder than the outdoors. "Your passport will do." Reading its absence on my face, he added, "We need it for the registration form we're required to turn in to the precinct."

"The precinct?" I gulped.

He stared at my soaked tennis shoes, the sagging cotton socks, my purple knees at the hemline of the juvenile plaid skirt, and sneered, "I doubt you have as much as a toothbrush on you. What kind of hotel do you think we are running? If you're still here in ten seconds I'll pick up the phone and call the police."

I was out the door in four, across the street in five more, and on the streetcar waiting at the curb in the next. I got off at the nearby Stachus, wondering which department store I should honor with my presence first, the *Kaufhaus* or *Herti*. Not that it mattered. The day was long and browsing up one store and down the other was the only option I had left. Then I remembered how I'd wanted to stop at the makeup counter in July, on my way to Vati's office, so I could to impress him with painted lips and a sample-dab of costly perfume. Maybe I could impress Lucius instead.

CHAPTER 40

IF I WERE A POLICE OFFICER SEARCHING for a girl like me I'd stake out the highway near Henry Kaserne, knowing that sooner or later she'd be drawn to it as a bee to a blossom. Then I would drag her to my well-hidden squad car and drive her back to the abbess.

But I was only Maria, out in bad weather and gathering dark, surrounded by ice and snow. I paused at the beginning of the access road to the base, dug a load of slush out of my sneakers, and furtively scanned the highway's shoulder behind me. It was covered in virgin snow except for my unwavering footprints. A war of two voices was raging inside me. One warned me to watch my step because danger lurked nearby. The other insisted I was far too unimportant for a city-wide hunt; no one really cared where I was or with whom. Nevertheless, it was the German way to be methodical and tie up loose ends—and I was a loose end.

I looked down the full length of the road, past the telephone booth all the way to the base gate, from which one lone guard soldier watched me lean into the desolate wind—hopefully only because he was bored and had nothing better to do. Was he as cold as me? Most likely he wore long johns under his thick winter uniform. I envied him his leather boots and white gloves.

It was noticeably darker inside the phone booth. The ceiling bulb was broken; I could barely see the numbers when I dialed the barracks. The soldier who answered yelled for Private Duncan. Seconds ticked by. Lucius was my last and only hope. What if he wasn't even there? I could hear men laughing, a radio tuned to AFN, an undecipherable conversation, and then the musical, familiar voice I'd so often imagined at night in the barred dorm. "Private Duncan here," it announced from the receiver's earpiece.

"Don't say my name," I whispered, although I wanted to shout with relief. "I'm at the gate. Can you get a pass?"

"Hey!" he said. "Don't go away. Pass or no pass, I'm coming out to see you."

That's when I began to believe he'd make everything come out right.

*

HE LOOKED just as I'd imagined while lying on my dorm cot: long-legged grace bundled in a beige camel-hair coat. I let his arms enfold me and closed my eyes, savoring the embrace. "I was in—uh—the place where they put bad girls," I told him, not knowing the English word.

Looking confused, he said, "The boarding school? In Augsburg?"

So Mutti had told him one of her little white lies.

"No, here in Munich," I said. "A prison for girls."

He stared. "You don't mean . . . reform school? Behind bars? That's not what your mother told me!"

I attempted a smile. "She took me there the morning after the police arrested me. Today I escaped. Now I have to find some place to hide. I tried to get a hotel room on my own. But the clerk said I needed papers."

He held me away from him to study my face, making me glad I'd wiped off every trace of the many lipstick tints I had tried on in the *Kaufhaus*. I'd scrubbed away the sample perfumes, too; they were making me queasy.

"I'm sorry," he said. "I had no idea you were locked up. After the Polizei took you away I started calling your house. By Thursday I was real worried, but then your mother invited me over and she was so nice and all, I just assumed you'd managed to bring her around."

Apparently he didn't get the urgent telepathic message I sent him from chapel on Tuesday before dawn. And I'd imagined it was a blast of thought-energy too powerful to miss.

Then the last vestige of daylight went out of the world. The wind turned ugly, throwing hard flakes at our faces. It blew up the sleeves of my paper-thin coat and down into my collar. I pulled at the blue scarf, adjusting it to close the only gap I could do something about.

"You need a place for the night? Let me run back to the barracks and ask Spider if he knows—"

"No!" I said. "Don't tell anyone I'm here. Especially not him. It's his fault they caught me."

"Say what?"

"He told you that restaurant would be safe when he knew it was not."

"Oh, Maria, come now!" Lucius said in that half amused, half irritable tone adults liked to use with children who were beginning to annoy them. "We stayed past the eight o'clock curfew."

"But they came on the dot. As if someone told them I would be there."

"It was bad luck, is all. Why would Spider tip off the cops, anyway?"

Because he is a snake, I wanted to say. Because he thought I'd be an easy catch and I got away from him, and he's the kind of man who makes girls pay for making him feel foolish. Maybe I was wrong but how could you trust a guy who wore sunglasses at night?

"We'll wait for a cab to show up," Lucius said. "Take it to some of the outlying inns. I'll get a room and soon as I'm in it I'll help you climb through the window. Then I'll leave and you'll have the room to yourself for the night."

The wind blew its icy breath through my soaked shoes and stiffened my wet socks. My toes ached. I jumped in place to pump more blood through them. It didn't work; the wind was too strong.

"I can't wait much longer," I told Lucius. "I'm wearing a stupid skirt!" Although the red-and-brown plaid was the warmest of the bunch Mutti had packed in the suitcase, it left my legs bare from the knees to the ankles, and allowed a draft to crawl under its hem and creep up my thighs.

"We'll have you indoors in a jiffy," he said, scanning the road to the highway.

"In a what?"

"Like that!" He snapped his elegant fingers and gently pushed me against the glass-walled booth. It proved a poor wind-break; after a few minutes I felt my hands go numb. There wasn't a single headlight in sight. I decided to call for a cab but when I went into the booth I could see neither the dial nor the roster of cab numbers posted next to the phone. I stayed inside, jumping in place until two beams stabbed through the glass.

Lucius rapped. "A cab. Quick, follow me."

*

AS SLEET battered the windshield the driver took us from one inn to the next and left the motor idling while Lucius ran in to ask for a room. He always came back with a long face, shaking his head, the smile he put on to encourage me getting smaller with each stop. Soon the driver became his coach, suggesting more out-of-the-way places where surely, on a freezing December night, at least one room was bound to be vacant.

It never was. We went from Gasthaus to Gasthaus, not even skipping the one in the middle of the forest where Spider had trapped me in his cognac web. The cab drove on to the far side of the woods where the night seemed even darker and the wind howled even louder.

We kept the meter running for two hours. Every now and then Lucius gave it a worried look. Finally the cab stopped again. The driver and I watched Lucius jog to a door and slip in. Then the man turned to me. "He won't get anything here either. Between the two of you, you're one unlucky couple. He's too dark and you're too young. I only hope he has enough money to cover the fare."

I knew at once he was right, and wondered how soon Lucius would realize that the inn-keepers were lying to him. When he came out I could see by the stiff flick of his lips that he'd been turned away again.

"Lucius," I whispered as he settled beside me. "We better go back to Henry. This is not working."

He nodded reluctantly and asked the driver to make a U-turn. Then he fished in his trouser pocket and pulled out a roll of cash, holding it low so he might count the bills without alerting the driver. Throughout the long return trip he recounted them several times between anxious glances at the relentlessly ticking meter. Neither of us had a good plan about where I could spend the rest of the night.

So I thought of a bad plan instead. When we passed Warner I adjusted my scarf and buttoned my coat up to the chin. Just before we came to Williams I asked the driver to stop. "I know someone from school who lives in one of these little houses," I told him. "I'll sleep on her couch."

Lucius handed over nine 10-*DM* bills. He gave the tenth to me. "I wouldn't want it to burn a hole in my pocket," he said with a tart little laugh. "Two hours of nothing. The amount of the fare could have paid somebody's rent for a month." He watched the cab's tail lights shrink and disappear. "You really got a girlfriend around here?"

"I wish."

"Just what I thought." He turned helplessly in a tight circle. "We're in a blizzard in the middle of nowhere and my pass runs out at midnight. Like in the fairy-tale. Now what?"

"I'll show you." I led him past the outlines of small, unlit houses until we came to the sheds. "Have you noticed that one of them is always open?" I asked.

"Right! With a black BMW motorcycle sticking out," he said, catching on.

We found it by bumping against the open door. Lucius dragged the BMW inside, shut us in, and rummaged in the inky interior, pushing at wooden crates and cardboard boxes until he'd succeeded in creating some space for us in the middle. He had to lead me to it, for I saw only black upon black. We sat on the dirt floor. In less than five minutes it sucked what little warmth I had left right out of my body. Then the door blew open, slamming against the outside of the shed wall.

"Freeze our butts off!" he muttered, struggling up to drag two crates into our space. He pushed them together and helped me sit on one. While I kneaded my fingers, hoping to avert frost-bite, he tried to reclose the shed door, but its latch was broken. It only stayed shut until the next squall sucked at it again. From where I sat, Lucius was a blurred sketch in a shadow-patch, crouching to sweep his hands over the ground until he found a brick that made a good door-stop. The wind rattled the door as soon as he pulled it shut. It wedged a gap for itself and then howled through it.

"Great place," Lucius muttered, sitting close beside me. "All snug and cozy."

"And dry," I added. "Don't forget dry."

"As dry as the North Pole." He wrapped an arm around me. I leaned into the teddy bear softness of his coat, suppressing a tremor. "Wish I had a flashlight," he murmured. "Might find something useful in that stack."

"We can't open the boxes. It would be wrong," I said.

"No worse than coming into the shed."

"But the door was already open. We didn't break in." My coat seemed to be getting thinner, the socks wetter. I pressed my face to his shoulder, trying to control my shivers so he wouldn't guess just how miserable I really was. And yet, I preferred this inhospitable storage shed to my white metal cot behind bars, the two blankets on top of the mattress tucked at precise angles. I even preferred it to the plump featherbed at home, for Lucius was with me and I was free.

"It all happened so fast." He shifted closer, the crate under him creaking in protest. "You should have let me go back to the barracks to ask Spider—"

"Uh-uh!"

He sighed. "Anyway—tomorrow's bound to be better. I'll get my CO's permission to go to the bank at Warner, first thing. Draw out some money for you. Maybe you'll find a place on your own. Things always look better in the morning." He told me how hard his first winter in Montpelier had been, when he didn't have any money and no place to stay. "That Vermont cold wore me down. After a while I got so desperate that I was willing to do anything to get out of it. Even join the Army, which was the last thing I had on my mind. I make a lousy soldier."

We leaned into each other and trembled in unison.

"I gave your mom some forms to fill out so we can get married. Think she'll do it? She seems very nice."

"She is," I admitted grudgingly. "But always afraid. It's O.F. who is mean."

"What about your dad?"

"What about him?"

"Maybe he could help."

I laughed, recalling how he'd slammed his door in O.F.'s face. And mine. "No," I said. "He wouldn't."

"Well, then. You have any friends you could go to? Grandparents?"

There was a lot we didn't know about each other.

"My mother's parents are dead," I explained. "My father doesn't speak to his. I only met them once, during school holidays. Separately. For a few minutes."

That long-ago summer, Anna and I had traveled with Vati on a ship down the blue Danube, in the same direction my little handball had floated. Only, we'd stopped in Vienna. Vati took us to the bank where his father worked. Was I five? Six? I recalled a man with curly salt-and-pepper hair who didn't seem to know how to smile. He leaned over the counter to put one Groschen (penny) into my hand. That's as close as he came to me, then or ever. My grandfather was and remained a gray-haired stranger who dropped a coin the size of a dime into the hand I held out in greeting. As far as he was concerned it was all I was worth.

Vati's mother, blonde and fluttery, had even less time for us. "You know very well that children make me nervous," she had reminded him. He *should* have remembered, for she had given him away soon after he was born to be reared in the house of his stingy, conservative father, where he wasn't welcome, either.

Vati and I were even more alike than I'd thought.

"Parents," Lucius said. "Hard to figure sometimes. Good thing we have each other. We'll be just fine once I get out of the service and we take off for California. You won't need a coat there. It gets so hot in L.A. you can barely stand wearing a T-shirt."

"A what shirt?"

He put my hand to his undershirt collar. "This thing."

"People in California wear undershirts in public?"

"It's not an undershirt if you don't wear anything over it. Too hot for regular shirts, see?"

I could no longer imagine that kind of heat.

After a few minutes of companionable silence, Lucius said, "I know a good way to warm us up. Guaranteed."

"What?"

"Let me kiss you. Just once. Then you'll see."

The one thing that had helped me through the past week and a half was that, no matter who said what about me, I knew I had done nothing wrong. I wasn't about to give that up now, so I pushed him away.

"Okay, okay," he said. "Just thought I'd mention it. You're the most stubborn girl I ever met."

"It helps."

He laughed. "Being that I waited half a year for one little kiss I suppose I can wait another six months."

"Especially since it's not just one little kiss you want."

"We do things different where I come from. I keep forgetting that," he said. "But I'm sure looking forward to May. Maria Duncan. How does that sound? Mrs. Joseph M. Duncan."

"Mrs. Lucius Duncan," I revised. What if spring never came? Right now I could hardly believe in tomorrow.

He put his arm around me again. "Funny, last Tuesday I woke up with the notion you were trying to call. I stayed close to the phone all evening. But after I met your mom and your sister I just assumed I'd been imagining that something was wrong. If I had known where you were I might have done something useful."

"You did," I said, snuggling against him. "You brought Mutti the forms. You told her you were serious about me. You're here now, freezing with me when you could be in your nice bed."

"I wish I could do more."

"Me, too," I admitted.

"I have to go soon."

"Already?"

"Almost a quarter to twelve. You wouldn't want me to turn into a pumpkin, would you?"

"Not even an icicle," I said.

"Where will I meet you with the money?"

"The bus stop at Warner." It had three solid walls and a real bench inside.

"Keep thinking about the California sun, Maria. Sunburn. Sunstroke. Hot desert winds. Ever hear of Death Valley?"

"No."

"Hot enough to die there if you run out of water."

"Like the Sahara?"

"Maybe worse. Hotter than hell."

"Is hell hot? I think it's cold, Lucius. Everything turned to ice. Hell is at the North Pole."

"Couldn't be," Lucius said. "It's where Santa Claus lives. You must mean the opposite end. On the bottom. The South Pole."

"And heaven?"

"It's got to be inside the earth. Molten rock. Liquid fire. You warm yet?"

"Not yet, Lucius."

"Here." He unbuttoned his coat and draped it around me. "I'll be okay. I'll run."

Greedy for warmth, I almost asked him for his dry socks too. But if he gave them to me—and he probably would—how could he run with those stiff leather boots?

"One day we'll laugh about this," he promised, putting his cold lips on my marble forehead. On his way out he pushed the door all the way shut. I heard the brick scrape as he propped it firmly against the wood from the outside.

Then he was gone and I had only the shrieking wind for company, which was so furious that Lucius had blocked the entry that it shook the flimsy walls, finding plenty of knot holes and cracks to whistle through. I could hardly feel my feet anymore. Figuring that wet socks and shoes were worse than bare skin I took them off and set them on the now empty crate beside me. I wrapped the unlined corduroy coat around my legs, pushing my feet into the shoulder openings of the sleeves, and put on Lucius's thick camel-hair coat, the padded lining inside still warm from his body. Nonetheless, I was too uncomfortable to nod off and the night stretched endless before me.

*

AT FIRST light I heard a muffled noise from the other side of the rickety walls: footsteps on crusty snow. I pulled my feet out of the sleeves and felt around for my shoes and socks. There was a dull thud as the brick was tossed aside. Then the door swung wide, and a burly male shape stood in the frame. I stopped breathing.

"Hello?" asked the husky-voiced man. "Ist jemand da (anybody here)?" His thick form blocked out most of the still dusky sky. He took a step in, feeling around for his BMW. He took another step, fumbling in his pocket for matches, or flashlight, or key.

I bolted past him. He shouted, "Halt!" but I was already veering on to the empty highway, running as fast as my bare feet allowed. He didn't bother to chase me. When I reached the bus stop at Warner I limped inside, cowered on the wooden bench, and sorted through my bundle. I'd lost both socks and my shoes were frozen solid. I put them under the bench and wrapped myself up as best I could, discovering that the coldest part of the night came just before dawn.

When the day's first car drove past I finger-combed my iced hair, hoping I looked presentable enough to fool the commuters who would soon come to surround me. My safety depended on them thinking I was a commuter, too. In any handful of Germans there was at least one who felt it his duty to call the police on someone like me.

In her polished-oak office across Munich, the abbess sat waiting.

CHAPTER 41

LUCIUS PEERED INTO THE CROWDED BUS shelter carrying a sealed paper cup. For the first time I saw him wearing what he called his "fatigues." The olive-green work-uniform, which included a lined cap with ear flaps and a padded jacket, made him look like a stranger until he beamed a smile in my direction. Drowsy commuters, following the smile's trajectory, grew wide awake and witnessed our self-conscious reunion.

"This coffee was the only hot thing I could find," he said, trying his best to ignore them. "It tastes kind of nasty so I put lots of cream and sugar in it for you."

I pulled a purple hand out of the camel-hair coat's pocket to take it from him. "Thank you, Lucius."

"Here's the dough," he whispered, stuffing an envelope into the same pocket. "Easy with the cash, Maria. I cleaned out my account for you—not that there was much in it. It'll have to last you a while. We've got to start saving toward an apartment and stuff."

"I'll return what I don't use, just as soon as I can," I promised, keeping my eyes firmly on him so I wouldn't have to see the disapproving German faces around us.

"Okay then. I've got to go back to Henry. Give me a call tonight to let me know you're all right." He stooped to look deep into my eyes. "Don't give up on us, Maria. This is just a little rough spot. We'll get over it as best we can."

I wrapped my hands around the cup, grateful for the heat it provided. "I know. I won't forget all you've done."

He grazed his knuckles over my cheek. "You'd do the same for me."

As he turned away, I asked, "Who is Santa Claus? The one who lives on the North Pole?"

He stopped. "You don't know Santa? With his sack of Christmas presents for good little boys and girls?"

"*Sankt Nickolas*?" I guessed. "The one with the funny hat and beard? The last time I saw him he was wearing Mutti's earrings. He doesn't live anywhere, Lucius. He's a lie, and the North Pole is *too* where hell is."

He cocked his head, as if trying to see me more clearly. "You best watch out that the cold doesn't sneak into your heart, Maria," he said so softly that I had to strain to hear him. "Then hell would be inside you. Neither one of us could live with that. So drink down your coffee, girl, and thaw out while you still can."

After he left most of the travelers lost interest in me, except for one woman who frowned with distaste as she studied my corduroy-wrapped legs and the dismal tennis shoes under my seat. Drawing on a cigarette, she raised a razor-pared eyebrow at me and blew out a lungful of spent smoke. I recognized her from the last time I ran away, in July. Back then, she had been sitting where I was sitting now, broadcasting an identical degree of disapproval at me. I had been mere minutes away from my first look at Lucius.

I pulled my gaze from hers and concentrated on sipping my coffee. When I was done she was still staring at me. She seemed about to speak, but changed her mind, peeled back a glove to glance at her wrist watch, ground the half-smoked cigarette out with her high-heeled boot, looked intently down the highway, and went outside. From the way the others queued up behind her I guessed the next bus into the city must be imminent. Once the last commuter vacated the shed to get in line I eased my feet into the frozen shoes, ready for boarding but unwilling to quit my shelter before it became absolutely necessary.

Then I remembered I had promised to call Anna this morning, so I shuffled as fast as I could to the payphone that stood next to the gate. Anna answered after the first ring, her voice terse.

"It's me," I said. "Can you talk?"

"Ja. Mutti's already gone. Where are you?"

I wasn't about to answer that question. "What happened in Würzburg yesterday?" I asked her.

"I managed to get Mutti calm by the time we pulled into the station. The two nuns storming our compartment looked like boxers in disguise. At first they thought I was you and tried to drag me off. Then I showed them my wallet. The only thing they found in it was a paystub made out to Anna Edel. Mutti and I could hardly wait to get out of there. All the way home, she agonized about you being out in the cold, and about all the trouble you brought on our heads, and about how it would end. And then she came up with a brilliant plan."

"Oh?"

"The only place where you'll be safe. Where no one will think to look for you."

"Where?"

"In Freidorf. On Hilde's farm."

I was hooked in an instant. But how could we ask her to take me in? Like Vati, she didn't have a telephone. "What do we do?" I scoffed. "Write her a letter?"

"Mutti already did. She wants you to come get it and deliver it to Hilde yourself."

A ruse? To pull me in with the best lure they had?

"I swear it's the truth. By St. Christopher. By the Holy Virgin," Anna said.

I was torn. "But—the girls who ran away from the Anstalt got caught because they went home. Their mothers called the police."

The wire hummed. Then Anna said, "Mutti won't. I swear it."

I wished I could believe her; her plan was the best offer I had. "Is there any hot soup?"

"Mutti stayed up late to cook one of your favorites—split pea with wieners," she said. "If you tell me when you'll get here I'll heat it for you. She sent me to the bakery for hot rolls already, smeared on butter, and heaped on sliced salami—all on the off-chance that you'd get in touch."

Anna was either more clever—or nicer—than I'd ever given her credit for. "Half an hour," I said, hanging up before I could change my mind. A real meal. Warm pants and my winter coat. Last year's lined snow boots, my wool cap and mittens. I'd stay just long enough to eat and change. What could it hurt?

Turning, I saw the bus had arrived and the final passenger was climbing aboard. If I ran I could just about make it. But I was tired of running—or maybe I no longer knew how.

*

I REACHED the apartments after the job holders had departed for work and the children for school, leaving only the retired and housewives at home—hopefully huddling near their stoves, far away from their windows, hugging cups of hot tea. I tiptoed upstairs, glancing apprehensively at Frau Forster's closed door as I tapped on our own. Anna opened at once, finger to lip, quietly engaging the dead-bolt after I entered the hall, and beckoning me to the living room, where she studied me from head to foot.

"You must have had a bad night," she said, keeping her voice low.

"I did," I replied, matching her tone.

"What happened to your socks?"

"Lost."

She prodded me toward the coal stove, which emanated luxuriant heat. "Sit. I'll bring you a some water so you can soak your feet."

I sank onto our comfortable couch, easing off the chafing shoes. My feet were unnaturally white, marked with purple bruises and blisters. Anna carried in a pail of tepid water, a towel slung over one shoulder. I dipped my toes into the bucket. They burned as if the water were boiling hot. Wincing, I lowered in the rest of my feet.

Next, Anna brought band aids and two plates of the promised Semmeln (rolls). The moment she left again I wolfed every satisfyingly greasy slice of salami off mine and followed up with the buttered rolls. Swallowing half-chewed bites, I looked around the room. It seemed more bleak than I remembered, and less familiar. Mutti's typewriter stood on the desk, a sheet of paper wrapping the platen, my old work book propped beside it. Who was doing my lessons? I swished my feet in the bucket, impatient at being pinned down.

Anna returned with two steaming soup plates, putting one on the coffee table before me.

"Have you been practicing?" I asked, indicating the typewriter.

She gave a discomfited cough. "Since the business school is refusing to refund the tuition I decided to attend in your stead. You don't mind, do you? I think it's fun."

"And the atelier? Horst Obdach?"

"I'm bored with drawing toothbrushes and toothpaste. Besides, the girls at your school get to wear fancier clothes. And I *like* learning secretarial skills. I'm still working at Horst's in the afternoons."

"Like mother, like daughter," I said, rolling my eyes. Then I fell upon the chunky soup, slurping it like a heathen.

She went to the phone. "I promised Mutti I'd let her know the minute you walked in." She dialed and murmured into the receiver, "She's here. . . Not good . . . I'll let you talk to her yourself." She tossed it to me.

"Hello?" Mutti said. "Mariandl?"

"My name is Maria."

"Ach Gott (oh God)!" she said with an exasperated sigh. "Not that again! Listen. Someone from the Youth Authority was waiting for me at the office. She insisted on a detailed account of what happened yesterday. In front of my new boss. Can you imagine? You'll have to disappear, fast. I meant what I said on the train, Mariann—Maria. You can never live at home again. I see only two possibilities. Either you stay in the village until you're of age or you marry Lucius, provided I regain custody soon. It's your choice to make. Think hard before you decide."

But I didn't have a thought in my head. "Did you pack my winter clothes?" was all I could come up with.

"Your warmest things. I'm afraid you've outgrown the snow boots. I slid an envelope full of cash into the side pocket before I hid the suitcase under your bed. Take out enough to buy a new pair and pay for your train ticket. Give the rest to Hilde. She'll need every D-*Mark*. You eat like a horse."

The doorbell shrilled. Anna peered through the curtain and blanched. "They're here," I whispered into the receiver, already groping for the towel. I shuffled to the phone to hang up, then went to stand behind my sister and gaped at the official-looking car parked at the curb. It was empty.

"Hide in the bedroom," she hissed, staring wildly about the room. "Don't make a sound!"

I pushed my soup bowl under the couch, the bucket and towel under the desk, and followed her into the hall. The bell shrilled again, longer this time.

"Ja?" Anna said, her eyes dark with fright.

"Fräulein Edel? Bitte aufmachen (open up)," a stern female voice barked.

I tiptoed to the bedroom. Behind me, Anna made a valiant effort to sound sleepy. "Einen Moment," she said, unbuttoning her blouse with clumsy fingers and pulling half of her hair out of the beehive. "Let me finish getting dressed first."

My mattress was stripped, the featherbed gone, probably already stored in the attic. Someone had ripped Ricky Nelson off the wall, leaving behind one single thumb tack. I opened the window and pressed my handprints all over the snow-covered sill, hoping to confuse the Youth Authority snoop. Then I considered the inside of Anna's closet. It was crowded with dresses and shoes and the two glamorous, puff-skirted gowns Mutti had helped her sew for her dance competitions. One was powder-blue, the other azure. I had a quick mental flash of the last time I'd seen her wearing the lighter gown, her lids caked with matching eye-shadow, a powder-blue satin bow centered in front of her beehive, a fake beauty-mark, twirled on with a gray eyebrow pencil, gracing one cheek.

Carefully, I climbed over the pile of shoes, parted the long garments, and squeezed behind them, leaving the wardrobe-door ajar. I heard voices in our hall—Anna's breathy and high-pitched, overridden by the commanding tones of a middle-aged woman. They moved to the living room where, I prayed, we'd left no obvious signs of my presence. For a few minutes the woman lectured at Anna, barely giving her a chance to respond. Then they came into the kitchen, from where I could hear every word. Chairs scraped. The woman said, "Whose dishes are those in the sink?"

"Mutti's. She had to leave early but kept breakfast warm for me. I slept in."

A pot lid was raised and slammed down. "Pea soup and salami? What an elaborate breakfast!"

"Leftovers, from the day before yesterday."

The woman sniffed. "Ja, wirklich (oh really)! Might I have a look in the bedroom you share with your sister?"

"It's all mine now," Anna said. "There's nothing to see. Hardly enough space for one person to turn around in. Mutti is going to take out Maria's bed but I'm keeping the wardrobe."

Stopping at the bedroom door, the woman said, "Mein Gott (my God), it's freezing in here! Was your window open when I drove up?"

"I like to sleep with plenty of fresh air. Don't you?"

The woman cleared her throat. "I leave that to the young. My bedroom is cold enough with the windows closed tight." She went to the sill, no doubt to lean out and examine the snow below for recent footprints. Scanning Anna's bed, she said, "A mighty fine featherbed you have on there. The old-fashioned kind, bulky but unbelievably warm. No wonder you're not bothered by the frigid air. May I?" I heard her flip back the covers.

"Hey!" Anna protested.

Already, the woman had moved on to Anna's closet, pulling the door open wider. "Look at those shoes!" she exclaimed, her voice alarmingly close. "And the gowns! All yours?"

"Excuse me," Anna said, her voice gaining strength. "Surely my clothes are of no concern to you?"

"Everything here concerns me," the woman said, backtracking to my wardrobe. "Your sister's? Hardly a stitch in it—but what a rat's nest of books!"

"I like clothes. She likes books." Anna sounded genuinely irritated.

"Fine, fine," the woman said. "Just you remember what I told you, Fräulein Edel. If your sister tries to get in touch—and she will have to in weather like this—you must contact us immediately. Otherwise you are violating the law."

"I remember," Anna huffed.

"Good. You have my card. Be sure to ask for 'Frau Hecht' when you call. I may return from time to time to check on things."

"No one will be here, Frau Hecht," Anna said, almost hostile. "Mutti and I both work all day. Why waste your time?"

"Oh, I never do that. And in case you're wondering—none of the girls who escape do so for long. We are too thorough for that. Thank you for showing me around. Guten Tag."

Now their steps retreated to the hall. Neither had anything more to say. Then the apartment door opened and closed. Perhaps Anna flung the lock home a bit hard or attached the safety chain with too much satisfaction, for Frau Hecht's descending steps halted, pivoted, and pounded across the landing. Seconds later, another bell rang, this one fainter, farther away.

Anna returned and slammed the window shut. "Maria?" she whispered, slowly parting the ball gowns I was hiding behind. I attempted a smile. She shook her head. "Can you believe it? She's talking to Frau Forster! I do hope that witch didn't see you come home." She went back to the window. "The instant Frau Hecht drives off you'll have to run. The reason she didn't check my wardrobe more thoroughly is because she made me open the one in the living room. I showed her Mutti's side, and when I said I didn't have a key to unlock O.F.'s part, her eyes started to gleam. I'm sure she suspects you're hiding in it. No telling what she'll do next."

I got on my stomach in front of my bed and pulled out the suitcase. The snow boots were lying on top. Mutti was right. I could no longer push my feet down past the insteps, especially with the blistered heels.

Anna rummaged in her sock drawer and tossed me a heavy pair of baby-blue socks. "I'm afraid none of my shoes fit your big feet. Shall we try O.F.'s waders?"

"Not on your life," I told her. "I'd rather walk barefoot on rusting nails."

I settled for a dry pair of tennis shoes since my leather shoes had smooth soles that were bound to slip on iced roads. A minute after the car finally drove off Anna dialed Frau Forster's number intending to lure her away from the spy-hole at her front door. I waited until the telephone in Frau Forster's kitchen stopped ringing and Anna, nodding vigorously at me, began to engage her in conversation. Then I cautiously made my way downstairs and hugged the long wall all the way to the far end of the building in an attempt to evade the neighbors' attentions.

As I passed the door to Frau Keppler's lobby it opened and her arm shot out to pull me into the foyer, suitcase and all. With an urgent "Shshsh!" she gestured me to put it down and beckoned me to look out over her bulky shoulder. Two policemen—the same who'd arrested me for violating curfew—were striding around Mutti's corner of the building and entering the lobby to our apartment.

Frau Keppler picked up my suitcase and waved me into her overheated living room, carefully locking her front door behind me. "As soon as I saw the patrol car slow at the curb I knew who it was coming for," she said, looking more serious than I'd ever seen her. "I'm only glad you got out in time."

CHAPTER 42

THE REALIZATION OF HOW CLOSE I'd come to being caught buckled my knees. I dropped heavily onto her couch, feeling the springs sag under my weight. Seppi uncurled from the other end and crept closer, wagging his rear and making little chirping sounds deep in his chest. Considering all that had happened to me lately, giving him to Frau Keppler had been one of my better ideas. At least I could now walk away from the city knowing he would not suffer for it. I took off my gloves, put a hand on his stove-warmed flank, and stared blindly at Frau Keppler's cramped floor-to-ceiling bookshelves, wondering just how much of an explanation she expected about current events.

Crossing her arms over her ample chest, she said, "We've all been highly entertained by the goings-on at your end of the building. Your Onkel Franz—"

"He's not my uncle!"

" . . . outdid himself this time. One night you're ushered home by the police. Then you're dragged off again by your dear family, along with a suitcase—only to return a couple of hours later. The next morning, in full daylight, Herr Hohner pulls you to his VW by the end of a rope. Tongues were wagging. And last Thursday—after dark, mind you, though we still noticed—a beautiful brown giant comes and disappears into your apartment for hours on end. Frau Forster reported gay laughter. As if it were a crime. And don't think I didn't see you trudge by a while ago, nose and knees purple. But I'll ask no questions; I am discreet. Now . . ." She rubbed her hands together briskly. "I'm about to make a pot of tea. I believe chamomile is called for. Calms the nerves. Munching cookies does, too. Here, have some."

She pushed a copper-bright canister at me. "You'd better stay a while. Give the police the opportunity to hie away and the neighbors enough time to untangle themselves from their curtains. Incidentally—I found some great used books for you near the university. I said to myself, I've got to buy these for Marianne. She's learning English. They'll be just the thing."

Rivulets of sweat had begun to run down my chest, soaking my undershirt. I rose, dislodging Seppi, who had trustingly put his big head on my lap. "I've changed my name to Maria," I announced, peeling off my heavy coat.

She chuckled fondly. "When I was your age I changed mine, too. One wants to have something of one's own, you see." She plopped a stack of books in front of me.

At first I thought all five were alike, for the same two words were written on each. Then I saw that "Zane Grey" was not a title but a name, and that the pictures on the jackets varied somewhat. They were all written in English. What a wonderful way to while away dreary winter afternoons on Hilde's farm! "But where will I put them?" I asked, picking a cinnamon star out of the canister. "I barely managed to stuff my Langenscheidt into the suitcase."

"You may borrow my old rucksack." She poured me a cup of pale yellow tea and tipped the canister, filling a plate with an assortment of Christmas Plätzchen (cookies). "I bake a batch every week. All the old family favorites." Her smile trembled and steadied again. Then she went to the window. "There. They're leaving. Empty-handed. Poor Frau Forster must be so disappointed."

"You think Frau Forster—?"

She shrugged. "There are only two telephones in the whole building. You want me to suspect Anna?"

"I bet it was that horrid Frau Hecht. She went to talk to Frau Forster after she finished scaring Anna half to death. Maybe she called the precinct from there."

Frau Keppler's eyes sparked. "Maybe Frau Forster suggested it. In case you forgot it was she who spoke against me after she found out I was a Protestant. Until that sad day the neighbors used to invite me over for coffee. Frau Forster is a proper Catholic witch."

She helped herself to an anise crescent and began to pace, alternately chewing and muttering to herself. "Now the question is, how do we get you out of here with everyone craning their necks for the next installment of your life-drama? They must have seen what I saw. No doubt they are still lurking near their windows, trailing dust cloths and cooking spoons. We'll have to fool them all. Find their blind spot. The angle from which they cannot see."

She paced a few more rounds, looking thoughtful. Then she planted her feet in front of me and asked, "Did you know that old women are nearly invisible?"

"No," I said, perplexed.

"Ah, but they are. And old ladies dressed in black cease to exist entirely. Come into my bedroom and I'll prove it to you."

*

A SHORT time later I shuffled out of the lobby door engulfed by one of her black trench coats. It was big enough to fit over my winter coat with room to spare. On my head, pulled low over my brow and all but obliterating every feature except for my nose, I wore a bulky black kerchief, tied under the chin. My feet were encased in Frau Keppler's second-best rain boots. The old black bike I was pushing had balloon tires and was even uglier than my painted green workhorse. Following Frau Keppler's advice, I did not take the foot path leading directly from her corner to the side-street, but hugged the back walls of the next two apartment buildings to the end of the block, where the newly plowed street curved toward Schleissheimerstrasse.

Anybody in our own building who was curious enough to lean out of a window, hoping to trade precious heat for potential gossip, might have caught a fleeting glimpse of the hulking, cumbersome shape of an elderly woman pushing her bike around that distant corner toward the stores for some shopping.

When I reached the intersection at Schleissheimerstrasse I was relieved to see that the sidewalk running alongside it had been cleared, too. I mounted the bike the prissy, old-lady way and pumped stiff-backed to my regular bus stop and then past it, pretending not to see the police car lurking on the far side of the bakery.

Half an hour later, long enough to feel the cold even under two coats, I stood at another bus stop, this one twenty blocks closer to town, the bike leaning against the shed. When the bus finally came into view I unbuttoned the coat, untied the head-scarf, and took the book-heavy rucksack out of the bike basket. The only person getting off the bus was another old woman dressed all in black. I pulled off the coat and scarf and thrust them at her in passing. In return, she slipped me a rumpled paper sack.

I got on, paid my fare, and made my way to the rear. One of the seats was still warm, the indent in it bigger than any I could have made. There were cookie crumbs all around it. My suitcase was in the luggage rack above. I wiped off the crumbs, settled on the indented seat, and opened the sack. As an ultimate sacrifice, Frau Keppler had emptied the entire canister of Christmas cookies into it.

They were a delectable comfort to me on the little black train as it wound its way south toward Freidorf, stopping at every village along the tracks.

*

IN THE middle of the afternoon I stood on the narrow platform at Waldbach, a small village in the woods, and watched the train puff away, leaving a long plume of smoke that soon drifted above the tree tops. I tossed the empty cookie bag into a bin and crossed both sets of tracks in my new snow boots, looking for a half-remembered shortcut through the dusky forest. Each tree was a perfect Christmas tree, laden with snow. After a while the suitcase grew heavy; I transferred it frequently from one hand to the other. At last the path widened and came out of the trees to meet a road undulating gently between white fields. In the distance ahead I saw a collection of red-tiled roofs surrounded by snow-covered farmland which was in turn ringed by the woods. The horizon was resplendent with steeply rising Alpine peaks, flawlessly white against a blue sky.

My chest tightened. The suitcase slumped and dropped to the snow. I collapsed on top of worn leather, unable to hold back an abrupt gush of tears. I cried for the little girl who had been hiding in Hilde's stable, ratted on by her best friend, found by Mutti, and pushed into the rear of the white VW to follow behind the moving van towards Munich. I cried for Putzi, my black-and-white cat, left behind. I cried over the many years of homesickness and alienation in the city the villagers called *Minga*. I cried for the loss of Hilde and Gabriel, and cried even harder because I was finally about to meet them again.

The act of forcing that little girl to leave the place of her birth had paled her existence in exile. Now the faded copy she had become was rejoining the original, waiting in the ether, and they aligned seamlessly to form one vibrant whole. All at once the colors around me grew sharper, purer, more alive. The world that had tilted awry eight years before finally shifted and clicked into its proper angle. The distant church bell gave a welcoming chime. I got up and strained forward, the suitcase weightless in my hand.

*

I FOUND Hilde in the farm yard on top of an enormous dunghill that was surrounded by a pond of sludge. With her pitchfork, she was emptying a wheelbarrow load of steaming hay and straw she had scraped from the stable floor. Then she stabbed the pitchfork into the heap, tipped the barrow to pour out a puddle of manure tea, turned the wheel 180 degrees, and guided it down the wide planks that serves as both ramp and bridge. She was wearing a tattered scarf tied behind her ears pirate-style, a heavy jacket, and a frayed woollen skirt, the legs underneath encased in a man's trousers and oversized boots—her mucking-out clothes.

I was standing still, making no sound, but she turned around anyway, as if I had been calling her name. For an instant, her gentian-blue eyes widened. Then she inclined her head without speaking.

"Grias Di (greetings), Hilde," I said. "Here's a letter from Mutti."

She took it, glancing briefly at the suitcase. Her face was weathered, her cheeks apple-red; the end of her nose dripped. She wiped it briskly onto her sleeve and stuffed the letter into a pocket, unread. "Gabriel sleeps in Frau Brandt's old room these days. Remember where it is?"

I nodded. Frau Brandt had died there and been laid out on her bed for a week, some months before we left. On our moving day I was still convinced the cloyingly sweet smell of death would linger in that room forevermore, even though by then the mattress had been removed along with the corpse.

"Tell him your suitcase goes in the little spare chamber down the hall. Tell him to fix you a bite to eat."

She went on with her work and I navigated through the snow, crossing the farm yard. I went through the humid stable astir with cows, into the equally warm and dank kitchen on the other side of a solid metal door, and through a dark hall and staircase up to the second floor. Halfway there, I heard a terrible bellowing from above. A hurt cow? A slaughtered bull in his last throes?

I knocked on Gabriel's door.

He said, "Herein (come in)!"

I left my baggage in the hall, went in, and cautiously sifted the air. It smelled as crisp as the outdoors. The brother of my heart was sitting on his bed, wearing nothing but long johns, his white-blonde hair in wild disarray. His featherbed was piled up in a wrinkled heap at the top end of the mattress. A pillow next to it was still balled from supporting his cheek while he had slept. The sheet had become dislodged at the foot of the bed, exposing smudged gray-and-white striped ticking.

He had kept the face that was carved into my soul—slanty blue eyes, sparkling and clear, a gentle half smile curving his wide, cherry-red lips. No more talkative than his mother, he nodded at me, shook the spit from the mouthpiece of a giant brass trumpet, and made it bellow again.

Like the supplicant I was, I sat timidly on the side of his bed, not bothering to take off my coat, for the only room ever heated on Hilde's farm was the kitchen, around meal times. For a full five minutes Gabriel blew his horn, his cheeks pale skin balloons. Then he shook fresh spit out of the mouthpiece, put the instrument tenderly to rest on top of the featherbed, and proceeded to wrestle me flat on to my back.

"Took your time coming home, didn't you?" he said. "We waited for years."

"Mutti wouldn't let me visit. She was afraid I'd want to stay." And now, oddly, she was hoping I would.

It wasn't until he rubbed a scratchy cheek against mine that I noticed he wasn't a boy anymore. He was, in fact, nineteen—the same age as Lucius. I found this amazing.

"I'm sorry I told your Mutti where you were hiding, that last day," he said. "Not that it made any difference. They would have found you anyway, in the end—but I'm sorry just the same."

On Gabriel's advice I had crouched inside the pig sty in the murkiest part of the stable, both of us hoping I'd be overlooked.

"You know I could never resist your Mutti's slightest request. And Mom threatened me with violence for delaying the van," he explained.

"I know it wasn't your fault," I said. "But, oh, Gabriel, how much better it would have been if they'd gone to Minga without me and left me here with you!"

Without warning, he hugged me so tight that my breath was expelled as a groan. Then the hard muscles in his arms loosened and I relaxed against him. Somewhere inside, a child laughed with delight. I closed my eyes and savored the familiar smell of his hair: damp feathers mixed with a faint whiff of cow manure. I had come home.

CHAPTER 43

I SLEPT IN AN ICE PALACE. Its many rooms were silent and cold. Outside, snow drove through arctic black air, covering the real shape of things. The farm was my limbo, where clock time had ceased to exist. In my narrow chamber, cocooned under down and floating on horsehair, I listened to the wind howl around solid walls. The curtain before my small window obscured the gradual waning of night. I drifted from dream to dream, allowing a kaleidoscope of childhood memories to flow through my mind.

Gabriel's horn woke me in stages, traveling the brass-scale from deafening blare to sputtering wheeze. Finally I roused enough to toss the featherbed over my face, attempting to muffle the sound. The abrupt move woke Putzi, my private bed-warmer. Curled against my neck, he began to purr loudly into my ear. I stayed in my feathery womb until hunger overcame lassitude. Then I kicked off my pajamas and dressed while gathering the courage to throw back the covers. Disturbed by my gymnastics, Putzi stretched, jumped off the bed and sat by the door. He knew that Hilde always milked the cows before sunup and ladled a generous amount of top cream on his saucer. I followed him downstairs, quickly retying my blue silk scarf before buttoning my bulky cardigan.

The kitchen was as empty as Hilde had left it on the way to her factory job. I added kindling to the coals in the cook stove. The easterly window beside the sink had become a pink square. While Putzi daintily lapped his cream on the sill I dashed arctic water on to my face, blotted it dry with my towel, and squinted at myself in the mirror. In the first tender light my image was flawless. A frail sunbeam put auburn highlights in my dark hair. I stared into my eyes, watching the pupils dilate as I moved closer, and shrink to pinpricks after I blinked. Alone in the farm kitchen, I was the ice princess wearing a crown of dawn light.

At last the horn blew its last note. I heard the faint rustling of satisfied cows browsing the autumn hay in their cribs. Their milk was already in a pail on the floor of the pantry, but a small pitcher of cream stood on the counter next to the breadbox. I poured it into a dented pan and set it on the stove top. While it warmed I measured two heaping spoonfuls of Ovaltine into a couple of mugs and stuck a third in my mouth where it soon melted to malty syrup. Then I settled on the sofa, a hand's breadth from the stove, and opened my second Zane Grey book.

When Gabriel came in he was carrying a book of his own, which he deposited on the table on his way to the sink. His eyes were sleep-swollen slits and his hair stood on end. After he plastered it down with a wet comb and rinsed the sleep from his eyes he cut eight very thin slices of rye. Then he smeared them with homemade butter, lathered on jam, stuck all the layers together, cut the concoction in two, and handed me my half of our breakfast. Carefully avoiding the broken center springs in the middle of the sofa, he sat at the far end, stretched his mouth wide enough to take a huge bite, and lubricated it with a sip of the Ovaltine.

"Cookies," he said, speaking the first word of the day.

I grunted encouragingly.

"Your Mutti's Christmas cookies," he elaborated, warming to his topic. "She let me cut them out. Stars, bells, crescents. Her kitchen would smell of anise and ginger and cinnamon." He sighed, looking at his rough, sticky bread. "Roasted hazelnuts. Slivered almonds. Powdered sugar." He took a dejected bite. "I got to brush on the icing while she chatted with me about school. When I was done she'd ask me to point to the cookie I liked best. Then she gave it to me. Still warm from the oven. You have no idea how much is used to envy you." It was the most he'd said since I arrived the week before.

"*You* envied *me*?"

"I wanted a mother like yours who took the time to talk and bake and was always there."

"Too much there," I said. "*I* envied *you*. Hilde never cared what you wore and where you went and when you came back. She gave you plenty of space to grow in any direction you chose. She left you free."

"She left me alone."

"My Mutti never left me alone. She told me what to think and when to think it."

"It's called guidance," he said, absently stroking the cat, who had curled up in the valley between us.

"It's called suffocation," I told him. "For instance—your trumpet. Did Hilde buy it for you?"

He nodded.

"Why?"

"Because I asked."

"And did she insist you practice at least an hour a day so you wouldn't be wasting your time and her money?"

"No. She just left me alone."

"Why *are* you practicing, then?"

"Because I want to."

"Right. In fourth grade I fell in love with a guitar. All I wanted was to sit on my bed with it in the evenings, stroking the strings and listening to the sounds they produced. But she insisted on sending me to a music teacher who tried her best to teach me classical guitar. My fingers grew calluses, and every evening Mutti reminded me how much the lessons cost and how I'd better not waste them. And while I practiced O.F. would tell her I had no talent for it and would never get it right. So I gave up."

He slammed his mug on the table. "That repulsive reptile! He should have praised your efforts instead."

"No. He should have left me alone to do it my way. Like Hilde. You can only be free if no one expects anything. What does Hilde expect of you, do you think?"

He shrugged. "To turn out all right in the end. Meanwhile, she goes about her business."

I slammed my cup next to his. "Let's trade. I'll take Hilde. You get Mutti. I'll throw in one O.F. for good measure.'

He wrinkled his nose. "I don't need him. Nobody does. The whole village thought he was an insufferable asshole. We were all hoping he'd move away—but not with your Mutti. She was one of our own."

I decided to keep my opinion on that subject to myself.

He put on his boots and coat. "Listen, I'll be working a short shift today and I'm getting the next two nights off, so I've invited some of your former classmates over for a musical evening tonight. I thought it was about time you socialized with old friends."

"You're playing for them?" I asked, trying not to wince.

"Of course. They love my music. And believe it or not Hilde has volunteered to fry up a batch of Hasenöhrl (pastries). Your Mutti's fool-proof recipe. Could you do me a favor and put on our bathwater before we get home?"

I told him I'd be delighted. In leaving, he handed me the book he'd walked in with. It was a photo album. "Your Vati's rejects," he grinned. "I used to rescue them from your trash bin regularly. Your village-school pictures, too. I guess your Mutti thought she wouldn't have room for them in the city. See if you'll recognize the four who are coming tonight. Karl, Wanda, Ursel, and Felix."

When he was gone I lost myself in my Wild West saga, marking the words I needed to look up in the Langenscheidt later. Once my mind numbed to English phrases I opened the album on my knees. At first I had to laugh—not only was I in every picture, but I was glaring at the camera in most of them. In one I was playing in the dirt with marbles, a small, tow-haired Gabriel patiently guiding my pudgy toddler-hand to a good shot. In another, he and I were shepherding the cows home from pasture in the late afternoon, both of us wearing nothing but our Lederhosen. On the next page we sat on the wagon atop an immense pile of new hay as a team of oxen pulled it toward the barn.

"Smile!" Vati used to demand before taking a shot.

How can I, my round, clear eyes said in these outtakes—when you've spent half the night yelling at Mutti? When you spanked me an hour ago for refusing to eat my cooked liver? When you just finished chasing us up a steep Alpine path as if the world were on fire?

I leafed through the pages, seeing not only the stubborn eyes of the child, but hearing Vati's biting tone, the insults calculated to prod the rest of us into instant obedience. "Look happy!" he'd order. "Don't waste my film!"

Gabriel had pasted my three early school pictures on the last pages of the album. There was the usual snapshot of the new first grader holding the traditional Zuckertüte (cone filled with candy). It was followed by a class portrait including the long-haired, glamorous new first-grade teacher who only lasted a year, framed by the traumatized faces of refugee children whose names I could no longer recall. But I recognized Ursel, standing in front, and Wanda, beside her. I found my face in the last row; as usual, I was one of the tallest pupils in class.

The most interesting picture of all was the last. It wasn't even glued to the page, as if Gabriel wasn't sure it belonged. Immediately, I knew why.

It was taken at the Freibad (outdoors pool) when I was two or three. The pool sat on a wooded slope near the river and had the charm of a natural swimming hole. All the children congregated there throughout the summer. It even had a high-dive board. In the photo Mutti was posing in front of it and I stood as if trying to shield her, my little arms extended to ward off something unpleasant. She was wearing a dripping two-piece suit that showed every curve and had not yet pulled off the bathing cap she had worn for her streamlined, spectacular dives. It was evening. Everyone but us had already gone home.

I was wearing nothing at all. The panties I usually donned in lieu of a bathing costume had snapped their rubber waist band during my last bathroom break. "Jump back in the pool without them," Mutti had urged. "There's no one here to see but us." Swimming in silken warm water with no barriers between it and my skin had been wonderful. But she'd been wrong about who was there to see.

Vati did his best to capture the lovely image Mutti presented. Earlier, he'd taken several shots of her flawless dives. Within a few years, half of those would end up in Mutti's album, half in his. I wasn't in any of them. The only reason I was in this outtake at all was that I refused to step out of camera range and was busy scowling at someone lurking behind the diving board. Someone who didn't belong, whose hungry eyes were glued to Mutti's pleasing curves. Vati must not have noticed him until after he developed the film. It was O.F., who soon thereafter insinuated himself into our lives, billing himself first as the loyal family friend, then as Mutti's trusted advisor as she talked of getting a divorce. Vati was right to throw the print into the trash.

I stoked the stove and damped it down, recalling the first time O.F. dared to insert himself into our attic apartment one frustrating Saturday evening after Vati had failed to arrive for the weekend. The interloper chose to visit after Anna's and my bedtime. She was already asleep but I was keeping vigil, certain Vati had simply missed the early train and was taking the next. When I heard the sound of a male voice coming from the next room I perked but realized almost at once that the whining, wheedling tones could never have been made by my father. Soon O.F. switched from telling Mutti that Vati did not deserve her to asking if he might unburden himself of his own domestic troubles.

"If *I* may cry on *your* shoulder next . . ." he began.

"By all means," she said graciously. "You've listened to me long enough."

He proceeded to catalogue the irreconcilable differences between himself and his wife, who had recently walked out on him, spiriting their daughter away with her. They left in the dead of night taking the suitcase and a week's allotment of household cash while he trustingly slumbered on in their matrimonial bed. Her good-bye note consisted of four words: "I want a divorce." He suspected she lied about him to the neighbors. Maligned his good name.

He was getting all worked up, his voice rising, wavering, breaking. To Mutti's unsuspecting ear, his sobs must have seemed genuine. But through the thin plaster wall separating the couch from my bed they seemed entirely false, meant only to sway my mother's guileless emotions.

Until I held the discarded photo in my hand I had been sure my dislike for O.F. originated that Saturday night. Could it be that I'd sniffed out his intentions at an earlier age?

I stuffed the snapshot back in the album, slapped it onto the table, and wrapped myself for my daily walk. It led down the same lane my parents had strolled upon in sunnier times, arms linked, trailed by Anna and me. But this harsh winter day I lumbered along on my own, fighting drifts. Past the shop of the carpenter who had built and stained all three of our wardrobes. Past the house of the elderly shoemaker who had measured our feet, traced their outlines onto paper, and presented to us fine leather shoes "with room to spare" every year for as long as we lived in the village. Old Frau Meier, who used to own the last house in the lane and had shamed Vati on our final family amble, had since gone the way of Frau Brandt.

Chin tucked inside my collar, I went to the brink of the Höllgraben (creek-bottom land) to peek down into the gully's white wilderness of thickets and trees. By late February the first Schneeglöckchen (snow bells) would break through the snow. By April the steep, icy slopes would have turned into a flower paradise, the creek roaring with melt water. Hopefully, I'd get to stay on the farm long enough to watch the May bells bloom.

Turning to the right, I ambled up toward the bakery, intending to skirt around it until I caught the scent of fresh-baked rolls. Cloaked and bundled, I paid for a half-dozen hot from the oven, ignoring Frau Hauser's puzzled look. She couldn't quite make out who I was under my hood and I liked it that way. I finished the third roll halfway between the little gray church and the butcher shop, where I bought a string of wieners. The butcher's wife recognized me and seemed delighted to see me again.

"How odd," she said. "Just this morning someone called asking if you were here. 'Of course she's not here,' I told him. 'She moved to Munich eight years ago and we haven't seen a hair of her since.' If only I'd known—"

"No, no," I quickly interrupted. "Don't tell anybody, please. It would spoil everything."

She looked taken aback, and as I went to the shop-door her eyes measured my waist line. Perhaps she was wondering why I had chosen the worst part of the year for a visit.

Veering toward Hilde's farm, I gulped three of the linked sausages, not tasting a bite. On a good day I could easily have devoured the contents of both bags before I entered the yard—but this was no longer a good day.

Who was fanatic enough to rout me out even here?

Feeling endangered for the first time since my arrival, I locked both the front door and the cellar door before filling Hilde's biggest pots and setting them on the stove top to boil. I mucked out the stable as conscientiously as I was able, every scrape of the blunt-edged spade asking, "Who?" When I'd dumped the last wheelbarrow load, I bolted the stable door from the inside. Then I spread fresh straw over the stall floors and collapsed onto a chair at the kitchen table, pulling the album close for another look at the pool picture. Something about the focus of O.F.'s predatory eyes was still bothering me. Could it be—was it possible that it hadn't been Mutti he was ogling, but me? Dangling the odious snapshot by one corner, I rushed to the stove and tossed it into the firebox, slamming its cast-iron door shut behind it.

The pots were at a rolling boil. As daylight began to wane I unhooked the tin tub from the stable wall. I filled it with steaming water and added enough cold so it wouldn't scald tender skin. Then I refilled the pots for Gabriel's bath. Lighting a small candle, I set it on an upturned bucket beside the tub, draped a decrepit sheet over the only window in the stable, and shut the metal door to the kitchen in an attempt to contain the most pungent odors. Then I immersed myself, leaving knees and shoulders exposed. There was a good reason Hilde and Gabriel took their baths with the cows. The beasts kept the air comfortable, and the tub-spills found their way to the same drain that took the herd's overflow.

Despite all my precautions I felt hunted, sifting nervously through gentle cow noises for more sinister sounds. Just as I realized my bathwater was cooling I thought I heard some pounding from far away. But then a cow mooed and when she stopped the sound was gone. I rose, shedding water, and had just reached for my towel when an unseen hand rapped on the outside of the stable window, dislodging the make-shift curtain and making it fall. The towel slipped from my grasp. I stood rigid, staring at the blurred shape on the other side of the glass.

"Maria?" It was Gabriel, pressing his face to the pane. "Are you in there? Open up!"

Panic and relief surged through me in piercing consecutive waves. Trembling, I retrieved the towel from the cement floor, shook off stray bits of hay, and draped it around me. As I stumbled to unbolt the stable door I hoped the layers of dirt on the window glass and the feeble candle flame had kept him from seeing more than the vaguest of outlines.

CHAPTER 44

GABRIEL TURNED ON THE LIGHT, frowning at me. "We never lock our doors! We're not in Minga!" His gaze swept over my bare shoulders and legs and then he looked away but not before I saw that he knew exactly what was under the towel I was clutching around me.

"I was scared," I muttered, sorry I'd let my fear crowd out good sense.

He held up a package and some letters. 'You done with your bath? I brought the mail. Half of it's for you."

"Wait in the kitchen. I'm getting dressed," I said.

He considered the tub. "Still hot?"

"Warm. Shall I pour it out?"

"No, leave it for me."

"But it's dirty."

"Not as dirty as it's going to be," he said. "Mom will be home in half an hour. Let her have the next lot of hot water. The sooner she gets done with her bath the more time she can devote to the Hasenöhrl."

Soon Gabriel was splashing in the tub and singing to the cows. I recognized Mutti's gothic script on the package, sawed off the twine with a serrated knife, tore into the box , and lifted out a large round tin and three gaily wrapped presents, one for each of us. Mine was the biggest, but a small gift card tied to the golden ribbon admonished, *DO NOT OPEN BEFORE CHRISTMAS!* The bottom of the box was lined with books, magazines, and several issues of the Daily Mail.

I pried the lid off the tin. It was filled with Gabriel's favorite Christmas cookies. Nibbling on a hazelnut drop, I sorted through the letters, picking out the two that were addressed to me. The thin one was from Mutti, the fat one from Lucius. After a quick look at the metal door I decided to read his first. He wrote that Mutti had invited him to dinner.

> *. . . Her Hungarian goulash was even better than the one you and I ate in that uppity little restaurant. When we said good-night she handed me a box of Christmas cookies. It made me the envy of the barracks. I wonder what I can give her in return . . .*

I noticed he wasn't wondering what to give me, but presently admitted to myself that I hadn't spared a single thought to what I might give him, either. Cramming another cookie in my mouth, I unfolded a copy of a story he'd written and sent off to an American magazine. He called it a mystery and said the proceeds would finance our apartment come spring. All ten pages of the manuscript were typed error-free. Apparently I was the only person I knew who couldn't learn that simple skill. When I heard Gabriel upend the tub on to the stable floor I stuffed Lucius's letter out of sight.

Gabriel came in with his hair damp and his face scrubbed till it was shiny. Stopping short in front of the open tin, he said in an awed voice, "*Ach*! Am I dreaming?" I pushed it toward him but before he could make his pick we heard a muffled pounding from the front of the house. He hurried down the corridor to let Hilde in.

She shook her head at me as she peeled off her coat. "It's the first time I've ever been locked out of my own house," she chuckled good-naturedly. "In the dead of winter!" She looked at the stove. "Is that hot water for me?" Then her eyes lit on the gift-wrapped parcels. I held out the one with her name on it. She gave it a squeeze. "That'll be your Mutti's brandy-soaked fruit cake. She used to bring down a loaf every Christmas Eve." Running a finger over Gabriel's present, she announced, "Stollen."

We helped her fill the tub. While she disrobed and bathed in front of God and the cows, belting "Alle Jahre wieder . . . (a Christmas song) " Gabriel tapped on the album I'd left on the kitchen table that morning.

"In those days no one could fool you about anything," he said. "It drove your Vati crazy. You were born knowing things, and not afraid of speaking them, either. Do you recall how you used to follow me to school when you were three? You sat under my desk and wouldn't let my teacher scare you away. Finally he gave you a chalk pencil, an old slate, and a worn-out text book. I was so proud of you, then. Not because you were smart, but because you stood up for yourself." He turned his full focus on me. It was like getting hit by blue lightning. "And now you've come back to hide and bolt yourself in, and your eyes have lost their sparkle. Take a good look at yourself and remember who you are!" He pushed the album at me. In the stable, Hilde was practicing her yodeling. A couple of zealous cows mooed along. Gabriel laughed. "Hot water always makes her daft."

He went upstairs to change out of his work clothes and I dutifully leafed through the album once more, studying the child I'd been: near bald as a baby; the downy locks of the two-year-old tamed into pigtails by time I was four; into braids at five. Even then the obstinate curls refused to stay confined. I examined the growing child's resolute gaze and tried to build bridges to her from my present self, so much less clear, less sure, less strong.

The photo I came back to again and again was a rare print that included Vati. It was taken by Gabriel, who'd just acquired my father's boxy, outdated camera. The entire Edel family was sitting on the wooden bench that used to stand in front of the farmhouse. It was a sunny spring day. Vati held Anna and Mutti was holding me. She looked at me, I looked at him, he looked at Anna, and my sister looked at her hands. Obviously, Gabriel hadn't known he was supposed to make us all smile.

Newly scrubbed, Hilde returned to the kitchen, weaving her towel-dried hair into a single braid, her mouth full of pins. She coiled the braid at the nape of her neck, stuck in the pins, and glanced at the mirror just long enough to ascertain that the bun was reasonably centered. Smiling at me, she exposed flawless white teeth. Her cheeks glowed like hot coals. "Company coming," she said. "I best start on my baking."

She sent me to the pantry for the ingredients but insisted on mixing them together all by herself. Soon her biggest cast iron pot was on the stove, the lard inside melting and then bubbling. The smell of frying dough drew Gabriel downstairs.

He was hiding his old second-hand camera behind his back until he found a good vantage point. Then he whipped it out without warning and snapped a picture of the unsuspecting baker. When she waved him away, he told her, "It's a once-in-a-life-time shot. I'm aiming to frame it and hang it on my wall."

She sniffed the drop dangling from the end of her nose back into her nostrils. "*Ja, du,*" she said. "You try running a farm singlehanded from dawn to dusk—never mind the winter factory work or a lazy son bent on puffing into a brass contraption when he could be helping out—and see how much you enjoy standing over a hot stove at the end of it."

"I'd rather go dancing," he laughed. "And interview candidates for the position of your daughter-in-law. So you can retire from hard labor."

"Really?" she said. "You're carousing every weekend for my sake? Well, don't force yourself, Bua (boy). I'm not ready to quit yet."

She scooped golden brown pastries out of the fat, spread them on top of a newspaper, and dropped in a second batch. When I reached for one of the fried tidbits she shook her head. "They'll burn your tongue. Besides, they're only half done—I have yet to sprinkle on the cinnamon and powdered sugar. Put your Mutti's cookies away. Tonight I'll tolerate no competition. It's my Hasenöhrl or nothing."

I stuffed our presents into the box and stored it on a pantry shelf, missing the moment our guests trooped into the kitchen. I was afraid they'd be strangers but when I gathered the courage to join them they were the same boys and girls Gabriel and I had chased maybugs with, jumped from the dusty rafters into the hay-pile with, filled milk cans full of blueberries with—though somewhat altered. The updated versions of Ursel, Wanda, Karl and Felix took over the couch, the two girls colliding in the middle as the worn springs collapsed beneath them.

Hilde piled the cooling pastries onto a platter, shook on the promised sugar and spice, and said, "Back zua (eat up). There's more on the way."

Gabriel took the first pastry, rescued his flour-dusted album and camera, and announced, "I'm going upstairs to fetch my instrument. Give it a chance to warm up in here before I start playing."

"Your trumpet?" I asked in a carefully neutral tone as I sat down on the chair he'd just vacated.

"That still needs some work, gell?" Hilde said with a grin after he'd shut the door behind him. "Though I don't know anyone who practices harder."

I sank my teeth into a Hasenöhrl but soon my chewing slowed. I could hardly make myself swallow the bite. Our friends weren't faring much better, yet we offered Hilde steadfast smiles.

In response, she grinned proudly and cut another sheet of dough into little rabbit ear shapes. "Don't be shy. There's plenty more." Rubbing a finger along the bridge of her nose, she deposited a coating of flour. "Maria, I need another stick of lard. This dough soaks it up fast."

It was only because I was in the pantry, fetching the lard, that I escaped what came next. I heard Hilde add dry sticks to the fire. They popped, exploding into flame, and the fat in the deep-fryer sizzled a bit harder. Putzi was slinking between my legs, looking meaningfully at the bucket of milk on the floor. The kitchen door opened again. I assumed it was Gabriel until the cat bristled, abandoned his campaign to get fed, and disappeared into the shadows. And then everything went quiet. Into the silence came the voice I had learned to loathe.

"Schönen Abend, (good evening) Hilde," it wheedled. "I was just passing through and thought I'd stop to wish you a merry Christmas. It's been a while."

"Herr Hohner," she said, giving no inflection to the words.

"Tag (good day)," my friends on the couch mumbled in relays, their voices equally flat.

I could hear him rubbing his hands. Perhaps he was warming them over the stove. "Your kitchen is just as I recollect it," he said. "Simple and, uh, . . . quaint. I see not much has changed around here. Gestatten (May I)? I haven't had a Hasenöhrl in a good many years." There was a small crunching sound before Hilde offered a joyless, "Ja, doch."

Then he spat the bite out. "Ach, pfui! I see your cooking hasn't improved any. These things are stiff with lard and you've left out the salt!"

A collective, angry hiss came from the couch.

Hilde said calmly, "Weisst was, Herr Hohner? Du konnst mi jetz' am Arsch leck'n, a' wenn's fast Weihnacht'n is (You know what? You can kiss my ass, even if it *is* almost Christmas)."

I couldn't have put it better myself.

One of the girls failed to suppress a nervous giggle. And then Gabriel's voice said from the kitchen door, "Excuse me, Herr Hohner—but no one invited you in. You are *not* welcome here. You never were."

There was an uncomfortable silence; perhaps O.F. had not expected to encounter the unabashed force of young male power. Then he huffed, "Ja, *der* Gabriel. All grown up. I was wrong about this place. It isn't quaint after all. In fact, it's as miserable a hole as it ever was and the stink is atrocious. I need some fresh air."

"The stink will leave when you do," Gabriel said, still from the door. "So I suggest you get out fast. And don't bother stopping by again. We're much too coarse for someone like you."

"Well said," O.F. replied, determined to have the last word as he retreated to the door, where he stopped briefly, explaining, "I came here looking for—"

"I said out!" Gabriel told him, his voice hard. "There is nothing here for you to find."

"Wiederseh'n!" O.F. croaked, shuffling past him into the hall.

"Auf Nimmerwiederseh'n!" the kids yelled at his receding back. "Sau Breiss! (We never want to see you again. Prussian pig.)"

Two sets of footsteps receded down the long hall. Only one set returned. I peered around the pantry door. Gabriel gestured me to a chair and deposited a shiny accordion on my lap. I handed Hilde the block of lard I'd been clutching and hugged the accordion, treasuring its cold weight as Gabriel adjusted the kitchen curtains and disappeared into the stable to re-bolt the door leading out to the yard.

"You were right, Maria," he said when he sat down beside me. "That man *needs* to be locked out. If he ever comes back I'm dunking him in the manure pond for you. As for now, his tail-lights are already disappearing toward Waldbach. Amazing how well a VW maneuvers on snowy roads."

"He's got a screw loose. Always had," Hilde grumbled, unwrapping the lard and dropping it into her pot. "Eat up, everybody. More's on the way!"

Gabriel shook a liberal amount of salt over the batch already on the platter, added an extra dose of cinnamon to deaden our taste buds, and stared hard at each of us until we picked up the delicacies and worked our way through them, praising the recipe along with the cook.

And then the cheerful sounds of the accordion filled the room. Mother-of-pearl and silver flashed as Gabriel's fingers flew over buttons and keys. The music quickly chased away the last bit of dissonance O.F. had left behind. And even though Hilde's pastries lay in my stomach like a stack of greased bricks I began to feel lighter and lighter. My brother Gabriel, adroit master of the accordion, would soon conquer his horn.

Hilde, lifting yet another scoop of a never-ending supply of unsalted Hasenöhrl out of the pot, gave me a vigorous nod, righteously proud of her boy. When the nod couldn't shake loose the latest nasal drip she carelessly wiped it on a flour-white sleeve.

I sat, listened and ate, joining the laughter of goodwill swirling around me, my eyes straying to Gabriel as often as his strayed to mine. If Hilde noticed the way we were looked at each other, she said nothing. Not then.

CHAPTER 45

W HEN KARL SUGGESTED WE CONTINUE our revels at his house, Gabriel lost no time packing up his accordion and urging me to get my coat and walk to the other end of the village with him and our friends.

"Nix (never mind)!" Hilde told him. "You'll have to do your celebrating without her. Maria's staying here to help me clean up this mess. And then she and I are going to bed. We've had a long day."

Gabriel started to protest but something in Hilde's eyes made him change his mind. Trailing the others on the way out, he turned and winked at me.

Hilde scraped flour from the table and I swept it off the floor. The first time I yawned she told me to carry my four-legged bed-warmer upstairs and leave her to see to the rest. Alone in my chamber, I could no longer convince myself that I was safe from O.F. What if he had only pretended to drive away but had since back-tracked to park somewhere nearby, the white paint of his car conveniently blending with the snow? What if he had watched my protector leave and was waiting for our lights to go out?

Despite Gabriel's pep talk, I locked myself in before crawling into bed to endure icy sheets. After persuading Putzi to curl at my feet I drew the covers over my face so that my breath could help warm my feathery cave. I wasn't aware of the moment I fell asleep but knew exactly why I startled awake in the middle of the night.

Out in the quiet hall someone was slowly pushing down my door-handle. I stared at the slit of light at the bottom and saw the soles of somebody's shoes. There was a clandestine knock. And then I heard Gabriel whisper, "Maria—open up. I brought you some *Glühwein* (hot wine) from Karl's." Forgetting to throw my robe over the nightgown, I felt my way to the door and opened it a virtuous crack.

He shook a glass jar at me, releasing the aroma of mulling spices. "You missed out on a great sing-along," he whispered. "I carried this home inside my coat, pressed to my heart, to keep it warm for you." He pushed the crack wider. I smelled wine from the jar, beer on his breath, and didn't like either—but couldn't bring myself to refuse his kind offer.

As I stepped out of his way a white-faced apparition swept out of the gloom and put a restraining hand on his shoulder. It was Hilde, barefoot, in an ankle-length flannel gown, her hair wavy and unbound. "Sie ist ein Kind (she's a child)!" she said, leading him to his chamber as if he were a small boy who'd lost his way. I heard her patient, lecturing murmur long after she closed his door behind them.

The next morning Gabriel did not appear in the kitchen. Nor did he play his trumpet upstairs. I heard him come down in the afternoon and leave by the front door.

That evening, when Hilde came home, I asked her where he was. She said he and his buddies had gone to a dance in the neighboring town. She looked at me sharply. "I'm trying to convince him that what works for a nineteen-year old boy is all wrong for a fifteen-year-old girl."

"Fifteen-and-a-half," I corrected.

"Exactly," she said with the ghost of a smile. "You best keep your door locked until he understands the difference. You and he have always been close. Right now that's not a good thing."

Out of sheer boredom, I re-read Lucius's story and wrote to tell him it was as good as any I'd seen in a magazine. In Mutti's short letter, she wished me happy holidays and said she'd decided to make a complete fool of herself in front of Herr Adler.

He has connections and is discreet. I'm sure he can recommend a good, affordable attorney to work on your case. I'll let you know how it goes.

I suspected Hilde had made Gabriel promise not to be alone with me anymore, for he only came into the kitchen when she was there, his smile subdued except for the rare occasions when she was focusing elsewhere. Then, for an instant, his eyes would shine and he'd dimple—and I knew if I waited long enough something would shift between us.

As soon as the snow began to melt off the highway he took the pay he had saved and bought a used BMW motorcycle with it. Karl and Felix did the same and then we didn't need Hilde to chaperone us anymore, for Gabriel only came home to sleep, though sometimes not even that. His footsteps awakened me no matter what hour of night he stumbled down the hall. He always paused in front of my door.

Mutti's next letter arrived in the middle of March. I strapped on Frau Keppler's rucksack early the next morning, went to Gabriel's room to wake him up, and told him I was walking to Waldbach to take the train into Munich.

His brow furrowed. "You *are* coming back—aren't you?" he asked, sounding anxious.

When I explained I'd only be gone for the day he offered me a ride to the train station. I mounted the motorcycle directly behind him, holding on to his shoulders. A fresh headwind brushed at my face, smelling of spring. Most of the snow in the fields we were passing had already melted and the tips of green shoots were thrusting up from sodden black soil.

He braked to a stop outside the station. I started to get off. Gently, he laid his hand on mine and kept it there for a few deliciously long seconds, not saying a word. When my train pulled away from the station, he stood on the platform and watched me leaning out of my compartment window. I cupped my mouth and shouted, "I'll be back on the last train!"

He yelled back, "And I'll be here, waiting!"

We waved to each other until the train went around the first bend and the forest swallowed both platform and boy. I slid the window shut, sat, and reread Mutti's letter.

"*Your sixteenth birthday is only two months away. Lucius's commanding officer has scheduled an interview with you on Friday afternoon. Lucius will meet you at the gate at one o'clock and take you to him. Be sure to wear something nice to make a good impression. Afterwards, go straight to my tailor. He needs your measurements for the wedding gown. Then take the next train back to Hilde's. Hannes said his attorney is confident he can turn things around any day now. Meanwhile, I'm thankful you're secure and happy just where you are."*

Hannes? Since when had she decided to call Herr Adler by his first name?

I leaned back in my seat and closed my eyes, trying to conjure the image of Lucius, but only managed a blur of brown skin and flashing white teeth. What I remembered more clearly was Gabriel's stricken eyes when I called my final good-bye from the train window.

At last I arrived at the Ostbahnhof, changed into the scratchy blue-and-white-plaid wool skirt I had brought, and slipped my grandmother's ring onto my finger. Frigid air crawled past my boots and up my thighs as I got first on a streetcar and then on the bus that would take me toward Henry Kaserne. Panic rose and caught in my throat. What was I doing in Minga? What was Lucius to me, now?

But when I saw him standing at the gate, tall and broad-shouldered in his fatigues, his face once more as familiar to me as my own, I had no trouble answering his gratified smile.

"Long time no see," he said. "You look better than ever."

"So do you," I told him, accompanying him to the guard, who checked the paper Lucius presented and waved us both through.

"So, what you been up to in the sticks?" Lucius asked as we walked side by side around the curve and onto the main avenue.

Although I'd read my way through every Zane Grey novel Frau Keppler had given me and had added to my vocabulary daily, I didn't understand what kind of sticks he was referring to.

"Our sticks are still covered by snow," I said. "I doubt there are many in the fields because they get plowed every year. But in the forest—" I caught him grinning and said primly, "Are you talking about our trees? They're too beautiful to be called sticks, Lucius. Even in winter."

"What do you do with yourself all day long?"

It was a meager list. "I read, eat, walk, and wait for spring. In a few weeks there will be flowers everywhere. And the air will be like velvet."

The buildings we passed looked a lot like his barracks but they faced in another direction. He pointed to the one at the end. "Battalion headquarters. The CO's office is in there." He stopped walking. "Listen. Listen good. The CO doesn't like me."

"I know that."

"He's going to try and change your mind about us."

"I know. Mutti told me the American Army doesn't want their soldiers to marry girls from other countries unless they're morally fit."

He hesitated, started to speak, and swallowed. The smile left his eyes. Taking my arm, he said carefully, "His first glance at you will show him you're fit, and there's nothing he can do to deny it. What he'll do, instead, is to try and make me look bad. That's what he did when Washington brought *his* girl in for an interview. She broke up with him on that very same day."

He made sure he had my full attention before going on. "Thing is, you can't believe anything my CO says. No matter what. But don't be calling him a liar. Just stare him straight in the eyes when he's done talking and say, 'Thank you very much, but I've made up my mind and nothing you say can change it.' "

"Thank you very much," I rehearsed, "but I've made up my mind and nothing you say can change it!"

"Yeah. Like that." He was still looking hard at me. "Promise?"

"But of course," I said airily, wondering what the fuss was about.

The corridor of the building we entered went straight from one end to the other. Lucius stopped at one door, knocked, and opened it just wide enough to stick in his head and say, "Sir, Maria's here for the interview, sir. Here she is now." He pushed me into the room, mouthing a soundless, "Good luck!"

The CO sat behind a scratched desk, writing something down on a form, his pasty face expressionless. Keeping his eyes on the form he said, "Please sit." I complied, though I had expected no less than a polite hand-shake. He wasn't the father figure I'd expected—stern, fair, with a piercing gaze and a resonant bass voice. On the contrary, he was slightly built, short, and only a few years older than Lucius. It explained why Lucius found it so hard to take orders from him. The CO kept me waiting for a good minute before he looked up and said,

"*You're* Maria Edel?"

"Yes, I am."

He watched me cross my legs in what I considered an adult fashion, nervously tugging at my school-girl skirt to make sure my knees were covered. I wished I had worn more impressive attire. I'd forgotten that American women liked wearing tent-like dresses that went all the way down to their calves..

"Pleased to meet you," he said, not reaching out to shake my hand. "I was just going over your application.—Are you *sure* you're the girl Duncan is trying to marry?"

I showed him the ring. "We are engaged."

"Yes. I see." He scribbled another word on the form. Then he put down the pen and folded his hands on the desk. "To tell you the truth, you're not at all what I expected."

My stomach knotted. "What *did* you expect?"

"You know . . . the usual. The kind our colored men seem to prefer. Women who hang out in colored bars . . ."

White-powdered slugs. I blushed in spite of my best intentions.

"I mean," he went on. "Why would someone like you want to marry someone like him? You're not . . ." He spoke in a drawl I had to strain to understand.

"Not what?"

He played with his ballpoint pen, thinking. Then he said, "Do you have any idea what you're getting yourself into, marrying a Negro?" He pronounced the word *niggra*.

"Pardon?" I asked, wondering where he was from.

"Do you know anything about our coloreds?"

I said, "I know Duncan."

His smile was fleeting. "I doubt that. Not even Duncan knows Duncan. Has he mentioned anything to you about the slums?"

"The what?"

"Slums. Where his people live. You don't have anything like it here in Munich. Slums are full of decrepit old houses that white people don't want anymore, though the coloreds like them just fine. Most of them grew up in dirt-floor shacks so they consider it an improvement." Putting his hands flat on the desk top, he leaned confidingly closer, "They're used to unbelievable filth. Rats and roaches. Garbage strewn in every front yard, usually including an abandoned mattress or two, disintegrating a bit more after each rain. If you marry Duncan that's what you'll get. Decent white folks never set foot in the slums. You'll be surrounded by coloreds. For miles and miles, in every direction. Who knows what they'll do to you the first time Duncan has to leave you alone for a while." He leaned even closer, his voice deceptively gentle. "You see, they hate us—God knows why. Envy, I expect."

"Why don't they just move?" I asked. "Why are those slums even allowed? You know the Schuttberg? That's where we buried *our* old buildings, after the war. Help them build new ones, like we did here."

Ruefully, he shook his head. "Believe me, we've tried. But it seems they like filth. A couple of years after we move them into new projects they run them right into the ground. Without fail. They have a habit of bunching up, too. Even here in the barracks they tend to stick together." He sighed. "A girl like you—I just can't picture it, Maria. All the coloreds I know are pretty much like Duncan. Or worse." He paused to give me a chance to catch up with his phrases. "Can't handle discipline. Can't follow instructions. Sometimes I wonder if our boy can even read. Never went past the ninth grade, you know."

I wanted to shout, "Neither did I but I'm sure I can read better than you!" Then I remembered Lucius's coaching, took a deliberate breath, uncrossing my legs and crossing them in the other direction, and yanked once more at my skirt hem. "He *can* read," I said, struggling to keep my tone civil. "And write, too."

"Just barely," the CO said. "But I bet if you tried to make him read a whole page from a magazine to you he couldn't go to the end." He ticked off three fingers. "Immature. Irresponsible. Incapable. You remember those words, Maria. Watch him and you'll see I'm right." He waved at an army-green file cabinet. "It's in his records. Never once made it past PFC. Never will." He closed his eyes to collect himself. Then he swung his chair around the desk corner and rolled it next to mine, his expression frank.

"Basically, Maria, our colored men remain boys their entire lives. They never really grow up. Most likely, if you marry Duncan and go stateside with him, he'll ditch you within a year. Two at the most. One day he'll simply. . ." He transcribed a wide arc, his wrist floppy. ". . . disappear. Leaving you with two kids at—what, eighteen? In the slums, where most colored girls have a new baby each year just so they can stay on the welfare rolls. Their men, they just up and walk out. Irresponsible. Immature. Incapable." He offered me a sincere, fatherly smile. "I don't want it to happen to you."

I said, "I like Duncan. My mother likes Duncan."

"He *can* be charming," the CO conceded, massaging his temples as if he could feel a headache coming on. "When he wants to be. Great smile. Dimples. But a boy like that, without a solid education, no skills—if he ever leaves the Army he won't qualify for any job except caretaker, janitor, gardener. Or shoe-shine boy. Is that what you want to be? The wife of a shoe-shine boy?"

"He has always been decent to me," I said, remembering Lucius's many kindnesses. "And I think you are supposed to decide if *I'm* good enough for *him*. Morally fit to marry an American. Not the other way around. Is that not so?"

Someone was shouting halfway down the corridor. Someone else laughed. I wanted to be outside, too—in mild sunshine, in the March breeze. The interview had gone on too long.

The CO gave another, heavier sigh. "Making life-time decisions for girls like you is a big responsibility. Sometimes I can hardly bear it."

I silently counted off ten seconds and asked courteously, "So—what have you decided, in my case?"

He considered the ceiling as if the answer was written there. Then he briefly glanced at my knees. "To be honest, I can't quite make up my mind. It's my job to find out if you're a liability for America or an asset. If you were to go with Duncan, and he were to vanish on you—what would you do? You're so young. Do you have any work skills?"

I blessed Mutti for making it possible for me to nod. "I've been to business school." *For a little while.* "I can type, take dictation, balance books." *Almost.*

His smile was ironic. "Good. Then you can take care of Duncan. He'll need all the help he can get." His words cut, like Vati's. "To tell you the truth," he said with an apologetic smile, "I will have to think about it for a week. We can continue this interview next Saturday evening. Perhaps over a light dinner."

"It would be nice," I said. "Only—my mother is ordering an expensive wedding gown today. So we need to know your answer now. Am I an asset or a liability?"

He raised his hands in surrender. "An asset, of course. I expect I'll have to write that down somewhere. It's Duncan who's the wild card. A mustang that can't be broken." He stood up. "As long as he stays in the Army I'll try to keep him in line for you. I can promise you that much at least." He offered his hand.

It was damp and slack when I shook it. I had already noticed that Americans did not know how to shake hands. It was no good trying to judge their characters by it. The truth lay in their eyes. This man hadn't looked straight at me from the moment I walked in. I hoped I'd remember it once his warning had a chance to sink in.

CHAPTER 46

LUCIUS WAS WAITING FOR ME in front of headquarters, looking less shiny than he had when I entered the CO's office. He fell into step beside me and glanced at me several times before asking, "So. How did it go?"

"Fine." I increased my pace, eager to quit the base, not caring if he stayed beside me or not, and left him to deal with the sentry.

He caught up when I was passing the phone booth. "I'll walk you to the bus stop."

"Don't trouble yourself," I told him. "It's not far."

He took my arm. "Wait. I can see you're upset. What did he say?"

"He talks funny. I could hardly understand him. And he's not very nice."

Lucius snorted. "All true—but what did he say about *me* that makes you want to run?"

In my head, I kept reciting the CO's "i" words, hoping I'd remember them when I got home to my Langenscheidt. "I'm running because I have a train to catch," I said. Then I brought out the cash envelope he had given me the last time I saw him. "Here's your money back. Most of it, anyway. Thanks for letting me borrow it."

He wouldn't take it. "Since you're obviously better at holding on to cash than I am, why don't you keep it? You'll need it soon enough, to find us an apartment for us."

"Who would rent to me?" I pushed it at him. "It would be like trying to get a hotel room all over again."

Reluctantly, he accepted the money. "That's what I'm afraid of. But at least you speak the language. Without you I won't even know how to read the ads in the newspaper—never mind finding a street address." He crooked his arm, inviting me to hook mine to it. I swiveled to see if the guard was staring after us. He was. I forged ahead, ignoring the invitation. At the highway I had to stop for a passing convoy of U.S. army trucks. Lucius stepped up, looking at me sideways.

"We should make a date to go house-hunting together," he said.

"That's not possible as long as I have to live in the village. It takes me half a day to get here and the other half to get home again." I started to cross the road. He followed me to the bus stop. I rummaged for change.

"I haven't seen you in months," he complained, leaning against the shelter. "You've changed. I don't want to marry a stranger."

"Neither do I."

His far-seeing eyes spotted the bus coming before I did. He gripped my hands. "Listen up, Maria—we have some serious talking to do. If we can't do it here I'll come out to where you're staying. Next Saturday. Just tell me which train to take."

The bus squealed to a stop. "Too late," I said, hurrying to get on.

"No, it's not." He got on behind me and trailed me to a seat. As usual the other passengers watched our every move. For once Lucius didn't seem to mind. He fished the cash envelope out of his pocket and pressed a pen into my hand. "Here, write your directions on this. I'll bring some more of our favorite pound cake. Let's have a picnic in that magical forest of yours." He tried for a crooked smile. "Don't worry—I won't do anything to embarrass you."

Unenthusiastically, I sketched a map and scribbled departure times. "It will have to be on Sunday morning." That way, the entire able-bodied population of Waldbach would be in church when the train pulled into the station. "Don't bother coming unless it's a nice day. We're *not* having a picnic in snowfall or pouring rain."

"Stands to reason. But I'm hoping for sunshine." He scanned the instructions and pulled the cord. Lurching to the exit, he added, "It'll be like old times." I had no trouble answering his smile with one of my own but as he disembarked and started to stride back toward Henry I was already praying for rain.

*

BACK ON the farm, I found the three words the CO had ticked off on his fingers: immature; irresponsible; incapable. During the empty week-days that followed I mucked out the stable in the mornings and afterwards sat alone for long hours next to the cook stove, trying to recall how I had come from sharing a plate of wieners and sauerkraut with a congenial stranger to being fitted for a wedding dress I had not asked for and did not want.

Getting married hadn't been my idea, either. I'd only agreed to Lucius's plan because of O.F. As it happened, I no longer needed the refuge Lucius had offered. But was cleaning up after cows or reading old magazines on a lumpy couch any better? What schools were there for me here? What life? If I got lucky Gabriel might help me get a job at the factory. I, too, could work the night shift and sleep my mornings away. Until I was of age. And then what?

No one was rolling out any fairy-tale carpets in front of my feet. No one was scheduling exciting career moves for me. I could almost see why, after being stuck in the village for a decade, Mutti had wanted to try something new.

*

THE SKY was clear the day Lucius breached my paradise. Hilde had gone to church wearing Freidorf's version of the Miesbacher Tracht (regional costumes), probably with woollens under the traditional, voluminous long skirt and apron. She would eat lunch with her sister and brother-in-law on the other end of the village and visit with various relatives most of the afternoon. I had accompanied her a couple of times and was soon bored with listening to monosyllabic conversations about last year's harvest, who had died during the winter, and what unlucky pair ought to speedily post their bans.

Gabriel, too, wore the regional Tracht—leather knickers, thick woollen knee socks patterned with green on gray, and a light-gray Loden jacket. I carried the accordion to his motorcycle. He managed to stow the instrument behind him and hung the trumpet from his neck, tying a cord around the case and his chest to keep it from swinging. He had been hired to play at the first *Bauernhochzeit* of the season. "A country wedding's the best way I know to get paid for having fun," he said. "Although, once I blow my horn, they might just pay me to shut up."

"Isn't it kind of early for a spring wedding?" I asked. "Why don't they wait until May?"

"Because they can't," he said drily, not bothering to enlighten me further. He pumped the motor to life, made it roar a couple of times and dropped it down to an idle. "You came at the most miserable time of the year, Maria. But it'll get better as soon as the weather warms a bit. Why don't you ride with me? The beer will flow like water. And we can do a few Landler (folk dance, similar to a waltz) together on my breaks."

Clearly, he had no idea how much I disliked drinking and dancing. I padded the accordion, which took up the rear of his seat. "Where would I sit?"

He patted the gas tank. When I was a toddler Vati often lifted me to sit on the tank of his cycle while Mutti and Anna settled behind him. I was a lot shorter then.

"Not this time, Gabriel," I laughed, stepping away. "I'm afraid you and your expensive instruments would arrive at the wedding in pieces."

*

I WAITED just inside the forest until the whistle blew and the train pulled away from the platform, leaving Lucius to stand there all alone—too tall, too dark, too alien and too close. A group of his fellow passengers, wearing their best, were scurrying out of sight as if he'd threatened to add them to his stock pot. I waited until the last of them disappeared into the station before I moved to a sunny spot just long enough to wave.

He waved back and leaped off the concrete slab and over the tracks while I studied the station windows for spying eyes. I was relieved when the curtains remained undisturbed.

"I think I triggered a stampede," he said with a grimace.

"These people are naturally shy, Lucius," I explained, leading him into green-filtered light. "And they've never seen anyone like you before. They don't have TVs or movies. This is an isolated region."

"The middle of nowhere," he agreed. "A beautiful nowhere, though. Are you sure this is a real forest?"

"What else could it be?"

"A movie set for *Hansel and Gretel*. Hope we don't get lost in the woods."

"We won't if you stay on the trail close behind me."

He brandished two cans. "Our favorite dessert."

It might be his but it sure wasn't mine. Canned pound cake was no more than a minor improvement over Hilde's Hasenöhrl.

Most of the snow was gone from under the trees but the layer of soaked leaf mulch under our feet was treacherously soft. There was no dry place to sit except for a game warden's look-out I found in a small clearing, standing on stilts under a humble roof. Lucius swatted my rear when I climbed up the ladder. I looked down at him, abashed.

"We *are* engaged," he said.

"But not married!"

A spatter of sun reached the rough platform above. We sat on the weathered bench from which the warden tallied deer, and I spread our picnic between us: a string of Landjäger (a dry sausage) from the butcher's; slices of buttered rye stuck together with Camembert ripened to the peak of perfection, and two wrinkled apples that had scarcely survived the winter in Hilde's root cellar.

"A real feast," Lucius said dubiously, smelling the cheese. "What's this? Limburger? You should have bought cheddar."

"Never heard of it," I told him, relishing my sandwich.

With open aversion, he tried chewing on his, giving up to gnaw on a link of Landjäger. "How long has this sausage been dead? I'm liable to lose a tooth before this picnic is over!"

"It's no worse than the rock-hard chocolate powder you brought to our last picnic," I pointed out.

He spat out his bite, grumbled, "Wish I had some right now," and pushed the remains of his sandwich at me. Gingerly, he picked up one of the apples and examined it from all sides, pronouncing it unfit for human consumption. "In Vermont, they use these to make apple-doll faces."

I was getting tired of his sour mood. "How much money does a janitor make, Lucius?" I asked, a hard edge in my voice. "Or a shoeshine boy?"

He busied himself with a miniscule can opener and sawed through both tin-can lids.

"What kind of job will you get in California?" I pressed. "What kind of work can you do?"

He concentrated on shaking out the first roll of pound cake and handed it to me with a flourish. Then he shook out the second and broke it to pieces. "What else did he have to say?" he asked quietly. When I mentioned the three "i" words, his eyes became pebbles. He gazed at a crow staring at us from an adjacent branch, hoping for crumbs. Then he asked, more quietly still, "What can *you* do? In California. Or Italy. Or anyplace else."

The Camembert stuck to my palate. Realizing I'd forgotten to bring something to drink, I climbed onto the bench, inspected the roof, scooped up a forlorn patch of snow, and crammed it into my mouth. Then we scowled at each other.

"You were already angry when you stepped off the train," I said. "You shouldn't have come."

"Can you blame me? Take a look at this!" He pulled a short letter out of his breast pocket and handed it over.

I read it out loud. "'Dear Author: We are sorry, but the story you submitted does not meet our standards. Due to the volume of mail we receive, we are unable to offer more detailed comments.' — I don't understand. What does it mean?"

"They don't think I can write," he said glumly, his eyes gathering moisture. "I told you, I was counting that money toward our apartment. Or else I wouldn't have bought this." He dropped a tiny box onto my lap. It was covered in blue velvet.

I opened it and saw a band made of red gold, inlaid with a stripe of white platinum. "But we already have rings," I said stupidly.

He held up his hand to show me its mate. "After they arrested you I started wearing your grandfather's ring. I forgot I had it on when I went to your house and your mother recognized it. Took it right off my finger. She'll pull your grandma's off your neck the next time she lays eyes on you. The other day she wrote down her ring size, which she said must also be yours since you're forever borrowing her jewelry. Besides—I thought it was time for us to have something all our own."

"Now? When we need all our money for an apartment? Can you take the rings back to the store?"

He gave an impatient sigh. "Already tried. You might as well see if it fits."

I took the ring out of its box but when I aimed it at my fourth finger, the little, seamless round band began to resemble a noose. "How much did they cost?"

"You don't want to know," he said. "I wanted something that'll last till death do us part."

He pronounced it as if it were a life-sentence. He was right. It was. All at once, I heard the Virgin Mary whisper inside my ear, "Remember— you can always change your mind . . ." The time was now. I pushed the band into its velvety slot, snapped the box shut, and set it onto his knee. "I've decided I don't want to get married after all, Lucius. I'm going to stay here with my friends."

He checked my face to see if I was kidding. Maybe he was waiting for me to giggle and say, "Not really!" But my immediate sense of release told me I made the right decision. "You shouldn't get married until you are older," I said flatly. "Nineteen is too young."

"But—I'm going to be twenty in July," he stammered.

"Too young," I repeated. "The only reason you asked me to marry you in the first place was so that you could live off-base, away from your CO. You must hate him as much as I hate O.F. But maybe hate is not as good a reason to get married as we both thought."

"Wanting to be part of a family is," he murmured.

I saw how cruel it was to take away his prospective mother-in-law, his future sister-in-law, and all the dreams he'd dreamed since we'd grown serious with each other. He picked up the box, turning it over and over again. "I came to tell you I found a pension for you to stay in on weekends, not far from Henry. Then we can look for a studio apartment together. You know—one room and a bath. If we both wear our rings people will think we're newlyweds. Everybody likes newlyweds."

I sat frozen, unable to believe I was actually cutting him out of my life, but saw no alternative.

"I was hoping you'd come back to Munich with me." He gave a harsh laugh. "I was so sure you'd want to, I already paid your fare." He opened his wallet, carefully extracted a ticket, and deposited it on the bench.

Still I said nothing.

"So this is it?" he asked. "We're through, just like that?"

I frowned at my watch. "The next train won't be here for an hour."

He attempted a cheery smile. "Enough time for you to show me some of your favorite places. That way I can picture you happy in them whenever I think of you."

It was the least I could do. I spread the remains of our meal on top of the roof for the crow, tidied the bench, stuffed the ticket and the rest of our trash into my bag, and climbed down the ladder to take Lucius to my special mushroom patch. From there it was a short stroll to the hedges where Gabriel, Anna and I used to fill our liter-sized milk cans with blueberries. The nearby brook gushed with melt water.

"Why is it so clean under the trees?" he asked. "The forest floor looks as if someone came and swept it with a broom."

I explained that the villagers were only allowed to gather dead wood for their stoves and must leave every tree standing. Lucius's last request was that I show him a glimpse of Freidorf. I led him to the rim of the forest. He scanned the expanse of rectangular fields to where the faraway white-washed village glistened, every rooftop brick-red.

"Our farm is the first one on the road, going in," I said, pointing.

"Is there a Gasthaus? We could have a farewell meal."

Perhaps there was a look of horror on my face, for he said quickly, "A silly thought. I would be an ink stain on immaculate linen. Hard to miss and hard to explain away."

I looked at my watch to hide the dismay I was feeling for the both of us. "Time to go," I told him with undisguised relief.

*

AS WE neared the station I saw through a gap in the branches that a few people were already waiting for the Munich train. I stopped where I was and primly offered Lucius my hand. He clasped it in his, admiring the juxtaposition the way he had so many times before. But then he pulled me toward him, buried his face in my hair, and whispered, "I need you, Maria. I can't even think of what my life will be like without the hope of having you in it."

My short and graceless answer was, "I'm sorry."

The train came. He got on it and leaned out the window, waving. All at once I was transported into the distant past. I was my mother and he was my father and everything was going wrong all over again. I suppressed the same urge to run after the caboose I'd felt when Vati left me all those years before. Forcing myself to turn away from Lucius's anxious receding face, I slipped in among the trees, but on my walk back to Freidorf I was no longer so sure I had done the right thing. After all, I'd worked hard for the right to marry him. Fought Mutti, the abbess, and even the weather. In sending Lucius out of my life, wasn't I giving in to public opinion? O. F. would think he had won—and so would the CO.

Walking between wet fields while the church bell struck the hour, I saw again how Lucius's dark hand had clasped my light one, attempting to bridge the abyss of ignorance that lay between us. And try as I might I could not quite imagine one hand without the other.

*

AT SUPPER that night I took the chair nearest the hearth, my cardigan buttoned to the chin.

"Seemed like everyone in the region danced at the wedding today," Gabriel said, buttering his boiled potatoes. "The tips were great. Half of Waldbach was there. Several couples came all the way from Minga." He sprinkled salt onto the rim of his plate. His tone remained casual even though his eyes had become watchful. "How about you, Maria? What did you do while we were gone?"

"Not much. I went for a walk."

"Where to?"

I shrugged. "Into the forest."

"All by yourself?"

Hilde tried to catch his eye but he refused to let her dissuade him.

"No," I admitted. "With a friend. From München."

Now he did look at Hilde, and she looked at him. Without saying a word they were confirming a rumor. He started to speak. She shook her head ever so slightly, then they both gazed at me with such unspeakable sadness, I was stunned. It was as if they had just realized I'd killed someone and were striving to keep on loving me anyway. And even though they continued to sit beside me and tried their best to keep on radiating good will, I suspected they would soon lose the struggle. Obviously, some wedding guests arriving by train had recognized me. Maybe they saw me greet Lucius and lead him into the most private parts of the forest, or watched me wave him off at the end. What better place to spread scandalous gossip than the first social event of the new season?

Hilde and Gabriel inhabited a homogenous world to which I could no longer lay claim, for I was the forerunner of a new millennium in which white would not be the only acceptable color. They had done their best to keep me safe, but maybe I was outgrowing the need for safety and was willing to take each day as it came. Besides, if I left Freidorf before I saw myself become less in their eyes, I would be able to keep this place intact inside me, a sanctuary in the uncertainties lying ahead.

"I have to go back to München first thing tomorrow morning," I told them, struggling to keep my voice free of emotion.

Gabriel lifted his hand toward me, but Hilde caught it and pressed it to the table.

"Your Mutti has sent for you," she said firmly. "I expect that's what your friend came to tell you today. I'm so glad you could spend the winter with us. You know, Anna was always your Mutti's child. You were mostly mine. We've always understood each other." She offered a somber smile. "But now you're growing up fast and must go your own way."

*

THE NEXT morning I gave Putzi a thorough massage before I let him out of my room. Gabriel sat outside the door, leaning against the wall fully dressed with his boots on.

I knelt down beside him. "I wish I could take Putzi."

"He'd die in the city. He belongs on the farm. Like you. If you stay—"

"I can't anymore," I said quickly.

He nodded his acquiescence. "Will you ever come home for a visit?"

"If I do I won't come alone. I'm getting married."

"You're too young for that, Maria. So am I." He shifted his weight, sitting up straight. "I always thought . . . one day, you and me . . ."

"I can't wait that long."

"Are you—?"

I stared into his eyes. "What do you think?"

He bowed his head, too easily defeated. I took his hand. "Next year I'm going to fly to the other side of the world. I'll take you with me. In here." I tapped my heart. "You and me, we can never be strangers."

He tugged at my arm. "I'll give you a ride on the motorcycle. It's a lot faster than walking."

"I don't want fast. I want to go the way I came, on my own two feet. To say good-bye slowly."

Then I left him behind. Frequently transferring the suitcase from one hand to the other, Frau Keppler's old rucksack strapped to my back, her second-best rain boots inside it, I walked until I came to my shortcut. There I turned, sat on the worn leather once more, and memorized every house I could see. My gaze brushed the church, the greening fields, the surrounding forest, and the spectacular peaks beyond, still capped with snow. Although my eyes burned I did not cry. Last time I left paradise it was against my will. This time I was choosing to go—and that made all the difference. In thirty years or maybe in fifty, change would come even to this quaint little village. Perhaps, in my own small way, I had planted the first seed.

Gabriel would forever remain in my past and Lucius was the only future I had. If I didn't yet love him, then surely I loved the idea of him.

My single regret was that I'd miss seeing the May bells unfurl on the gulch meadow.

CHAPTER 47

TWO WEEKS AFTER MUTTI REGAINED full custody of her wayward daughter and two days before our wedding, an enthusiastic young rental agent drove Lucius and me to a vacant mansion outside the city. The bathroom was bigger than Mutti's living room. Most surfaces in it were tiled in turquoise and white but the sunken tub was lake-blue. It was big enough for a swim. One of the long walls was made of glass, overlooking a lush walled garden. The other was covered with a vast mirror. The rest of the house was a beautiful empty cavern. There wasn't a piece of furniture in it. If we lucked into renting the place Lucius and I would have to sleep on the flawlessly varnished parquet.

"He must think all Americans are rich," Lucius whispered when the agent forged ahead to show us the picturesque French-country kitchen.

"A bargain," the agent told us, giving us a tour of the spacious walk-in pantry.

Neither Lucius nor I had the courage to ask how much the mansion was renting for. "Very nice," Lucius said when he turned it down. "But don't you have anything closer to a bus line?"

The realtor offered to put our names at the end of his agency's long waiting list. He'd been our last hope.

In late afternoon Mutti showed up at my pension wearing a superior smile and waving a couple of keys. "Geschafft (done)!" she said. "I found you a place on Hohenzollernstrasse. On the outskirts of Schwabing. Only one block from a streetcar stop."

She couldn't have given me more welcome news. But when she saw my relieved smile she raised a cautionary hand. "It's a . . . starter apartment. Well, actually—it's only one room on the fifth floor of an ancient building without elevators."

"I don't mind," I said, accepting the keys.

"No running water. Not even a sink. And you share the bathroom with three other tenants. I've already paid a month in advance and hired a mover to take your trunks there tomorrow afternoon. You'll have to meet him at the curb and guide him to Room 5D. It's fully furnished. And remarkably clean."

"However did you find it?"

She smiled proudly "An ad in the classifieds, so small I skipped right over it the first time I scanned the pages."

I'd seen it myself—every day since returning to Munich. And every day I had wondered who, in the city's ever-mounting housing shortage, was desperate enough to pare down her expectation to one dinky room no one else wanted. Turned out it was me.

*

I ARRIVED just in time to see a blistered pickup cough to a stop in front of the address. The two wooden shipping trunks Mutti had donated to us were crowding the truck bed along with Lucius's suitcase and mine. A short, skinny man emerged from behind the wheel, a cigarette wedged in his mouth. "You must be Maria," he said, wrestling the first trunk over the tailgate.

I considered his thin arms. "The room's upstairs," I warned. "I'll carry the back end."

"Oh no you don't. I've already been paid." He looped a strap to the handle and heaved the trunk on to his back. "Just lead the way."

The first thing I noticed upon entering the lobby was the immaculate stone floor. Even the stairs had been robbed of their last dust particle. The little man paused on the second-floor landing. It smelled of perfumed detergent. He took a quick drag on the cigarette still clenched in his mouth and gazed stoically up the stairwell before moving on.

He paused again on the third-floor landing, which smelled of distilled vinegar. "How much farther?"

"Two more flights," I admitted.

He spit on his palms, rubbed them together with a whispered incantation, centered the trunk between his shoulders, and climbed on. The fourth-floor landing smelled of pernicious ammonia, making our eyes burn. He loosed his grip during a coughing fit. The trunk sagged but stubbornly he locked his knees and pulled it upward again, straining his ropey biceps. At last we reached the fifth floor.

He sniffed. "Pfui (phew)! Bleach! But since we seem to have run out of stairs, this must be it. Quick, open the door!"

Searching my pockets for the right key, I glanced at a neat row of labels next to a single bell button. "Schmied—1 ring," I read. "Hofer—2 rings. Nagel—3 rings. Duncan—4 rings." Lovingly, I polished the last label before unlocking the door. The mover gave a desperate puff and followed me into a large square hall. I glimpsed a tub at the opposite end, then found Room 5D two doors to the left. My second key slipped easily into its matching lock, admitting me into a narrow room.

With a groan, the mover eased the trunk onto the spent but well-scoured linoleum. "Where do you want me to park this?"

I pointed to the floor at the end of the primitive counter, a rough, three-tiered structure made of bricks and weathered boards. He slid the trunk perpendicular to the wall and looked at me with pity. "Only two more trips up those ghastly stairs for me. You'll have to fight them every single day from now on. I don't envy you that." Abruptly, he turned on his heel to fetch the second trunk, leaving me in my nest.

I ran my hands over the rough pine-board counter top. Mutti's housewarming presents were the only things sitting upon it. After she'd cinched the deal with the landlady she'd gone to the nearest department store and bought us a large plastic reservoir with lid, a matching plastic bucket for fetching clean water from the bathtub spigot, a metal pail for scrubbing the floor and hauling off spent water, and a white-enameled basin for washing the dishes.

A gloomy, lusterless wardrobe divided the kitchen area from the rest of the room. A daybed sat half-hidden behind it, and at the only window stood a small, rickety table complete with two equally rickety chairs. I decided to fetch my first bucket of water. As I crossed the hall, a pretty young woman, wearing a beige cardigan over a pleated navy-blue skirt, was just coming out of the next room and arrived at the bathroom before me. She looked at me with a strange little smile and said, "Ah! It's you! I *thought* you'd wind up here sooner or later."

Her face was faintly familiar. So was her no-frills chignon. I said "Grüss Gott!" and she laughed at my blank expression before bolting herself in. In vain I searched my mind to match her face to a name. It would come to me later. Unwilling to queue, I returned to my room to unpack what Mutti had triumphantly called my "trousseau."

The pillow she had insisted I must wear to the house tomorrow lay on top, already studded with safety pins. When I'd asked her what it was for, she had said, "For your own good." I figured out the rest for myself. None of the neighbors could find fault with a mother whom circumstances *forced* to let her pregnant daughter get married. On the other hand, they'd have vociferous objections to my union with Lucius if they thought it wasn't absolutely necessary. In other words, Mutti was still more concerned with *her* reputation than with mine. Scowling, I tossed the silly cushion onto the bed along with a half-dozen new, starched sheets and an old comforter she'd used to protect a complete set of matched dishes from our brand-new yellow-enameled pots and pans.

As I lingered over a graceful tea pot, admiring the drop-stopper Mutti had already attached to its spout, there was a sharp rap on the half-open door. I expected the new neighbor, but found a tiny, grim-faced woman who looked like a brown mouse with sharp, beady eyes, her sparse hair scraped into a tight bun.

"I'm the landlady," she said. "Your mother told me you'd be coming today." She walked in without waiting to be asked and nodded at the furniture. "I know it's not much but this is all I have vacant on the fifth floor at the moment. As soon as one of the other girls moves out you get to transfer. The rest of the rooms have sinks."

"Yes," I said. "Mutti explained that to me. Uh . . . don't you have any vacancies on one of the *lower* floors?"

She gave a grating chuckle. "Several. But not for the likes of you." She studied the new pots on the shelves. "I believe I told your mother that cooking is strictly verboten. And I like things kept neat." She looked pointedly at the messy daybed. "No loud music, no cigarettes, and no gross vulgarities. Do you understand?"

"Yes," I said, finding the last remark puzzling.

"First month's rent has already been paid. Be punctual with the next payment and you'll have no trouble from me. If there's anything you need, I live on the ground floor." She turned to go, but not before directing her penetrating *Röntgen* (Xray) eyes at the trunk as if she could see the used two-burner hot plate Mutti had hidden away on the bottom, wrapped in old newspapers. Or maybe she didn't, for she concluded the interview with, "I think you'll do. I don't normally rent to couples but your mother was very persuasive."

From the gleam in her eyes I deduced Mutti had paid a hefty security fee. When the mover stumbled through the hall with the second trunk she stepped aside, snatched the crumpled cigarette from his mouth, fixed him with a severe gaze, said "Smoking is not allowed anywhere in my building!" and took it off with her.

The mover slid the second trunk behind the first, reached into a pocket, and pulled out another cigarette. He lit it, laid the spent match on the end of the would-be counter, took a long drag, and said, "Only one more round trip for *these* tired legs," as he pivoted toward the stairs.

It occurred to me, upon unpacking the elaborate silverware, that the first trunk held my poorly planned future and the second my entire past. My life at home was now completely erased except for the pristine, custom-tailored wedding dress waiting to be worn just once. Strange that Mutti, who turned every Pfennig five times before spending it, had insisted on outfitting me so thoroughly.

"Es gehört sich eben (it's only right)!" she'd said when I pointed out that I could just as well get married in one of my old school-girl dresses, and that a few mismatched cups, bowls and pots would do me just fine. As I put the silverware tray onto a shelf I could feel the entire trousseau, including the trunk, weighing me down, making it harder for me to imagine flying away before the end of the year.

Unaccountably tired, I decided to unpack the second trunk tomorrow—or, more likely, the day after—and left soon after the mover brought up the suitcases. A few minutes later, clutching a sack containing the pillow, I was walking across the Kurfürstenplatz, enjoying my first enticing whiff of grilled Polish sausages and shashlik. My gaze wandered to the corner around which the Wurstbude (sausage shack) waited, but not before it found the upstairs window belonging to the Hungarian photographer. Mutti had forbidden me to ever go to his studio again. But then, what could she do to me if I disobeyed now? Technically, I was already beyond her control.

Before I could follow the impulse, however, there was a commotion on the bus unloading at the curb. A determined woman swinging a bulging briefcase elbowed her way out of the dispersing crowd, calling, "Marianne! Marianne Edel!" It was Frau Bischof, my favorite tyrannical teacher.

In a flash I metamorphosed into a slouching student. She stood before me, critically eying my flawed posture. I said meekly, holding out a hand, "Frau Bischof! Grüss Gott*!*"

She gave it a firm shake. "I've been wondering what happened to you. After all the learning I managed to cram into your skull, how *could* you drop out?"

"Uhm—you see—I'm getting married," I said, abbreviating nine months of my life.

She blinked, and the hand carrying her briefcase went slack. Then the man behind us stepped on her heel and she hissed in sudden pain, clenching her teeth as he apologized, steadied her, and moved on.

"Married," she repeated, looking strangely helpless on the bustling sidewalk, the crowd parting around her.

I'd finally managed to catch my teacher off-guard. "Tomorrow," I added with relish.

"But why?" she asked, her eyes straying to my waist.

"Because it's my sixteenth birthday and I'm finally old enough to be a wife."

She shifted the briefcase to the opposite hand, then clamped her relentless fingers on my arm and steered me into a small coffee shop, where the aroma of freshly baked pastries and rich, dark chocolate mingled with that of roasted coffee beans. Propelling me past the display case lined with a tempting assortment of cakes, she crammed me into a corner seat at a farthest table, positioning her chair to block my exit.

"You're doing it because you're pregnant? Is that it?" she asked bluntly, proving to me that she'd never really known me at all.

"No. I'm doing it because I want to," I said, resolute. While the waitress approached and Frau Bischof placed our order without bothering to ask me what I might like, I grappled with the old Marianne still lurking within me, reminding myself that I was no longer a docile schoolgirl forced to appear obedient, subject to this beloved dictator's iron will.

The waitress jotted down two coffees and *Nusshörnchen*, although I wanted a slice of Linzertorte and peppermint tea. She hurried away before I could gather the courage to change the order. Frau Bischof folded her hands on the white linen-cloth and trained the full force of her gaze upon me.

"You were my best student. Almost perfect recall. Clear-minded. Logical, too. I was sure you'd go far."

"I am," I assured her. "All the way to America. To start a new life."

"A *new* life? You haven't even started your old one yet! Are you unhappy at home? As I recall, your Mutti remarried. You took it hard. That's it, right?"

If she had known I was suffering why had she not offered a sympathetic ear? A few words of clarifying advice? I felt my heart contract with anger. "There's something I've been meaning to ask you."

"What?"

"How come you never told us about Hitler, the Nazis, and six million Jews?"

Her face drained as she stared at the wall behind me.

"You were a Nazi, too, weren't you?" I pushed on. "You were on Hitler's side."

Now her eyes blazed, and I readied myself for lightning and thunder, but she merely touched the fingertips of both hands to her forehead. The waitress chose that moment to set down our order. Porcelain and metal clinked. Frau Bischof busied herself with sugar-cubes and a tiny pitcher of cream, stirring them into her coffee so vigorously that it swamped her saucer. With shaking hands, she raised the cup halfway to her lips, spilling coffee onto the table cloth. Staring at the widening stain, she carefully lowered the cup, poured the contents of the saucer back into it, and set them both down. Only then did she permit herself to drill me with a withering look.

"You can't be blamed, of course," she said, keeping her tone measured. "It's to your credit that you've discovered our recent history and cared enough to ask questions. I'm only sorry you didn't find out from me."

She waited until I had thoroughly masticated my first bite of straw-dry pastry. Then she asked, "What makes you think I was on Hitler's side?"

"Was there another?"

"There must have been, since I was dismissed from teaching during the Hitler years precisely because I was *not* a Nazi. I refused to join the party. So did my husband. They took *him* to Dachau and I never saw him again. When I was rehired to teach after the war I actually had to prove that I was not involved with the party. Luckily I'd kept every piece of paper the Nazis ever sent me. Even the one informing me about my husband's terminal bout with pneumonia, at the camp."

"I'm sorry," I mumbled, feeling small and stupid. "My Mutti won't tell me anything. There's no one else I can ask."

She sighed. "It's a hard question to answer. But you do have a right to know. There are two reasons why I don't discuss that period of history with my class. First, it's not in the curriculum. Too raw, I suppose, too recent for the administrators to want to risk a wrong word. As for the second—*Kind*, don't you know how confused and torn up we all are? What was self-preservation then is called a crime now. My husband spoke up and lost his life as a result."

It could have been me.

"When they came to arrest him he said, 'Ride it out, Elisabeth. It must end sometime. It always does.' "

"Why did he have to die, if he wasn't a Jew? Or was he?"

Her eyes steady upon me, she said, "Jews weren't the only victims. Only the most prevalent. Whole tribes of Gypsies were wiped out too."

"What did *they* ever do?"

"They were too dark," she said.

It could have been Lucius.

"Do you know what Hitler's dream was?" she went on. "Pure white blood, untainted by any mixture."

It could have been our children. But I wouldn't have stayed in a country that supported a Hitler. "How come people let him? How come you all let him?" I demanded, twenty years after the fact.

She pushed her Nusshörnchen at me and relieved me of my coffee. When she raised the cup this time, her hand remained steady. "Fear," she said. "We all stank of it in those days. And an inborn need to survive. It wasn't callousness, you see—just an ever-increasing numbing of our senses. Even now I have to remind myself daily that I'm safe."

She smiled drily. "Sometimes I have nightmares of the Americans going away, and of all the little Nazis still left—and there are plenty— starting the whole thing up again, with the help of the big Nazis flocking homeward from Argentina and Brazil. And then everything I said or thought since the end of the war will be held against me, even my husband's outspokenness. The truth is, child, no one quite trusts anyone these days. No one knows what to believe or what the future will bring. Sixteen years after the war Germany is still a morass, full of ugly things writhing under the mud. I don't blame you for wanting to leave. But I must say, I *am* sad to see you go. Germany needs question-askers like you. And you could have been anything. I saw the university for you."

I forced out a laugh. "It's too bad my Vati didn't see it. He made me leave school to become an apprentice."

She snorted. "I could have told him it wasn't for you. Would have, had he just asked. You're too thirsty for knowledge. I suppose it seems frivolous to people like him. But all is not lost, Marianne. I have some advice for you if you want it."

"I've changed my name to Maria. Maria Duncan, after tomorrow," I told her. "What do you mean, all is not lost?" I tapped our empty plates together, comforted by the sharp click they produced.

"Read," she said. "Read everything you can get your hands on."

"I already do!"

She looked pleased. "In any book, there's information to be ferreted out. Get a library card in America."

I recalled the woman with plastic curlers, driving a convertible down the alley inside Warner Kaserne past the arrowed "library" sign. After tomorrow I'd follow the sign, too.

"Say you read a paragraph about Gypsies," Frau Bischof said. "Search through the index cards. Find out where they came from, what countries they traveled through. Then read about those countries and their neighbors, and theirs. On and on, Marian . . . Maria. Knowledge is a chain you pull to you link by link."

"Click-click," the plates said, though I stayed silent.

Frau Bischof raised a restraining hand, lowered it again, and took a shaky breath. "If you like dogs, read about the different breeds. Then read about wild dogs, wolves, coyotes, foxes, hyenas . . . the list goes on and on. You understand?"

I laughed again, this time with delight. "You're asking me to do what I love best, although everyone thinks I read too much already. Except for one neighbor."

"Yes," she said. "I remember now. You live in the Harthof. Marshall Plan housing." She sniffed. "They have a different school system in America. Something they call 'college.' Easier to get into. Less math. As long as you can keep from having children right away you can *still* do everything you want."

Now *there* was a question I wanted an immediate answer to. Embarrassed before I even asked it, I leaned toward her and whispered, "How do I do it?"

"What?" she asked.

"Keep from having children right away."

A flush crept over her face. She glanced at her wrist. "Goodness, it's late!" she said, jumping up and grabbing the check. "I've got to run. I have a briefcase full of essays to grade. None of them as good as your worst. I always looked forward to yours." She finished the last drop of my coffee.

"Thank you for being so open with me," I said as she started to go. "And for letting me wear jeans to class when no one else was allowed to."

Her mouth twitched. "Your book about Africa was excellent," she admitted. "I was impressed." She extended her hand. "And now I wish you a happy new life in your new world." She shook again in that no-nonsense way of hers, picked up her briefcase, and pushed in her chair. Then she said, "I expect your Mutti will want to have a talk with you tonight. Ask *her* that question. She's the proper person to answer it. Not me." She walked away, each step crisp and determined.

It was obvious she didn't know much about Mutti who had no talent for answering touchy questions even when I *did* have the nerve to ask them. I bought two pieces of *Linzertorte* and asked the server to pack them up nicely. While I watched her skilled hands cut, wrap and bag, I wondered if Frau Bischof was of the faith. Surely, in the staunch Catholic realm of Bavaria, a Protestant teacher would not have been allowed to teach thirty impressionable Catholic girls. Or an agnostic, God forbid. No wonder she'd clammed up. Unfortunately I hadn't paid enough attention to the subject of birth control when I was reading my sex manual. In fact, I'd swear it wasn't mentioned at all. Perhaps doing so would have been a punishable offense.

Slowly making my way out of the coffee shop, swinging the pillow-sack in one hand, cradling the wrapped cake with the other, I crossed the square toward the photographer's drab stairs and tried to find the answer to that important question by simple logic.

It was this: Mutti had three miscarriages before Anna and I came along. Gitta did, too. Even Frau Huber from downstairs had to work awfully hard for her baby. What they all had in common was that they'd prayed for years for the privilege of motherhood. Therefore, reason told me that as long as I refrained from praying for an infant I'd remain foot-loose and child-free.

Half-way to the Hungarian's studio I abruptly remembered where I'd seen my new neighbor with the chignon before. She was the teacher-look-alike I'd met in the precinct station on the night I was arrested for violating curfew. How strange that our paths should cross again, now that I teetered on the brink of respectable matrimony.

CHAPTER 48

WEARING MY LOOSE RAINCOAT under immaculate blue skies, I crossed Schleissheimerstrasse toward home the next afternoon. Unfortunately the sidewalk took me past Regina, who stood in her miniscule yard, leaning against the same slender tree trunk she'd leaned on in July. She was still smoking but her hair was now bleached the color of straw and her neon-bright bobby-socks had faded to dull orange. This time she was not alone.

I barely recognized Heinz, standing beside her. He had transformed himself into a leather-jacketed Halbstarker (rebellious teen). An unfiltered cigarette was sticking out of his mouth at a tough-boy angle. While I stared at his duck-tail hairdo, glistening with grease, his gaze skimmed over my face and got stuck on my well-padded middle. Then his cigarette drooped and his dark complexion grew several shades lighter.

Regina sucked on her cigarette, narrowed her eyes, and tittered, "Hey, Marianne! You got a pillow under your coat, or what?"

"Good guess," I said woodenly, registering Heinz's skin-tight jeans as he plucked a black comb from its rear pocket and smoothed it over the ends of his duck-tail as if his life depended on it.

Regina barked out a laugh and elbowed him in the side. "Miss High and Mighty's beastly uncle must be tearing out what's left of *his* hair."

With a groan, Heinz bolted down the path and away, proving once and for all that he would have been a most unfortunate choice for a boy-friend. I forced myself to walk on at a leisurely pace, hoping Regina couldn't guess how much her words rankled. She called after me, "Hey, I'm *grateful* you decided to give the neighbors a new scandal to gossip about!" It was just as well I had refused her clumsy overture last summer. She would have made a terrible friend.

I made a big detour around Frau Keppler's end of our building, afraid I'd see Heinz's stricken look repeated in her eyes. Passing the Hubers' open bedroom window at Mutti's end, I heard the lusty wail of a baby and saw first one head, then two, gazing at me from behind the curtains.

After I entered our apartment, I unbuttoned the raincoat, took off the pillow, and tossed both onto a kitchen chair. "I hope I'm done with this dumb thing," I told Mutti. "You don't expect me to wear it under my wedding dress, do you?"

"Of course not," she said, calmly stirring the milk she was heating for my prenuptial snack. "I expect you to wear it *over* the dress until we're in Hannes's car. Anna will let you borrow her white cardigan for the occasion." She crooked her head, then ran her fingers through my hair. "It could use a good wash with that nice egg shampoo you like. But first let's go to the bedroom for a minute." She turned off the gas under the pan, covered it, and preceded me through the door.

Anna was at the mirror, spraying a heavy cloud of perfumed hairspray over her beehive. Mutti shooed her into the kitchen, asking her to heat the water kettle for my shampoo. Then she sat on my sister's bed. They'd moved it to the center of the long wall now that my bed was stored in the attic. Staring blankly at the white lacy gown hanging on the outside of what used to be my wardrobe, Mutti said, "You'll be a beautiful bride. This will be a day of big changes for you. You are literally going to enter the *Standesamt* a girl and leave it a woman. We need to talk." She seemed unaware that she was wringing her hands. "About your wedding night. So you'll know what to expect."

"I did read that sex manual before you destroyed it."

She averted her gaze. "Was there anything written in there about wifely duties?"

"Probably not."

"I thought so," she said, looking pained. "But as you'll soon find out, men are different. From us."

Good grief. She was starting with basics. I stifled a grin. "Yes?"

She twisted her wedding ring around and around. "It is your wifely duty to submit to your husband. In all things. Particularly . . ." She cleared her throat. "Particularly . . ."

"Yes?" I asked again, watching her knuckles turn white. Seconds ticked by. Then a light dawned in my befuddled brain. "Oh—I see!" I said. What I saw was my beautiful young mother lying next to an old goat who considered her a prized possession. I saw her closing her eyes to remove her inner being to elsewhere while her body became his play-thing. I'd always wondered how she could stand it. Did she recite the duty-phrase to herself each time she lay down beside him? Was that her nightly prayer? And the first consoling thought the morning after?

"Is it your motherly duty to pass on that information to me?" I asked gently. "Did *your* mother pass it to *you*?"

Her eyes clouded. "I was too young when she died." On reflection, the radiant woman in my favorite family photo, her eyes overflowing with love, knew nothing of duty. "Your aunt, then," I guessed. "The one who took you in when you were orphaned. The one who worked you so hard. She told you that?"

Unable to speak, she gave a stiff nod. I considered the text of every romantic novel I'd ever read. "I think things might have changed since your aunt gave you that bit of advice," I told her. "But thanks for mentioning it." A towering wave of daughterly affection was rushing clear through me. Spontaneously, I pulled my grandmother's ring out of my blouse, slipped the string it was attached to over my head, and held it out to her. "Here. You need it more than I do."

She took the ring with a grateful smile, string and all. "It's one of the few things of hers I have left." Rubbing a finger around the inside of the band, she said, "Smoothed by her skin but miraculously whole long after the finger that wore it is gone," and worked the string carefully over her elegant coiffure. "I don't know why I kept it locked away in the attic. It belongs next to my heart." Rising, she planted a damp kiss on my forehead. "There's one more thing I want you to know—I can't say I've always understood you, Maria, but it's been a pleasure watching you grow. I hope Lucius realizes how lucky he is."

Anna came in as soon as Mutti was gone. "Well?" she asked with a smirk. "Has she properly prepared you for your womanly role?" Detaching the veil from the gown, she draped it over my head and studied the effect. "How about letting me do up your hair for the occasion? I'll even wash and dry it for you. Consider it my one and only wedding gift."

I winced. "A beehive? Nein, danke. Then I wouldn't be me. And today of all days I need to be me."

Rolling her eyes, she huffed, "I was right the first time—you *are* utterly hopeless!"

"If you want to shampoo it for me, be my guest." I untied my blue silk scarf to keep it from getting soaked, folded it into a small square and slipped it into my miniscule bridal purse. Then I unclasped the St. Christopher's medallion and returned it to her. "You wanted it back on my wedding day. It was a big help."

Anna started to take it, then said, "Are you sure? You *could* keep it until after the ceremony, just in case . . ."

I gave a carefree, liberated laugh. "What could possibly go wrong now? Mutti has arranged everything down to the smallest detail. Besides, I might not remember to give it to you in the Standesamt bustle."

She lost no time restoring the silver chain to its rightful place around her neck, seating the medal against her cleavage. "I hope you're happy with the way things are going, Maria. If not . . . it's not too late—"

"It is," I said with unalterable conviction. "Unless you've found a better alternative."

She gave a sad little shrug. "Not for you. But as for me, I have decided to focus entirely on becoming a career girl, buy great clothes every season, vacation in Italy twice a year, and go dancing with a slew of discreet Latin lovers." We went into the kitchen, where I watched her prepare for her last act of sisterly love. Half-joking, I put on my raincoat again, buttoning it to the chin. "In case you miss. I don't need a bath."

Mutti reheated the milk to kill any germs that might have escaped the first boiling and started slicing a loaf of rye. I bent over the sink, pressing the dry washcloth Anna thoughtfully provided over my eyes. She dunked my hair in a bowl of warm water, raised my head just enough to slide the bowl out from under, and snipped off the end of the little plastic pillow containing my favorite shampoo. I inhaled its soapy sweet fragrance, heard Anna squirt the creamy liquid into her hands, and waited for her to massage it onto my scalp. Then I heard something else: a ring of keys rattling on the landing, one key thrusting into the front door lock.

I jerked upright, hardly aware of the water streaming over and under my collar. Anna ran to the chair and threw the pillow at me, hissing, "Put it on!" She didn't have to ask twice. I stuffed my soft armor under the raincoat an instant before the kitchen door crashed against the wall. Mutti dropped the loaf and the knife and clutched at her mother's ring. Anna touched her fingers to the St. Christopher medallion, bracing her hips against the table edge.

O.F. paused dramatically in the door frame. I heard my own pulse, the low, steady gas flame under the pan, and the soft swish of water cascading down my raincoat to puddle on the linoleum. Then O.F.'s agitated breathing drowned out the other sounds. "So you think you've won, you slut," he said, starting out in the same low voice he always used at the beginning of his tantrums. "Well, you haven't. You never will."

Clasping the front of my raincoat to keep the loose pillow from sliding, I glanced uneasily at the wide-open window, suspecting the neighbors were about to get the concluding installment of our long-running family drama.

His eyes glittering, O.F. pointed a gnarled finger at me. "Hure (whore)! Teufelskind (devil's child)! Traitor of the German race! I *will* have my say!" He aimed the finger squarely at my padded middle, like the tip of a poisoned arrow, stabbing it toward me afresh with each phrase, his voice rising. "Marianne Edel, I pronounce you unlucky today and for the rest of your life. I curse you and your man and your children and your children's children to live in poverty and die in poverty. Nothing will ever go right for your family. Every one of you will slide into the gutter where you belong. Everything you try to build will crumble, and those you love most will hate you, making your life hell on earth. Henceforth you are damned. Your husband is damned, and so are your spawn. That is my curse and your just reward, so help me God."

The last stab of his finger shot a power-bolt straight at my belly. Desperately clasping the pillow under my raincoat, I did not dare cross my fingers to ward off his evil spell. Because I'd removed all three of my shields, the bolt hit its mark dead-center. Picture-fragments streamed through my mind—of a homeless family; abandoned babies; a grieving mother; a raped daughter; a bloody, dead son; mangled, weeping grandchildren. I raised a sluggish hand to block the awful stream and to bring Lucius's ring to my lips. But there was no magic in it; perhaps it was too new. O.F.'s curse was turning my marrow to ice.

White-faced and grim, Mutti snatched up the bread knife and advanced on him, thrusting it like a sword. "You said you'd stay away today. You broke your promise. Maybe I'll break mine." She pointed the knife tip at him, then at the door. "Get out! Now!"

Spent, he blanched, turned, and was gone. A board creaked in the hall. The apartment door clicked shut. The nightmarish scene should have been over, but it was not. Clutching my belly, I could feel something slimy boring its way into my womb. The first cramp doubled me at the sink. Mutti pried my hands off the edge, led me to a chair, and dabbed a towel at my neck. "Curses don't work if you don't believe in them, Maria. We are not Africans, after all."

But the part of me already connected to Lucius believed every word— backward and forward in time. That's why the foul, searing worm created by the wizardly curse was able to swim up my tubes toward my stock of precious eggs. Hadn't I read in my sex-book that every woman held a life-time supply that could not be renewed?

"Maria!" Mutti shook me until my brain rattled, then put a trembling hand to my forehead. "Never mind the shampoo. Dry your hair with the blower and lie down for a while. But first, drink this." I was afraid she meant to offer the scalded milk but she produced a bottle of cognac and three shot glasses, sat beside me, and poured. Anna emptied her tumbler first. Mutti was second. Having developed a distaste for the stuff, I was a poor third but nonetheless grateful for the thawing heat it provided.

My sister tittered nervously. "He got the idea for that speech straight out of Sleeping Beauty. The bad fairy's curse. I wonder how long he rehearsed it before the stunning performance." She went to test the temperature of the heated water. "We could still—"

"Never mind," I groaned, rubbing my eyes. "Can I rest on your bed for a while?"

She looked at the wall clock. "Sure. You've got an hour before you have to get ready. We'll wake you in plenty of time." She grabbed the cognac flask for a refill, but Mutti snatched it from her, capped it, and put it away.

*

AN HOUR later O.F.'s scene no longer seemed real. Mutti stood by the bed, wearing a gorgeous lilac dress I'd not seen before. "Time to get ready," she whispered. I was struggling to sit when the doorbell rang. "Now who could that be?" she murmured, vexed, listening to muffled voices moving from the hall to the living room. Then Anna came in, her freckles in stark relief.

"It's for you, Maria. A neighborhood delegation, led by Frau Forster. She's bristling mad." She pulled a robe out of her wardrobe and tossed it to me. "Wear this. And pin on the pillow, for God's sake!"

My temples were beginning to ache. One more crisis and I'd be stuck with a headache. What else could go wrong on the first day of the rest of my life? "I'll be out in a minute," I said, busying myself with pins and buttons before I got up to confront the hostile mob.

The living room swarmed with faces. The Hubers had brought their baby. Frau Stöhrenfried glared at me from behind them. Frau Forster and Wolfi stood shoulder to shoulder with grouchy Herr Braun, who'd left his spy glass at home. Even Peter's mother was there.

As usual Frau Forster spoke first. Pushing Wolfi toward me, she cried, "We all heard what your uncle said. This time he's gone too far. We want nothing to do with him from now on. Wolfi and I made an honest mistake, and we're both sorry for it." She twisted his arm.

"Sorry," he muttered, not meeting my eyes.

Frau Forster pressed an envelope into my hand. "We wish you the best."

I accepted both card and apology. Frau Keppler gave me a small, well-polished silver spoon tied with a pink ribbon, and a tiny used book full of names. "For your baby," she said almost shyly. "If you haven't picked a name for it yet." I shook her hand, barely able to keep myself from confessing the truth about my bulging midriff.

Then I took the layette Herr Huber held out. "Yellow is a neutral color—and it goes well with brown skin," he volunteered, beaming. Frau Huber added, "It's going to be a beautiful baby. Don't let that old monster frighten you anymore. You should hear how bizarre he sounds from our side of your floor."

Herr Braun, trying for a friendly smile, failed miserably and stuck his envelope straight at my face. "Taufgeld (christening money)," he said. "It's only right. Herr Hohner has never been a friend of mine."

I couldn't keep from giving Mutti a helpless look. She answered with a nearly imperceptible twitch of her shoulders. "Thank you," I stammered. "Thank you all. I'm not sure I deserve it."

"Ja, doch," Peter's mother said sternly. "We've known you a long time. You were always a pleasure to us. A sweet young girl, no matter what some might have thought." Her gift was a small box of truffles, tied with a white ribbon.

"Heavens!" Mutti exclaimed. "It's almost time for us to go. If we don't get Maria dressed in a hurry she'll be late for her own wedding."

The neighbors filed out, satisfied with their errand of mercy. I returned to the bedroom, divested myself of the cushion, slipped into everything Mutti had so neatly lined up for me, and borrowed Anna's brush to smooth out tangled curls while she was in the bathroom refreshing her makeup. Then I sat on the bed and opened the two envelopes. Each contained a ten-DM bill enclosed in a gold-rimmed card—guilt, purged and transferred. "Christening money," I moaned when Anna came in for her pumps. "If they ever find out that I lied they'll surely demand it back."

"Just stay away from this crummy place and they won't know the difference," she said. "Believe me, you don't owe these people a thing. Besides, who cares what our neighbors think? They'll always see what they expect to see, no more and no less. Listen. O.F. may be lurking nearby to watch your escape. There's a part in the wedding vows that goes something like, 'If anyone objects to this union, let him speak now or forever hold his peace.' So, for the last time—don't forget the pillow." I put on her bulky white cardigan, stuffed the pillow underneath, and rearranged my wisp of a veil. We went to the living room, from which Mutti had stepped out onto our narrow balcony, squinting down the street.

"They're coming," she said. "There's Horst's BMW. And Hannes is turning the corner behind him. Are we ready to go?" She snatched up her purse and a cloth coat matching her new dress, and went toward the hall. And then the telephone shrilled, sounding so menacing that I dropped the box of truffles I had planned to tear into in the backseat of Herr Adler's car. Mutti eyed the receiver with obvious distrust. "Anna, you take it. If it's O.F., I don't want to speak to him for the rest of the day." I joined her at the door and she fluffed my veil, my hair, and my skirts.

"Ja, Vati," Anna said into the mouthpiece. "A message? But she's right here. Why don't you speak—well. All right then. I'll listen." Some seconds later, she said, "Oh, I understand, all right. I'll tell her. But I think you're mean!" She slammed down the receiver. We waited. "It was Vati," she began.

"I got that part," I told her.

"He wants you to know that if you go through with the wedding he will consider you dead. As he so delicately put it—you'll cease to exist for him."

The wall clock ticked loudly—or was it Horst's car at the curb? "I thought I already had," I said with as much nonchalance as I could muster. "Is that all?"

She nodded, her eyes moist.

"I can live with it," I said. Then my knees caved and I sank onto the couch. "Mutti," I said. "May I please—"

"Of course," she replied. "I'll get it at once." Anna sat down beside me and reached for one of the tumblers Mutti held out to us. Mutti filled them with cognac. We emptied them fast.

"Some men are bad losers," Mutti said.

"Men who are bad losers deserve to lose," Anna amended, holding her shot glass out for seconds. This time Mutti obliged. Downstairs, an engine revved politely. Our composure restored, we descended the stairs together, Anna on my left in a powder-blue shift embroidered with daisies, Mutti on my right with pink and silver silk blossoms on her lilac ensemble. I was a fluffy white cloud, surrounded by flowers. When we rounded the building Lucius rolled down the rear window of the BMW, grinning at us. He had on his forest green dress uniform. A soft cap, like an upended boat, sat on his hair. His skin glowed a rich, earthy brown. Anna got in next to Horst, who was wearing a fine suit and looking as good in it as Anna had said.

Herr Adler came around his Mercedes, opened the front door for Mutti, the rear one for me, and said, "What an agreeable way to spend this lovely afternoon. I'm so glad you are letting me be your chauffeur today." I smoothed my starched petticoats and got in. Then Horst's car rolled away from the curb and I unpinned the pillow, tossed it on the seat next to me, and put the white cardigan on top.

Herr Adler managed to keep the little tan BMW in sight until we got to the Kurfürstenplatz, where Horst began zipping in and out of slow moving traffic. Herr Adler soon gave up the chase. "Lotte, don't worry. All roads lead to the Standesamt," he said, placing a calming hand on Mutti's and giving it an encouraging squeeze. She, lifting her chin and squeezing back, replied,

"I think I'm ready for those driving lessons now, Hannes, if your offer still holds."

"Excellent," he said. "We shall begin tomorrow."

From the back seat, I could see heavenly handwriting appear on the nearest wall. It said, "Exit O.F."

CHAPTER 49

W
E FILED INTO THE ANTEROOM of the Standesamt and immediately became the center of attention. I counted five groups before us, every bride among them wearing regular street clothes. I felt quite overdressed, realizing belatedly that my frilly gown was more appropriate for a church nuptial. I was also the only bride below the age of thirty that afternoon. Neither perfumed, painted or permed, I was an oddity even without my sky-scraping groom wearing an American military uniform with an upside down boat on his head.

Along our route, thoughtful Herr Adler had stopped at a flower shop to buy me a bouquet of rosebuds, giving me something solid and prickly to hold on to. I was beginning to understand that I would never again fit in anywhere, no matter what I might wear. Since every eye in the room was upon me I forced myself to look from face to face, smiling until each smiled in return. It was like lighting candles one by one.

This was going to be an assembly-line wedding. Every ten minutes a group surrounding one bride and one groom would file out of the inner sanctum through the door on the left. Then a thin, harassed clerk wearing a suit that was too big for him popped his head out of the door to the right and called out the names of the next couple on his list, who then entered with their entourage to the strains of classical music.

My heart didn't start pounding until we were at the head of the line. Then the clerk shouted, "Duncan and Edel," and we poured into the sanctum. It was an austere chamber with no place to sit—which was probably why people called it the *Stand*esamt.

A dignified silver-haired man wearing glasses and a funereal robe leafed through a folder of papers, picked up a sheet, and proceeded to read in a grave, guttural monotone, in English—perhaps in the hope that both Lucius and I would begin to comprehend what we were getting ourselves into—"Dearly beloved, we are gathered here . . ."

As he continued to speak I became aware of an odd tension building within me. Someone seemed to be knocking on the inside of my skull.

"Do you, Joseph Maddis L. Duncan, take Marianne Edel . . ." the justice droned on.

I wanted to correct him but didn't quite dare. I could only hope Holy Maria was not watching, or if she was, that she found it in her heart to forgive me for my singular bout of cowardice. Between the music and my wildly beating heart, I couldn't understand much of what the judge was saying. But I did I heard Lucius squeak, "I . . ." and then, after some throat-clearing, ". . . do."

Now the judge was focusing his attention on me. "Do you, Marianne Edel . . ."

A voice inside my head shouted, "No!" so loud that it obliterated every other sound. A gaunt, graying woman appeared on the screen of my mind, her hair spiked and dry, with dark circles under inflamed, tired eyes. I couldn't suppress a small gasp. Mutti looked at me sharply. Herr Adler's silver irises gleamed like two newly minted 50-Pfennig pieces. Lucius, half wed and half not, held my ring suspended between us.

The echo of the gray woman's protest-shout faded back into the future, and then an even older voice, nearer my heart, said with unshakeable conviction, "The answer is yes!" It belonged to an ancient, vaguely familiar face appearing on the same screen the other had vacated. This face was criss-crossed with lines and framed by lichen-like scraggles of fluorescent white. Her eyes, too old for color, seemed kind and at peace. "Yes," she prompted again before she returned to the next century, where she belonged.

She was right. For me, who loved meadows filled of flowers of every hue and shape, it was the only answer worth giving. Kunterbunt (A Riot of Colors) was Life's eternal response to racist dictators. And so I repeated not only the crone's word but also her firm tone, choosing to belong to a time to come that no longer made room for the likes of a Hitler. Recalling the harried look on the gray woman's face, I knew the path to it wouldn't be easy.

Lucius and I exchanged rings. The black-robed judge pronounced us wed and invited Horst Obdach and Hannes Adler to witness the event on two identical dotted lines. Then the clerk with the oversized suit maneuvered us all to the exit and rushed to the entrance, calling the names of the next group in line. Our entire so-called ceremony couldn't have lasted more than five or six minutes.

Outside the front portals Lucius gave me his arm. We descended an array of stone steps in synchronized fashion. When we were halfway to the sidewalk the Hungarian photographer climbed off a wine-red Lambretta, his camera at the ready. "Well done, my beautiful Gypsy princess," he said, clicking away. "Now stand still. Turn head this way. Ist gut (is good)." Twitching his trigger finger, he recorded the instant Lucius and I looked at each other in the first pangs of wedded bliss, his face tender, mine trusting.

We descended two more steps, then the Hungarian captured the groom's capable arms enclosing the bride's slender waist while hers lovingly encircled his muscular neck. They exchanged a chaste kiss. "*Wunderbar*," the photographer said. "Keep walking, Maria, one step at a time. Look at the lens and say hello to children and grandchildren who will one day study every detail of photos. Next a group picture, yes? Family portrait. Goes on first page of new album." *Snap*, went his finger. "Now you go to the car. That nice Mercedes is yours? Open door, please." *Snap, snap.* "Chauffeur in front. You sit in back and wave. Good shot. You come to studio for prints in one week. Last picture is of bride and groom riding off into sunset."

We drove away laughing. Horst and Anna lagged behind, busy engaging the photographer in a short conversation, then posing in front of the BMW for a potential family portrait of their own. Herr Adler took us to our new address, gently coming to a full stop at the curb. I thanked him for his help. Smiling, he asked me to call him Hannes. Then he studied the house number posted over the entrance and stopped smiling. "Is *this* where you'll live? However did you find it?"

"Mutti picked it for us, ' I said. "From the classifieds."

"The ad that never stops running?" Crestfallen, he looked at my mother who was nervously picking lint from her lapel. "Schade," he told her with infinite tenderness. "But," he continued in English as he helped me disembark, "I dare say you'll find something more suitable soon." And then he chauffeured Mutti away.

"What did he mean?" Lucius asked, shifting his attention from the disappearing Mercedes to the recently white-washed façade of our new home. An unkempt woman, leaning out of a third-story window, beckoned to him and shouted something I couldn't quite hear. Lucius gave an incredulous laugh and draped a protective arm around me. "Pay her no mind. I bet she's the neighborhood drunk. Hey, aren't we close to the Kurfürstenplatz? It'll be easy to catch a streetcar and bus to work every morning."

Arm in arm, we entered the lobby and climbed to the second floor, where two ruby-haired women dressed in drab house-coats were leaning over the banister, drinking beer from a shared bottle. "Look!" said one. "Fake newlyweds in the old rat trap." Her drinking-buddy slurred, "Now I've seen everything."

I gave them a puzzled "Grüss Gott," and Lucius added a hesitant, "Wie geht's (howdy)," but they did not reply. Climbing on, I said, "It's a small room, Lucius. On the top floor."

"That high up, huh?"

"Like a castle. A hard-to-reach castle of our own." I was beginning to understand that my dream had really come true—I never had to go home again. The relief made me giddy.

We paused on the third-floor landing to catch our breaths. "Good for the heart," Lucius said, tapping his chest. "And for the thighs," I agreed.

A man wearing a business suit emerged from the hall, knotting his tie. He was trailed by a plump blonde, buttoning her quilted robe, who pulled at his sleeve and held out a hand. "You're five D-Mark short."

"You're not that good," he answered, staring at Lucius and me. "Place is going to the dogs," he muttered in German as we sailed past.

On the empty fourth landing, Lucius just sighed, and when we finally arrived on the fifth, he said, "Back o' the bus!" But then I showed him the pretty bell label marked, "Duncan 4 rings," and he caught his second wind. I extracted my keys from the bridal purse, unlocking the front door. Without warning, he snatched me up in his arms and carried me across the threshold—to the delight of the schoolmarm-like neighbor I'd met yesterday, who was watching our grand entrance with undisguised amusement from inside the hall.

"Old American custom," he told her, lowering me to the floor.

She clapped. "Nice game. Can I play?" Then she asked me, "Will he live here too?"

"My husband and I will live here together," I confirmed, unlocking our room door. Lucius picked me up once more. Over his broad shoulder, I saw the schoolmarm cover her mouth to stifle a giggle. I wondered what it was about us she was finding so funny. Then Lucius shut and locked the door from the inside and put me down.

The room seemed even smaller today than it had yesterday. I smoothed my skirts. "That woman is a teacher, Lucius. This whole building is full of single career women. Like a cloister. The landlady doesn't like renting to couples."

"Is that right?" he said, sounding perplexed. "I don't think nuns would dye their hair bright-red. Teachers, either. Or secretaries. How did you say you found this place again?"

"M-Mutti . . ."

"Ah!" he said. "Well, then. Case closed." He took a leisurely look at our new refuge. The few homey touches I'd added the day before did little to disguise the overall shabbiness of the place.

"It seemed bigger yesterday," I told him. *And* emptier!

He swallowed. "That's okay. At least we'll have our privacy. Yessir, this'll do us fine. For a while. We're together, aren't we?"

So we were. Suddenly, those words took on a whole new meaning. I put the bouquet on the counter. "Shall I fix us some tea?" Then I remembered that I hadn't fetched any water and that the schoolmarm was most likely still sneering out in the hall.

"Not now," he said, untying his shoe laces.

I lifted the veil from my hair. He unbent—and expanded in all directions. I backed away, coming to an abrupt halt when I bumped into the table. I knew what wedding *nights* were for, but I'd neglected to consider wedding afternoons. Small as the window was, it let in far too much daylight. I climbed onto a wobbly chair to pull at the stuck curtain and noticed an abandoned spider web in an upper corner of the casing. Finely woven and dust free, it held a baby fly, still iridescent though sucked dry.

I imagined the new hatchling catching an updraft from the sidewalk below, soaring five stories on its maiden flight only to come to this unhappy and premature end. Gently, I drew the curtain shut over it and turned to see Lucius pull off his tie, pinning me with an intense gaze. I flattened myself against the wall. He unbuttoned his uniform jacket and advanced.

Looking at the narrow, uninviting bed, I saw the wan face of a ghostly, see-through Maria emerge from under the covers, staring up at the ceiling and waiting to submit. Every page I recalled from the sex manual was meaningless gibberish now.

Lucius stopped moving when he got to the daybed, a mute question forming in his dark almond eyes. With an awkward, self-conscious grin he held out his hand to me. I wanted to run away from this place while I was still able, but I couldn't get around him; he filled the whole room. There was only one path left for me to take—straight to him. "Lucius," I said, reaching out, my voice high and thin. "Catch!" And then, hair and skirts flying, I jumped to his spreading arms.

GLOSSARY

Note: The author took care to weave most translations of German words into the text. The following terms might need additional explanation:

Ach oh
Ach du lieber Himmel oh, dear heaven!
Ach Gott oh God
Ach ja oh yeah
Ach wo oh come on, now
Achtung attention
Adventskranz Advent wreath
alle Jahre wieder every year
Also, ich komme dann sofort mit dem Fahrrad. Ich freue mich schon. So, I'm looking forward to meeting you right away on my bike.
Ami, Amis American(s), American soldiers
Anstalt institution
Aufmachen open, open up
Auf Wiederhören until we hear each other again
Auf Nimmerwiederseh'n may we never meet again
Augenblick A moment
Ausgeschlossen impossible, out of the question
Ausgestossen ejected
Basta! and that's that!
Bauernhochzeit country wedding
Bauernhof farmstead
Behüt dich watch out, watch yourself **behüt dich Gott** may God watch over you
Belegte Brote open-faced sandwiches **belegte Brötchen** open-faced rolls (Semmeln) finger sandwiches
Bist du wirklich ein schwarzer Neger? Are you really a black Negro?
Bitte! Please **bitte?** What do you mean? What did you say?
Bitteschön it was a pleasure (you're welcome)
Bitteschön . . . Jetzat there you are . . . now let us proceed
Bockwurst large wiener made mostly with veal
Braten roast
Bua, buabal boy (in Bavarian dialect)

DM acronym for **Deutsche Mark** **D-Mark** abbrev. of same **Mark** common usage for Deutsche Mark

Da liegt es/ihr Kinder/auf Heu und auf Stroh Here [he] lies, children, on hay and on straw

Danke, dankeschön thanks, thank you very much (**donkey shane**= heavy American accent) **vielen Dank** many thanks

Das auch noch What else [do I have to endure]?

Das ist aber komisch That's odd (weird, funny)

Das ist nicht nett that's not nice

Datschi fruit topping on something that tastes like sweet, baked pizza dough

Deine Dichliebende your loving

Der Gabriel the Gabriel

Der schwarze Teufel the black devil

Deutsch ist eine Weltsprache German is an international language

Dunklem, hellem variations of dunkel, hell [or] dunkles, helles—dark, light

Ein feiner Apparat a fine camera [apparatus]

Ein schöner Tag a beautiful day

Eine Notlüge a white lie

Eine solche Frechheit What nerve! (cheek! impudence!)

Einen Schwarzen a black man

Einmal eins, zweimal zwei lit.: your one x one, two x two i.e. do you know what's what? [or] do you know your way around?

Ein richtiger Neger a real Negro

Einser, Zweier As and Bs

Elvis ist tot Elvis is dead

Erziehungsanstalt, reformatory **Erziehungsheim** reform school

Es ist zum heulen I could cry [scream, howl] I feel like screaming

Es tut mir leid I am sorry

Euer Stammtisch your [reserved] table [from now on, this is your special table]

Fachwerk medieval half-timbered house

Freibad spring-fed outdoor pool

Gastarbeiter guest worker, in those days mostly Italian

Gell an affirmative question, such as *isn't it, doesn't it, don't you think?*

Genau exactly

Gemütlich cozy, comfortable

Geschafft it is done

Gewiss certainly, absolutely

Glühwein mulled wine

Griesnockerl semolina dumplings
Grias Di Bavarian dialect for **Grüss Dich [Gott]** I greet you [or] may God greet you
Groschen small Austrian coins, worth approx. 1 cent, 2 cents, 5 cents, 10 cents, or 50 cents
Guten Appetit good appetite
Guten Abend, guten Morgen, guten Tag good evening, good morning, good day
Halbstarker young tough (lit.: half-strong one)
Halt's Maul shut up
Handelschule trade school, business school
Hasenöhrl small deep-fried pastries shaped like rabbit ears
Heiland savior
Heilige Holy (feminine)
Herein come in, enter
Herrgott noch mal swear-word, lit. Lord-God-and-again , meaning *damn it all*
Höllgraben hell's ditch
Hure whore
I hob di gean I really like you
Ich bin mit den Nerven fertig my nerves are shot
Ich bitte dich I'm asking you (also: please don't)
Ihr Kinderlein kommet Come, little children
Im Notfall in case of an emergency
Ist gut that's good
Ja, doch sure; sure you do
Ja, du approx: Listen, you!
Ja, gut...und? All right (then)...and what else?
Ja, gut, zwei Essen okay then, two dinners (meals)
Ja mei, tja mei Bavarian lament, the second one more deeply felt
Ja, wirklich you don't say, or, really or, is that so
Ja, und? So? or, So what?
Jawohl yes, of course
Jetzat now, then
Jugendamt youth authority
Kaffee und Kuchen coffee and cake
Kaiser Schmarrn emperor's scramble (German butter-and-egg pancakes, lightly scrambled, topped with powdered sugar)
Kalte Platte an assortment of sliced sausages on a platter, with butter and sliced bread
Kasperl Bavarian clown-puppet

Kind child
Kleine little one, young one
Knödel boiled dumplings of wheat(bread, rolls) or semolina
Krankenkasse state-administered health insurance
Kuck, ein Neger look, a Negro
Kunterbunt higgledy piggledy (all mixed up)   **Kunterbunte Blumen** A mix of flowers in a riot of colors
Landjäger a flat, hard sausage the size of a wiener, dark brown, spicy, in links
Landler a country dance, a slow waltz
Läuten ring (the doorbell)
Leberkaas, Leberkäse lit. liver-cheese, a sausage-loaf, usually eaten hot
Lebkuchen,   famous gingerbread pastries mostly made in Nürnberg for the Christmas season
Liebchen . . . nicht wahr? My dear . . . isn't that so?
Liebes, also **Liebe** or **Lieber** dear
Lieder lyrical folk-songs or hymns
Likör cordial; a thick, creamy alcoholic drink, often home-made from various fruits or eggs
Limunade a bottled, sparkling lemon drink often mixed with beer to produce "Radlermass"
Mädchen girl
Mahlzeit! Same as **Guten Appetit!** enjoy your meal
Mariandl Bavarian version of Marianne
Mass, Masskrug, Mass Bier a measure of beer, fitting into a liter mug
Max nix GI slang for **es macht nichts** makes no difference [to me]; I don't care
Mein Schatz my treasure
Mein Gott my God
Mein Kind my child
Miesbacher Tracht quintessential Bavarian costume from the city and region of Miesbach
Minga countrified name for the city of Munich
Mittagessen the noon-time meal
Mittlere Reife final exam in secondary schools
Neewahr a Prussian form of "nicht wahr" transl. as "isn't it right?"
Neger Negro
Nix slang for **nichts** nothing, nothing doing, oh no, you don't
Nusshörnchen, Bienenstiche, Negerküsse lit. little nut-horns, bee-stings, Negro-kisses—small inexpensive sweet baked goods

O seht in der Krippe im nachtlichen Stall Oh see in the manger in the stable in the night

Oberschule German high school

Ochsenschwanzsuppe oxtail soup

Onkel uncle

"O seht in der Krippe/im nachtlichen Stall　oh see in the manger in the nocturnal (night-dark) stable . . .

Ostbahnhof East Train depot

Panzer tank

Pfiat Di broad dialect version of Bavarian **Behüt Dich**

Pfui Teufel yuck! In the dialogue given, it is inferred that Maria is a yucky devil

Plätzchen cookies

Polizei police

Prozess trial, court case

Quark curd cheese, akin to cottage cheese, but dry

Rezept recipe

Rohrnudel yeasty, sweet, oven browned dumpling

Röntgen eyes Xray eyes

Sau Breiss variation of **Sau Preusse**, which means Prussian pig

Sauerampfer an edible, sour-tasting meadow plant

Sauwetter nasty weather

Schade too bad; it's a pity

Schau, ein Neger! Look, a Negro!

Schau mal her look at this

Scheisse shit

Schneeglöckchen little snow bells (flower)

Schnellzug speed train

Schnürsenkel shoe lace

Schützenverein(e)　gun club(s)　note: **Schützen** are volunteer marksmen protecting Bavaria's mountainous borders

Schweinehund lit,: pig dog; swine

Servus so long, good-bye also: hello

Sie ist ein Kind she's a child

Sie Schwein you pig

Sprudel, sprudeln bubble

Standesamt city-clerk's office;

Stollen Semi-sweet Christmas bread

Stossverkehr rush hour

Stub'nmusi Bavarian folk music, parlor music

Sudetenland former East German province

Südtirol South Tyrol
Tag abbreviated version of "guten Tag"
Taufgeld christening money
Teint complexion
Teufelskind devil-child
Tracht regional costume **Trachtenjacke** man's jacket, as part of regional costume
Tschüs so long
Uhre clock --note: as in "Wieviel **Uhr** ist es?" (lit.: how many o'clock is it? i.e. what's the time?)
Unglauben unbelief, disbelief
Verboten forbidden, not allowed
Vielleicht maybe, perhaps
Von wegen! No way! That's what you think! Think again!
Warte wait
Weissbier light beer
Weisst was? You know what?
Weltbürger citizen of the world i.e. someone without a country or passport; global citizen
Wies'n lit. meadow; local term for Oktoberfest, derived from **Theresienwiese**, the meadow on which the celebration takes place
Wir machen ein Bild mit uns dreinen We'll take a picture of us three
Wirt proprietor
Womit kann ich dienen? How can I help (serve) you?
Wunderbar wonderful
Wurstbude sausage-shack
Wurstbrot open-faced sausage sandwich
Wurstsalat sausage salad
Zwei Wasser? Kein Bier? Two waters? No beer?
Zwieback "twice-baked" toast —very crisp oven-baked toast, is sold like cookies, often given to teething babies
Zuckertüte a large, cone-shaped paper container full of sweets, traditionally given to a child to celebrate his first day of school
Zwetschgendatschi Datschi topped with Italian prune-plums

www.ingramcontent.com/pod-product-compliance
Lightning Source LLC
Chambersburg PA
CBHW031132260626
47153CB00021B/31